Joyful Morning

Shauna Lee

Joyful Morning

Copyright © 2015 by Shauna Lee

All rights reserved. No part of this book may be used or reproduced by any means, graphic, electronic, or mechanical, including photocopying, recording, taping or by any information storage retrieval system without the written permission of the publisher except in the case of brief quotations embodied in critical articles and reviews.

This book is based on a true story, All interpretations of events are based on the author's perception and in no way reflect the feelings of any of the characters portrayed in the book.

Scripture quotations are from the King James Version, the New International Version or the New Living Translation as noted.

THE HOLY BIBLE, NEW INTERNATIONAL VERSION®, NIV®, Copyright© 1973, 1978, 1984, 2011 by Biblica, Inc. ™. Used by permission. All rights reserved worldwide.

Scripture quotations marked (NLT) are taken from the Holy Bible, New Living Translation, copyright © 1996, 2004, 2007 by Tyndale House Foundation. Used by permission of Tyndale House Publishers Inc., Carol Stream, Illinois 60188. All rights reserved.

"Everyone has their own dream. I would urge all to try to give their best and not succumb to that which requires the least action on our part, or dulls our sensitivity to those whose needs are much greater than our own."
– Ruth Peterson, Accepting Reality.

Dorcas,
enjoy the story of love, life, happiness & challenge
– Shause Lu

This book is lovingly dedicated to
Ruth and Waldemar, who were
brave enough to change the way
society judged one another.

This book is based on a true story. All interpretations
of events are based on the author's perception and in
no way reflect the feelings of any of the characters
portrayed in the book. Some names and identifying
details have been changed to protect the privacy of
individuals.

Chapter 1

"Therefore do not worry about tomorrow, for tomorrow will worry about itself. Each day has enough trouble of its own." Matthew 6:34 NIV

February 27, 1949

Gerry and Ruth

The sound of a bleating lamb filled Waldemar's dream. His mind cleared, realizing that it was the sound of his six-week-old son, Gerry, crying out from the wicker bassinet. He looked over at his wife, Ruth, who was sleeping with one arm hanging off the bed, resting on Gerry. His feet hit the floor and he hastily circled around the bed to scoop him up before he woke Ruth.

"Shhh, shhh. Daddy's here." Waldemar held Gerry against his chest with one large hand covering his back and cupping his bulky diapered bottom. "Are you wet?" he whispered.

Waldemar shoved his feet into his slippers and went down the hall to the living room. He turned on a lamp. Gerry was quiet and still now, looking up at his dad with wide blue eyes. Waldemar smiled and said, "Hello, little guy. Let's get you changed."

Waldemar laid him down tenderly on the couch on a blanket that Ruth had left. He grabbed a cloth diaper off the pile of laundry that was perched precariously on the coffee table. Waldemar hummed as he unpinned the old, wet diaper. Gerry's lips curled up in a half smile. Waldemar threw the wet diaper into a pail that Ruth had for soiled diapers and then went to work pinning on the new one, nice and snug. He buttoned Gerry back into his sleeper and then picked him up.

"Now, are you in need of a bottle?" he asked. Waldemar walked to the kitchen with Gerry held tightly against his chest. Gerry's limbs wiggled. Waldemar opened the fridge with his free hand and pulled out a bottle of formula that Ruth had mixed before going to bed. He put it in the pot on the stove, still full of water from heating the last bottle. He turned the element on and waited while the water came to a boil. He moved around the kitchen, slowly dancing with Gerry, trying to soothe his cries. Waldemar carefully pulled the bottle from the water and placed it on a towel on the kitchen counter. He dried off the sides and then squirted a drop onto his wrist. "Just right."

He took Gerry to the armchair in the living room, grabbing a burp cloth off the coffee table before sitting down. Gerry's mouth opened widely. Waldemar put the nipple in his mouth but Gerry's mouth did not close down on it. It remained open, his jaw wiggling from side to side. "Close your mouth now," Waldemar said softly, coaxing Gerry's mouth shut around the nipple. "There we are." Gerry's arms waved madly while he ate. Waldemar pulled him in close, holding his arms down with his hand. "Just calm down. Daddy's got you." Gerry sucked and then began to cough and sputter. Waldemar pulled the bottle out and sat him up. Gerry coughed and wretched until everything came back out, right onto the burp cloth. "Oh man," Waldemar sighed. He carefully wiped Gerry's chin. "What's the matter? Are you drinking too fast?" He laid Gerry back down and again attempted to get him to latch on. Once Gerry was rhythmically sucking, Waldemar let go of one of Gerry's arms. The arm waved around. Waldemar offered his finger to the splayed out little hand but Gerry would not grasp it.

Waldemar's brows knit. "Hold on to my finger. Just grab on." Gerry's hands defied his father's words and continued to wave. Waldemar pinned the little arm back down against his body. "Maybe next time."

The sun rose as Waldemar walked Gerry, still fussing, back and forth across the living room. With one hand, Waldemar made a pot of coffee and boiled some water for oatmeal. When it was six o'clock, he went to wake up Ruth so that he could get ready for work.

"Ruth," Waldemar said softly as he shook her shoulder. "I have to get ready for work. Can you take Gerry?"

Ruth groaned as she rolled over in bed. "Yes, I can." She fumbled for her glasses on the nightstand. She put them on and slowly sat up, her bare feet hitting the carpeted floor. "I'm tired."

"I know," Waldemar said sympathetically. "You're still recovering. Your body has been through a lot."

"Yes it has." Ruth smiled up at Waldemar. "Who would have thought that I would need fourteen transfusions to survive this whole ordeal?"

"We're lucky — really lucky that you and Gerry made it through all of that." Waldemar offered Gerry to Ruth. "He had a bottle a couple hours ago. I can put another one on if you'd like."

"Did it stay down?"

"Most of it. He did have one big spit up at the beginning but he was able to get through the rest."

"Well that's promising."

"He had trouble getting onto the bottle though…does he do that with you?"

Ruth nodded sadly. "Yes, he seems to have trouble getting his mouth to close over the nipple of the bottle."

"Hmmm."

Ruth looked at her little boy. He still had his dark newborn hair. It stuck up in every direction, reminding her of a little squirrel. Tears spontaneously burst from Ruth's eyes.

"What is it?" Waldemar asked tenderly.

"Do you think he's going to be okay? I mean, he seems okay, right?"

"He's going to be fine. Just because he had a rough start doesn't mean anything. Look at him…what's your gut feeling?"

Ruth shrugged.

"He smiles, he responds…when you look in his eyes you know he can hear you."

Ruth wiped the tears away with her nightgown sleeve. "I guess," she sniffed.

"You're a nurse, you're trained to worry. Gerry's okay. We've been through the worst."

Ruth nodded, not admitting the uneasy feeling she had in the pit of her stomach. "Yes, he'll be fine. We just need to keep praying for him."

"And we will," Waldemar agreed. "Every day." Images of Gerry's splayed out hand, seemingly unable to grasp his finger, flashed into his mind. He pushed the thought away. "He's going to be fine." He looked at the clock on the wall. "I better get going before I'm late."

Ruth lay back down on the bed with Gerry beside her. She touched his velvety skin and stroked his soft hair. "Hey, Ger? We're going to be okay, right?" Gerry cooed and looked at his mom. "Oh, I love you." She looked up at the ceiling of the bedroom. Whispering she said, "He's going to be fine, right God?"

Ruth and Waldemar had been married for two-and-a-half years now. Waldemar was an RCMP officer and Ruth a nurse. The pair had met while working together in St. Paul, a small town in northern Alberta. Gerry was their first child who had just barely survived his birth. When he was born, he wasn't breathing. The delivery nurses had worked frantically to save him. After ten minutes, he finally drew his first breath. Ruth also had endured great physical trauma from the birth. She had lost so much blood that the doctors had feared that she might not survive. Thankfully, now six weeks later, the family was home and settling into everyday life.

At work, Waldemar looked through his desk drawer for a file he had been working on. His desk was as neat and orderly as he was. Last night they had been meeting with some of his informants. It was always a very colorful experience. Right now, he was working on another robbery. He worked on all kinds of cases but robberies were common. Talk would usually surface on who had done what, if you were patient. Most nights he worked from dark until two or three o'clock in the morning when most criminal activity had settled down for the night. He would drop into headquarters occasionally and work on his case files, doing paperwork and preparing for court. He also had to type his reports for Ottawa and get in touch with officers to keep himself on the pulse of criminal activity.

Waldemar swiveled in his chair and looked at the large board on the wall behind his desk. He and his fellow detectives had a collection of names and photographs so they could keep up with who was who.

Waldemar studied the faces and thought about the raid that they had planned for tonight. The previous night, his informant had told Waldemar that there was a poker game going on at a well-known downtown hotel, and some of the stolen money and goods might surface.

The RCMP and the Edmonton City Police worked closely together. Tonight, another RCMP officer and two city police officers were all going to be a part of the raid.

He was only in the office for a short time to coordinate the raid. Then he planned to go home for a bit to rest up. His time was his own. He could come and go as he pleased, as long as he was producing results. As long as he solved cases and brought the cases to prosecution, he was doing his job.

Waldemar picked up the phone and dialed the city police.

"Edmonton City Police, how can I help you?" a pleasant voice answered.

"Hello, may I speak to Frank Harrison please?"

"Certainly. One moment please."

Waldemar waited for a minute.

"Harrison here. How can I help you?"

"Hi, Harrison. It's Detective Peterson. I'm calling to talk to you about the raid tonight."

"Hello, Pete! Good to hear from you. I was just working on my paperwork for the raid. I have good news. I've been able to find a car for us to use."

Cars were scarce in the Force so the City Police and the RCMP had to alternate between who would be providing the police car for the night. Cars were very basic: four wheels, an engine and a steering wheel. Officers joked that if they ran it was a bonus. They were unmarked cars and they didn't even have a radio for music. A simple portable red flashing light and siren were thrown onto the dash when needed. Most City

Police patrolled on motorcycle. Everyone else had to share the limited resources they had.

"Great. Where did you want to meet?"

"Ah," Harrison said, "I'll pick you up on the corner of Jasper Avenue and 99 St. around ten o'clock."

"That would be fine."

"And Nixon? Will he be with you?"

"Yes, he's joining us."

"Fine then. Sounds like we have everything in order."

"We sure do," Waldemar agreed.

"Hey, I've heard through the grapevine that you're a dad now."

Waldemar grinned, "Yes! We had a boy, Gerald. He's six weeks old now."

"Well, congratulations."

"Thanks, Harrison. How about you? Any more kids in your future?"

Harrison laughed. "No, sir. Six kids is enough!"

"I'll say!"

"Good chatting with you, Pete. I'll see you tonight."

"See you then." Waldemar said goodbye and hung up the phone. He put his files away and closed up his desk. He too was going home for the afternoon, to rest and spend some time with Ruth and Gerry.

Just as he was leaving, a clerk came by.

"Hi, Detective Peterson, I have a message from the telegram office for you."

"Thanks," Waldemar's brows furrowed as he looked at the envelope. He tore it open.

He read, *"Waldy, Mother is gravely ill. Please arrange to come to Winnipeg as soon as possible. Margaret."*

Waldemar's mother, Alina, had been having trouble with her health for a number of years, but this was the first time he had received a message like this from his sister. He ran his hands through his blonde, wavy hair and sighed. He needed to talk to Ruth. He wondered how she would feel about a trip to Winnipeg.

Early the following morning, Ruth was waiting for her father and stepmother, Edith Bohlman, to arrive from their home in the nearby town of Leduc. Edith was going to stay with Gerry while she and Waldemar went to Winnipeg. Waldemar was at the office to wrap up some final things before they left.

Ruth had been pacing for hours, trying to get Gerry to stop crying. Finally, he had begun to give in to exhaustion and relax. Ruth didn't dare lay him down for fear that he would cry again. She knew that babies should be laid down to sleep, but with Gerry it was such an effort to get him to this point, thus it was simply easier to hold him.

She settled in the armchair, closing her eyes for a moment with Gerry lying on her chest. His little hand was spread out on her breast, showing each tiny finger. She loved every detail of this child, each nail, each dark hair on his head, each wrinkle in his baby skin.

The doorbell rang. Ruth rose carefully and quietly to answer it. She clutched Gerry to her chest while motioning Herman and Edith into the modest apartment.

"Hello," she whispered.

"Hello, child," Herman replied as he came in. The cold winter air rushed in behind them as they brushed off their boots.

"Hello, Ruth," Edith said as she shut the door behind her.

"Hello, Mother."

Edith pointed at Gerry. "Why don't you lay him down while he sleeps? You need to have him learn to sleep on his own."

"I know, but he is very fussy and he never sleeps for long. I'd rather hold him than hear him cry."

"Well, he'll never learn to sleep alone if you spoil him like that."

Ruth groaned, "Really, Mother, must you criticize?"

Herman interrupted, "How is Pete?"

Ruth smiled at her father and stroked Gerry's small back, "He's worried about his mother, of course. He's anxious to get on the train today. As you know we leave at noon."

The three adults visited for nearly an hour as Ruth explained everything she could about Gerry before he began to stir. He grunted and groaned, as newborns do, and turned his head back and forth, looking for milk.

Ruth handed Gerry off to her father and said, "I'll go heat up a bottle." She left for the kitchen while Herman admired his grandson. He loved Gerry's hands. He held out his own wrinkled finger for Gerry to grasp as Gerry looked around for something to eat. "It'll be here in a minute, *Schatsi*." Gerry did not grasp Herman's finger but instead the two put their palms together.

Twenty-eight years earlier, in December of 1921, Herman had lost his first wife, Ruth's mother, during childbirth. It still haunted him. He had fears of the worst when his daughter had hovered between life and death while delivering this baby. When Herman held his grandson in his arms, he thought of all he had left behind in Russia. When he left for Canada, in 1913, he was merely a young man. He had left his mother, sisters and brother, who he would never see again. He came to start a better life in a new country. He had promised them all passage to Canada, unaware that they would be victims of the Russian Revolution before he could save them. Coming to Canada now seemed a worthwhile sacrifice when he held this small boy.

Ruth entered the living room with the bottle, looking tired and pale.

"Sit down, Ruth, you look like you need to rest," Herman commented, his brows knit.

"I can feed him," Edith piped up, taking Gerry from Herman and the bottle from Ruth.

"Thank you, Mother." Ruth sat down and closed her eyes. "I'm really tired." She groaned. "I still have to pack and get ready but I just haven't been able to put him down."

Edith struggled to get Gerry to latch onto the bottle. "I remember when Lorne was born. I thought I'd never feel rested again."

Lorne was Ruth's younger half-brother. He was Herman and Edith's only child. He was now living in British Columbia.

"Yes, those were long days and nights," Herman agreed.

The three adults talked while Edith managed to get Gerry to take most of the bottle. She paused to burp him and managed to hold him upright long enough for most of the formula to stay in his tummy. She tenderly wiped his lips when he spit up.

"Are you sure you're going to be okay, Mother?" Ruth asked.

"I'll be fine, Ruth. I've raised a baby before."

"I know. It's just that Gerry — he cries a lot. He's hard to settle, hard to feed. When his legs spasm, you need to massage them. He has terrible colic."

Edith looked at Ruth sternly. "Child, there isn't much of a choice here. You need to go and I need to be here. I will manage with Gerry."

Herman looked at Ruth and smiled. "I'll be here too. I'll come up as often as I can. It's going to be okay."

Tears welled up in Ruth's eyes. "I should go pack."

Chapter 2

"She is clothed with strength and dignity; she can laugh at the days to come. She speaks with wisdom, and faithful instruction is on her tongue. She watches over the affairs of her household and does not eat the bread of idleness. Her children arise and call her blessed; her husband also, and he praises her: 'Many women do noble things, but you surpass them all.' Charm is deceptive, and beauty is fleeting; but a woman who fears the Lord is to be praised. Give her the reward she has earned, and let her works bring her praise at the city gate." Proverbs 31: 25 – 31 NIV

February 28, 1949

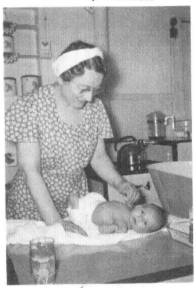

6 weeks
Edith and Gerry

Waldemar sat next to Ruth on the train, holding her hand and looking out the window. As the prairies rolled by, the memories rushed over him — threatening to overwhelm his normally calm exterior.

As he saw the cows in the farmer's fields, he thought of his own childhood on the farm. He thought of his mother and all the times she had been there for him.

He distinctly remembered being four years old, atop the wagon full of all of their worldly goods, moving to the farm. He remembered his pregnant mother walking the trail with strength and confidence, leading the family to their new life. His mother had been governess to the royal family in Sweden, caring for the royal prince and princess when she and Otto, Waldemar's father, decided to move to Canada for a better life. The landlords in Sweden had oppressed the people and taxed them to the point of poverty. Waldemar thought that it must have been quite an adjustment for Alina to face the Canadian wilderness back in the 1920s when they first arrived. She never complained though; she worked tirelessly on the farm, making the best of things for their family. She watched her children grow up and take on the responsibilities of the farm when Otto had injured his back. Victor, Waldemar's older brother, still ran the farm, caring for his parents and making his living. Waldemar enjoyed the farm as a young boy, milking the cows, working the fields and playing in the woods on and surrounding their property. He remembered his mother singing to him, giving him hugs and taking special attention to care for him in the early mornings and late nights. She had always let him be himself, be independent and expend his seemingly endless energy. She had quietly shown her appreciation for all of his hard work on the farm. At nights when he would come home late from working his trap line, she would leave fresh bread on the table for him. Every Christmas she would knit him mitts, scarves or socks — even this last Christmas she had sent him a pair of navy wool socks, which he had lovingly folded and placed in his drawer, not to wear, but to cherish. Through his adult life, her love and prayers had followed him through his days working at

Gunner Mine and into the Force. Her letters came faithfully, always filled with news of the family and neighbors.

Waldemar admired and loved so many things about his mother. She had instilled in him his core values, his faith in God and his strong work ethic. She had taught him what it meant to love your children unconditionally and let them be who God had planned for them to be. He hoped that he could be that kind of parent to Gerry, as Gerry grew up.

Waldemar squeezed Ruth's hand knowing that she too was filled with emotion. It had been a long spring adjusting to the arrival of Gerry, worrying about his frequent illnesses. Now she was leaving him for the first time, with Edith.

Ruth looked over at Waldemar and smiled. She was glad that she had him to hold her fragile world together. She felt ill at leaving and yet was anxious to be in Manitoba, meeting many of Waldemar's family members for the first time. She hoped that this would not be the last time she would meet Waldemar's mother. From the urgency in Margaret's telegram, it seemed to be a grim possibility.

When they arrived in Winnipeg, one of Waldemar's younger sisters, Singhild, and her husband Nick were there to greet them.

Sing, as everyone called her, rushed toward Waldemar when she saw him exit the train. "Waldemar! How good to see you!" He gave her a big hug. She dissolved into tears.

"Now, now," Waldemar said as he took her hands in his own. "How are you?"

"Oh, Waldy," Singhild exclaimed, "it's good to see you!"

"It's good to see you too." Waldemar extended a hand to Nick. "Nice to see you, Nick."

Nick shook Waldemar's hand vigorously. "And you, Waldemar."

"This is Ruth," Waldemar introduced, "and this is Singhild and Nick."

Ruth put out her hand, shaking each of theirs, "Nice to meet you."

Singhild pulled Ruth into a warm hug. "Nice to finally meet you as well. We've heard many wonderful things about you."

"What's happening with Mamma?" Waldemar asked.

They began to walk down the train platform toward where Nick had parked the car.

Sing looked downward, clearly having a hard time holding back her emotions. "She is in St. Bonafice hospital. They say she has bleeding lungs."

"She's had this for some time though, hasn't she?"

"Yes, she's been ill for a while; she always downplays it though."

"Do they fear she is near the end?"

Sing said nothing, only nodded, brushing away the tears.

Ruth offered a hug. "My deepest sympathies."

"I know she's had a good life," Singhild sniffed, "but I'm not ready to say goodbye."

"Of course not," Waldemar soothed.

Nick wrapped his arm around his wife. "Come now. Let's get to the hospital so we can see her. That will help us all feel better."

"Is Pappa there?" Waldemar asked.

"Yes, Victor brought him up from the farm a few nights ago," Nick answered. "Margaret is here too."

The three came up to the car. Nick drove them to the hospital. He let them off at the front door and then went to park the car.

After entering the hospital and walking the white echoing halls to the ward for the dying, they found members of the Peterson family huddled outside a private room. After introductions and some small talk, Waldemar and Ruth entered Alina's hospital room alone. Waldemar took in the sight of his Mamma. She was pale and thin, looking ashen against the white bed linens. Her lips were cherry red. She held a bloody cloth to her lips as she coughed.

"Hello, Mamma," Waldemar said softly as he approached her.

She opened her eyes and saw her handsome young blonde-haired son standing in front of her. "Am I dreaming?" she asked in Swedish, a smile playing at her lips.

"*Nej*, I'm here. I've brought Ruth."

Alina looked up at Ruth and said, "Hello, Ruth, wonderful to finally meet you. Congratulations on the birth of your son." She began to cough violently. Ruth looked at the dark blood she coughed up. Her nurse's instinct told her that Alina did not have long for this world.

"Thank you, Mrs. Peterson."

Alina smiled weakly and took Waldemar's hand. In Swedish she asked, "How are you, Waldemar? I've missed you terribly."

"I am well, Mamma, I've missed you too."

"How is that boy of yours? Do you think he will insist on running everywhere like you did?" Alina began to cough again. "When Waldemar was a boy, he never walked from one point to the next, he ran."

"Gerry's been sick lately but he has such a sweet personality. When he looks into your eyes," Waldemar paused, "well, there's nothing like it."

Alina started to cough again. Waldemar began to worry that the visit was putting too much of a strain on her. "Let's just sit, Mamma, we don't want to wear you out."

Alina nodded, closed her eyes and laid her head back on the pillow. Waldemar held her small, fragile hand and thought of her in her younger days. He remembered the day she had told them to stay out of the creek that ran across their property. Of course he, Gus and Victor, being mischievous little boys, had gotten so involved in chasing frogs that they had waded into the creek so that the water came over the top of their rubber boots. When they returned to the house, Mamma said nothing, simply making them take off their wet socks so that she could smack them in the back of the head with them. Waldemar smiled as he thought of so many other memories where she had caught him when he was up to no good and essentially said nothing, but had got her message across nonetheless. When he was a young boy, he had decided to roll up a leaf and try smoking it behind the barn. She had seen the fiery embers from the house. When he came inside, she told him, 'I know what you're doing. You're going to burn the barn down if you keep it up.' That had been the end of smoking leaves. She had always been so gentle and kind, loving all of her children in their own special way.

When they left the hospital room that day, Waldemar gave her a kiss on the forehead and said, "I love you, Mamma."

"I love you too, Waldemar. I have always had a special place in my heart for you."

"I know, I know, Mamma."

Waldemar felt the sting of tears in his eyes. He gripped Ruth's hand tightly as they left the room. Singhild and Nick sat in the hallway waiting to go in after them.

"You can go back to our place, Waldemar. Margaret and Victor are there. They'll let you into the house. Catch a taxi out front of the hospital; there should be a few waiting."

"We'll see you later then." Waldemar and Ruth walked out of the hospital and got into a waiting taxi. Waldemar looked at Ruth and sighed. "Well, what do you think?"

"About?" Ruth asked tentatively.

"Her health?"

"I'm not sure…"

"But if you had to say?"

"I'm sorry…" she squeezed his hand. "I think you know as well as I do."

Waldemar nodded. He turned and looked out the window, watching people do their everyday things around the city, as if they had no concerns. Ruth laid her head on Waldemar's shoulder, wanting him to know that she was there. Waldemar wondered if that was the last time he might ever hear his Mamma say that she loved him.

Anna Alina Peterson died the next day with her husband by her side. The family held services and spent time grieving together. Before long, Ruth and Waldemar were back on the train to Edmonton to see how Edith had fared with little Gerry.

*

"We're back," Ruth called softly as she opened the apartment door.

Edith brought her finger to her lips. "Shhh." Gerry was sleeping in Edith's arms.

Ruth was drawn to Gerry as a magnet to a pole. "Oh, I've missed him!" She took the sleeping baby from Edith's arms. She cradled him tightly to her chest. "Oh, Gerry!" She peppered his head with kisses.

Edith sighed and sat down on the sofa. "Welcome home."

Waldemar sat down in the armchair. "How are you, Mother?"

"Good." She looked at Ruth beaming at Gerry. "Fine. And how was the train ride back?"

"Uneventful."

Edith slid to the edge of her seat. "You look worn out, Pete. Can I get you some coffee?"

"Sure. That would be great."

Edith stood up and walked toward the kitchen. "Ruth? Coffee?"

"No thanks. I'm fine. It's good to be home. Thanks for taking care of Gerry."

Edith smiled. "You're welcome."

Ruth moved into the kitchen after Edith. "How was it? How did he do?"

Edith poured coffee into a cup. "He was fine. He's not an easy baby."

Ruth sighed and said, "I know. I appreciated every night of sleep I had while I was away."

"He never sleeps very long…a few hours at best. He seems like his stomach is always hurting. I think he has a bad case of colic."

"It's terrible."

Edith stood, frozen with the coffee cup in her hand. "And did you notice how his arms flail? Is that normal at his age?"

Ruth squeezed sleeping Gerry a little tighter. "Yes, it's normal…until about four months. He's still young."

"What about the spasms? Is that normal?"

"I don't know…" Ruth hesitated, her voice catching in her throat. "I don't know."

"You're a nurse, shouldn't you know?" Edith walked back to the living room while they talked and handed Waldemar his coffee.

"Thanks," he said, taking the hot cup.

Edith sat down on the sofa again, looking up at Ruth, standing in the doorway between the kitchen and the living room.

"I am a nurse, and I don't know if that makes things better or worse. I'm not an expert on everything. I don't think I want to be. Perhaps ignorance is bliss."

"How's Dad?" Waldemar asked, changing the subject, preferring not to think about Gerry's troubles.

"He's fine. He came up every Wednesday to help out, in between purchasing for the store and driving home."

"What time is he coming today?"

"He should be here by three o'clock. We'll try to get back before it's dark."

"That sounds good," Waldemar said.

Gerry began to stir in Ruth's arms. He opened his wide blue eyes and looked up at his mom. Recognition passed over his face. "Hi, Gerry!"

Gerry's arms began to wiggle in his tightly swaddled blanket.

Waldemar stood up and came over to Ruth. "Hi, Gerry! We're home!"

Gerry gave his little half smile at his mom and dad's beaming faces. Waldemar put his hand on Gerry's head. "Good to see you, little man!"

Edith excused herself and went to pack up her things from the bedroom. Ruth sat down on the sofa with Gerry. She began to tell him all about the train ride to Manitoba and about all of the aunties and uncles that he would one day meet.

"One day you can go too. When you're a little bigger."

"Can you imagine him riding the tractor with Vic?" Waldemar laughed. "I think they'd both love that."

Ruth smiled and said, "Yes, we'll have to go once Gerry is a little older, so he can see Lac Du Bonnet and meet all of the family."

"Pappa is a Grandpa now…" Waldemar mused, "weird to think about. Can you imagine that we could be grandparents one day?"

Ruth burst out laughing. "No! I can't imagine that!"

Chapter 3

"What I feared has come upon me; what I dreaded has happened to me. I have no peace, no quietness; I have no rest, but only turmoil." Job 3:25 & 26 NIV

<u>August 1949</u>

Ruth and Gerry

Ruth and seven-month-old Gerry were on the bus on the way to another doctor's appointment. Ruth had many concerns. Gerry had one chest cold after another and certainly had not slept through a single night. He was always fussy, couldn't keep down any of his food or milk, had trouble swallowing and had frequent muscle spasms. Ruth was at her wits' end trying to solve his problems and ease his pain. He was not progressing very well with his grasp; in fact, he did not grasp at all, and wasn't building any core strength so that he might be able to sit up on his own at some point. Waldemar would often sit with Gerry and put a rattle in his hand. He would then wrap his big hands around Gerry's tiny fist and show him how to grasp it. Every time Waldemar let go, Gerry dropped the rattle. Ruth kept telling herself that all of this was of a temporary nature, that in time he would catch up. As the months wore on she knew, deep down, in places she dared not admit, that something was wrong. She told the doctor again and again that things were not right but he dismissed her as the worst type of worrier, a combination of a first-time mother and a nurse.

Today, though, she was going to lay down the law. She wanted answers. She had been asking for answers for months and today she was going to get something — some reason why Gerry was having such a hard time. As they sat on the bus, Gerry's little arms flailed, much like a newborn's. Ruth held them close against his body and bounced him on her knee, trying to keep him content. He was such a sweet little baby. His dark newborn hair had fallen away and in its place he had soft blonde curls. She leaned down and kissed his full cheeks.

"I love you," she whispered.

Gerry smiled.

She waited patiently in the pediatrician's office, among the other young mothers and babies. She watched the other children Gerry's age sit up strongly on their mothers' laps. She saw some grasping toys and bringing them to their mouths, and others making wonderful babbling noises, "ma ma ma," and "ba ba ba." She was proud of Gerry, there was no mistaking that, but she wanted him to be progressing, as he should be. Watching these other children made her feel once again that something was amiss.

"Mrs. Peterson," the receptionist called.

Ruth stood, clutching Gerry and the diaper bag. "Hello."

"The doctor will see you now."

Ruth was ushered into a white room. On the left side of the room, there was a counter with medical equipment laid out. On the right side of the room was a hard wooden chair next to the examination table. She sat down in the chair and talked to Gerry while they waited.

Within a few minutes, the doctor came into the examination room. She watched as he carefully looked Gerry over. Once the doctor finished, Ruth wrapped Gerry back up. He invited her out of the examination room and into his office across the hall. She settled herself across from the doctor with Gerry on her lap. The expansive oak desk sat between them. The doctor sat there, twirling a pair of scissors around and around, most annoyingly, saying nothing and looking away from Ruth and Gerry. Ruth waited for answers to the many questions she had posed while he had examined Gerry, and yet the doctor said nothing. Gerry sat quietly, watching the scissors twirl.

Ruth looked at him penetratingly. She scrutinized his face. She felt unease seep through her again. Finally, she said, "Okay, now tell me what is wrong with my baby."

He stopped twirling the scissors. The room was oppressively still. He said, "You know Gerry didn't breathe for about ten minutes after his birth, right?"

"Yes." She examined the doctor's face, looking for clues about his revelation. The silence hung heavily over Ruth.

He ran his finger along the edge of his desk. He began to twirl his scissors again. Finally, he said, "He has Little's Disease, Cerebral Palsy, so named after a doctor who did research on newborns with difficulties like Gerry's." He paused. Ruth said nothing, just stared at this man who was sentencing her child. "He will be hopelessly crippled due to a blood clot in his brain, which has blocked out the part of his brain that controls muscle coordination." The scissors stopped twirling. "The damage is permanent."

Ruth sat there, taking in the information. *The damage is permanent; the damage is permanent...* The words echoed inside her head. Her world threatened to come crashing in around her. She felt the room spin. She held Gerry tightly. He looked up at her and cooed.

The doctor's next words came slowly and deliberately, without concern for the heart of a mother. "My advice to you is to put him in an institution and forget you ever had him."

Ruth felt the ground shake beneath her as his words sunk in. Her brow furrowed and a rage built up from the core of her being. She stood up, clutching Gerry. She banged her fist on the desk, looked the doctor in the eye and seethed, "Oh no I won't! Over my dead body, neither you nor anyone else will put this child in an institution!"

The trip home was a blur. Once she was home and in their apartment, she gently laid Gerry down in his bassinet. He was sleeping soundly. She left him there and went into the living room where she stormed back and forth, raging, grieving, crying and mourning all at the same time. *Why, God? Why?* Ruth asked again and again. *Why my baby? My son who responds to our every touch, this baby boy who conveys love and understanding to us, why him? No, no, no!* She felt out of control. Anger and grief were spinning about into an internal tornado that threatened to destroy everything in its path.

Gerry slept on, unaware of his mother's pain. The hours passed and Ruth felt no relief. She cried an ocean of tears. She sent angry prayers heavenward.

When Waldemar walked through the door, he saw his wife who was standing, looking out the window, her arms crossed across her chest. He said softly, "Tell me."

"I went to the doctor today," she said with her glazed eyes fixed on a spot outside the window.

He came to her and put his hand on her shoulder. She was rigid. "What happened?"

"He looked Gerry over, he listened to me explain all of his symptoms and then – he…" She brought her hands to her face, her eyes still fixed in the distance.

"What?"

She looked him in the eyes. "He said that Gerry has Little's Disease."

"What is that?"

"Cerebral Palsy — a permanent problem with his brain and muscles."

Waldemar looked at his wife, perplexed.

"That's not the worst part," she whispered, looking away again as her eyes welled up with tears.

"What?"

"He told me that we should give Gerry up and pretend we never had him. Like the last seven months have meant nothing to us." Ruth sat down on the couch.

The silence that surrounded them was absolute.

Waldemar rolled Ruth's words over in his mind. "Like he is a worthless, broken object to be cast aside?" he whispered into the stillness.

Ruth cried. "How can this be happening?"

"I don't know." He shook his head and began to wipe his own tears.

"What are we going to do?"

"I don't know."

They both sat quietly, thinking things over.

"Maybe we can help him work through it," Waldemar suggested quietly. "What do you know about Cerebral Palsy?"

"Not a lot…let me get my Gray's Anatomy text." Ruth got up off the couch and went to her desk. She pulled down the book and went to the index. She found Cerebral Palsy and flipped to the appropriate page. "Inability to control muscle coordination due to brain damage."

"Hmmm."

"That's not helpful."

"No."

"I need to talk to people, experts, and find out more."

"I think that's a good first step," Waldemar answered, his tone turning more cheerful. "Maybe we can find people who have been through this…people who have cured their children."

"Okay," Ruth wiped at her face, "I'll do that."

He hugged her. "We'll figure this out. Somehow."

Gerry slept on peacefully, unaware of the earthquake of pain that had hit their family.

*

Ruth and Waldemar were at the Bohlman home on a sunny Sunday afternoon. They had just finished lunch. Ruth helped Edith take the dishes to the kitchen while Herman and Waldemar went into the living room.

Waldemar sat down with Gerry in his lap.

Herman looked at his grandson and smiled. Softly he said, "He'll get better, Pete."

Waldemar looked up at his father-in-law. "I don't know, Dad."

"You have to pray on it. Pray and God can do anything."

Waldemar shrugged. He was beginning to hate this conversation. "I don't know."

Herman leaned forward in his seat. "Do you believe it, Waldemar? Do you believe that God can do anything?"

"I guess."

"If we take Gerry to God…" Herman paused, "God can."

"Does that mean that God takes away all the bad things that happen to us?" Waldemar spit out the words, trying to keep his tone even.

"No," Herman ran his hands over his trousers.

"Has he answered every prayer you've uttered? Did he spare your wife?"

Herman looked wounded for a moment. "No."

"Then we don't know if he'll heal Gerry. Respectfully, Dad, we just don't know."

"I suppose."

"He's our blessing and we're happy to be his parents, Cerebral Palsy or not."

"Indeed, Waldemar. Indeed. And we're happy to be his grandparents."

"Good. Right now that has to be enough. We love Gerry for who he is today, not who he might be someday…limitations or not."

"You're absolutely right." Herman reached out his arms. "Let me hold him."

Waldemar handed Gerry to Herman. Gerry vocalized and reached his arms toward Herman's face.

"Hello, little fellow!" Herman laughed as Gerry's face split into a wide grin. "Aren't you cute! Come sit with Grandpa for awhile." He hugged Gerry tightly and kissed the top of his head.

Ruth brought the last of the dishes to Edith who was standing at the kitchen sink, washing. Ruth sighed as she set them down. "Here you are, Mother."

"Thanks."

The previous weeks had been spent breaking the news to family and friends. Each time Ruth explained the situation, she wept a little less. Her heartbreak was not for herself but for Gerry. Every time she tried to explain Cerebral Palsy, she realized how little she knew. She prayed that the doctor would be wrong; that with therapy she could teach Gerry to walk and talk one day. It was the hardest to tell her parents; to shatter their dream of a normal, happy existence for their first grandson.

"Do you want me to dry?" Ruth asked.

"Sure."

Ruth picked up a dish off the drying rack and began to rub it dry.

"Do you know the meaning of *Sindenschult*?" Edith asked quietly.

"Yes," Ruth answered, perplexed by the question. Edith rarely spoke German to her. "Of course I do. Do you?" She set down the plate she was holding.

"Sin guilt. People have been saying that." Edith's hands continued to scrub the dishes furiously.

"People who?" Ruth squeezed the dishtowel tightly. She glared at her mother. "What are you saying?"

"I am saying," Edith said, her eyes still focused on the dishes, "that there is nothing that God doesn't give us that we don't deserve." Edith looked up and made eye contact with Ruth. "That you must be wickedly sinful to be given such a burden – "

"How dare you!" Ruth stepped toward Edith menacingly. "Is that what you think?" She pulled the towel tightly between her two hands. "Perhaps it is your sins that cause *me* to suffer!" She quoted Exodus 34:7, "'Yet he does not leave the guilty unpunished; he punishes the children and their children for the sin of the fathers to the third and fourth generation!' If anyone has guilt and shame," she seethed, "it isn't me!" She snapped the towel down on the counter.

She turned swiftly and left the kitchen before the tears could erupt. She took one look at Waldemar on the way out the door and mouthed the words, "It's time to go." She walked out the front door, leaving it hanging open, like a gaping mouth. She ripped open the car door, flung herself down on the seat and began to cry.

Inside, Waldemar hastily wrapped up Gerry and thanked Herman and Edith for the meal. He laid Gerry on the backseat and then slipped into the driver's seat. He patted the bench seat next to him.

"Slide over here."

Ruth slid next to Waldemar. She laid her head on his chest, sobbing. "Just go. Just get out of here."

Waldemar started the car, his right arm wrapped around his wife. "Tell me."

Ruth sobbed. "She said…" another torrent of tears came down Ruth's flushed cheeks. "She said that I must be…" The sobs racked her body. Waldemar stroked her hair as he drove down the quiet street.

"It's okay."

Ruth sat up, pulling away from Waldemar. She wiped her face on her sleeve. "It's not okay, Pete. Nothing is okay. She looked back at Gerry in the backseat. He was about to roll on the floor. She leaned over the seat and pulled him into the front seat with her. She wrapped her arms around his flailing arms as he started to cry. "Shhhh…shhhh, Gerry. It's okay. Mommy's okay."

"What did she say?"

"She said that I must be wickedly sinful. Can you believe that?"

Waldemar banged his fist on the steering wheel. "Really?"

"Yes," Ruth carried on crying, all the while stroking Gerry's hair. "She said that it was my sin that did this to Gerry."

"That's bullshit, Ruth," he said angrily, "and you know it."

She wept the entire drive back to Edmonton. She cried as though she would never feel happy again. With each tear, she mourned the loss of a normal life, the affliction of judgment against both them and Gerry. With every tear that fell, she begged God to reconsider.

"Please, God," Ruth begged between sobs, "heal our son."

Waldemar put his hand on Ruth's knee. He looked over at her reassuringly. "We'll get through this, honey. We will. You and I can do anything together. You've always said that. Now here we are."

Ruth put her hand on top of Waldemar's large, strong hand. She felt his calmness. "I hope you're right."

Chapter 4

"I am the vine; you are the branches. If a man remains in me and I in him, he will bear much fruit; apart from me you can do nothing." John 15: 5 NIV

October 1949

Ruth and Gerry

    Ruth was walking to the premier of Alberta's office. She had an appointment. She was going to get some answers about children with Cerebral Palsy. The premier was someone who could make a change and she didn't think it would be impossible to convince him. On this fall day, the trees in the river valley were displaying their most vivid reds, yellows and oranges. She liked the cool air on her face as she walked. She could hear the distant sound of the fountains that graced the grounds of the legislature.

It had been a few months since that first day of receiving the news of Gerry's condition. Ruth had spent hours and hours both denying his diagnosis and thinking about what she could do for him. There was an institution in Red Deer called Alberta's Provincial Training School for the Mentally Defective, and Ruth knew with one hundred percent certainty that it was not an option. It was not an environment where children could thrive. She found out that the life expectancy for children with Cerebral Palsy was only about fourteen years. She had agonized over this statistic.

Ruth had agonized over many things lately. She kept feeling like this was a terrible nightmare that she would wake from. She kept praying that Gerry would be whole and healthy. The guilt consumed her. What — what had she done to cause this to happen? Even though Waldemar had told her that Edith's accusations were rubbish, she often wondered if there was any merit to it. What terrible sin had she committed to contribute to Gerry's condition? She struggled day and night, through every untold hour of crying, wondering why things had turned out this way. She lashed out at everyone. She loved Gerry so deeply that she didn't want to accept the permanence of his condition — not for her sake, but for his.

She had used her nursing connections and put in a phone call to the minister of health to try to find some help. She remembered the phone call vividly.

"*Hello, I'm Nurse Peterson, I am calling to speak to you regarding children in Alberta with Cerebral Palsy.*"

"*Good afternoon, Nurse Peterson,*" said the minister.

"*I'd like to talk about what sort of support you have for parents of the disabled.*"

"*Support? Why would they need support?*"

Ruth sighed and said, "I'd like to start by asking how many children in Alberta have Cerebral Palsy?"

"Well, Nurse Peterson, I am happy to report that there are no children in Alberta with Cerebral Palsy."

Ruth could feel her anger building up inside as this conversation began to be more and more pointless. "I beg to differ, sir, mine does! What are we going to do about it?"

"Well..." the minister paused, "I suppose there is the option of the hospital for the mentally def–."

Ruth had slammed down the phone in total frustration. It seemed to be the only option society had. Forget you ever had him. Ship him away. Out of sight, out of mind. The words of the doctor rang over and over in her head every time a door closed — forget you ever had him.

In her mind over the last few weeks, many verses had come to mind, but one in particular seemed to keep coming up from John 15:5.

"I am the vine; you are the branches. If a man remains in me and I in him, he will bear much fruit; apart from me you can do nothing."

Apart from me, you can do nothing. This seemed to be particularly true with Gerry. If she thought about her entire future — Gerry's future — it was too overwhelming to imagine. When she thought about getting through today and conquering each challenge, she kept coming up with 'apart from me you can do nothing.'

Ruth arrived at the legislative building and walked inside. She was unsure of what to expect. The one positive thing was that the premier also had a child with a disability. This gave Ruth some hope that he might be willing to hear what she had to say. She was going to talk to him about putting programs in place so that disabled children could attend school and be integrated into family life, to get therapy and support right in their community. The premier was someone who could bring awareness to this issue — if he so chose.

She looked around the grand entrance of the legislative building and went to the information desk to speak to the clerk there.

"Hello, I'm Mrs. Peterson. I'm here to meet Mr. Premier."

"Good day," the clerk smiled at Ruth. "If you'd like to have a seat I'll have someone take you up to his office."

Ruth nodded and sat in a plush chair, waiting to go in. After some time, one of the premier's assistants came and escorted her to his office. She walked in the room and took in the man behind the desk. He was tall and thin. He had a narrow face and small glasses perched upon his sharp nose. He wore a dark suit and every hair on his head was neatly flattened down.

"Hello, Mr. Premier." Ruth stuck out her hand as he stood to greet her.

"Hello, Mrs. Peterson. Thank you for coming in today. Please have a seat." He gestured to a chair opposite his desk.

"Thank you for your time. I'll get right to my purpose for coming."

He nodded and looked at Ruth. "Please do."

"As you know I am here to speak to you about the disabled in Alberta."

"Yes." His tone was cool.

"I feel like we are vastly short of resources in Alberta and I'd like to present you with some ideas for change."

"Mmmm."

"I think that the disabled should be able to live at home, and with the right support from government programs, they could be integrated into society."

He raised a thin eyebrow. "Integrated?"

"Yes." She carried on despite a cold feeling she had. "I think that we should talk about getting some therapeutic programs started for those children who have physical disabilities. We could get experts together who can identify the child's needs, who can work with…"

"Excuse me, are you not aware of the Alberta Provincial Training School…"

"Yes, I am. And I believe you are all too familiar with the conditions at the school. Not everyone can afford or wants to send their child away."

His gaze was distant. "Perhaps you should look for a facility out east with better programs."

"Why should the disabled be sent to a facility when they could be cared for at home?" she asked.

"Not every mother is a nurse, Mrs. Peterson."

"I realize that but I am not a teacher and I want my son to be educated."

"Mmmm," he said skeptically.

"Educating a child with Cerebral Palsy is worthwhile. Every human being deserves basic dignity and a sense of purpose."

He raised his eyebrow.

"Nursing isn't all of it," she continued, "even as a nurse I am limited by what I can do. We need facilities, clinics and resources for education. We need them here in Edmonton."

"Well thank you for coming in today, Mrs. Peterson," he said in a dismissive tone.

"I'm not through, Mr. Premier."

"I get the point of what you're saying. You want the government to care for your son but you don't like the options you have."

"No, sir, that is not what I'm saying. I'm saying the options could be a lot better. You have the power to make that happen. Parents and government could work together, I am sure it would even be less expensive than the current setup…"

"Well I must be moving on with my next appointment. Good day."

Ruth let out a sigh and rose from her chair. The premier had picked up his pen and started to write at his desk. She didn't even bother with a handshake but picked up her purse and left the office. She was furious. She needed help and support and there was none. People didn't even want to talk about children with disabilities — as though if you ignored the problem it would disappear. If you shipped them away or shut them in your home then everything would be normal. As she walked home, every muscle in her body was tense. She crunched the leaves under her feet.

Once she was home, she opened the apartment door. She found Waldemar sitting in the armchair with Gerry sleeping on his chest. He smiled at her and whispered, "Hello."

Ruth plopped herself down on the couch and sighed.

"How did it go?" Waldemar whispered.

"Not well," she whispered back.

"Let me put Gerry down and then you can tell me what happened." Waldemar left the living room and went to lay Gerry down in his crib. When he returned, he sat on the sofa and put his arm around Ruth. "Tell me."

Ruth started to cry. It was about the millionth time she had cried in the last few months since Gerry's diagnosis. Waldemar held her close and let her release her torrent of emotions.

Between sobs, Ruth said, "I'm – I'm frustrated!"

"I know."

"I thought – I thought for sure he would listen, and even be excited by what I had to say."

"It's okay."

"It's not okay, Pete! It's so maddening! Why doesn't anyone want to help these kids — our son?"

"There is someone," he said quietly and calmly.

"Who? Who cares about Gerry?"

"We do, Ruth." He looked into her teary eyes, "We care."

"It's not enough!" she sobbed on.

"It is enough, Ruth. We need to find the right avenue. You can't give up at the first closed door."

"It's not the first closed door! There's been so many! I thought that since he knew firsthand that he would be…"

"He's not the answer. Now you know. Now you have to pray and listen for God to show you the next step."

"Why, Pete?" Ruth cried, "Why does this have to be happening?"

He held her close. "I don't know, I don't know." He quoted a verse from Proverbs 31: 8 and 9 that suddenly had new meaning to the couple: "Speak up for those who cannot speak for themselves: for the rights of all who are destitute: Speak up and judge fairly, defend the rights of the poor and the needy."

*

After many tears and much prayer, Ruth had decided to keep searching for other avenues of help. Waldemar was right: she was Gerry's voice in a world that wanted to shut away the disabled. Ruth had to persevere and pray that God would give her the strength to find answers for Gerry's future. Ruth had written the Department of National Health and Welfare, to which she had received limited information on who to contact for written information on Cerebral Palsy therapy. Ruth had received a response from a doctor in Baltimore with a recommendation of a book she could read. Even though this was helpful, it felt like a grain of sand on the beach. She was the one who fed Gerry many times a day and had it spit back out at her. She was the one who massaged his spastic muscles endlessly. She was the one who awoke in the night to his tortured cry. She wanted someone to lead her through this battle, someone to guide her and tell her what Gerry needed. She wanted concrete answers and direction. There were none.

Every morning she started the day with a cup of coffee, and if time allowed, the morning paper. She read the articles about the surplus of money that the government had. She read the letters to the editors and would occasionally find another parent who was searching for help with their specific problem. On one such morning, she found an article that seemed to be written just for her.

Gerry lay on a blanket on the floor next to her, looking around with his bright eyes and making little grunts to remind her that he was there. Waldemar was sleeping in the bedroom, catching up from a late night of undercover police work.

The headline in the Edmonton Journal read: "Edmonton Children Need Help To Overcome Spastic Paralysis." She read Jane Becker's article intently.

> "How old's your little boy?" the kindly looking matron at the Santa Claus parade asked the mother with the child in her arms.
>
> The mother told her.
>
> "Hm, crazy, eh?" was the rejoinder.
>
> The mother was utterly stunned, for her five-year-old, though small for his age, was considerably less crazy than the woman who made that incredibly thoughtless remark.
>
> But, like about thirty other children in Edmonton, this five-year-old had a handicap. He had been born with almost no coordination between the brain and his muscles — a condition known as spastic paralysis. Estimates of the number of children so handicapped are about 1000. In the United States, where a campaign to bring spastic paralysis under control is starting soon, about 200,000.

Like a sudden squall, spastic paralysis comes unheralded. It knows no rules of class or type, and can't be traced to hereditary causes. It is most often acquired at birth, but sometimes a bad fall or other accident later in life will also damage the part of the brain that is detailed to send messages, so effortlessly in a normal person, to the muscles of the body to act harmoniously and with control. A particular type of blood in either the father or the mother known as RH negative, severe nervous strain or a fall to the mother before the baby is born may be other contributing causes.

Although the crippling effects of spastic paralysis are as prevalent as those of the much-publicized poliomyelitis, it was until recently a sad dark splotch on the field of medicine for which doctors had no name. A child had a scant chance to fight it, unless he had a light case, or an extremely fortunate set of circumstances to help bring about its control. Now, however, the problem is not knowledge but opportunity, and funds to form clinics in centers wherever there are numbers of spastic children.

Doctors and therapists can win the long war with spastic paralysis if they take up arms soon enough, and use them constantly against a stubborn enemy. Children at the Red Cross "workshop" at Windsor, Ont., at schools in New York and Wichita, and in many other places, have learned to walk, to speak clearly, and eventually become completely independent. The harnessing of the energy that the disease lays waste; their capturing of the freedom of movement by control, and finally, their long-awaited gaining of happiness and self-respect, are the results that make the years of treatment more than worth the trouble. In many Canadian cities, notably in Ontario, service clubs have set up clinics for spastic children who otherwise would have no chance for a normal life

Need Help

At least two mothers of Edmonton children who have spastic paralysis, Mrs. Cameron and Mrs. Allen, don't see why they should accept the fate of their little boys being handicapped this way all through life.

Yet Edmonton hospitals, badly overcrowded and lacking enough therapists to even set up the field of combat, can't admit the children. Public schools can't take them either, even if their mental capabilities are equal to other children their own age, until they are able to care for themselves physically as well.

Eight-year-old Jordan Cameron spent a year in the Junior Red Cross hospital for crippled children in Calgary, where he first learned the exercises to strengthen and control his muscles, which are the chief weapons of his recovery. Last year, his mother took him to a Spastic school at Wichita to see what could be done about his treatment. Wichita's fee for helping Jordan was $300 a month, and hospital officials wanted him to stay for at least two years. So now Jordan takes his exercises at home, with his mother as therapist, launching a daily routine of control to make his legs work so he can walk on them; help his hands and arms to hold and lift; and his teeth and tongue to shape itself around the words his quick mind tries to form.

But Kenny Allen, who is six, has had no special training. His tight little muscles call out for therapeutic treatment, which his parents neither know of nor can afford.

Clinic Is Dream

"We want to give our children and others a chance to help themselves while they are young," explains Mrs. Cameron and Mrs. Allen, for nowhere more than here is "the sooner the better" a necessary rule.

Their dream is a clinic, where children could be brought each morning, to be given therapy training along with schoolwork according to their capabilities, and brought home again at night. This way, parents would know all possible was being done for their children; and children would absorb the benefits of this help, without losing touch with their parents and more fortunate brothers and sisters, as a morale requirement is important to recovery.

"But even a parents' group would be a beneficial," said Mrs. Cameron. "We could take turns looking after the children and giving them exercises while the other mothers took a much-needed rest."

Mrs. Allen, whose telephone number is 75939, and Mrs. Cameron, at 74326, hope they will hear from other mothers of children handicapped by spastic paralysis, so they may foil this menace to their happiness before it's too late.

Ruth smiled down at Gerry. "I think I've got an idea, little man. I think I may know my next step."

Gerry waved his arms excitedly. His baby noises grew louder. He grinned his two-toothed grin at her. She bent down and picked him up, holding his arms against her and kissing his cheeks. "Shhhh, shhhhh, Daddy's sleeping. I think that a phone call is in order."

Ruth folded the paper with one hand and then kissed the top of Gerry's head. She instinctively rubbed his little chubby legs while she thought about her plan. She would call these other moms today. Perhaps if the government was unwilling to listen and fund her ideas, then maybe a service club, such as the Kiwanis, might help. She needed to get in contact with the president of the club, to discuss fundraising and leadership on a Cerebral Palsy clinic.

"Should we pray about it, Gerry?"

He made an excited noise.

"Dear Lord, thank you for this article today. Thank you for reminding me that I am not alone. I come before you today to ask you to lead me in the right direction. I want to do the right thing for Gerry. I ask that you would open the hearts and minds of those I will need to approach for assistance with this idea. In your Holy name, Amen."

Waldemar came into the kitchen in his pajamas, his blonde hair tousled and his eyes still blinking, adjusting to the sun pouring in the kitchen window.

"Morning, Ruth." Waldemar rubbed Gerry's head and bent down to kiss his wife.

"Good morning, Pete. How was your sleep?"

"Fine."

"I want to tell you about this," she tapped the paper on the table.

"What is it?"

"It's an article by parents who are coping with Cerebral Palsy. As I was reading it, I've had an idea." Ruth handed Gerry to Waldemar who gave his son a warm hug and a kiss. "Let me get you some coffee."

Waldemar watched Ruth turn to the counter, take out a cup and pour some hot coffee for him. "Is it something for me to build?" Waldemar was used to coming up with new contraptions for Gerry that might help him in his day-to-day life. He had already built a chair with a post in the center so that Gerry could sit up on his own.

"No, for a school…therapy, a program — a clinic." She handed him his coffee.

"Another politician in mind?"

Ruth scoffed, "No, I'm fed up with politicians at the moment. I was reading this article and I'm thinking that I might be able to get a service club on board with raising funds and setting up a program. You know, like the Kiwanis. I think these moms are on to something."

"What would the clinic offer exactly?"

"A place to learn — traditional school and then also physical therapy. It could also be a place for parents to find support and learn in home techniques for dealing with the spasms."

Waldemar nodded his head and smiled. "That's a good idea. It's worth a try."

"I hope so. I don't know if I can really make it happen, but nothing ventured, nothing gained."

"Can you contact the parents?"

"Yes, they put their numbers in the paper so I'll give them a call. See if we can come up with a strategy. Just from reading the article, it sounds like they are ladies I can really get along with."

"That's good. I'm proud of you, Ruth. You're never sitting still. You're always trying to do the right thing for Gerry."

Chapter 5

"...The Lord does not look at the things people look at. People look at the outward appearance, but the Lord looks at the heart." 1 Samuel 16: 7 NIV

September 1950

Dale Douglas

Nearly a year later, Ruth lay Gerry down by the door and carefully maneuvered the stroller down the front steps and onto the lawn. She then went back, groaning as she bent down to pick up Gerry.

"Wow! With this baby on board, it's getting nearly impossible to pick you up!" Ruth was pregnant, only a few weeks away from delivery. Her back ached terribly from the pregnancy and from having to lift Gerry constantly, now twenty months old. Soon though, she thought, the baby would be here and her body would belong to her once again. Gerry scowled as Ruth carried him to the stroller.

"What's the frown for?" she asked, with a half smile. "Did Mommy say your least favourite word?" She laughed. "How can you possibly know what's going on? A baby will be fun! You'll have a brother or a sister to play with..."

Gerry grunted his distinctive 'no.' She was sure that if he could have crossed his uncooperative arms across his chest, he would have.

Ruth laughed. "Oh, Gerry!" Her back strained as she leaned over the stroller, carefully guiding Gerry's awkward legs through the seat and around the post that kept him from sliding out of the stroller.

It was the Labor Day weekend and because Waldemar was working, Ruth decided to break up the day by taking the short walk from their apartment down to the legislative grounds. As she approached, she could see that the grounds were buzzing with people. Some were playing in the fountains and others were strolling through the gardens. In the distance, Ruth could hear the thump of a tennis ball connecting with a racket. Gerry was looking around as they walked, smiling at all of the hustle and bustle. It was a beautiful fall day and the sun warmed Ruth as she walked.

Things with Gerry were good. She had made amazing progress this last year. She had taken her anguish over the reality of Gerry's condition and put her energy into caring for him and teaching him. She had given the issues of his health and short life expectancy over to God, knowing that she did not have the energy to waste on something she could not control. She had found *some* measure of acceptance regarding his abilities. As she brought Gerry into all of their everyday activities, she realized that God was calling her to change attitudes. She felt as though He wanted her to be the one to strip away the prejudices of society and to show people that every creation of God was important. Every child deserved the dignity of a purposeful, meaningful life and that somehow or another she would have to make that happen for Gerry and for other children with birth injuries. She wasn't sure what that would look like but she was ready for God to guide her through it. She thought about the verse that He had whispered to her after Gerry's diagnosis: *apart from me you can do nothing*. She was willing now to accept that and to try to be productive. She still prayed daily for healing for Gerry, to change his fate. She still longed for him to be whole and well. She could not yet accept that this was his reality — forever.

The pair of them had learned to communicate. Gerry was able to tell her 'yes' and 'no' in his little voice. To anyone else, 'yes' and 'no' might have sounded the same but the body language that accompanied his grunts expressed exactly what he was feeling. As any mother knows, a child can get his feelings across with or without words. She had begun to label all of the things in the house so that Gerry could become familiar with the words and names of household objects. She was sure that his comprehension was equal to that of any child his age. As she worked around the house she talked and sang to him so that he could be stimulated by her voice. She and Waldemar had come up with a system to handle the long nights. They simply alternated who would get up. One night she could sleep while Waldemar tended to Gerry's needs and the next she would be up. Mainly his muscles needed to be massaged because they cramped badly.

Gerry had lost his baby face and had slimmed out into a cute little toddler. His blonde curls were cut short by the clippers. His many expressive faces let you know how he was feeling. He would furrow his brow and frown at you when he was mad. He would smile and his eyes would light up when he was happy. Ruth loved the little individual he was becoming. His personality shone through his physical problems.

She came to the tennis courts and sat on a bench. Gerry loved to watch the tennis games. He was mesmerized by the thunk of the ball as it bounced from racket to court and back again. She placed her hand on her belly and felt the next little member of the Peterson family move about. The baby seemed to be all elbows and knees, poking and prodding her from within.

Since that day last fall when she first read the article about Mrs. Cameron and Mrs. Allen, she had made some phone calls and met face to face with the president of the South Side Kiwanis Club.

Funds had been raised and Ruth had gone to the media, both the paper and the radio, to spread the awareness of their need. She talked to anyone who would listen. She had offered her nursing skills to Mrs. Cameron and Mrs. Allen, and in April the three of them had banded together to form the Cerebral Palsy Association. It felt good to be a part of a group, finally to be unified with someone else in taking on the government.

They put in their own funds, government funds and public money raised by the Kiwanis, to form a temporary downtown clinic on 105th Avenue and 105th Street. They had appealed to the Department of Health who supplied staff and equipment. Other organizations donated building supplies and furnishings. The Edmonton Club of Associated Travelers provided a bus to transport the children, and Edmonton firemen volunteered to drive the children back and forth. Already the mothers had seen improvements in their children. It was exciting and encouraging and yet all of them knew that there was still a long way to go.

The flood of parents requesting help for their children was overwhelming. They could already see that a new, larger facility was required as well as government leadership to oversee the therapeutic and educational programs.

An Edmonton surgeon, Dr. Frederick George Day, had been appointed last spring as the director of Cerebral Palsy treatment services. His appointment had begun at the beginning of the summer. He was in charge of the temporary clinic and eventually the permanent clinic, which was intended to be complete in the next year or so.

Ruth felt hopeful but knew that it was a long way from fully integrated education. She had read about schools and programs in Europe and she often thought that it might be beneficial to go there one day and see how they ran, firsthand.

Every Wednesday when her father came to Edmonton to buy supplies for the store, he and Edith would come by to visit. Ruth often spoke of her success and hopes for Gerry. Herman loved Gerry intensely and accepted him. He was deeply saddened by Gerry's condition and seemed to want to ignore the fact that this could be a lifelong condition. She had talked about her desire to go to Europe and he had been reluctant, saying, "Nothing the old country had to offer could be good."

Gerry wiggled in the stroller, waved his arms and vocalized to his mom.

"All done, Gerry?" Ruth stroked his hair. He was wiggled restlessly. "We'll go, sweetheart. Let's go home for some lunch."

Gerry smiled at his mom. She bent down to kiss his cheek. She groaned as she sat up. "Are you ready for your new sibling, Gerry? We're going to have a new baby pretty soon." Gerry's smile disappeared. Ruth began to push the stroller back through the legislative grounds. She smiled at the people she passed. A pair of women walked past her. She could hear them talking. They pushed strollers of their own with small children, a boy and a girl, inside. As they passed, Gerry waved his arms and vocalized excitedly about a squirrel he saw running up a tree.

One of the women gasped, "I think that boy is handicapped. Can you believe she takes a handicap outside?"

"I know! I mean, really, handicaps should be left inside," said the other.

Ruth bristled. She wanted to turn around and slap them. She heard the comments often and sometimes chose to confront them and sometimes she ignored them. She hated their ignorance. What right did they have to judge Gerry? The older he got, the angrier the comments made her. He knew what they were saying. He could understand. Why did people have to be so callous?

She approached the apartment and left the stroller out front, pulling Gerry out and carrying him inside. She sat him in the wooden chair that Waldemar had built and started making sandwiches. She cut up squares of soft fruit for him with a vengeance. She took a deep breath and said a prayer. She thought of a verse she had memorized as a small child: *Be still and know that I am God*. It was hard to be still. So hard. She had to let it go. She fed Gerry the fruit while she ate.

Since it was a holiday, Ruth had planned a roast for supper with scalloped potatoes. She needed to get started on that after she put Gerry down for a nap. She hoped that Waldemar would be home for dinner. He always tried to join them, however, his work was unpredictable. He never knew where he might be or what he might be working on any given day. Sometimes he would be gone for days on end. It was always unnerving to wake to an empty bed, but she was busy with Gerry and she tried not to dwell on the dangers of Waldemar's work.

After lunch, she changed Gerry and gave his cramping muscles a rub before he went to sleep. She knew she didn't have long before he would wake up so she went straight to the kitchen to prepare supper. She tied an apron around her large middle and started cutting up potatoes.

Before long, Gerry woke up and she laid him on the couch. She talked to him from the kitchen while she worked.

As she was sitting down with her plate of supper, Waldemar came through the front door.

"Hello," he called cheerily.

Ruth got up from the table to greet him. "Hi, Pete! You made it home!" She gave him a hug and a kiss. "I'll get you some supper."

"I don't have long but I wanted to come by and say hello, and of course get something to eat!"

"That's great!"

Waldemar went and picked up Gerry while Ruth served him supper. "How's my little man?" Waldemar tickled Gerry's stomach, which resounded in an eruption of giggles from the little boy.

"So, are you ready for the new baby?" he asked his son who was smiling widely at his dad.

Ruth answered instead, thinking the question was intended for her, "Yes, I've got the cradle out and I've washed the clothes that Gerry wore. It's much easier with the second baby; you know what you need and most of it I already have."

"I can't wait," Waldemar said. Gerry stopped smiling and made an angry noise.

Ruth laughed and said, "I think we may have a little sibling rivalry already."

*

In the evenings, after supper, Waldemar liked to take Gerry for a walk in the stroller. He watched his son who enjoyed looking all around. Waldemar smoked a cigarette and decompressed from the stress of work. He loved his time with Gerry. He liked the stillness of the legislature grounds, the din of the wind in the grand old trees, the loud noise of the water in the fountains and the crunch of his feet as he walked the pebbled sidewalks. Gerry was always relaxed while they walked. Waldemar could imagine how Gerry would be when he grew out of this — when his development caught up.

He didn't know when but he figured someday, with Ruth's determination and his patience, they could teach him to walk and talk. He looked down at Gerry. His eyes were closed. He looked peaceful and cute. Ruth had put Gerry in his pajamas and wrapped him in a blanket to keep him warm against the cool fall night. These quiet moments reminded him of when he was a boy, walking in solitude along his trap lines. While he walked, he prayed for the health of his son. He prayed for strength for Ruth and for the safe arrival of their new child. As he came back toward the apartment, he put out his second cigarette, rubbing it out with the toe of his shoe. He parked the stroller outside their front door and carefully lifted his little sleeping boy from the stroller and carried him to his bed.

The phone rang. Waldemar rushed to answer it before it woke Gerry. "Hello?"

"Hi, Waldy. It's Margaret." Margaret was one of Waldemar's younger sisters.

"Hi, Margaret! How are you?"

"I'm fine. How are you?"

"Good, good."

"How is Ruth?"

"She's well. Busy with Gerry of course."

"And you? How are you and Ron?"

"Well, busy with the fall work in the yard."

"Ah yes, we're waiting for our first snowfall."

"Listen, I know it's late. I'll get straight to the point. I called to talk to you about Pappa. I've got a letter here from him."

"Okay."

"I know there's nothing we can do, but it left me feeling sad for him. I had to call you and tell you about it."

"Sure."

"May I read it to you?" she asked.

"Of course. I'm listening."

She cleared her throat and began to read the words penned in Swedish.

"Hello Margaret,
I should have written before but I know you understand how lonesome my days are. I have become very nervous — something I've never been before. Wherever I go, it is so empty and dark for me, everything seems worthless. There is nothing that gladdens me now that the best is gone.
I had a funny dream the other day. She came to me, she was so beautiful. She was dressed in the same dress that she had on when she came to Winnipeg. I woke up and then looked at the clock; it was 5 am the same time she woke me in the morning she passed away. She was so strong then she even sat up and called me over, so I asked her if there was anything she wanted, she answered, sit here with me. So I sat on the bed for a few minutes. I said I really should go, I am too heavy. No sit awhile, she said. Shall I call Singhild? I asked. Let her sleep, she is tired, she said.
I've written so much that probably doesn't interest you so I will stop. With much love...

You will have to excuse me, I am so shaky I can hardly hold the pen.
I never did thank you for all that you did for us but I think Annie told me that she had written thanking you.
A funny thing — former summers when Mamma was home and the sun was warm, Mamma would go and sit on a stool behind the summer kitchen. Now there was no stool there but there was a pail in the same place so I sat there when the sun was too warm.

One day when it was really warm, 104 degrees, I went and sat in the same place Mamma used to sit. I had probably sat there a half-hour when a bird came and sat on my head. I tried to catch it with both my hands but there was no bird there just a cool breeze past my face.

Goodbye, Margaret. You must have a hard time reading all this. It is poorly written this time so excuse me.

In all love — your father."

Waldemar exhaled. "Wow."

"I feel badly for him," Margaret lamented.

"I do too."

"What can we do?"

Waldemar gave the situation some thought. "This is the time of life he's at. He's missing Mamma and nothing we can say or do is going to change that. We've had him out to visit us — to meet Gerry and you've had him out to Vancouver to be with you."

"And he wasn't content here either."

"No. What did he keep telling you?"

"That he just wanted to go home. I mean, he enjoyed the diversion but after three weeks he'd had enough."

"No change of scenery, no family joy — even a new grandson can't displace his grief. This is a road he must travel."

"It's hard."

"We can pray for him, and for wisdom for Victor."

"I will."

"It's going to be okay. We can't do anything other than be with him."

Margaret sniffed. "You're right. All we can do is grieve with him."

"He is not alone. He has Victor, he has Annie, Sing, you and the others to support him."

"Thanks, Waldy. I'm glad I called. I really needed to hear your voice."

*

It was the first week of October. Ruth and Waldemar were coming home from the hospital with their new son, Dale Douglas. His arrival had gone smoothly, to everyone's relief. He was cute as a button and looked very similar to Gerry, when he was a baby. Edith was staying at the apartment while Ruth was in the hospital. She was caring for Gerry. Dale had been named after Waldemar's youngest brother, Douglas. He shared a birthday with Dale, September 25. Waldemar sent a telegram home to Manitoba and everyone there had been elated, especially Douglas.

Herman was at the apartment with Edith to welcome them home.

They came in the door and called out, "We're back!"

"Hello, child." Herman rose from the sofa and came to the door to hug Ruth.

"Hi, Dad." Ruth smiled at her dad. "How are you?"

"I'm very well. But more importantly, how are you feeling?"

"Not too bad. I guess the second time around is a little easier."

Ruth turned her attention to Edith who was sitting next to Gerry. "Hello, Mother."

"Hello, Ruth," Edith smiled.

Ruth came to Gerry and kissed him. "Hi, sweetheart! I missed you!"

Gerry reached out his arms and Ruth hugged him.

"It smells good." Ruth looked at Edith. "Do you need help with supper?"

"It's fine. Can I get you some tea? You should sit for a while."

"That would be nice." Ruth sat down next to Gerry. She longed to pick him up. He was suddenly looking much larger compared to Dale. Waldemar saw the look in her eyes. He placed Dale in the bassinet. He went to the couch and scooped Gerry up in his arms.

"Hello, little man! Mommy has missed you! Come and sit with her." Waldemar placed Gerry onto Ruth's lap. She wrapped her arms around him and kissed him. He wiggled excitedly.

"How are you doing? Did you have a good time with Grandma?"

He looked at her with wide eyes and smiled.

"Do you want to see your baby brother?"

Edith made tea for Ruth and brought it on a tray into the living room.

"Thank you, Mother." Ruth smiled and set her tea down on the side table to cool.

"You're welcome."

"How was everything while I was gone?"

"It was good; I think he missed you though."

Ruth gave Gerry a squeeze, "I missed him too!"

Gerry vocalized.

"Pete, can you come and take Gerry to see Dale?" She looked at her dad, seated on the floor next to the bassinet. "Dad, can you grab the camera?"

"Sure." Herman took the camera off the coffee table.

Waldemar got up from where he was sitting on the floor and came to Gerry. He picked Gerry up and stood him next to the bassinet. Gerry's hands held the edge of the basket. Little Dale had his eyes wide open, looking all around.

"Look, Gerry," Waldemar coaxed, "look at your baby brother."

Gerry refused and looked in the opposite direction.

Herman started laughing and snapped a photo. "I don't think he's too interested in his brother just yet!"

"It will come," Edith said.

"He'll have to look at him sometime," Herman laughed.

Gerry arched in Waldemar's arms, pulling away from the bassinet.

"Okay," Waldemar laughed, "I get it. You need to catch up with Mommy before you're ready to accept your little brother."

Ruth sipped her tea. "Will you be going back tonight?"

Herman nodded. "Yes, your mother is ready to be back in her own bed. Right?"

Edith agreed, "Yes. I'd love to stay but I have a lot of commitments at home."

"Oh," Ruth said softly.

"You'll manage." Edith looked at her pointedly and said, "You always do."

"I guess. I suppose I'm a little nervous about it."

"One child, two…it won't make a big difference."

Ruth thought about how much work Gerry was all on his own. She looked at Dale who now was going to demand all the same things of her…diapers, feeding, rocking, soothing… "I guess I'll be fine."

"I'll be here too," Waldemar reassured her, "when I'm not working."

"I know. I'll get through it."

Edith got up. "Supper should be ready. Why don't we all move to the table?"

The family ate. Afterwards, Herman and Edith left. Ruth went back and sat on the couch. She sighed.

Dale cried out from the bassinet, where he had been sleeping.

"Will you bring him to me, Pete?"

Waldemar laid Gerry on a blanket on the floor and went to pick up Dale. He laid him in her arms. He went to the kitchen to prepare a bottle of formula while Ruth admired her newest son.

As she held him, he grasped her finger with his tiny hands. She gasped as she felt the strength of his grip. For her it was more than just a grasp, it was an intense realization that he would not suffer the same challenges Gerry did. She stroked his soft cheeks. He opened his mouth and turned to her.

"Hello, little one," she said softly. "Daddy's getting the bottle."

Dale began to cry. Ruth rocked him gently in her arms. She hummed an old German hymn to him. She smiled at Gerry who was looking at her from his place on the blanket. "Hello, sweet Ger."

Gerry vocalized.

She turned toward the kitchen and asked, "Pete? Is the bottle warm?"

He brought it to her and she began to feed Dale. He gulped excitedly as he drank, grunting and squirming in her arms. Before long, his eyes grew heavy and his sucking slowed. His fists relaxed and his outstretched hand lay on top of his mother's. She looked at his little hands, a reflection of her own. His tiny pinkie fingers were curved, just as hers were. It warmed her heart to see the physical connection between the two of them.

She looked at Pete, on the floor, talking softly to Gerry and then she looked at Dale, sleeping soundly in her arms.

"Thank you, God, for my family," she whispered in the stillness of the moment, "thank you."

She brought Dale to her face and pressed his cheek against her own. Warm tears flowed from her eyes and dropped onto this perfect child.

"I love you, Dale Douglas," she breathed.

Chapter 6

"But if it were I, I would appeal to God; I would lay my cause before him." Job 5:8 NIV

April 1952

Gerry with fireman volunteers

"Buh – Buh," Dale shouted as he stood at the front window.

"Is the bus here, Dale?" Ruth asked as she was bent down lacing Gerry's tennis shoes.

Dale squealed excitedly and clapped his chubby hands.

"That sounds like a yes, doesn't it, Gerry?"

Gerry verbalized a sound, meaning yes, which Ruth understood. They all heard the sounds of boots coming up the front walk.

"Fi-yuh!" Dale bounced up and down, holding on to the edge of the sofa.

"Yes, yes, Dale, the fireman is here." Ruth stood up and opened the front door.

"Hello, Petersons," the man at the door greeted them warmly. He looked down at Gerry, who was sitting in his half chair. "Are you ready to go?"

Gerry grunted yes. Ruth pulled him out of his chair and maneuvered his wild arms into his coat. "Relax, Gerry," she coaxed, "when you get so excited it takes me longer."

Once Ruth had Gerry's coat on and zipped, the fireman scooped him up. "See you later then."

"Bye! Bye!" Dale waved madly.

"Bye, Dale!" The fireman laughed and said, "What a happy little guy you are!"

Ruth smiled and ran a hand through her hair. "See you later, Gerry."

The fireman, with Gerry in his arms, walked toward the van that transported the children to the Cerebral Palsy Clinic.

Ruth closed the door and sighed. She sat down in the armchair near the window and watched the van pull away. She was thankful for the clinic. It had been good for Gerry so far. She kept thinking forward to when he would need to go to kindergarten. He was as bright as any other child his age. There weren't any schools in Edmonton — in Canada for that matter — that could accommodate a wheelchair or any of Gerry's special needs. He couldn't communicate with others. Ruth had started teaching Gerry common words and how to spell them. He was catching on quite rapidly. She would name each letter of the alphabet and then when she got to the letter he wanted, he would vocalize to her. They would slowly spell out the word he wanted. So far it was simple words: eat, drink, up, down, sleep. Since he only had a few words, she could guess after hearing the first letter. She didn't know any other three-and-half-year-olds that could spell. They also used the twenty-questions method until she narrowed down what he was trying to get across. She worked constantly in their everyday lives to educate him. She loved the summer time when she could take him out in the garden and teach him about the flowers in the yard, the way that the plants grew and about the insects they found.

He loved all kinds of books and would always sit quietly while she read to him. He absorbed every word she said. She could see his mind processing all of the information. She had read articles about schools in Europe that had disabled children in regular classrooms. Washrooms were made accessible and stairs were replaced with ramps so that the children could navigate the school. It seemed that Canada was in the dark ages when it came to children with disabilities. It wasn't just the physical layout of the school, it was the attitudes of the people who ran them.

There was attitude everywhere Ruth went. From the grocery store to the park — judgment followed her and Gerry. She took a deep breath and let it out slowly. Everything was hard for him.

As she sat in the armchair she prayed, "God, you can do anything. I will do whatever you want if you make Gerry better." Tears started to fall. "Please heal him — make him whole. I am sorry for whatever I may have done to deserve this. Heal him not for my sake — but for his…" she took off her glasses and wept into her sleeve.

Dale peeked over the side of the armchair. "Mama?" he giggled and then started to run away, unsteadily, across the living room floor.

Ruth looked at Dale — so hopeful and innocent. She laughed and jumped to her feet to pursue him. "I'm going to get you!" She crossed the room in three steps and whisked him up, under the arms, and cradled him close. She tickled his tummy. He giggled until tears began to spring from his eyes. She kissed his cheeks and set him down. "What am I going to do with you?"

"Mama!" he shrieked as he ran into the kitchen.

She followed behind him, making a mental list of all she had to do this afternoon. She put her anguish behind her. There were dishes, laundry and supper to prepare.

"Dale, it's nap time. Come to Mommy, we're going to go read a story."

Dale toddled over and into Ruth's open arms. She scooped him up and carried him to the bedroom that he shared with Gerry. Dale was nineteen months old. He was such a wonderful addition to the family. He was always happy and excited about everything. He was already showing his independence, by saying 'me' more every day. Ruth didn't mind his independence. She was happy to let him do what he could on his own. She had her hands full, especially when Waldemar was away with work.

She changed Dale's diaper and tucked him into bed. She stroked his short, light brown hair. She picked a book off the shelf and began to read, taking him away to a land of little pigs and big bad wolves.

He fell asleep quickly. Ruth went back into the kitchen to wash the lunch dishes. They had moved from their apartment when Dale was six months old and were now in an area of Edmonton called King Edward Park. The house originally was a three-bedroom bungalow. Shortly after moving there, Waldemar had converted one of the bedrooms into a dining room. Ruth entertained Herman and Edith every Wednesday night. She also hosted dinner parties for neighbors, church families and members of the Force. It was lovely to have a separate dining room to accommodate their guests.

It was also wonderful to have a nice big backyard. Waldemar had made a sandbox for Gerry and Dale last summer. Ruth was anxious for the weather to warm up so that she could send them out there. Waldemar had plans to build a garage with some friends of his when the weather changed.

Tomorrow was Herman and Edith's twenty-fifth wedding anniversary. They would all be driving out to Leduc to celebrate. There were festivities planned at Temple Baptist and at Herman and Edith's home. Ruth was planning to bring some baking. Normally, she loved to bake but today she wasn't feeling well.

It was hard to believe it had been twenty-five years since Edith had come on the scene. She remembered the day she had first met Edith. She was four years old, full of childish dreams. Back then, she was sure she would be getting a new mother who would dote on her. She dreamed that Edith would be the type of woman who would play dolls, have tea parties and cherish her the way that her friend Artrude's mother did for her. She was wrong. She squeezed the dishcloth tightly.

She finished up the dishes and sat down at the kitchen table for another cup of coffee. Gerry was getting over another chest cold. The last two weeks he'd barely slept at all. She had been up tending to his cough, checking his fever and massaging his spastic muscles. Last night was better though. He was over the worst. She was happy to have him back to the clinic today where he could work on his physical therapy.

She was tempted to lay her head down on the kitchen table, just for a minute. She took off her glasses and rubbed her eyes. The phone rang, shattering her moment of peace.

Ruth grabbed the receiver and picked it up, "Hello?"

"Hi, sweetie."

"Oh hi, Pete. How are you?"

"I'm fine. Listen I wanted to ask you something…"

"Sure, what is it?"

"One of the constables here has a dog, she's had puppies. They're Cocker Spaniel mixes. I was thinking…"

"A puppy?"

"For Gerry. It would be a good companion for Gerry."

The line was silent.

"Ruth?"

"I'm here."

"Well, what do you think?"

"Now?"

"Yes, they're six weeks, ready to be weaned from their mother."

"I don't know. I've got a lot on my plate."

"For Gerry."

"Yes but he can't care for him."

"But the dog will be there for Gerry. The upkeep is a small price to pay for the companionship…"

"I guess…" she said hesitantly

"Great!" said Waldemar excitedly. "Don't say anything to the boys. I'll pick it up and bring it home around supper time."

"Okay," she said reluctantly, "we'll see you then."

"Bye."

Ruth placed the receiver back into the cradle. "A puppy," she sighed.

As promised, Waldemar came through the door while Ruth was dishing up supper. Dale was seated in his highchair. Gerry had his own special chair at the table where he was waiting. Ruth had mashed Gerry's vegetables to make them easier to swallow. Choking was a concern, even more so now that Dale was on the scene. He was constantly making Gerry laugh, which wasn't appreciated at the table.

"Hello, boys!" Waldemar had a box in his arms. "Daddy has something for you!"

Gerry wiggled excitedly in his chair while Dale yelled, "DADA, DADA!"

Waldemar slowly lowered the box. A small black Cocker Spaniel puppy came into view. It had long floppy ears, covered in wavy black fur, wide black eyes, a small yet muscular little body followed by an excited tail, wagging vigorously. The boys went crazy with excitement, clambering in their seats, trying to reach the puppy.

"Whoa, whoa, whoa. You'll scare him!" Waldemar laughed. "One at a time you can pet the puppy. Gerry first."

Dale crossed his little arms and stuck out his bottom lip.

Ruth came over from the counter to help Gerry pet the new puppy. She took his arm and brought it to the dog's back. Gerry moved his fingers over the dog's soft fur.

"Soft, isn't he, Gerry?"

Gerry vocalized 'yes.'

Waldemar looked his three-year-old son in the eyes. "When he grows up he'll keep you safe. You can take care of him. Sound good?"

Gerry grunted in agreement.

"What will we name him?" Ruth asked.

"Scout?" Waldemar wondered.

Gerry vocalized 'no.'

"Rover?"

Again Gerry vocalized 'no.'

"Puppy?" Dale suggested.

They all burst into laughter.

"No, I think we can do better than puppy," Waldemar teased as he brought the dog over for Dale to touch. "Be gentle."

"Soff," Dale smiled as he pet the back of the dog. "SOFF PUPPY!"

The dog wiggled in Waldemar's big hands. Gerry started making a lot of noise.

"What is it, Gerry?" Ruth asked.

"Do you have a name?" Waldemar questioned.

Gerry vocalized 'yes.'

Ruth thought for a minute, looking at Gerry and trying to read his mind. Waldemar brought the dog back to Gerry who seemed to point purposefully at the dog's black coat.

"Blackie?" Ruth asked.

Gerry vocalized 'no.'

"Midnight?"

"Nah."

"He's jet black…"

Gerry waved his arms excitedly, vocalizing 'yes.'

"Jet?" Waldemar asked.

'Yes!'

Ruth laughed. "Jet it is then!"

"JET! JET!" Dale called out from his highchair.

Ruth brought over the plates of food. She fed Gerry slowly and carefully, allowing him to chew everything thoroughly. She fed him his milk with a cup and straw. With some coaxing, he was able to close his lips over the straw and drink. Dale ate his meat and vegetables with his fingers, stuffing it in until he was finished.

When Ruth was done, she leaned back in her chair. "Are you going out tonight, Pete?"

Waldemar looked at his wife, noticing how tired she looked today. "No I don't need to. I can stay in. I'll help get Jet settled."

"That sounds good."

"Are you feeling okay?"

"I'm exhausted. It's been a long couple of weeks."

"I'll be up with Gerry tonight. You can rest."

"Thanks. Don't forget we have Mother and Dad's anniversary party tomorrow night."

"Right." Waldemar bent down and started picking up the food that Dale had thrown on the floor. He tossed them into the box where Jet was being held captive.

"Can you occupy the boys for a bit?" Ruth asked. "I'll do the dishes."

"No problem."

Waldemar took the boys down to the basement to play with Jet for a while before bed. They both laughed and squealed as they watched Jet run around in circles. Waldemar sat on the floor with Gerry propped up between his legs. Gerry's eyes followed the swift puppy like he was watching a tennis match at the park. Dale toddled around trying not to get knocked over by the rambunctious dog.

"Come here, Jet," Waldemar called enthusiastically.

The dog bounded across the room and skidded to a stop in front of Gerry. He started licking Gerry's face. Gerry laughed and wiggled happily in Waldemar's arms. Waldemar rubbed the puppy, causing him to flip over on his back, exposing his tummy.

"See that, Gerry? He wants a rub!"

Gerry reached his arm to Jet's belly. Waldemar steadied Gerry's hand, bringing it to Jet.

Gerry vocalized.

"Do you love him?" Waldemar asked tenderly.

Gerry vocalized 'yes.'

Gerry tried to pet the dog on his own but his hands clamped and caught Jet's fur in his tight fist. The dog yelped and Gerry's body denied him what he wanted yet again. His arm jerked back, pulling out the dog's soft coat. Jet snarled and bit Gerry's hand, coming down with sharp puppy teeth and causing little pinpricks of blood to erupt from Gerry's hand.

Gerry started to cry. Waldemar shooed the dog away.

"Love 'im! Love 'im!" Dale piped up.

"Are you okay?" Waldemar soothed.

Gerry sniffed as his dad rocked him back and forth, wiping the drops of blood from Gerry's hand.

"You'll be okay."

Gerry turned his head into his dad's chest.

"Dale, go get me a ball." Waldemar said, trying to coax Gerry back into playing with the dog. He pointed toward a box of the kids' toys.

"Ball! Ball!" Dale walked over to the toy box and started pulling things out looking for a ball. Before long, he pulled a red tennis-sized ball from the box. "Ball!" he exclaimed, holding up the ball for Waldemar to see.

"Good! Bring it to Dad."

Dale walked back to his dad, holding the ball out in front of him.

"Can you throw it, buddy?"

Dale threw the ball. Jet eagerly ran and chased after it, yipping. Dale clapped his hands excitedly. Gerry looked at his baby brother and frowned.

"It's okay, Gerry. It was an accident. Next time I'll do a better job helping you."

Gerry looked down at his hand and cried again.

"It's going to take time but soon he'll get to know you."

Gerry vocalized.

"Don't be discouraged." Waldemar whistled Jet over to them. "Let's try again." He held the puppy firmly with one arm and guided Gerry's hand over the dog's back. Then he released him.

"There you go. See, we can do it together."

The next morning, Waldemar woke to find the bed next to him empty. He wondered where Ruth was. Perhaps she had fallen asleep on Gerry's bed. He thought about the upcoming day. They would need to get the boys ready and start the drive to Leduc. They wanted to leave this morning so that Dale could have his afternoon nap at Herman and Edith's. The boys loved going to Leduc. Herman and Edith were always equally elated to see the boys.

He decided that he should go and start some oatmeal and coffee for himself and Ruth.

With a stretch, he rose from the bed. He was on the way to the kitchen when he heard Ruth in the bathroom. He put his ear to the door and listened to her — throwing up.

"Ruth? Are you okay?"

Waldemar heard the water running in the sink and then the door opened a crack. Ruth looked awful.

"Are you okay?" he questioned her.

"I have good new and bad news…" she half smiled at him.

"Bad news?"

"I feel awful…"

"Good news?" he asked, his brow furrowed.

"Maybe it will be a girl."

Chapter 7

"If only my anguish could be weighed and all my misery be placed on the scales! It would surely outweigh the sands of the seas…" Job 6:2 NIV

December 5, 1952

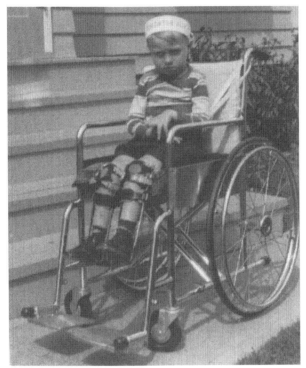

Gerry

"I can't do it!" Ruth cried. "I can't deal with these stupid things anymore!"

Waldemar rolled over in bed as Ruth crashed into their bedroom, flinging small metal leg braces onto her side of the bed.

He rubbed his eyes and looked at the clock. Six. "What is it?"

"These!" She picked up the braces and shook them menacingly.

"Gerry's braces?"

"He screams all night! He's been crying all night for the last week we've been trying these STUPID, STUPID THINGS!"

"Okay," Waldemar soothed. Three-week-old Brian began to cry from the bassinet.

Ruth sat on the edge of the bed and started to cry. "Great! Just great! Now Brian is awake!"

"I'll handle it." Waldemar rose from the bed and picked up Brian. He came around to Ruth's side of the bed and sat down next to her. He wrapped his free arm around her as she began to cry. "Tell me."

"I am tired, Pete. Between Brian feeding every two hours and Gerry's spasms and these horrible braces..."

"Why are we using these anyway?" he questioned.

"Because the doctor thought that they could stop the spasms by holding his legs in place."

"Ruth, you know best. What's your instinct telling you?"

"That it's a terrible idea," she sobbed, "and that it won't work. Not now, not ever."

"We are Gerry's voice. If this isn't what's best — we don't need to do it. Right?"

Ruth sniffed, "I guess. I want him to be better. If only – "

"Stop. There's no sense in that. If God wants Gerry to be healed — He will heal him. Maybe one day Gerry will rise up and walk. However, this is our reality now."

Ruth cried, "What did we do to deserve this? What did Gerry – "

"Nothing. He did nothing to deserve this. We need to make things easier for Gerry now. We need to think about the present. Not what should have been, not what could be. What can we do now to help him through this? That's what we need to focus on." Waldemar passed a now sleeping Brian to Ruth and picked up the leg braces. He rose up off the bed and left the room. Ruth could hear him walk to the back door. She heard the door open and the sound of the braces being tossed in the trashcan.

Waldemar came back to the bedroom with a smirk on his face. "Problem solved."

Ruth started to laugh. "That was easy."

Waldemar hugged her. "It sure was. We'll get through this. Back to bed with you. I'll make Brian a bottle. There's a few more hours until sunrise — take advantage of it."

Ruth put the baking sheet of shortbread in the oven and shut the door. She set the timer for twelve minutes and sat at the kitchen table.

Gerry was at the clinic this afternoon and two-year-old Dale was napping. The newest addition to their family, Brian Lorne, was sleeping soundly in the bassinet next to her. He had arrived on November 14, and although he was not the girl Ruth had hoped for, he was treasured and loved as much as Gerry and Dale. Jet was curled in a ball on the rug by the back door, sleeping contentedly.

Ruth watched the timer tick down the minutes until the cookies were ready. She looked at the baking dishes next to the kitchen sink and sighed. She should get up and wash them, she thought, but the energy it required simply wasn't there. Life was tiring. It had been three weeks since Brian's arrival and she had been home from the hospital for one. It felt like the longest week of her life. All of the work required to care for three boys was draining her completely. Gerry and Brian were tiring at night. Dale was more tiring during the day. His independence had cultivated a bit of an attitude. As with most two-year-olds, he wanted everything his way and when he didn't get it, he let you know how he felt about it. His favorite word was 'no,' and if it wasn't his idea, it wasn't a good idea.

On his second birthday, she had taken his cake and sat him out on the back steps so that she could take a picture. He had dipped his pudgy fingers into the icing and licked them clean. After one taste of the chocolate icing, he declared that it was 'mine' and that he wasn't going to share it with anyone. After much convincing, he decided to come inside and share with Grandpa, Grandma, Gerry and his dad. When he wasn't driving her crazy, his independent spirit made her laugh. She thought of herself as a little girl and she knew that the apple hadn't fallen far from the tree.

It was hard to believe that tomorrow was her thirty-first birthday. Herman and Edith were coming from Leduc to join them for lunch. Edith was going to bring a cake and Ruth had planned a simple meal.

The delicious smell of the cookies filled the kitchen. Brian wiggled in the bassinet and maneuvered his arm from the tight swaddle he was in. He brought his tiny fist to his mouth and sucked at it. The timer buzzed. Ruth jumped from the chair to silence it. Brian started to wail as she briskly pulled the cookies from the oven. She had already made his bottle. It sat on the counter in a glass-measuring cup full of warm water. She pulled it from the water and toweled it off. Jet looked up at her from his spot on the rug, his head cocked to the side.

"It's okay, Jet." She scooped up Brian. "Shhhhh, shhhh, shhhh. Mommy's here. I've got your bottle."

She walked to the living room and sat down in the armchair. She put the bottle in his open mouth to quiet him. He sucked hungrily, his tears subsiding.

Jet strolled into the living room and lay down at Ruth's feet.

"Are you waiting for Gerry?" she asked as she rubbed the dog's head with her slipper. At the sound of

Gerry's name, Jet leapt to his feet and wagged his tail. "No, no. He's not here yet." Jet paced anxiously to the front door and then back to Ruth.

Jet and Gerry had developed a special connection. The dog would sit next to Gerry's half chair or by his bed while he slept. When Gerry cried, Jet would pace anxiously until Ruth came. The first few months with the dog had been a bit trying. Jet had bit Gerry because of his spastic movements. The dog had first thought that Gerry meant him harm. In time, however, the dog adjusted to Gerry and had become a constant companion.

"Hi, Mama."

Ruth was startled; there was Dale next to her chair, with sleep-tousled hair, holding his bear.

"Hi, Dale." She smiled at him. "How was your sleep?"

"Good," he yawned. He came over to Brian. "Hi, baby."

"Do you want to give him a kiss?"

"No." Dale padded over to a basket that Ruth had put in the corner of the living room. He pulled out a few wooden blocks and began to build.

Ruth finished giving Brian his bottle and returned to the kitchen. Dale followed her.

"Cookie?" he asked.

She used the flipper to slide the cookies from the baking sheet onto the Formica kitchen counter. "Sure, sweetheart. Sit at the table."

Before long, Dale was perched on the edge of his chair, munching away on his shortbread cookie with Jet lurking below. Brian was back in the bassinet, sleeping yet again.

Ruth sat next to Dale at the table and pulled out a pen and paper. She was preparing for a lecture she was giving at the Kiwanis Club next Monday.

Over the last three years, she had spoken frequently in Edmonton and surrounding cities. She wanted to raise awareness about children with disabilities as much as possible. She wanted to challenge people to change their thinking. She would talk to anyone who would listen.

"What doin', Mom?" Dale asked.

"I'm getting ready for next week. I'm doing a lecture at the Kiwanis Club."

"Leck-shure?" He cocked his head to the side, looking a little like Jet. "That silly."

She laughed. "You're silly."

The following day, Ruth woke to sounds from the kitchen. It had been another long night with Brian, but thankfully, Waldemar had taken his turn with Gerry. She could hear Gerry and Dale's whispers and laughter from the kitchen as well as pots clanging. Brian was sleeping in the bassinet next to the bed. She rolled over to admire him. He had long, dark eyelashes and he looked a lot like his brothers. His nostrils flared slightly as he breathed in and out. Ruth always felt peaceful while watching him sleep.

The door opened a crack and Ruth saw Dale peek in. He was wearing his blue pajamas and his hair stood on end. He looked at her and shut the door.

Ruth heard, "Awake! Awake!" as Dale ran down the hall back to the kitchen.

Ruth could hear Waldemar's low, calm voice and then Dale's little feet coming back to the bedroom. Dale swung the door open and behind him stood Waldemar, holding Gerry and a tray of breakfast.

"Happy birthday!" Waldemar grinned at her.

Ruth slowly sat up in bed. "Well, what a lovely surprise!"

"Mommy! Beck-fest!" Dale shrieked. He clapped his hands excitedly.

Gerry grinned broadly from his perch in his dad's arms.

"Happy birthday, sweetheart." Waldemar leaned down to give Ruth a kiss as she took the tray from him. He moved around the bed and laid Gerry next to her. Dale scrambled up on his own, pulling himself up by grabbing onto the bed sheets.

Brian started to squawk from the bassinet. Waldemar picked him up, rocking him back and forth. "Good morning to you too," he said as he kissed Brian.

Ruth started to eat her eggs and toast. "What a nice way to start my day."

"Grumpa? Gramma?" Dale asked, wide-eyed.

"Yes, Grandpa and Grandma are coming today." Ruth tousled Dale's hair.

Dale began to hum 'Happy birthday to you' and swayed back and forth enthusiastically.

Waldemar left the room with Brian in his arms. He returned with a cup of coffee. "Okay, boys, we'll let Mommy finish her breakfast." Dale turned over on his tummy and slid off the bed while Waldemar expertly picked up Gerry in one arm while holding Brian in the other.

"Thanks." She leaned back against her pillow and sighed.

A few hours later, Ruth was working in the kitchen preparing a roast and vegetables when the doorbell rang.

"Grumpa! Gramma!" Dale ran around the living room excitedly. Jet barked and ran to the front door.

Waldemar went to the front door and opened it. "Hello, Mom and Dad!"

Herman and Edith came in from the cold and stamped the snow off their boots. Waldemar hung their coats in the front closet while the pair came into the living room.

"Hi, boys!" Herman went to Gerry and kissed him on the top of his head. "How's the biggest brother of the house?"

Gerry vocalized.

"Do you like your baby brother?" Edith asked.

Gerry vocalized 'yes.'

Dale skipped across the room and came up to Gerry, nose to nose. "Wike me?" He grinned broadly, waiting for a response.

Gerry looked away from Dale. The adults laughed.

Herman came over to Dale and picked him up. He pressed his nose against Dale's. "Grandpa loves you an awful lot!"

"Wuv you, Grumpa!" Dale wrapped his little arms around Herman's neck, giving him a big hug.

"Pete, how is work?" Edith asked once everyone was seated.

"It's good. I'm glad that nothing has come up this week that's been out of town."

"We won't even think about that," Ruth said as she came in from the kitchen. "Hello, Mother, hello, Dad."

Herman came over to Ruth and embraced her, giving her a kiss on the cheek. "How are you, child?"

"Worn out."

"I can tell. Three boys keeping you a little busy?"

"Just a little!"

"Well, happy birthday all the same."

"Thanks. I had breakfast in bed this morning, thanks to my boys."

Gerry vocalized. Waldemar picked up Gerry and sat with him on the couch next to Edith. She stroked Gerry's hand while they talked.

Dale came up to Edith. "Hi, Gramma."

"Hello, Dale. Do you like the new baby?"

"Yup. Baby cries."

"Does he?" Edith smiled. "Babies do that, you know."

He bounded off to the basket of blocks. "Play, Grumpa?"

Herman got down on the floor with Dale and began to build a fort. Dale started to show his grandpa exactly how the fort should be built. Edith and Waldemar sat on the couch, chatting while Ruth worked in the kitchen, putting the finishing touches on lunch.

The family gathered at the dining room table. Herman gave thanks for the meal, "Dear Heavenly Father, thank you for the food we are about to eat. Thank you for Ruth, and her strength. Thank you for all these wonderful little boys that fill our lives with joy. In your name I pray, Amen."

"Amen," chorused Dale, Edith, Waldemar and Ruth.

After lunch, the family gathered back in the living room. Brian began to stir in his bassinet. Herman went to him.

"May I, Ruth?" he asked.

"Of course," she smiled, "Mother and I will do the dishes and you two can watch the boys."

Herman sat in the armchair with baby Brian. Brian cried and waved his arms madly. Herman began to sing softly to him. At that point, he noticed Brian's hands.

Brian's tiny fingers, the middle and ring finger, were fused together by skin. They were webbed. A wave of emotion rushed over Herman as he held his tiny hands in his own.

"Are you okay, Dad?" Waldemar asked.

"His fingers…"

"Oh yes. Ruth didn't mention it?"

"No…" tears started to fall.

"It's okay. Ruth says it is a simple procedure. They'll fix it when he's a little older."

"No," Herman paused, staring at Brian's hands.

"They just snip," Waldemar carried on, oblivious to Herman's thoughts, "and he'll be fine. Really, Dad, it's okay."

Herman explained, "My grandfather, Gottlieb Bohlman, he too had webbed fingers. It took me back to the old country. It seems like a lifetime ago, it feels like all of my past was wiped away…and yet, here it is. A simple connection to my family. To my past."

Waldemar sat silently, holding Gerry.

"I'll never forget the day I left. I was so sure I was doing the right thing. Maybe if I had been there I could have protected Mother and Martha."

"You had no way of knowing."

"Regardless, it is astounding to see that family continues. That you are my family; the boys are my family. This remarkable child is connected to me." Herman pulled out a handkerchief from his pocket and dabbed his eyes.

He gently fingered Brian's tiny hands. "Incredible, just incredible."

*

Three weeks later, it was Christmas Eve. Waldemar and Ruth were wrapping gifts for the boys. They had attended a candlelight service at First Baptist Church that night and then had put Gerry and Dale to bed. Brian lay on the bed, wiggling and cooing.

"Do you think we've got everything covered?" Waldemar asked.

"What should we do with this?" Ruth pointed at the large ride-in car that they had bought for Gerry.

"Maybe put a big bow on it?" He shrugged.

"Yes," Ruth dug through a box of Christmas bows, "here's one."

Waldemar placed the big red bow on the top of the hood. The car was perfect for Gerry. It had a metal grill on the front, a small plastic windshield frame, a black steering wheel and the words 'Fire Chief' on the side of the car. Waldemar always took the boys for a walk in the evenings, and Gerry was getting a bit big for the stroller. He was sure that Gerry would love their walks even more if he could 'drive' the car. Once everything was ready, Waldemar took all the gifts and carefully arranged them around the living room.

The next morning, Dale tiptoed into his parents' bedroom.

"Cwistmas!" he whispered excitedly, his face about an inch away from Ruth's.

She opened one eye and looked at Dale who was smiling at her.

"Mommy, Cwistmas!" he clasped his hands together. "It's Cwistmas."

Before Dale could announce it again, Ruth answered, "Yes, sweetie, it's Christmas."

"Gerry awake."

Ruth smiled and said. "Is he?"

"Get 'im."

"Really?"

"Yep."

Waldemar joined in to the exchange between mother and son, "What is it time for?"

Dale shrieked, "Pwesents!"

Waldemar jumped up from his side of the bed. "You're right!"

Ruth got up and stretched. She looked at Waldemar. "I'll get Brian and you can get Gerry."

He nodded and went to the boys' bedroom. Gerry vocalized excitedly from his bed.

"Good morning, Gerry!" Waldemar greeted his son.

The family all went to the living room. Dale looked at the gifts beneath the tree.

"A car!" he gasped, his jaw hanging open.

"It's for you, Gerry," Waldemar announced.

Gerry's smile stretched from ear to ear.

Dale's brow furrowed as Waldemar leaned down to set Gerry into the driver's seat. Understanding dawned on him. "No, no, no, Daddy. MY car." He made an attempt to push Gerry out of the car.

Waldemar placed a large hand on Dale's chest. "No, Dale, it's for Gerry," he said sternly.

Dale's bottom lip stuck out and his eyes began to well up. As though in slow motion, his little mouth opened with a silent cry before he began to wail, "MIIII-NE!"

Ruth tried to help. "It's for Gerry."

"MINE, MINE, MINE!" Dale stamped his feet.

"Look," Ruth explained, "there are lots of gifts for you."

Dale continued to scream and cry. Suddenly, there was silence as Dale held his breath and clenched his fists at his side.

Waldemar started to laugh. "That's one way to negotiate."

Ruth joined in the laughter. "Dale, sweetie, Daddy will go and get you a car tomorrow. Okay?"

He let out his breath and sniffed. He made a small smile. "Okay."

After breakfast, Waldemar laid Gerry on the floor. Dale took a turn in the car. Following that, he joined Gerry on the floor and drove around some of his new matchbox cars while Gerry watched intently.

Waldemar stood at the kitchen counter drying the breakfast dishes. "Well, Mrs. Peterson, another Christmas together."

"Our seventh." She came up to him and wrapped her arms around him.

"It gets better every year." He smiled down at her.

"It sure does." She reached up for a kiss.

"MOMMY!" Dale ran in from the living room disrupting their moment together. "Gerry say me dwive."

"Does he?" Waldemar laughed, "Let's go ask him."

Chapter 8

"Therefore I will not keep silent; I will speak out in the anguish of my spirit…" Job 7:11 NIV

March 1954

Gerry

It was a crisp winter day in March. Ruth stood in her blue suit with her pillbox hat perched neatly on her brown curls. She held her papers tightly in her hands and looked around the legislative assembly room. The room was buzzing with politicians talking, laughing, and opening and closing their books. She began her walk up to the microphone. She steeled herself to deliver her speech. She said a quick prayer, that God would open the hearts and minds of these men and show them the need to integrate disabled children into society and into the education system.

"Good afternoon," Ruth spoke hesitantly into the microphone. The room quieted slightly, but as Ruth looked around many politicians were still rustling their papers and talking amongst themselves.

"Good afternoon," Ruth said, a little louder and more confidently. The noise in the room continued. Ruth began once more, "Good afternoon, gentlemen. I will not begin until I have the attention of every single person in this room. Please put down your papers and give me your full attention for what I am about to say is of utmost importance."

The room went silent. Every eye in the room turned to this young lady at the microphone. Papers had ceased shuffling. Every lip was closed.

"Thank you." Ruth cleared her throat and pulled her shoulders back. She took a deep breath and began to read the brief she had prepared.

"Mr. Hardy, Chairman of the Education Committee, and members:

"This brief is being presented on behalf of those children in the province of Alberta who are handicapped by reason of Cerebral Palsy.

"Cerebral Palsy is a disability of the neuro-muscular system, which results in the inco-ordination of the muscles. It is the result of an injury to the brain before, during or after birth.

"Cerebral Palsy is one of the foremost types of crippling among all types and classes of people. Based upon the best information available, there are 1,000 Cerebral Palsy children in this province. We can further estimate that there will be fifty born next year, and an increasing number born every year as the population increases."

Everyone in the room had their eyes fixed upon this passionate young lady. Ruth made eye contact with each man as she spoke, hoping to stir in him the desire to help her with her cause.

Ruth continued, "Cerebral Palsy children are handicapped all their lives, but 75 percent can be habilitated by proper treatment to become useful, independent citizens. This has been proven by the National Conference on Cerebral Palsy. The treatment is a prolonged process of training the muscles affected. To teach a child the simple art of sitting, of standing, walking and talking — processes we take for granted — requires intensive treatment plus educational facilities, geared to his individual needs.

"In Alberta, there are two parent groups of Cerebral Palsied children, the Edmonton Cerebral Palsy Association and the Southern Alberta Cerebral Palsy Association in Calgary. The need for such groups arose from the individual desire of parents to band together in order to provide treatment for their children.

"The province has provided clinics for physiotherapy, occupational therapy and speech therapy in Edmonton and Calgary.

"Three hundred and thirty cases of Cerebral Palsy have been diagnosed at the clinic in Edmonton. Present facilities enable each clinic to treat twenty children per day from the age of three to sixteen years. The one schoolteacher at our Edmonton Clinic is doing a wonderful job. Statistics show that Cerebral Palsied children are able to be educated. These children display all degrees of mental ability, as do all children. A child who is severely handicapped physically may make an adequate educational adjustment in a school that provides special facilities, while a child of higher intelligence fails to make satisfactory progress in a school that does not provide such facilities."

Ruth took a deep breath. She held her head high and spoke with authority. "The present educational program provides one hour per week per child. With that limited amount of time, the children attending the clinics have made considerable strides.

"We feel that our children warrant an education, that they may take their places among their fellow men, and above all, retain their human dignity and not become wards of the government or misfits in society."

Ruth paused to let the words soak in. The room was still and quiet.

"We are requesting that schools be constructed in Edmonton and Calgary, in conjunction with the clinics now in operation, and that the necessary staff and equipment be provided to give instruction to the children on a reasonable individualistic basis.

"These schools should be geared to accommodate all educatable Cerebral Palsied children in Alberta.

"The Province of Alberta has made provision in the amount of $750 000 for a school for the 120 deaf children who now are sent out of the province for educational training. We submit that the educational needs of 1,000 Cerebral Palsied children are of prime importance.

"During the past three years, through the efforts of the two Cerebral Palsy Associations and with the assistance of several service clubs, almost $200,000 has been raised and spent for the extra clinical services our children require. We believe that by doing so, we have established what the needs of these children are and we plan to continue our efforts in this regard. However, even with the most generous assistance from voluntary organizations, it is impossible for any group of parents to build, equip and service the educational institutions that are so vitally needed if these handicapped youngsters are to take their rightful place in society.

"We want our children to have an education."

Ruth looked up. Hushed whispers broke out as this request was discussed around the room.

Ruth had one more thing to say. "That, gentlemen, is the end of our brief, but if I may I would like to refer to a statement in yesterday's *Edmonton*

Journal, page 19, column 8. Dr. J. D. Ross asked the question:

"'Does the government plan establish special schools or classes for children with cerebral palsy?'"

The minister said, 'Children with Cerebral Palsy who are able to walk and care for themselves are accommodated in regular classrooms.'"

Ruth added her thoughts, "This, gentlemen, I submit, represents only a very, very few of the children concerned."

She read on, "The minister continued: 'Others are taught in special classes operated by the Edmonton Public School Board.'"

Ruth put down the article and said, "As a mother of a Cerebral Palsy child, I have not heard of any such classes for Cerebral Palsy children, which are operated by the Edmonton Public School Board."

Picking up the article and reading on she said, "The minister added: 'Other classes are given at the Edmonton Cerebral Palsy clinic…a teacher paid by the Edmonton School Board is employed at the clinic.'"

This, of course, is correct but as I have implied in our brief, these children are taught only during their stay in the clinic, which on the average is three months each year. I feel that this should be made clear to you."

Ruth looked around the room, hoping that her words had been taken to heart.

Following her presentation, Ruth answered questions from the members of the assembly. When the questions had been answered, she stepped away from the microphone.

The room was silent as Ruth left. No one shuffled a paper or lifted a pencil until she had exited the double doors.

Once outside, she let out a deep breath.

"Mrs. Peterson?" A man in a blue pinstriped suit approached her.

"Yes?"

"I'm Nathan Burgess from CJCA Radio." He flipped open a notepad. "I was wondering if we might be able to have an interview with you?"

"Now?"

"No, ma'am, perhaps tomorrow morning at your residence?"

"Ah – sure. That would be fine."

"Perfect, I'll see you at nine?" He jotted down her address. "Looking forward to it."

"Thank you."

Waldemar came through the door a little after midnight to find Ruth on her hands and knees polishing the kitchen floor. Her usually neat curls were in disarray.

"Hi," he whispered so as not to wake the boys.

"Hi," she whispered back as she vigorously scrubbed the floor.

"What's going on?"

She looked up at him and hissed, "I hate this job. I've always hated washing the floors. I hated when Mother used to make me scrub those wretched wooden floors."

He raised his eyebrows while standing on the mat at the backdoor. "Why are you washing the floors so late?"

She smiled for the first time since he had come through the door. "I have an interview tomorrow."

"Oh yes! How did your address go today?" He slipped off his shoes and carefully made his way to a kitchen chair where he sat down.

"Brilliantly." She stopped scrubbing and pushed up her glasses.

"Were they receptive?"

"It's hard to say for sure but they listened. I made sure of that." She told him how she had demanded everyone's undivided attention before she had started her address.

Waldemar laughed. "Only you would tell the legislative assembly to be quiet."

Ruth got up, came and sat on his knee, and wrapped her arm around his broad shoulders. "Well you know if I've got something to say, you had better be listening."

He smirked. "*I* know!"

"I'm exhausted," she sighed.

"Who is your interview with tomorrow?"

"With CJCA."

"You know the house doesn't have to be clean, it's a radio interview," he teased.

"Ha, ha, very funny." She gave him a big hug and a kiss on the cheek. "I'm glad you're home."

Waldemar helped her clean for another half-hour and then the pair headed to bed. He stopped to check in on the boys on the way to their bedroom. The three boys slept contentedly in the beds he had made for them. Dale slept on the top bunk, Brian beneath and Gerry's bed came away from the bunks in an 'L' shape. The beds had big deep drawers underneath and each bed had its own lamp. Now that Brian was two years old, he was excited to sleep in a 'big boy bed.' Brian had watched his dad building in the garage all through the fall. He sat quietly as Waldemar hammered and nailed the bunks to life.

Brian was curled up in a ball. Waldemar tucked the blankets over him and kissed him on the head. Then he looked up at Dale who was sprawled out, his arms stretched to each side. He kissed Dale on the forehead. Next was Gerry, looking content for now. Jet was curled in a ball at the foot of the bed. Waldemar didn't dare kiss Gerry for fear of waking him. He walked quietly from the room.

"Goodnight, boys, I love you," he whispered as he shut the door behind him.

In the morning, Ruth received a phone call from a local television station asking if she would do a live interview for the evening news. She sent the boys to the neighbors. The neighbors were comfortable with Gerry. They had a daughter named Maureen that often came to play with him. Brian and four-year-old Dale went along, promising that they would be on their best behavior. With the kids out of the house, Ruth tidied up once more, to calm her nerves more than for necessity.

The doorbell rang and in came Mr. Burgess with two other gentlemen who were carrying recording equipment.

"Good morning," she said as she gestured the men into the house.

"Good morning, Mrs. Peterson." Mr. Burgess shook Ruth's hand warmly.

"Let me take your coats." Ruth hung the coats in the front closet. She ushered them into the living room. "Please, have a seat."

In a matter of minutes, she had served coffee and baked goods. The interview was ready to proceed.

"Mrs. Peterson, let us begin by asking you, what is Cerebral Palsy?"

"Cerebral Palsy is a disability of the neuro-muscular system, which results in the inco-ordination of the muscles. It is the result of an injury to the brain before, during or after birth."

Mr. Burgess went on to ask her for some of the Cerebral Palsy statistics in Alberta and how it affected her personally. The two talked about the lack of educational resources in Edmonton and what Ruth proposed could be done to improve the situation.

"And why," he asked, "why have most people never seen a crippled child before if there are so many as you say there are?"

"I believe there's an element of shame that people feel when they have a child with a disability. I want to change that, Mr. Burgess. I want people to know that there is no shame in having child with a disability, be it physical or mental. Every individual has a purpose. God has a purpose for every life. Who are we to limit them with our judgment?"

"Let's instead support each child to become a worthwhile member of society. Let us be thankful for the wonderful individuals they are and the marvelous gifts they have to offer."

"Thank you, Mrs. Peterson; I believe that is the perfect way to end our conversation."

"Thank you."

"That's a wrap," one of the crew members announced.

Mr. Burgess and Ruth stood and shook hands. She led everyone to the door and handed them their coats.

"Thank you sincerely," Mr. Burgess said as he put on his coat. "I do believe you have begun to crack open the consciousness of the general public. I hope that your crusade to empower handicap people continues."

"I am glad that you were able to come today."

"My pleasure."

And with that, the crew left. Ruth let out a deep breath.

"Thank you, Lord, for the opportunity to be heard." Again the verse from John 15:5, came to her mind, *Yes, I am the vine; you are the branches. Those who remain in me, and I in them, will produce much fruit. For apart from me you can do nothing.*

She put on her coat to go and pick up the boys. Aloud she said, "Apart from me you can do nothing. Indeed."

*

The months passed with a flurry of interviews, lectures and time at the Cerebral Palsy Clinic. Spring turned into summer and Ruth was happy to get the boys out into the backyard to play. There were imaginary camping trips in the yard and treasure hunts in the sandbox. Sometimes Dale would pull Gerry in the wagon and Brian would walk alongside. Ruth could watch them from the front window, going up and down the sidewalk in front of the house. Gerry loved to help Ruth with the gardening, watching attentively as she planted flowers and tended to the weeds. Brian loved to give a hand with the watering, although he had to be reminded to 'keep the garden hose only on the plants.'

The boys loved to play camping. Ruth made them a tent and sent them out with camping dishes, flashlights and sleeping bags. They spent hours in the yard with Dale directing the playtime.

Waldemar built his garage, the beds for the boys and spent the last few months studying a design for a tent trailer by reading his *Popular Mechanics* magazine. He was determined to build it for their summer vacations to the mountains. She had no doubt that he would succeed.

Today, Ruth could hear the three boys in the camping tent she had set up as she did the gardening. Dale was talking, as usual, and Brian and Gerry were his captive audience.

"Do you know where babies come from?" Dale asked his brothers.

Ruth's ears pricked up. She walked softly toward the tent to listen — and perhaps interrupt if the content of the conversation became more than two-and-a-half-year-old Brian should know.

"No," Brian said softly, having never considered such a matter.

Gerry vocalized 'Mom.'

Dale did not understand Gerry, but Brian did. "Mommies?" he asked.

"No, no, no. Well, not exactly. I'll tell you how."

Ruth crouched outside the tent, listening eagerly to hear where exactly Dale thought that babies came from.

"Well Mommies and Daddies make babies together," Dale explained, "in their bedroom."

"Oh dear!" Ruth gasped. She was about to open the flap of the tent.

"Mommy gets the broom and dustpan…"

Ruth stopped to listen again, letting out a little sigh.

"Ya?" Brian's high-pitched little voice questioned with wonderment and fear.

"Yes," Dale said with authority, "And then she sweeps under the bed for dust. Then she holds the dust in her hands like this." Dale illustrated his point by cupping his hands that were full of imaginary dust.

"Oh." Brian's eyes were wide, watching intently to see if Dale had the power to create a baby on his own.

"And then Dad comes and POOF! He blows on the dust and it turns into a baby."

Ruth started to laugh quietly outside the tent. She turned away to return to her flowerbed.

"I learned that in Sunday school you know. The Adam and Eve story of course. Sunday school is very boring, Brian — but one day you'll go too."

Gerry vocalized 'No.' He didn't think Sunday school was boring, he found it fascinating.

"I'd rather sit in the service with Mom. All we do is coloring and singing and they make you try to remember verses."

"Dale," Ruth called from her place in the garden, "that's enough."

Dale popped his head out of the tent. "What?"

"Enough stories of babies and Sunday school."

"It's true!"

Ruth looked at him sternly and said, "Dale."

"Okay Mom — okay!"

"Why don't we go inside for lunch? Boys, go inside and wash your hands." Ruth approached the tent and raised the flap. Brian grinned at his mom. She reached past him and picked up five-year-old Gerry off the sleeping bag. She groaned as she stood up with Gerry in her arms. "What a big guy you are!"

Gerry smiled at his mom.

"Are you boys ready for lunch?"

Gerry vocalized 'Yes!' Brian echoed, "Ya!"

"Let's go then. Brian, Dale, inside."

The four of them went inside. After a thorough hand washing, they sat down at the table for lunch. Ruth made them peanut butter sandwiches with a cut-up piece of fruit on the side and a glass of milk. Brian started eating right away. Gerry was happy to be fed by Ruth. Dale sat with his arms crossed, his bottom lip sticking out.

Ruth looked at him and sighed. "What is it?"

"I don't want peanut butter."

"Well that's what I made — and besides, you like it." Ruth sighed again.

"I don't want it." He glared at his mom. "I don't want it today."

"Then you're going to be hungry."

Dale burst into tears. Ruth ignored the outburst and continued to feed Gerry. Brian kept his head down and continued to eat his sandwich.

"I hate this family!" Dale stood up from his chair. "I want a new family!"

Ruth raised an eyebrow. "A new family?"

"Yes! I'm leaving! I'm going to find a better family who does what I want to do!"

"That's fine. I'll pack up your lunch for you and you can find a new family."

Ruth put Gerry's sandwich down and stood up from the table. She grabbed one of Waldemar's red handkerchiefs that were by the back door. She wrapped up the sandwich and fruit into the handkerchief and then tied it to a walking stick that the boys had brought in from the yard. Dale stood watching her.

"Here you go." She handed him the 'hobo' stick with his lunch. "Good luck."

His brow was deeply furrowed as she opened the back door for him and motioned him out. Not to be the one to back down, he grabbed the stick and bravely walked out into the backyard. Within a few minutes he was in the alley, walking away, fully prepared to seek out a new family.

Ruth went and sat down at the table to continue to feed Gerry. She smiled to herself and took a look at Brian. He was wide-eyed — horrified.

"It's okay, Brian," she soothed, "he'll be back."

Brian started to cry and Gerry started to laugh all at the same time.

Meanwhile, Dale headed determinedly down the back alley. He was headed for the park. Perhaps there would be a nice family there. His feet were already getting tired. The midday summer sun was beating down on the top of his head. He should have brought his hat. He was hungry too.

He stopped when he got to a boarded area at the park. It was the skating rink in the winter months but now it was merely dilapidated boards in the middle of the park field. Dale sat down with his back against the boards, trying to find some shade.

He sighed. There was no one else at the park. He decided to open his lunch. He ate the sandwich and the fruit, and wiped his soiled fingers on the handkerchief. He wished he had that cool glass of milk that was on the kitchen table.

Ruth finished feeding Gerry, wiped up Brian and took them to their bedroom for a story and a nap.

She was washing the lunch dishes when she heard a small knock at the back door.

She dried her hands and went to the door. She opened it and saw little Dale, with his 'hobo' stick in hand. He said nothing but walked past her, leaving his stick at the door. He walked to the table and picked up his glass of milk, which was still sitting there. He drank it back, relieved to quench the thirst that the sweet peanut butter had caused.

Ruth shut the door and returned to her dish washing. She heard Dale go to the bathroom and wash his hands. Then he came back into the kitchen.

Ruth turned around and took in the sight of her little boy. His hair was damp with sweat around his face and his shirt had drippings of fruit. He had a small smear of peanut butter on his cheek.

"Come here." She gestured him toward her. She took the dishcloth and got down on her knees as he came toward her, dragging his feet. She tenderly wiped his face. She wrapped her arms around him.

"I love you, Dale."

"Love you too, Mom."

"I'm glad you came back."

"Me too," he whispered as he hugged her back.

Chapter 9

"What do you think? If a man owns a hundred sheep, and one of them wanders away, will he not leave the ninety-nine on the hills and go to look for the one that wandered off?" Matthew 18: 12 NIV

August 1955

Waldemar

It had been a very long summer. Six weeks ago, Waldemar had been called out on a case. He had been investigating a murder in a small town south of Edmonton. It had taken considerable effort to crack the case. They had questioned every resident, tracked the individual's whereabouts prior to his death, and had even tracked leads to the United States and Italy to try to gain some insight on the case. Waldemar had spoken to Ruth briefly a couple of times on the phone requesting clean clothes and a home-cooked meal. She had driven out to him, even taking laundry for some of the other officers.

As the weeks dragged on, she missed him more and more. Even though he was typically busy with his work, he did devote himself completely to Ruth when he *was* home. She not only missed his help with Gerry, she missed his companionship. The boys were wearing on her nerves, fighting all the time and complaining that they had nothing to do. She worried about him, out there, trying to track down criminals — although she constantly told herself not to think about what he was up to. There was nothing she could do about his absence or the nature of his work. There was no point letting it get the best of her.

The day he walked in through the back door was a good day for everyone in the Peterson family. Even Brian and Dale, who were typically oblivious to their dad's absence, felt a sense of relief to have him back. If nothing else, it would put their mother's nerves at ease.

Following his six weeks away, Waldemar decided that it would be wise to take his vacation time. After a few days at home, he packed up the new tent trailer and attached it to the back of their Ford Fairlane.

The tent trailer was a thing of beauty. He had built the camper on a trailer chassis. It had a wooden frame with foldout beds on each side. The top had a frame that held a large canvas in place. At the back was a screen door, an awning and one step that could be removed for travel. The canvas snapped securely into place over a collapsible frame. Northwest Awning had taken his specifications and made the canvas for him. It also had a cover when it was folded down. Waldemar thought it looked even better than the one in *Popular Mechanics*.

It was six in the morning. He had already been up for over an hour, getting everything ready to go. He came in through the back door. "Are you ready to go, Ruth?" he called.

"Almost," she hollered from the boys' bedroom.

Waldemar came down the hall and into the room. Ruth had all three boys dressed in matching trousers and little jackets. The jackets had elephants embroidered on the pockets.

"Did you make those?" he asked.

"Yes I did. The pants are from your old uniforms. Cute, aren't they?"

"They sure are!" Waldemar smiled at his three boys in a row, Gerry, six years old, Dale, a month away from his fifth birthday, and Brian, nearly three. They were all sitting on Gerry's bed. Ruth was tying everyone's sneakers.

"Are you three ready?" he asked.

"Yes," they all answered in unison.

"Well let's hit the dusty trail!"

Dale jumped off the bed first. "Let's go, guys!"

They all loaded into the car. Ruth had packed a picnic lunch, which she placed at Gerry's feet. Jet settled in on the opposite side at Brian's feet. Dale sat in the middle, sandwiched between his two brothers. Ruth had books, small toys and coloring to keep the boys busy. She had sewn an organizer to hang off the back of the front seat to keep all of the playthings contained.

The trip to Johnston Canyon in Banff National Park was about five hours. Banff National Park was nestled in the Rocky Mountains and had wonderful areas to camp.

Within thirty minutes, Ruth and Waldemar heard their favorite words from the back seat.

"We there yet?" Brian asked.

"Ya, are we there yet?" Dale chimed in.

Waldemar chuckled, "Not even close."

The boys colored, looked at books and played with their matchbox cars within the first hour. Soon they were all sleeping, leaning up against one another. Waldemar pointed to the back seat.

"Look," he whispered to Ruth.

Ruth turned around in her seat and saw the three little boys in their matching outfits all sleeping soundly.

They arrived in Calgary just before ten. They stopped for gas and let the boys use the washroom and stretch their legs. Jet was also happy to be out of the car.

Waldemar was holding Gerry in his arms, walking around a grassy patch next to the gas station. Brian and Dale were running around, pretending they were airplanes.

"Zooooomm!" Brian had his arms stretched out as he circled around his dad. He stopped and looked up at Gerry in his dad's arms. "Dad?"

"Yes?"

"Gerry fly too?"

Waldemar smiled and said, "Sure I can." He flipped Gerry onto his stomach, holding him firmly under the arms and around his waist. He spun him around in the air. Gerry giggled like crazy.

"See, Gerry? You be airplane too!" Brian continued to circle around.

Ruth sat on the seat of a picnic bench a few yards away. Another family walked over to let their kids have a stretch as well.

"Well for goodness sakes," the mother exclaimed loudly, "you have triplets!"

Ruth laughed, "No, not triplets,"

The chubby lady plopped down next to Ruth, jostling the picnic table. "Well aren't they dear in their matching outfits!" She grinned at Ruth, her bright pink lipstick smudged on her teeth.

"Thanks," Ruth replied. "Where are you headed?"

"Oh, we're from Montana, we're heading back from a trip to the mountains. We just had to let the kids have a break. You know how it is! Complain, complain from the back seat!" She let out a hardy laugh.

"We're off to the mountains too — Johnston Canyon."

"Oh, the hiking is wonderful there — well I can't hike, you know — bad ankles and all! But Roger –" she pointed at her thin, gamely looking husband, "he'll take the kids up and down those trails all day!"

"Sounds wonderful." Ruth excused herself, "We'd better get back on the road."

"Well, honey, you have the most beautiful children. Have a great trip!"

"Thanks," Ruth rose from the bench and walked toward Waldemar who was still zooming Gerry around and watching Dale and Brian chase one another.

As they left Calgary, the Rocky Mountains loomed ahead of them. The prairie landscape turned into pine trees and rocky terrain. The boys were content to look out the window for deer and the occasional black bear.

"Do you know grizzly bears can eat you?" Dale asked Brian.

Gerry laughed.

"They can?" Brian's eyes were wide.

"Yep, in one gulp."

Waldemar laughed, "Dale."

"It's true! I saw it in a book." He used his arms to show Brian quietly how the bear could chomp you. "Arrrrmp."

Brian's eyes began to fill up. "I don't wan-new go camping!"

Ruth turned around in her seat. "Really, Dale, don't scare him!"

Gerry laughed again.

"Don't worry," Dale whispered in Brian's ear, "if you're a fast runner you can run away and you can climb a tree! Then they can't get you."

Brian considered the matter quietly as he watched the trees fly past his window. *Yes*, he thought, *I am a fast runner. I can climb too. But what about Gerry? What if a bear came after him? He couldn't run at all.*

Before long, the woods thickened and the winding road led them to the campsite. Waldemar and Ruth were busy setting up the trailer while the boys looked around for pine cones. Brian brought each one he found back to Gerry who was sitting on a blanket, on the ground, in his half-chair. Jet sniffed around the campground, occasionally coming back to Gerry.

After his quest for pinecones, Dale chased squirrels up the trees and poked around with a stick in the old campfire, left by the last campers.

Once the campsite was set up, they ate lunch. Waldemar announced that he would be taking all three boys for a hike. Ruth filled each of their canteens with water and made sure they had their hats. Then she waved goodbye as they trekked off into the woods.

Waldemar carried Gerry in his arms. The two younger boys walked in front of him along the trails. The canyon was breathtaking. A huge waterfall broke out from the side of the mountain and poured into the canyon. The water was crystal clear and flowed swiftly over a rocky creek bed down the mountain. Rocky cliffs stretched upward along the sides of the canyon. As they walked along the trail, the sound of the rushing water drowned out the boys' voices. Waldemar stopped the boys at some points along the way and pointed out certain birds, squirrels and even the occasional spider that had woven a beautiful web between the pines. The trail took them through rock caves and right along the edge of the rushing water.

They hiked for more than two hours, from the lower falls to the upper falls and back again. By the time they returned to the campsite, Brian and Dale were thoroughly worn out.

"Hello, boys," Ruth called from the trailer. "Did you have fun?"

"Yes," Dale answered excitedly, "We saw really big waterfalls!"

"Did you?"

"And the river was really noisy!" Brian exclaimed.

"What did you think, Gerry?" she touched his cheek softly.

Gerry indicated that he had a message.

"You have a message?"

Gerry vocalized 'Yes.'

"A, B, C…" Ruth continued until she reached 'P.'

Gerry indicated that was correct.

"A, B, C…" Ruth continued again until she reached 'R.'

Gerry indicated that was the next letter.

"Pretty?" Ruth asked.

'Yes!' Gerry vocalized.

Ruth hugged Waldemar who was still holding Gerry. "Why don't you put him inside the trailer to rest awhile? Brian, Dale, you too, come inside to rest for a little bit. You can have a snack."

The boys agreed and all came into the trailer where Ruth fed them crackers and jam.

"Remember when you ate all the jam at Mother and Dad's?" Ruth laughed, looking at Waldemar.

"Yes," he chuckled, "who knew it was such a valuable treasure at the Bohlman house?"

"We've had some fun times, haven't we?"

"Yes, we have."

"Did a bear ever try to eat you, Dad?" Brian broke in, the thought of the ferocious grizzly lurking in the woods still weighing heavily on his mind.

"No, Brian, if you make enough noise the bears will usually be scared away."

"Oh," he considered this for a minute. Gerry *could* make noise.

Later they cooked beans over the campfire for supper and finished off the evening by toasting marshmallows. Waldemar took the boys to the outhouse before bed. Ruth changed them into their pajamas. She tucked them into the bed on the left side of the trailer. She and Waldemar would sleep on the right side. She laid out their clothes for the next day.

"Okay, boys, your Dad and I will be out at the campfire. Jet will stay in the trailer with you. Not too much chatting."

Ruth had no need to worry. They were asleep as soon as their heads hit the pillows. She went and sat next to Waldemar on a log bench next to the fire.

"This is nice," she reached out for his hand.

He took her hand in his own. "It's good, isn't it?"

"I thought I was going to lose my mind when you were gone for so long."

"I know," Waldemar sighed, "I am sorry."

"But you're here now."

"I am, and I'll get up with Gerry tonight."

"Thanks." She smiled at him. "I love you."

He leaned over and gave her a kiss. "I love you too."

Ruth rolled over in bed and saw Waldemar sleeping soundly. She had slept all night, tuning out any noise that he and Gerry may have made. She felt good. There were no household chores, nothing but relaxing vacation time with the family. She could make breakfast whenever she was ready — perhaps eggs and toast this morning.

She sat up to peek at the boys. Dale was still sleeping and Gerry too. She sat up a little further looking for Brian. Where was he? Her heart began to pound. She scanned the trailer and then noticed that the door was open slightly. Where was Jet? She jumped out of bed. She crashed open the screen door. She looked around. Jet was pacing at the edge of the campsite.

"PETE!" she screamed.

Waldemar came out of the trailer in seconds asking, "What?" He could hear the panic in her voice. "What's wrong?"

"BRIAN!" she sobbed, "I can't find Brian!"

Waldemar's mind swiftly switched to detective mode. "Get back in the trailer, see what's missing. Let's see if we can figure out what he's up to. Maybe he tried to find the outhouse on his own."

"Okay…" she wiped her tears on her nightgown sleeve and dashed back into the trailer.

Waldemar was looking in the dirt for Brian's little footprints. Where would he have gone?

Ruth popped her head back out of the trailer, "His clothes are gone! His blue shorts, red T-shirt and his sweater. You know the cream one with the red squirrel on the front?"

"Okay. I see his tracks leading to the camping road. Then it's hard to see where he went from there. Take Dale and Gerry to the people in the next campsite and we'll start searching. Ask anyone you see if they've seen him."

Ruth went back inside to hurriedly dress Gerry and tell Dale to get ready.

"Ruth?" Waldemar called.

"What?" She stuck her head out the door again.

"Is the flashlight there?" There was a large flashlight they kept by the door of the trailer.

"Yes," she called back to him.

"Then he must have left in daylight — sometime after five am."

"Oh," Ruth gasped, "it's already eight! He could be anywhere!"

"Mom," Dale interrupted, "I'm hungry."

"Your brother is missing!" she exclaimed. "Breakfast can wait!"

Dale rolled his eyes and continued to get dressed.

Brian was having a great morning. He had woken up to find everyone still sleeping. He didn't want to bother anyone so he got up, put on the clothes that his Mom had set out and decided to go for a walk. Jet had come out of the trailer with him but then had yipped and growled when Brian started along the camping road.

"You stay with Gerry," he had said. *"You keep him safe from bears."*

Jet obliged. Brian headed down the road alone. He thought it might be nice to see those big waterfalls again. Too bad he couldn't remember exactly how to get there.

Waldemar went calmly, but rapidly, from campsite to campsite asking if anyone had seen a little boy in a squirrel sweater. No one had. Most had just gotten up for that matter. His heart began to beat faster as he thought of all of the dangers that Banff National Park had to offer a little boy. Bears, water, elk, coyotes, mountain lions...

"Oh God," he whispered, "keep him safe." In the distance, he could hear Ruth calling Brian's name over and over. The minutes ticked agonizingly by and still no sign of Brian.

Brian was starting to get tired. He couldn't find those waterfalls they had seen and the trail was getting really thick. He looked around. Actually, it wasn't a trail anymore. He was in the woods. He wondered which way it was to get back to the campground. He was starting to get hungry for breakfast. He wondered if everyone would be awake when he got back.

Ruth had gathered up a number of fellow campers to help. Waldemar called for everyone to meet out on the main camping road.

"Okay everyone," he explained, "we're going to search the area in a grid pattern. Take a stick and comb through the underbrush. Depending on what time he left, he may have fallen asleep."

Ruth hadn't even considered this. She felt her stomach lurch.

"We'll make this our starting point and then work out in opposite directions. Call his name. Be quiet so you can hear if he answers you. He's wearing blue shorts and a cream sweater with a red squirrel on the front. He's two-and-a-half, almost three, he's a little over three feet tall."

All of the search party nodded.

"We'll go in a grid, ten-yard sections. Be thorough."

Everyone agreed and set off in the direction Waldemar had instructed.

Brian sat down on a log. *Which way to the campsite?* Dale's Grizzly demonstration came to mind. *What if there were grizzlies out here?* He hadn't considered that before. He had better keep walking. His dad had said to make some noise. Maybe he should sing too.

"Jesus loves me, this I know," he sang, "For the Bible tells me so…"

Waldemar's heart was racing. The minutes had stretched into an hour and still there was no sign of Brian. The more people that they met, the more people were looking and yet there were no sightings of the little boy. What if he had fallen into the creek? He had seen many horrifying things as a police officer, but if he came across the body of his little boy…He stopped his train of thought.

"He's fine," he reassured himself. "BRIAN!" he called even louder and listened for a reply.

Brian was really getting tired now. And really hungry. He saw a clearing up ahead. *It must be a trail.* He wondered if that would take him back to the campsite. He hoped that Mom had made a big breakfast.

Suddenly, his dad appeared out of nowhere, walking alongside him.

"How are you doing?" Waldemar asked.

Brian looked up and smiled. "Good."

"Are you out for a walk?"

"Yep."

"Do you know where you are?" They continued along the trail.

"Yep. Banff."

Waldy smiled. "Do you think it's time to go back to the campsite?"

"Yep."

"You're lost, aren't you?"

Brian looked up at his dad. He was big. He was tall. He was smart. And, Brian considered, he could definitely tell when you were lying.

Brian nodded his head.

Waldemar reached down and took Brian's small hand into his own. "Let's go back."

When they returned to the campsite, they gathered up the search party — including Ruth. Everyone was relieved that Brian was safe and sound.

Once back at the campsite, Ruth took one look at her wide-eyed little boy. Anger and relief charged out at once, "Brian, how could you? We were worried! You should never, never – "

"Ruth," Waldemar cut in, "let it rest."

"But – "

"He's back now."

Brian looked up at his dad and smiled. Waldemar gave his hand a little squeeze. "No more walks — right, buddy?"

"Right, Dad."

Chapter 10

"How good and pleasant it is when brothers live together in unity!" Psalm 133:1 NIV

August 1956

Ruth, Gerry, Dale and Brian

Dale sat glued to the television. Mac the Mailman was on CBS. Ruth and Waldemar bought a television at the beginning of summer vacation. Dale had been sitting cross-legged in front of it every spare minute he had. Four-year-old Brian was playing on the living room floor with his matchbox cars. Gerry laid on the carpet next to Dale also watching Mac the Mailman intently.

"Dale?" Ruth called from the kitchen.

Dale's eyes were fixed on the television.

"Mom's calling you," Brian piped up.

"What?" Dale called back to his mom.

"You boys need to get out for some fresh air." She came into the living room, wiping her hands on her apron. "There's not too many days until school starts up again."

"Ah, Mom," Dale complained.

"All three of you," she pointed at Brian, "put your cars away."

All of the boys grumbled and groaned as they obliged. Dale turned off the dial on the television. Ruth bent down and picked up Gerry, carrying him to the backyard.

Waldemar had built a new contraption for Gerry to sit in. It had a metal frame and four wheels. It had a bicycle seat in the center and was large enough that Gerry couldn't tip over. He had enough control over his right foot that he could push himself down the street with Dale and Brian.

The three boys headed out into the neighborhood to find some other kids to play with. Brian kept close to Gerry as they walked down the street. Jet tagged along at their heels.

Gerry vocalized to Brian.

"Maureen?" Brian asked.

Gerry vocalized 'Yes.'

"Sure, we can look for Maureen."

"How do you know what he's saying?" Dale asked, somewhat annoyed that *he* couldn't figure out exactly what Gerry was saying.

Brian shrugged and answered, "I just know."

Dale quickened his pace and headed for a couple of neighborhood boys that were up ahead, playing marbles. He knew them from his last year at kindergarten.

"Hey, guys," Dale called out.

They greeted Dale and turned to watch Brian and Gerry come down the street.

"Those your brothers?" a boy named Henry asked.

"Yup," Dale smiled, "Brian and Gerry."

Brian and Gerry had caught up and joined the group.

"Hey guys," a boy named William greeted them.

"What's wrong with him?" Henry asked, pointing at Gerry.

"Nothing," Brian answered, "he's fine — see he's smiling!"

Gerry smiled at the neighborhood kids.

"No, I mean why can't he walk? Why can't he talk?"

"Oh," Brian considered, "gee — I don't know? Do you know?" he asked Dale.

Dale shrugged and said, "Beats me. That's how he is. Maybe Mom knows."

"I'll go ask," Brian stated. Before anyone could respond, he dashed toward the house. Jet barked after him.

"Bring our marbles back with you!" Dale called after Brian.

"Is Gerry in school?" Henry asked.

"My mom teaches him at home," Dale answered. "They don't let kids who can't walk go to school."

"Gee, that's too bad."

"Mom?" Brian yelled as he crashed in through the back door.

Ruth was in the living room folding laundry. "What?"

Brian kicked off his sneakers and came into the living room. "What's wrong with Gerry?"

"What do you mean? Did something happen?"

"No — the other kids were asking. You know, why can't he talk and stuff?"

"Oh, I see." Ruth thought for a moment. "He has Cerebral Palsy. He had problems when he was born and it hurt the part of his brain that makes him walk and talk."

Brian smiled and said, "Thanks, Mom."

Ruth rose from the couch and went to the kitchen window to watch Brian run down the alley. She stood there for several minutes before returning to her laundry pile.

Brian re-joined the boys a few minutes later. They stopped their conversation to hear what he had to say.

Brian smiled widely. "He has Threezy Palsy."

Henry and William smiled. "Okay."

"He can understand you and everything," Dale added. "He can even answer 'yes' and 'no' if you ask him a question."

"That's cool," Henry said.

"Ya, no sweat," William agreed.

"You wanna play marbles?" Henry asked Gerry.

Gerry vocalized 'Yes,' excitedly.

"He says 'yes'," Brian explained.

The boys played marbles and Gerry happily watched until Ruth called them home.

After lunch, Ruth announced that she would be driving them all to Leduc. Waldemar was away and she was going out of town to deliver a speech about children with disabilities to a charity club. She knew the boys would enjoy staying with their grandparents. She was planning to be away for three days. Herman and Edith were eager to help.

"I'm taking you to Grandpa and Grandma's house for a few days."

"Yay!" they all cheered.

"Will we sleep there?" Brian asked, clasping his hands together.

"Yes," Ruth answered, "for a few nights."

"Wow," Dale breathed.

"I want you to be on your best behavior." Ruth looked each of her sons in the eyes. "Got it?"

"Yes, Mom!" they chorused.

"Come and help me pack your things."

"Can I bring my teddy bear?" Brian asked.

Ruth tousled his hair. "Of course, sweetheart."

"Can we bring Jet?" Brian asked.

"No, he'll visit the neighbors."

Brian frowned and looked at Gerry. "What about Gerry?"

"He'll be fine."

Ruth carried Gerry down the hall and laid him on the bed. She gathered up his things and took Brian and Dale's clothes, packing them neatly into a small hard-sided suitcase.

She loaded the boys into the car and headed off down the highway. Leduc was forty-five minutes away. The boys were too excited to be bothered by the time spent in the car. They chattered about what they would do while they were there.

They pulled up to Herman's hardware store, parking out front, on Leduc's main street. The younger boys jumped out and ran inside while Ruth came around to Gerry's side of the car to carry him in.

She grimaced as she picked him up and pulled him to her body. She used her hip to shut the door. She carried Gerry inside the store, struggling with the store's main door as she came in.

"Hi, Dad!" she called out.

"Hi! I'm back at the bikes."

Just then, Dale came flying toward Ruth on a small bike with training wheels, followed closely behind by Brian on a tricycle.

"Hi, Mom," they smiled as they whizzed by, barely missing a display of china dishes.

"Boys!"

Herman came from the back of the store toward Ruth. "Hi!"

"Dad! That is not a good idea!"

"Oh, it's fine. They said they'd be careful." He grinned broadly. "They're just having a little fun."

Ruth sighed. "Here, can you take Gerry? I'll go get his half-chair from the car."

"Sure," Herman took Gerry from Ruth's arms. "Boy, Gerry — you're getting to be a big guy!"

Gerry vocalized 'Yes.'

Ruth rushed out to the car for the half-chair. She went out the front door narrowly missing Brian and Dale biking by at breakneck speed.

She returned in a moment with the half-chair and set Gerry up near her dad's office. As soon as Gerry was settled, she nabbed Brian off the tricycle first and then Dale off the bike.

"No biking!" she hissed at them.

"But Grandpa – "

"I know. Just stop. You can look around the store on your feet. Stay off the wheels."

"Come on, boys," Herman laughed, "come and take a look at some new things I've got in the tools section. Your mom and I need to talk. We'll take some bikes outside a little later."

"Okay," Dale shrugged. He and Brian went off to look at the different tools that Herman had for sale.

"Come into the office for a minute, Ruth. I'll bring Gerry in too." Herman bent down, pulling Gerry from the half-chair. He sat in his desk chair with Gerry perched on his knee. "I wanted to show you this catalogue I have."

"Sure, Dad," Ruth sat in the chair opposite his.

Herman flipped open a medical supply catalogue to a page of wheelchairs. "This might make it easier on you — until he can learn to walk on his own."

Ruth looked at the two different types of chairs they offered. One for children and one for adults — both collapsible.

"What do you think?"

"I think it's not a bad idea…he's not getting any lighter."

"What do you think, Gerry?"

Gerry vocalized 'no.'

Herman laughed.

"The only thing," Ruth looked at the price of the wheelchair, "I don't know if it's something we can afford just now."

"Your mother and I will take care of that for you," he offered.

"No, Dad, you don't need to."

"It's our pleasure. It's for Gerry. A gift for our grandson."

Gerry frowned. He was quite mobile in his half-chair; he was able to push himself where he wanted to go.

"I guess…" Ruth hesitated.

"Think nothing of it. I'll have it shipped to the store. It takes time. I'll bring it up next time we're in Edmonton."

"Thanks, Dad."

The next morning, the boys had a wonderful breakfast of homemade cinnamon buns and hot cocoa. They played in the backyard after breakfast. Herman showed Gerry all the different flowers he had planted this year as well as the different vegetables that were ready to harvest.

In the afternoon, they went to the store with Herman. They spent the day there, playing, exploring and even helping Herman at the cash register. It was heaven on earth. The wood floors shone brilliantly. Gerry found it easy to push himself around in his half-chair. There were barrels of nuts and bolts, tools, household items, toys, bikes, china, appliances and furniture. They loved to play with it all — pretending they owned all of these wonderful, new things. By late afternoon, Dale and Brian decided that they should go for a walk around town and explore Main Street, Leduc. Herman approved and the two set off.

They looked in shop windows, walked past the bank and then they stopped in front of the Capitol Movie Theatre. The building was a grand Victorian built in the 1900s. The boys were awestruck by the bright lights and the flashy movie posters outside the building. They saw a poster for 'The Beast of Hollow Mountain.'

"Oooo," said Dale, "that looks good."

"Grandpa will never say yes," Brian said, his eyes fixed on the black and white poster of dinosaurs terrorizing mankind. "It looks cool."

Dale looked at his younger brother, the wheels turning in his head. "Maybe we can." Herman and Edith didn't like movies, not at all. It would be a tough sell.

The next morning, after considering the matter all night, Dale approached the subject of the movie with his Grandpa. They were all around the breakfast table, eating the rest of the cinnamon buns.

"Grandpa and Grandma," Dale smiled sweetly, "do you think that we could go to a movie today? It is our last full day here"

"I don't – " Edith began.

"Well," Herman interrupted, "what movie were you thinking of?"

"Movie's aren't good for your soul," Edith announced.

"It's about dinosaurs," Dale told them.

"Well, let me think about it. Go out in the yard and play and your Grandma and I will talk it over."

The boys obliged. Herman carried Gerry outside and set him up on the lawn in his half-chair.

Five minutes later, Herman emerged from the house. "We can go, after lunch."

"Yay!" they all cheered.

A few hours later, after they had eaten, Herman pressed a quarter into Dale and Brian's palm.

"Now each of you hang on tight to your money and I'll go get the wagon to pull Gerry in. Then we'll walk to the movie theatre together. I'll keep your quarter safe, Gerry. Okay?"

Herman walked around to the back of the house to the garage. Dale and Brian started running around — full of excitement for the upcoming movie. They chased each other all over the front and side yards shrieking and laughing. A few minutes later, Herman returned with the wagon.

"Is everyone ready?" He picked up Gerry and settled him in the wagon.

"Grandpa?" Brian started to cry.

"What is it, child?"

"I lost my quarter!"

"I put mine in my pocket." Dale reached into his pocket and showed Brian his shiny quarter.

Brian sobbed, "Now I can't go to the movie!"

"Now, now," Herman soothed, "we'll find it. Where were you standing?"

Brian continued to cry.

Dale piped up, "We were running all over the place."

Herman ran his hands through his hair. "Oh dear."

Brian continued to wail.

"Don't worry, Brian, I have an idea." Herman left the front yard and went around to the garage to get his rake.

Dale sat in the grass next to Gerry in the wagon while Brian frantically searched in the lush grass for his lost quarter.

"Okay, child. I'll find it. Not to worry." Herman went to work raking the large lawn, one small section at a time. He looked on his hands and knees around the garden. Each minute ticked by, growing closer to the movie time.

Edith opened the front door and called out, "Why don't you take the two kids and Brian can stay here with me. Otherwise we'll all miss the movie!"

Brian erupted into tears again. Herman tried to calm him once more. "No, no. We're fine, we'll walk a little faster to the theatre."

Finally, a few minutes later, Herman yelled out, "Ah-hah!"

Brian rushed over, "Did you find it, Grandpa?"

"I sure did!" He smiled at Edith, who was still standing in the front door. "Triumphant!"

She smiled. "Yes you are. Now we had better get going."

Herman, Edith and the boys headed down the street, walking at a quick pace, with Herman pulling the wagon.

The movie theatre was stunning. They had been to the Paramount in Edmonton but this one was even grander. The front doors opened to a beautiful foyer, lined with golden pillars. Ushers in uniform took you up a triple-wide marble staircase and into the theatre area where lush velvet curtains covered the screen.

By the time they found their seats, the boys were ready to burst with excitement. The lights went down and the big screen whirred to life. Letters and symbols clicked across the screen and then the MGM Lion appeared, giving his mighty roar.

They ate the most delicious popcorn at the movie. Brian fed Gerry one piece at a time. The afternoon passed in a flurry of man-eating dinosaurs. Soon they were on their way back to the Bohlman house.

"That was fun, wasn't it?" Brian asked.

Edith shook her head and frowned. "Terrible!"

"It was fun!" Herman answered. "Shall we go again some time?"

"Oh yes," Dale replied, "I loved it!"

Gerry vocalized enthusiastically.

Ruth picked up the boys the next morning. On the way home, Dale and Brian spewed out all of the exciting things that they had done. When Dale announced that they had been to a movie, Ruth was surprised.

"Really? With Grandpa *and* Grandma?"

"Yes," Dale said, "both!"

"How did that happen?" she asked, perplexed.

"I asked and Grandpa said yes."

Ruth scowled. "What movie?"

"The Beast of Hollow Mountain," Brian said innocently.

Ruth banged her fist against the steering wheel. "No kidding."

*

The last few weeks of summer faded away. Dale began grade one at King Edward Park Elementary. As Ruth walked Dale to his classroom on the first day she thought of Gerry who had never experienced his first day of school. He would be in grade two now, if only. She home schooled him but between his physical care and the demands of the other children, she wondered if she was educating him to his full potential. There was also the problem of communication. Some days both she and Gerry were brought to tears with the frustration of it all.

Dale was unconcerned about starting his new routine. He said goodbye to her with ease. She walked home on her own. Waldemar was home in the morning with Gerry and Brian. Brian had cried his eyes out when Dale left that morning. He couldn't understand why Dale had to be gone *all* day.

Gerry had developed pneumonia once again and he was really struggling. The nights were long and painful for everyone as Gerry struggled for each breath.

Ruth prayed as she walked, "Why, God? Why me? Why Gerry? If you would only make him better — I would do anything if you would make him better." Sometimes she wondered if God was listening. She had prayed these words over and over in the last seven-and-a-half years. If only God would answer her prayer.

Once she was home, Waldemar left for work. She checked Gerry's temperature again and called the doctor. He promised to come by in the afternoon to check on Gerry. She tried to settle him in bed. He was crying and in terrible pain each time he coughed. She sang to him and rubbed his spastic muscles. Brian came into the bedroom.

"Hi, Brian," she smiled and motioned him over.

"Mommy," Brian came up to his mom and said softly, "I miss Dale."

"I know, sweetheart. It's hard. At least you have Gerry here."

"Ya, that's good. Right, Gerry?"

Gerry wheezed, 'Yes.'

Brian took one look at Gerry, in so much pain. He swallowed the lump in his throat.

"Are you feeling alright?" she asked him.

"Uh huh." Brian felt the tears coming to his eyes. He rapidly turned and left the room. He didn't want to worry his mom.

The doctor came in the afternoon as promised and listened to Gerry's chest. He spoke to Ruth outside of the children's bedroom.

"It's pretty bad, Mrs. Peterson. I'm going to send a nurse to help you through the night. You'll most likely have to drain his lungs. If it gets too bad, take him to the hospital."

Ruth agreed. She said goodbye to the doctor and then called a neighbor to see if they would walk Dale home from school. She tried calling Waldemar at work but there was no answer.

"Where is your dad?" Ruth wondered out loud to Gerry as she rubbed his legs.

The neighbor arrived with Dale shortly after school.

"Thanks so much," Ruth greeted them at the front door. "Gerry is sick. I hate to take him out if I don't have to."

"No problem," the neighbor replied, smiling. "Any time."

Waldemar called while they were eating dinner. "Hi, honey."

"Hi, Pete. How are you?"

"I'm good. I got word that I need to take the train out to Vancouver tonight."

"Oh."

"Are you okay?"

"I'm fine. Gerry's having a really hard time. The nurse will be coming to help me drain his lungs."

"I'll be praying for you."

"Thanks," she said, her voice hollow.

"I'll be back in two days. I'm transporting a prisoner."

"Be safe," she whispered.

"I will. I love you."

"Love you too." Ruth hung up the phone after saying goodbye.

Dinner was a quiet affair with Ruth and Brian thinking of poor Gerry, coughing away in the bedroom.

"Do I have to sleep in the same room as him?" Dale asked.

Ruth glared at him. "What are you talking about?"

"Well if he's going to cough all night it's going to be hard for me to sleep."

"Really, Dale! Deal with it! Have a little sympathy."

Dale scowled at his green beans and potatoes. "Stupid pneumonia."

Brian pushed his plate away, unfinished.

"Are you okay, Brian?" Ruth asked.

"I'm fine, Mom," he wrung his hands. "I'm not hungry."

She frowned and said, "Clear your plate then."

He excused himself from the table and went to their bedroom. He lay on his bed and watched Gerry labor for each breath. Jet lay faithfully at the foot of Gerry's bed. Brian turned over and cried into his pillow.

"Dear God," he sobbed, "save Gerry."

Chapter 11

"'The virgin will be with child and will give birth to a son, and they will call him Immanuel'" – which means, 'God with us.'" Matthew 1:23

Christmas 1956

Dale, Gerry and Brian

A tree had been cut off crown land a few weeks earlier. Ruth and the boys had decorated it while Ruth sang Christmas carols. Now it stood, with its twinkling lights, awaiting the joy of little boys on Christmas morning.

Dale and Brian crept quietly out of bed and down the hall into the living room. Jet followed behind them expectantly. When they turned the corner, they saw the beautiful tree and marveled at what was beneath it.

"We should go get Mom and Dad," Brian whispered to Dale.

"Okay," Dale waved Brian away. "You go."

Brian's eyes were fixed on the toys, "You go."

"Good morning, boys," Ruth came up behind the two boys, followed by Waldemar who was carrying Gerry.

They turned around, startled. "Hi! Did you see – " they both said at the same time. Jet barked excitedly.

"Yes, we see," Waldemar said softly as he and Gerry went into the living room. "The farm is for you, Gerry."

Under and around the tree was the most wonderful display of Louis Marx play sets. There was a farm, complete with plastic animals, fences, people and a tractor. For Brian there was a Fort Apache play set. There were wooden fort walls, lookout towers, countless soldiers and horses. For Dale there was a magnificent castle. The castle had a tower in each corner, knights and horses. Ruth and Waldemar had spent Christmas Eve setting up the play sets.

"Whoa," uttered Dale, "this is amazing!"

"I love it!" Brian exclaimed. "Thank you!"

"Yes, thank you!" Dale dropped to his knees in front of his castle and looked at all the knights and horses.

Gerry vocalized.

"You're welcome"

The boys played all morning, unaware of anything else. Ruth sat on the sofa with Waldemar, drinking coffee and watching the boys.

"No fighting this Christmas, is there?" Waldemar said softly to Ruth.

"It's too soon to say," she laughed.

Ruth set the three boys up in the basement with their play sets. She put each boy on his own carpet with his toys and laid down the law that no one was to trespass on the other's space. They immersed themselves in imaginary worlds of cowboys, farm animals and knights for the rest of the morning, surfacing to the living room only briefly upon the arrival of the grandparents.

Ruth came out of the kitchen to greet her parents. "Merry Christmas!"

"Grandpa, Grandma!" Dale shouted.

"Hello!" Herman greeted Brian, Dale and Gerry with warm hugs.

Dale and Brian took turns hugging their Grandma.

"Merry Christmas, boys," Edith patted Brian and Dale on the head. Ruth watched as Edith leaned over and touched Gerry's hand. "Have you had a good day?"

Gerry vocalized 'Yes.'

"I hear you two are taking piano lessons," Edith smiled at Dale and Brian.

"Yes, Grandma," Brian answered. "Dale is really good."

"I'd love to hear you play sometime. You know your Uncle Lorne took piano lessons when he was a little boy."

Ruth turned and walked back to the kitchen.

On a cold January afternoon, once Dale was back in school and Brian and Gerry were playing downstairs, Waldemar and Ruth sat at the kitchen table looking over their bills. Jet was sleeping under the table.

Ruth sighed as she looked at the pile of paper, "I'd really like to hire a teacher for Gerry. Do you think it's possible?"

Waldemar ran his hands over the stubble on his face. "I don't know. It doesn't seem like that's something we could afford right now."

Ruth sighed. "I just don't feel like I am doing everything I can for Gerry."

"He's learning, right? He seems to be comprehending when we read to him."

"Well he is, but I feel like now that he's a few days away from being eight — I don't know if I can meet his educational demands going forward."

"What are you thinking?"

"I've heard of a retired school teacher through a contact at the clinic. She's done some home schooling on the side."

Waldemar drummed his fingers on the table. "How much does she charge?"

Ruth sighed again. "Too much I'm sure."

"I'm sorry," he flipped through the bills on the table. "With the doctors' bills and everything else…"

Ruth pounded her fist on the table. "Why does this have to be so hard?"

He shook his head. "We've got a lot of things to be thankful for."

"I know, I just want him to be in grade two with all the other kids."

"Me too. I guess we keep praying."

"How can we cut down our costs?"

"We can't — we're not doing anything aside from the absolutely necessary."

They sat at the table, drinking coffee and thinking things over.

"What if I went back into nursing?"

Waldemar looked at her questioningly. "Really? How would that work?"

"I could make enough to pay a housekeeper to watch the younger boys and a teacher for Gerry. I would work enough to cover their expenses."

"Is that something you're prepared to do? There's not too many working moms."

Ruth laughed. "Do I ever do the typical thing?"

He smiled. "I guess not."

"Besides," she rubbed his hand, "it's what is best for Gerry, and that's what is most important."

"True."

"Let's try. This is what Gerry needs and I really want to make it happen. It can't hurt to try."

"Then I'll support you."

"Thank you."

Waldemar smiled and took the last sip of his coffee.

Ruth was thinking of the upcoming weekend. "Hey, do you have curling practice this weekend?" she asked.

"No, a game. Part of the Canadian Police Bonspiel."

Waldemar played curling with some other officers from work. They had a great team. The best part about curling was the camaraderie. On the rink, rank disappeared and the only orders were to win the game.

"We're playing a team from Lethbridge."

Ruth smiled. "That's wonderful."

"Will you go visit your parents?"

"Maybe I will."

Within a matter of weeks, Hilda was hired to live with the Peterson family. Waldemar finished a bedroom in the basement. She was going to live with them, with room and board as part of her salary.

Ruth had introduced Hilda to all aspects of their daily routine and the things that Gerry required. She introduced her to all of the boys. Dale and Brian reluctantly shook her hand.

Ruth would be nursing at the University Hospital from three o'clock until eleven at night on general duty. She would be home for the bulk of the boys' day. Hilda would be in charge of suppertime and bedtime. Gerry's new teacher would be coming twice a week, on the days he was not at the Cerebral Palsy Clinic.

It was a big change in lifestyle for everyone. Gerry enjoyed his time with his teacher. It was nice to have someone besides his mother telling him what to do. Hilda kept the boys in line — although Dale constantly complained about her.

One afternoon, right after Ruth had left for work, Hilda called Brian up from the basement to come and help her with some of the household chores. Dale was at school for the afternoon and Gerry was at the clinic. Brian was busy playing cowboys with his dart gun, pretending his was a part of his Fort Apache play set. He didn't want to be interrupted.

"Brian," she yelled, "get up here, you've got work to do."

"No," he yelled, "I'm not coming up." He hated chores and even more than that he hated being alone with Hilda.

Suddenly, he heard her stomping down the basement steps.

"Boy! You listen to Hilda!"

Brian crossed his arms defiantly. "I'm playing right now!"

Her face turned red and she thundered toward him. "I don't have time for this," she hissed at him.

She grabbed him by his short brown hair and pulled him, kicking and screaming to the cellar door.

Once Brian saw where she was headed, he started to protest even harder. "No, no! Not the cellar!"

"You will listen to me!" She shoved him in the cold, damp cellar and slammed the door shut. He heard her fiddle with the door. She was wedging a chair under the handle so that he couldn't escape.

Brian looked around, stunned. It was pitch black in the cellar with only a sliver of light coming from beneath the door. The walls were unfinished. The floor was dirt. There was a crate that Brian promptly sat down on, pulling his bare feet up so that the spiders wouldn't walk across his feet.

"You can't lock me in here all day!" Brian screamed from his perch on the crate.

There was silence. Brian realized that he could hear her footsteps in the kitchen above.

"What? She left me here!" he gasped. He fingered the dart gun in his hands. He knew there was no use in screaming for her. He could hear the radio on and the water running. "How can she do this?" he whispered into the cold, dank air. He wished Jet wasn't in the backyard. He could bite Hilda.

Brian sat there for what seemed like an eternity. He kept swishing his legs, brushing off the bugs he was sure he felt crawling on him. Oh, he hated the cellar. It was a place where no one should ever be alone.

"I hate you, Hilda," he muttered over and over again. He wondered when Gerry and Dale would be home. He wondered if Dale would even notice that he was missing. He kept holding his dart gun, ready to kill any monsters that might materialize from the basement walls.

"Dear God," he prayed. "save me from Hilda."

As the minutes turned to hours, Brian got angrier and angrier. He had never felt so angry in his whole life.

"She'll pay," he seethed, "she'll pay."

Dale and Gerry returned from their day out. Dale was trying to watch TV but Gerry kept vocalizing. Dale wasn't too sure what he was trying to get across. Hilda was busy in the kitchen making dinner. Jet whined at Gerry's feet.

Gerry vocalized yet again.

"I don't know what you're saying," Dale said, exasperated. He turned from the television show and looked at his older brother.

Gerry vocalized again.

"I don't get it, Gerry! I can't understand you. Is something wrong?"

Gerry vocalized 'Yes.'

"Okay, I think that was 'yes,' right?"

Gerry vocalized 'Yes' again.

"I wish Brian was here," he sighed.

Gerry vocalized excitedly.

"Brian? Ya, where's Brian?"

Gerry went crazy, waving his arms and trying to get Dale to understand.

"Okay!" Dale said excitedly. "I get it! We need to find Brian!"

Hilda came into the living room. "What's going on? What's the ruckus?" she scowled.

Dale looked up at Hilda from his spot on the carpet and asked, "Where's Brian?"

"He's playing. Downstairs."

"I need to go get him," he jumped to his feet. "Gerry has something to say."

She looked at him with steely eyes, "I'll get him. You sit!"

Dale promptly sat back down. Hilda stomped off to the basement.

"That's weird," Dale commented. He turned his attention back to the TV.

Gerry was concerned for Brian. Usually he was waiting at the door when they got home. Why would he be in the basement?

Hilda stomped down the stairs and went to the cellar. She kicked the chair out of the way and opened the door.

There was a pop and a whiz of air as the dart flew through the air. Brian had pried the rubber tip off his dart from his dart gun. The sharp wooden end pierced Hilda's neck.

Brian bolted past her and up the stairs before she even had a chance to scream.

Ruth came through the back door. It had been a long night at the hospital. She couldn't wait to get out of her uniform and into bed. It was almost midnight. The boys would be up before she knew it and the daily routine would begin again. She wondered how many hours she had before Gerry woke up in pain.

She was startled as she suddenly noticed Hilda sitting at the kitchen table.

"Oh, Hilda! What are you still doing up?" Ruth noticed a white bandage wrapped around Hilda's neck with a small stain of blood at the front. "What happened?" she said, her eyes wide.

"Mrs. Peterson, your children — they are wicked!" She fingered her neck. "Your son, he nearly killed me!"

Ruth gasped and sat down at the table with Hilda. "You are kidding me!"

Hilda shook her head and glared at Ruth.

"What did Dale do?"

"Not Dale," she said abruptly.

"Gerry?" she asked, wondering if Gerry had hit her with something by accident.

"No."

"Brian?" she asked, in total disbelief.

"Yes, Brian. He was terrible!"

Ruth shook her head. "Well you can be assured I will talk to him. Is your neck okay?"

Hilda gave Ruth her most pathetic look. "I think I'll manage."

"Do you need me to take a look at it?"

"No. We will speak in the morning regarding his punishment," Hilda said.

Ruth rose from the table. She watched her turn and head for her bedroom. She stood there for a few minutes, replaying the conversation over and over. *Brian?* Suddenly, her heart began to pound and she rushed down the hallway to the boys' bedroom. She went to Brian's bed and touched him softly.

"Brian?" she whispered, "are you awake?"

He turned from the wall and by the light in the hallway, Ruth could see his tear-stained face. She pulled him into her arms. He sobbed.

"What happened?"

Between choking sobs he said, "She – she locked me in the cellar…I – I shot her!"

Ruth listened as Brian poured out the heartbreaking story of his terrifying afternoon in the cellar. By the time he was finished, she had tears pouring down her own face. She held him and rocked him as he cried.

"It's okay, sweetheart, Mommy's here now. You're safe now. Mommy's here."

Chapter 12

"We are hard pressed on every side, but not crushed;
perplexed, but not in despair; persecuted, but not
abandoned; struck down, but not destroyed."
2 Corinthians 4: 8 & 9 NIV

June 1957

Dale, Brian, Ruth and Gerry

It was already a hot morning. Waldemar listened to the oscillating fan whir behind him, blowing only a small breeze on the back of his neck. He opened the file on his desk, trying to decide what his next move would be. Malcolm Holmes had been on his radar for quite some time. Holmes and his father were suspected of committing a murder in Alberta just this year. Unfortunately, they had incinerated the body so they could not be convicted. Waldemar knew that it was only a matter of time before Holmes would put himself on the wrong side of the law again. The Devon creamery had been broken into and Waldemar was assigned to the case. Informants had suggested that Holmes might be good for it. He ran an illegal distillery off his property in the Devon area.

"Hey, Pete," Corporal Jefferson came up to Waldemar's desk.

"Good morning, Corporal," Waldemar stood up and shook his hand.

"I've heard you're looking at Malcolm Holmes for a robbery."

"Yes." Waldemar tapped the file on his desk. "In fact, I was just trying to decide if I should apply for a warrant to search his property. I think that's my next move."

"Well this may be your lucky day," Jefferson smiled and waved the paper in his hand. "I happen to have a warrant for the Holmes property."

Waldemar sat back down in his swivel chair with a big smile on his face. "No kidding! That's great." He began to lock his cabinet drawers.

"Are you ready to go?"

Waldemar finished putting away his things and jumped to his feet. He grabbed his gray tweed sports coat from the coat stand next to his desk. "I'm ready. Let me get a constable to come along and we'll meet you at your car."

"I'm bringing a civvy along. We're busting up a big illegal still there." A civvy was a civilian who worked or volunteered with the force.

"Sounds good." Waldemar pulled his badge from his desk drawer and put it in his breast pocket alongside his wallet.

The four men met in the parking lot and got into the car. They loaded their weapons in the trunk and slammed it shut.

Waldemar sat in the back seat with Constable Irwin and explained the case he was investigating.

"Have you done this before?" Waldemar questioned the young rookie.

"Yes, Corporal Peterson, I went on a search warrant last week." Irwin ran his hand down his tie several times.

"Do you have any questions? Do you understand the procedures?"

"Yes, sir, I understand."

"You cover me while I search the premise."

"Yes, sir."

"Good man."

When they arrived, they parked the car at the edge of the property, near the road. The four men quietly came down the narrow dirt drive. Woods flanked each side of the drive. At the end of the drive was a clearing, a front yard of sorts with a shack standing in the middle of the clearing. The shack was small and run down. The window in the front was cracked and coated with dirt. The front door hung weakly on its hinges.

Corporal Jefferson knocked on the dilapidated door. "POLICE, OPEN THE DOOR!"

The door opened slowly.

Jefferson pushed the door open rapidly. He shoved the warrant in front of the man who had opened the door. "Here's the warrant, step aside please."

The man, Malcolm Holmes, backed away from the door. Waldemar entered the home flashing his badge as he entered. Irwin stood by the door, next to

Holmes. Jefferson stood at the door for a moment. He and the civilian left to look for the distillery.

Waldemar scanned the shack, trying to decide where to start his search. The shack was dark and dingy. He noted that tucked behind the door there was a stash of firearms. To the right of the door there was a black wood stove. To the left there was a rundown countertop, single sink with a broken faucet and next to it an electric range. There was a beat-up armchair and a double bed in the far corner of the room. Suddenly, Waldemar noticed a woman in the bed. She was lying on her side with one arm beneath her pillow and her other bare arm above the sheets.

"Excuse us, ma'am," Waldemar said. She didn't stir, so he continued, "we have a job to do and when we're finished we'll leave." He motioned to Irwin who had started to walk into the shack. "Stand by the door."

Waldemar starting searching a pile of papers next to the bed, flipping through to see if he could find anything that related to the robbery at the creamery. Holmes' eyes darted back and forth between Waldemar and young Constable standing in the open doorway.

Waldemar said nothing as he searched. He picked up odd pieces of paper, placing them in the breast pocket of his sports coat. The noise made by Jefferson and the civvy breaking down the illegal distillery filled the shack. The crack of boards and the snapping of wood echoed across the property.

Waldemar bent down and peered under the bed. He pulled out a few boxes and began to leaf through them. After he was satisfied that there was nothing of interest, he moved into the cooking area. He looked in the kitchen drawers, finding only worn, chipped enamel dishes. In the bottom drawer were tea towels. He looked in the cabinet under the sink, finding a smelly trash bin and the wash bin for dishes. He closed the cabinet.

Holmes shifted from his right foot to his left. Waldemar ignored him as he continued.

Waldemar searched the space above the range. He noticed cheques. They were cheques from the creamery, pay cheques from employees of the creamery and other incriminating documents from the office. Waldemar slipped them all into his pocket, feeling satisfied that he had found what he needed to get Holmes to trial. He continued to look through the papers as the sound of the still being smashed apart carried on.

There was a sharp jab in Waldemar's back. He jumped.

"Get out," a gravely voice hissed.

Waldemar's eyes darted to the doorway. It was empty. He slowly raised his hands in surrender.

"Get out, Detective," Holmes ordered. His rifle prodded Waldemar to the door of the shack.

Waldemar complied and walked into the yard. He could hear the voices of the other officers off in the bush as the breaking of wood continued.

Holmes came around from behind Waldemar. They stood face to face. The rifle was aimed at Waldemar's chest.

The noise was deafening — CRACK!

Ruth slammed the wooden spoon against the tabletop.

"If I have to tell you one more time to settle down I'm going to send you to your room!" she barked at Brian and Dale.

They were eating lunch. Brian and Dale insisted on being ridiculous and making Gerry laugh. Ruth loved to hear Gerry laugh — but not at mealtime.

Ruth had fired Hilda the morning following the cellar incident. Within a few weeks, she hired Irene who had turned out to be a perfect fit for the family.

Ruth continued her shifts at work while Gerry made great strides with his teacher. It was Saturday; Irene had the day off and Waldemar was working.

She fed Gerry each bite of his lunch slowly, allowing him to chew each piece of food thoroughly. Brian and Dale continued with their tirade of silly faces and inside jokes.

Gerry continued to laugh.

"Boys," Ruth shouted, "cut it out!"

Suddenly, Gerry was quiet. Ruth turned to him and saw the panicked look in his eyes. Jet stood up from his spot beneath Gerry's chair. His ears pricked up.

"Gerry? Gerry!" Ruth rose from her seat and jerked his chair toward her. "Cough it up, Gerry! Come on!"

Gerry wiggled in his chair madly, trying to free the food trapped in his throat. Jet started to bark.

"Come on, Gerry," Ruth coaxed but within seconds she realized that he was not able to get any air to muster a cough. Dale and Brian sat frozen in their seats. Ruth could tell by the look on Gerry's face that he was getting more and more frightened.

Ruth's mind was going a mile a minute. She crossed the kitchen and went to the block of knives on the counter. She hesitated only for a split second before pulling the sharpest paring knife from the block.

"Oh God, oh God…" She placed the knife on the table. She yanked him out of his chair and laid him on the kitchen table. His lips were turning blue. Jet barked madly.

Dale and Brian's eyes were wide, as their knife-wielding mother put the blade to Gerry's throat.

"Give me the papers," Holmes said, his hands shaking, his finger twitching on the trigger.

Waldemar went to reach into his pocket.

"STOP!" Holmes shouted. "Give me — give me the coat!"

Waldemar slowly eased off his coat and tossed it on the ground between the two of them.

"Back up!" Holmes ordered, "Back up!"

He took several steps back, suddenly aware that the noise from the still had ceased. *God,* he prayed, *keep them away.*

Holmes looked down at the coat. "Go," he whispered frantically.

Waldemar didn't need to be told twice. He walked backwards for a minute and then turned his back and jogged away, into the woods where he figured the others were. Once out of sight of Holmes, he broke into a run. He reached the clearing where the illegal still had been. It reeked of moonshine. The liquor had all been poured out. The building was completely broken down, beyond repair.

With no sign of the others, Waldemar carried on through the brush in the direction of the police car. His heart thudded madly as he pushed the branches out of his way. He raced toward the car. The others were ahead, about ten yards from the car.

There was a crack as the rifle discharged. A bullet whizzed through the air above the officers' heads.

"Get to the car," Corporal Jefferson whispered fiercely to his men.

The four of them sprinted to the vehicle. They heard the bullets flying through the air around them. They all crouched down behind the car as Holmes came down the drive toward them firing. He stopped a good distance away and took cover behind some larger trees, still firing.

Jefferson whispered to all of them, "Get down — lay down." He laid face down on the ground with his hands over his head. He was quiet for a minute, trying to come up with a plan. "We can't leave here without him."

They all nodded in agreement as the rifle continued to boom, sending bullets in their direction.

"We can't let him leave without us," Jefferson hissed.

"Right," Waldemar agreed, the rocks from the driveway digging into his torso.

Holmes continued to fire, seeming to have an endless supply of ammunition.

"Can you reach the rifles from the trunk?" Irwin questioned.

"No," Jefferson shook his head, "too risky. We'll wait it out for a bit."

They all lay there, breathing rapidly, hoping that none of the bullets would ricochet off the trees and strike any of them or disable the car.

Jefferson reached for his radio. "Devon Headquarters, come in."

The radio buzzed and whined. "Headquarters. Go ahead."

"Corporal Jefferson, Corporal Peterson, Constable Irwin and Civilian Dunn. Under fire at the Holmes property. Pinned down. Requesting backup."

"Hold on," the four men listened to the radio whine while headquarters radioed for backup.

"Units enroute."

"Roger that…"

The minutes turned to hours as Holmes continued to hold them under fire. Backup didn't approach the property. Waldemar thought that they must have been waiting out on the highway, setting up a perimeter. He hoped that they had chosen wisely.

He heard Holmes' footsteps as he came out from his cover and started down the drive toward the police car. The gunfire intensified as he approached. The bullets continued to whiz over their heads. He thought of Ruth and the boys as he listened to Holmes' feet crunching the gravel, all the while the rifle was still firing.

Ruth paused before she touched the steel blade against Gerry's throat. Suddenly, she dropped the knife on the table. She had a different idea. She picked his flailing body off the table and grabbed him around the middle. She squeezed with all her might. There was a pop and the piece of food flew across the table, directly at Brian and Dale. Gerry gasped for air and burst into tears, taking big deep sobs as the oxygen flooded back into his body. Jet paced around Gerry's chair.

Ruth sat down in her seat, shaking, Gerry in her arms. "Boys, go to your room."

Brian and Dale jumped from their seats and rushed down the hall to their bedroom. Ruth stood up on her quivering legs and carried Gerry to the living room. They sat on the couch together where she held him, letting him cry. His limbs were particularly wild, mirroring his wild emotions. She held him close, bringing his limbs in, soothing him with her voice and her touch.

"It's okay. It's okay now."

Eventually, Gerry fell asleep in her arms on the couch. She gave a mighty sigh and carried him to his bed. She tucked him under his covers and kissed his head. She glanced over at Dale and Brian's bunks. They had fallen asleep in their clothes, on top of their covers. Dale had his comic books all around him. She walked out of the room. They could stay that way. She returned to the kitchen. She picked up the lunch dishes and angrily scraped everyone's uneaten food into the garbage can. She dumped the dishes into the sink and turned on the water. She washed the plates and cups and laid them out to dry. She wiped the counters and turned to wipe the Formica tabletop. As she picked up the knife, the tears began to fall. She flung it into the sink and turned out the kitchen light.

"Why, God? Why?" she sobbed as she went into the living room. There was so much anger churning inside. She needed to take her mind off things for a bit. She decided to turn on the radio and listen to the news.

Holmes came toward the men, firing. He turned and then suddenly bolted into the woods, away from the four men. They all heard an engine come to life and a car door slam. The car peeled away, leaving a cloud of dust behind it. Jefferson radioed headquarters to let them know the suspect was heading north, away from the property.

They got up, crouching near the car, listening for the sound of the car returning. Satisfied that Holmes was gone, they decided to go back to the shack and see if they could recover any of the evidence that Holmes had taken, along with Waldemar's badge, wallet and coat.

Waldemar came into the shack and noticed the woman still in the bed. The wood stove had come to life. The smell of smoke filled the shack. He opened the stove door while Jefferson looked around. Irwin stood at the door while the civvy waited outside. Waldemar recognized the ashes in the stove to be the documents that had been in his pocket. He used a poker that was leaning next to the stove to fish out his badge. His wallet and all the cash in it were burned.

"Man," Waldemar muttered, "I just cashed my paycheck." He picked up his tweed sports coat off the floor and walked out the door. Jefferson followed behind.

As they walked back down the drive, Irwin timidly asked, "Everything gone, Corporal?"

Waldemar glared at Irwin. "Yes, Constable."

Back in the shack, the woman fingered the revolver under her pillow.

Ruth turned the volume up on the radio.

"Four RCMP officers were held at gunpoint this afternoon in Devon, Alberta."

Ruth's stomach flipped. She leaned forward.

"The suspect has been apprehended and we have reports that all officers…"

She flicked the switch on the radio and stood up. She paced the living room floor, praying. She didn't want to hear that anyone had been killed.

"Wherever he is, Lord," she paused, "be with him. Protect him." The phone rang, making her jump. She rushed to the kitchen to answer it.

"Hello?"

"Mrs. Peterson?" Ruth's knees felt week.

"This is Corporal Jefferson. Corporal Peterson was involved in an altercation today."

"Yes," her eyes began to well up.

"He's fine. He'll be on his way back to Edmonton shortly."

"Thank you. Thank you for calling."

Ruth said goodbye and placed the receiver back on the cradle on the wall.

She sank into the kitchen chair. It had been a long day.

*

Several weeks later, the family was once again loading up the car for a vacation. They were all off to Seba Beach for a week of tenting and relaxation. Ruth had the boys settled in the back seat with Jet. Waldemar shut the trunk and came to the driver's side door.

"Oh, I forgot my sunglasses," he remarked. "I'll be right back."

He went into the house. Ruth heard the phone ring as she sat down in the passenger seat. She listened.

"…I guess now then…" his voice trailed off from inside the house.

"Now what?" Ruth wondered out loud.

"We're ready!" Dale exclaimed from the back seat.

"I know, me too!" Ruth smiled at Dale.

"…okay, I'll see you soon." Waldemar came out of the house, shut the back door and locked it behind him.

He came out and got into the front seat of the car.

"Who was that?" Ruth asked.

"Ah, work."

"Work?"

"Yes, I'm needed for a case."

Ruth threw up her hands. "We're on vacation!"

"Well, not yet." He said calmly.

"The car is packed!"

Waldemar put his sunglasses on and glanced at the boys in the back seat. "I'm sorry. I'll tell you what; I'll drive you out to Seba Beach and get you all set up. I'll join you as soon as I'm through."

Ruth sighed as he put his arm on the back of her seat. He turned around and backed out of the drive.

Dale and Brian ran up and down the beach while Gerry sat in his half-chair. Waldemar hammered the last stake into place. He stood back and admired his handiwork.

"There! All set."

Ruth looked at the tent begrudgingly. "Yes. All set. Now all I have to do is make a fire, cook supper, entertain an eight-, six- and four-year-old for a few days until you come back."

Waldemar laughed and said, "That's the spirit."

Ruth chuckled, despite herself. "Oh, Pete, I was looking forward to spending time with you."

He hugged her as they stood in front of the tent. "I know. I'll be back as soon as I can." He leaned in for a kiss. "Okay?"

She kissed him. She turned to Gerry and said, "We'll manage, won't we, Gerry?"

"Yah," Gerry said clearly. Jet barked in agreement.

Waldemar said goodbye to everyone, got in the car and drove away. Ruth started the campfire, cooked beans for the boys and fed Gerry his supper. She carefully disposed of her garbage in the designated bins so that she wouldn't attract any bears overnight. The food she had in the tent was all in cans or glass jars, sealed.

Before bed, she let the boys explore the beach while she carried Gerry up and down the waterfront. Jet bounded in and out of the water, barking happily. As the twilight began to fade, she snuggled them all into the tent, in their sleeping bags. She told them stories and sang to them until they drifted off. Jet curled up by the flap of the tent. She switched off her flashlight.

"Goodnight, Pete," she whispered, "wherever you are."

Ruth woke up to the soothing sound of the rain.

"Rain!" She sat up and looked around the tent. They were still dry. Brian and Dale were awake, whispering to one another. Ruth had been up with Gerry several times during the night. He slept right next to her. She groaned as she sat up. She went to the boys' bags and pulled out warm clothes for the day.

"Hi, Mom," Dale said, smiling. "It's raining."

She smiled back at him, "I can hear that."

"What are we going to do today?"

"I don't know just yet. Let's see if we can figure out getting dressed and breakfast and then we'll decide what to do."

"Okay," he shrugged.

Ruth helped the boys into their clothes and put on her raincoat to go outside. She eventually got a small fire going, despite the rain. It didn't seem to be getting hot enough to boil a pot of water.

"Hello," a friendly voice called out.

Ruth turned. A lady in a yellow slicker was coming down the beach toward her. "Hello," she called back.

"I couldn't help but notice that you're camping alone with your dear children."

"Yes, my husband was called to work."

"You poor thing! If you'd like you can come up to our cabin and join my husband and I for breakfast. It's going to be pretty tough to keep the fire going in the rain."

"That sounds great," Ruth responded. "I'm Ruth Peterson."

"Eve Thomas," she stuck out her hand and shook Ruth's.

Ruth gathered the boys from the tent and headed up to the cabin.

The week dragged on with endless rain. Dale and Brian were still happy to explore the beach. Ruth and Gerry spent time with Eve at the cabin. Ruth tried to keep a positive attitude. Late one night, Waldemar had come by to dig a trench around the tent, to keep water from seeping in. He couldn't stay though; he was trying to get through his work as quickly as possible so that he could join them.

On their fifth night, Ruth laid awake, listening to the sound of the rain falling softly. She listened to the three boys breathing, sometimes accompanied by a tiny snore. Suddenly, Jet popped his head up and started to growl.

She sat up and looked at the dog. "What is it, boy?" she whispered.

Jet got to his feet. She grabbed his collar. She picked up the flashlight so that she could clobber whatever or whoever was outside the tent. She silently moved to the tent flap and peeked out. There was a small black bear, not a cub, yet not full grown, nosing around in the fire pit.

Jet continued to growl. Ruth was frozen as she crouched at the tent flap. She held her breath while she watched the bear.

"Oh, Pete," she whispered, "where are you now?" She made a mental plan that she might be able to hit the bear over the head with the back of the axe, grab Gerry and make a run for the Thomas cabin with Dale and Brian. The bear moved slowly around the tent, brushing up against the side at one point. Ruth held Jet's collar tightly.

"It's okay, Jet," she quietly soothed as she held his snout with her hand. "It's okay."

The bear eventually meandered on, back into the woods. As she watched his tail end disappear, she let out a big sigh. "Thank you, Lord!"

The next morning, Waldemar arrived. The rain had finally cleared but Ruth decided she had enough of camping. After spending the day together swimming in the lake, they all loaded back into the car and headed home.

"Did you boys have a good time?" Waldemar asked from the front seat.

"Yes!" said Brian excitedly, "We had so much fun!"

"I loved it! We should go back again soon!" Dale shouted.

Gerry vocalized enthusiastically.

Waldemar turned to Ruth. "And you, Mrs. Peterson?"

She shook her head. "I think I've had my fill of solo camping for now." She winked at him. "Thank you very much."

Chapter 13

"When the storm has swept by, the wicked are gone, but the righteous stand firm forever."
Proverbs 10:25 NIV

April 1959

Gerry

It was a warm spring day. Everyone was packed into the car. The family was returning from an anniversary party in Leduc. Herman and Edith were celebrating their thirty-second year together. Giggles began to erupt from the back seat. Ruth turned around and looked at Gerry.

"What?"

Gerry vocalized.

"Do you have a message?" Waldemar asked, looking in the rearview mirror as he drove.

Gerry vocalized 'Yes.'

"Is it about today?" Ruth asked.

"Is it about Grandpa and Grandma?" Brian guessed.

Gerry vocalized 'Yes.'

"About the party?" Ruth asked.

Gerry said, "Na."

"Spell it out," Waldemar suggested.

"A, B, C…" Ruth began.

Gerry stopped her at 'Y.'

"A, B, C…" Ruth continued.

Gerry stopped her at 'O.'

"You? Your?" she asked.

Gerry vocalized 'Yes.'

"A, B…"

"Aye."

"B?" Ruth asked.

"Aye."

"A, B, C…"

Gerry stopped her at 'I.'

They continued on for quite some time until Ruth decoded, your birthday too soon, wedding anniversary. Ruth glanced at Waldemar knowingly. Dale and Brian had lost interest in the long message. Gerry continued to laugh.

"Ah, Gerry," Ruth began.

Waldemar looked at her, smiling.

"You know, it's best if we explain that when you're older. Okay? Let it go for now."

Gerry stopped laughing and looked out the window, smiling. He had figured something out that none of the children had ever noticed. Why were his grandparents celebrating their thirty-second anniversary when his mom was thirty-seven?

"I guess his schooling is effective," Waldemar laughed. "Mathematics at least!"

*

Last November, Waldemar was promoted to Sergeant while he was on a training course in Rockcliff, Ontario. This enabled Ruth to quit nursing and focus on the needs of the boys at home. She was also consumed with her activism. She volunteered with the Easter Seals society and was still trying to find a way to change the educational system. She didn't know how but she was determined to get Gerry an education, in a school. Now that Gerry was nearly eleven, she knew that his educational needs were greater than she could handle. He needed someone to challenge him. His teacher was wonderful at home but Ruth wanted Gerry to experience school, as every child does. She needed to find a way for him to communicate and speak freely to the world.

It was Sunday. Ruth was washing lunch dishes at the kitchen sink. They had been to church and finished a late lunch. Brian and Dale had gone out into the backyard to play. The snow had melted, revealing the brown spring grass beneath. The boys were eager to enjoy the yard again.

Gerry was resting in the master bedroom with his dad. The two were having an afternoon nap together. It had been Waldemar's turn with Gerry last night and it had been especially tiring. Waldemar would never complain but Ruth could tell by the three cups of coffee he had already consumed that he was beat. Some nights Gerry would cry for hours on end, in terrible pain. The massaging helped but it did not take away the pain.

Ruth yawned as she looked out the window. Dale was coming out of the garage with something in his hand.

"What's he up to?" she questioned as she grabbed a tea towel and dried her hands. She looked at Brian who was kneeling next to a tree stump with his hand oddly spread out on top. Dale suddenly gave a war cry and raised one of Waldemar's camping knives above his head.

In a heartbeat, Ruth was out the back door. "STOP! STOP! STOP!"

Dale looked at his mom, racing wildly toward him. "What?"

She ripped the knife from his hands. "ARE YOU GOING TO STAB YOUR BROTHER?"

Dale's brow wrinkled. "What's the big deal? We were playing Last of the Mohicans."

"WHAT!" Ruth bellowed.

"I was going to stab *between* his fingers."

Ruth felt as though her blood was going to boil. "Get me your comic books."

Dale stomped his feet. "No, Mom! No, it's just a game!"

"Get them," she seethed.

"No, Mom! No!"

She grabbed Dale by the arm and shook him. "Get the comic books now, or I will!"

He reluctantly turned to go inside but not before shouting, "Last of the Mohicans is the *only* bad one!"

"Get them all!" she screamed back at him. She suddenly pointed at Brian who was cowering in his sacrificial spot on the lawn. "YOU! Get inside!"

Brian didn't have to be asked twice. He jumped to his feet and raced inside the house, letting the door slam behind him. Seconds later, Dale emerged from the house with a stack of comics in his arms.

"What are you going to do?" Dale asked fearfully.

"You'll see." Ruth grabbed a large metal pail from the garage and some matches. It didn't take long for Dale to figure out her plan.

"No, Mom, no! Don't burn them! The Last of the Mohicans one is the only one that gave me the idea!"

She scowled at him before she lit the match. "Go inside."

Dale stomped his feet, cried and ran inside the house, bawling. "You're the worst, Mom!"

Ruth set the whole lot on fire and stood there watching them burn. The flames licked the colorful pictures on the covers. She could see Dale's face twisting in agony as he watched through the kitchen window. She shook her head.

"That is the last of the Mohicans," she breathed.

*

In May, the family relocated to a new neighborhood. They had outgrown their first home. Now that Gerry was older and in a wheelchair, they realized their house needed to suit their needs a little better. For the last few weeks of school, Ruth drove them to King Edward Park, explaining that next year they would start somewhere new.

The new house was a bungalow in a newly built neighborhood. The front and backyard were black soil. The land was barren of trees. Behind the house was a double garage. To the left of the front door was a living room, which opened up to the dining room. At the rear of the house were steps leading to the basement and the kitchen, which faced the backyard. Down the right side of the house were three bedrooms and the bathroom.

Waldemar was in charge of the exterior and Ruth the interior. He had plans to landscape that summer, starting by seeding the lawn as well as planting trees and shrubs. Ruth loved the extra space that the new house provided. Because the house was on a cul-de-sac, the boys could play out front or out back with very little concern for traffic. Waldemar went to work building a ramp across the front of the house, leading to the front door so that they could wheel Gerry in and out easily.

They didn't speak of the Mohican incident again but Dale was still angry. Ruth suggested that Waldemar help them find something more productive to do. He decided to build them a stage for their new playroom in the basement. A few weeks later, the stage was complete. The boys kept busy writing scripts and putting on puppet shows.

When Herman and Edith came to visit, they were seated in the audience while the puppets danced, sang and acted out the stories that Dale had written. Brian acted as the stagehand, keeping the show running by passing Dale the puppets he needed.

Another method to keep the boys busy and all together was to send them for walks. Each time she allowed them to go a little farther from home. Gerry was ten years old, Dale eight and Brian six. Ruth was beginning to trust them to explore the new neighborhood. Today she had sent them out with Dale pulling Gerry in the wagon. They were to go through the ravine, pick a treat from the local dime store and return home. While they were gone, she decided to take the time to write a letter to the paper regarding the educational system.

Dale pulled Gerry along the trail in the ravine, asking Brian to help him on the uphill bits. Now that Gerry was getting bigger, Waldemar had built a guardrail around the wagon to hold him in. Ruth had settled Gerry in with a soft blanket before they left. He was riding comfortably looking for birds in the ravine. Brian and Dale were not comfortable as they heaved Gerry up the hill.

"Oh man, Gerry!" Dale gasped.

"It's okay," Brian said calmly, "we'll be fine."

At long last, they reached the dime store. Dale rushed to the candy aisle leaving Brian to steer Gerry's wagon down the narrow aisles on his own.

"No wagons in the store, boy," the shopkeeper called out to Brian.

"My brother," Brian explained, "he can't walk, he has Cerebral Palsy."

The shopkeeper was taken aback. "Where's your mother?"

"At home," Brian said simply. "We're fine."

"Well hurry up and get out of here so my customers don't have to trip over your wagon," he said sharply.

Brian looked around but could see no other customers in the store. "Okay," he shrugged.

The shopkeeper shook his head as Brian chose out a candy bar for himself and Gerry. Dale paid for his candy bar and then left the shop, saying nothing to his brothers. He knew it would be much easier to walk home without the wagon. Brian patiently paid for his and Gerry's bars and headed out into the sunshine.

Gerry vocalized.

"Ya, where's Dale?"

Neither boy could see Dale so they decided to walk back alone. The first part of the trip was fine. Brian pulled the wagon along the smoothly paved sidewalk. Once the sidewalk ran out, they began their descent into the ravine. Gerry vocalized to Brian. He could see his little brother struggling to keep the wagon in control.

"Mah!" Gerry exclaimed.

"Mom?" Brian asked.

Gerry said "Yah!"

"No," he panted. "I don't need Mom."

Dale walked in though the back door. Ruth looked up from the table.

"Where are your brothers?" she asked, concerned.

"I dunno," Dale remarked as he went to the kitchen sink to wash his sticky chocolate fingers.

"What do you mean you don't know?"

"They're walking back from the store."

"Alone?" She crossed her arms.

Dale shrugged. "I guess. Don't worry, they'll be fine." He went to the living room and flipped on the television.

Ruth sighed and hastily put on her shoes. She shut the back door behind her and headed out to the direction the boys should have been coming from. Before long, she saw Brian in the distance emerging from the woods of the ravine. He was leaning at a forty-five-degree angle, pulling with all his might.

"Brian," she called out.

He looked up and waved cheerily. "Hi, Mom!"

She quickened her pace. When she reached him, she went to grab the wagon handle. "I'll get it."

"Oh, I'm fine, Mom. I can do it." He waved her away.

Ruth smiled down at her youngest son. "Okay. I'll walk with you then. Sound good?"

Gerry vocalized 'Yes' and Brian agreed.

Ruth gave Brian a little squeeze around the shoulders as they carried on down the sidewalk and back to the house.

That night when the boys were in bed, Waldemar and Ruth sat in the living room. Waldemar was home for the evening, for a change. He had been away for a week, traveling with the Royal Family on their tour across Canada.

"How was it?" Ruth asked.

"Pretty uneventful," he replied.

"Did you see her?"

"Only when we arrived in Edmonton. Other than that, the Queen and Prince Phillip stayed in their train car. We patrolled the exterior of the train at every stop — to keep the public away."

"Where were you on the train?"

"We had our own car, at the back."

"It's exciting," Ruth sighed.

"Not really," he laughed.

"We should do our own Royal tour someday."
"Tour Canada?"
"Yes, wouldn't that be fun?"
"Only if we leave the kids at home," he smiled.
"Yes, that would be an unbearable amount of 'Are we there yet?'" she laughed.

*

It was a hot afternoon in the middle of August. The kind of day where sweat trickled down your spine, even when you were standing still. The mosquitoes hummed loudly in Waldemar's ears. He swished them away and dabbed his forehead with his handkerchief. He was at the scene of a homicide — or so he figured. There was no body, only an abandoned tractor, splattered with blood. He studied the scene, trying to make sense of things in his head, before he spoke. He had a few possible suspects in mind. Fellows that would be up to this sort of trouble in this area.

"Any ideas, Pete?" his fellow officer Jensen asked.

"I'm thinking about it." His eyes looked over the freshly plowed fields. The dirt was soft, all turned over, as far as the eye could see. The farmer had had a busy day. He was nearly done when he had been shot in his tractor seat. *Why, why, why...* Waldemar thought, *and more importantly, how?* He paced around, studying the tracks the killer had left that were still intact. In Alberta, in the summer, most days came to a close with a late-night thundershower. It had been a few days since the crime and a heavy downpour had washed away the direction the killer had gone. The only thing Waldemar could determine was that he had approached the tractor from the rear, and with the loud noise of the tractor, the farmer would have been completely caught off guard. Hopefully, he hadn't heard it coming. Hopefully, he had been dead before he had a chance to know what was happening. There were a few prints at the side of the tractor where the killer had most likely stood to drag the body off. They were protected from the rain by the tractor.

"Jensen, come and take a picture of these prints for me," Waldemar commanded.

Jensen came to the side of the tractor and clicked his camera, recording the evidence.

If the killer could ensure that the body was never found, then he could never be charged with the homicide…*so*, Waldemar thought, *what better place to hide a body than acres and acres of freshly plowed fields?*

"I'm thinking," Waldemar said slowly, "that we need to start in the fields. The dirt is freshly turned and the simplest place for the killer to hide the body would be right here…right here on the farm."

Jensen groaned, "It's hot."

Waldemar laughed, "Yes, it sure is."

The men radioed for assistance and were able to have a few other officers come out to give them a hand. They fired up a neighbor's tractor and began the tedious task of searching the property.

Three days later, they had captured the suspected killer, who confessed to being on the farm that day. He did not, however, want to tell them what became of the farmer and where his body had ended up. Waldemar didn't tire though. Day after day in the hot sun, he carefully combed each square yard of the farm with the precision one needs when searching for a needle in a haystack.

He had given up on his detective suits and had come to the farm in his work boots, denim jeans and a loose plaid, short-sleeve button-up. He had also brought a hat to keep the sun from burning the top of his head.

Today his good friend Ronald McGovern dropped by the crime scene.

"Hello, Pete!" he called out as he approached the team of officers.

"Hi, McGovern!" Waldemar stopped and mopped the sweat from his brow. He walked toward McGovern, away from the others who continued working, with a smile. "What brings you by today?"

"I'm defending your suspect."

"Ahh…" Waldemar smiled knowingly. "I see."

"Did you tell him that I'm going to find that body, if it takes me until Christmas?"

McGovern smiled knowingly. "Really? It sure is hot."

"Yes it is. A real cooker…"

"And you're going to search every acre of the property?"

"You got it."

"How do you know it's here?"

"Just a hunch. If not, I'll look elsewhere. I've got to start in the most logical place and work myself away from here."

McGovern's eyes settled on the tractor in the distance. His eyes then went to a dirt road only a few hundred yards away that disappeared through a patch of birch trees. "Well, Pete, best of luck. I don't envy you."

"I'll give you a call when I find the body. Then you can buy me a drink."

McGovern chuckled, "Sure thing, friend, sure thing."

The phone rang and Ruth jumped to answer it, "Hello, Peterson residence."

"Mrs. Peterson?"

"Yes, this she."

"It's Mrs. McNally, you know, from the other side of the block over."

"Uh-huh…"

"Well, I'm calling about your son."

"Okay," Ruth's fingers touched the curly telephone cord.

"You know, the crippled one."

"His name is Gerry."

"Right, Gerry." Mrs. McNally's voice was dripping with insincerity, "Well, I hate to be the one to tell you this…"

"What is it?" Ruth said impatiently.

"He's escaped."

Ruth felt all the muscles around her shoulders tense up, right up into her neck and jaw. On previous occasions, well-intentioned neighbors had dragged Gerry in his walker through the streets like a lost dog, back to the house with Gerry protesting the whole way. Ruth had always given Gerry the freedom to do whatever he pleased and since he was able, he enjoyed strolling around the block in the walker Waldemar had made. He could push himself down the sidewalk and was very skillful at maneuvering himself around. She had no problems with this, and encouraged him to venture out on his own. Through clenched teeth she replied, "He's not a caged animal, Mrs. McNally. He's a ten-year-old boy who happens to be perfectly capable of going for a stroll around the neighborhood on his own. Where are your children right now? Out playing in the neighborhood? Out for a walk as well perhaps? Am I calling you to question your parenting?"

"Well," Mrs. McNally stuttered, "Well… he – ah, I thought you should know. How am I supposed to know what you let him do?"

"I let him do what any other child his age would do. Thank you for your concern."

"Okay then, goodbye."

"Goodbye," Ruth snapped. She slammed the receiver back into the cradle. "He's escaped?" She seethed to herself, "Escaped? For heaven's sake! When will it end?"

Brian sauntered into the kitchen. "Hey, Mom."

She stood with one hand on her hip and the other gripping the kitchen counter. "Hi, Brian. Gerry's out for a walk. Can you go and join him before someone tries to drag him home again?"

Brian tensed at his mom's words. "Sure, Mom, no problem."

She exhaled loudly. "Thanks."

Waldemar drove down a country road, looking for the next farmhouse. He had decided to quit plowing the fields and try another angle. The others remained at the farm, going inside the farmhouse, taking a break from the sweltering heat.

At the first farmhouse, the couple who lived there said that they had seen a car heading north on that day, a car they didn't recognize. Waldemar thanked them and carried on down the road to the next farmhouse. The breeze coming in through the car windows felt good. He smiled and said to himself, "I think our plowing days may be over!"

At the next farm, Waldemar found the farmer in his barn, milking. The familiar smells made him feel right at home. He called out so as not to startle the man, "Hello, RCMP."

The farmer emerged from a feed room, carrying a bucket. "Hello. How can I help you?"

Waldemar showed the farmer his badge. "I'm Detective Peterson. I'm investigating a murder."

"Bentley?"

"Yes, sir."

"Poor fella. Could have been me. I can't say I ever watch my back when I'm out in the field."

"No, sir, and you shouldn't have to. That's why I need your help."

"Anything I can do…" the farmer's voice trailed off.

"Have you seen anyone over the last week, anyone you didn't recognize? Any cars go by that you don't normally see around here?"

The farmer thought for a minute and replied, "Actually, last Tuesday. A car came down the road and got itself stuck — something awful — and the young man came to my property to have me tow him out."

"And did you?"

"Yes I did. He was a nice young man. We don't get too many…wait a minute, you think that's the one?"

Waldemar kept a poker face. "It's hard to say. Do you mind showing me where that mud puddle was?"

"No, sir, I don't mind. Right this way." The farmer walked out of the barn, down to the main road and pointed out the spot where he had towed the car out.

"Mind if I have a look around?"

"Feel free." The farmer left Waldemar alone, heading back the barn.

Waldemar stood in the middle of the road and slowly turned around. He looked in all directions, trying to reason what the killer would have done. He started walking back down the road. His eyes scanned the side of the road until he found what he was looking for. Slightly trampled, hardly visible, the grass led into a wooded area. Waldemar walked into the woods, his senses heightened, searching for a sign of Bentley, the dead farmer. He wasn't more than one hundred feet off the road when he saw a boot sticking out of the brush.

He pulled the brush aside and groaned, "Here you are."

Chapter 14

"Come to me, all you who are weary and burdened, and I will give you rest." Matthew 11: 28 NIV

September 25, 1959

Brian, Waldemar, Gerry and Dale

"Happy birthday," Ruth smiled at Dale as he came into the kitchen. "I made your favorite breakfast." Dale smiled half-heartedly and sat at the table with a sigh.

Ruth chattered on as she stood at the stove, "I'll make whatever you'd like for supper tonight. You pick — I'll pick it up at the store and cook it up."

Dale shrugged. "I don't know."

"Chocolate cake?" she asked excitedly.

"I don't feel well," Dale complained.

Ruth turned from the stovetop and looked at him quizzically. "In what way?"

"My stomach," he looked at his mom with big, sad eyes, "it hurts."

"Dale, you're going to school. It's Friday. You've already missed two days this week. What's going on?"

Dale didn't answer.

"Brian?" Ruth drilled. "What's going on at school?"

Brian hung his head. "Nothing."

"Well then you're both going." She handed them their metal lunch boxes as they finished their breakfast. She kissed them both. "Have a good day then. It's your birthday, Dale, cheer up!"

He rolled his eyes.

"Sweetheart, you're nine years old today! It's a good day!"

Dale muttered incoherently as they trudged out the back door. Halfway to school, their troubles began once again.

"Dale is a nincompoop!" a grade-five boy called out.

"Just keep walking," Dale hissed to Brian who was now in grade two. Dale pushed up his horn-rimmed glasses.

Brian clutched his lunch kit a little tighter as they walked faster.

"Come on, Dale," the boy hissed as he approached them from behind, "are you going to cry for your Mommy?"

Dale spun around and shouted, "Shut up! Just shut up!"

The boy stopped in his tracks. "What did you say to me?"

"Nothing," Dale mumbled and continued walking with Brian by his side.

Every day it was the same. The Peterson lunch boxes were the envy of the school and every day Dale surrendered his lunch to avoid getting a punch from the school bully.

The boy raced in front of Dale, stopping the boys in their tracks. "What's in the box?" he said savagely. Before Dale could respond, the boy ripped the metal lunch box out of Dale's hands. He popped open the metal clasps and pulled out the turkey sandwich that was wrapped neatly in wax paper.

"I'll take that," he snarled. He continued to look though the lunch box. He took the entire contents of Dale's lunch: fruit, sandwich, a chocolate cupcake and a tiny packet of jellybeans that Ruth had lovingly wrapped in a wax paper envelope. She had jotted 'Happy Birthday' on his napkin. His thermos was full of chocolate milk, his favorite.

The boy opened the jellybeans and threw them into the grass. "Stupid jelly beans!" He tossed the lunch box into the bushes. He jammed the other contents of Dale's lunch into his own bag. "Thanks a lot," he read the napkin that had fallen to the ground, "and Happy Birthday, baby boy."

Dale sighed and bent down to pick up the jellybeans that weren't too dirty. The boy wound up and punched Dale in the arm before he left.

"Tell your mom to pack more cookies!" he hollered as he laughed and ran away.

Brian felt the tears spring to his eyes as he watched Dale look through his thick glasses, searching for salvageable jellybeans. Brian dabbed his eyes and sucked in a deep breath of air. His legs were trembling.

Dale popped a few jellybeans in his pocket, picked up the thermos and then motioned to Brian. "Come on, let's get going. We're going to be late if we don't hurry."

"Go ahead," Brian said softly. "I'll get your lunch box."

The lunch box had been flung into the bushes. Brian scrambled to retrieve it as Dale walked ahead, his head hung low.

At lunchtime, Dale didn't even want to open his lunch box. He dreaded facing the emptiness. He knew his stomach would pain him all afternoon. He was a good student but with the mix of anxiety and hunger, it was hard to concentrate.

The teacher would ask him why he wasn't eating if he didn't open his lunch box soon and he didn't feel like explaining his problem. He was embarrassed that even with a cop for a dad he was still getting picked on.

He opened his lunch box and was surprised to see that there was half a turkey sandwich, half of a chocolate cupcake and an entire packet of jellybeans. Under it all was the crumpled napkin, stating, "Happy Birthday, Love Mom."

Dale smiled. "Maybe it's not such a bad day after all."

When the boys returned home, Ruth set them up at the kitchen table to work on homework. She was trying to get Brian to practice his reading but he couldn't focus.

"What's going on, Brian?"

Brian looked at her and shrugged. "Nothing."

"Dale?"

"Nothing, Mom."

"I know something is happening at school, why don't you tell me about it?"

The boys sat silently. Ruth sighed and smoothed her skirt. "Whatever it is, I can handle it. We can work on your problem together."

Dale sat squeezing his pencil while Brian looked stony-faced at his reading book.

Ruth rose up from the table, exasperated. She went to the living room to talk to Gerry, who was lying on the couch.

"Maybe I can have a decent conversation with you," she winked at Gerry as she sat down.

Gerry laughed. He began to spell out a message.

The next day, Dale was riding his new bike up and down the alley. It had been a wonderful surprise for his birthday. Waldemar was working out in the garage, cleaning up his tools when Brian came out to join him.

"Hey, buddy." Waldemar smiled at his youngest son.

"Hi, Dad." Brian settled himself on a milk crate near the door.

"What's new?"

"Not much," he said glumly.

"How's school?"

Brian hesitated. "It's okay."

Waldemar paused, looking at his youngest son. "Anything you wanted to talk to me about?"

Brian took a deep breath and shuddered.

"Are you having a problem at school?"

"Dale is," Brian blurted out.

"Ah," Waldemar said knowingly.

"It's okay — no big deal." Brian scuffed his sneakers in the dirt that covered the garage floor.

"Is there a bully?"

Brian nodded. It wasn't easy hiding things from your dad when he was a detective.

"Is he hurting Dale?"

Brian nodded again. "But don't tell him I said so!"

Waldemar gave Brian a hug. "It's okay, we'll take care of it."

Within a few minutes, Waldemar was off to the hardware store. He waved to Dale who was coasting down the alley toward him.

"I'll be back soon. Tell your mom for me, okay?"

"Okay." Dale left his bike in the garage and went inside the house with Brian.

Waldemar returned an hour later and took his purchase to the basement where he drilled and bolted it into place. He then rounded up all three boys.

He carried Gerry to the basement. Brian and Dale followed behind. Waldemar sat Gerry down in a comfortable spot and had Dale and Brian examine the newest addition to the basement.

"What's this for?" Dale asked, looking at the punching bag curiously.

"I want to teach you some things."

Dale turned to Brian and glared at him. "Thanks a lot!"

"Now, now," Waldemar interrupted, "this is a lesson for all of you, regardless of what's happening at school. It's something you should know."

Waldemar took an aggressive stance and wound up, hammering out a vicious hit to the punching bag. The sound of his fist against the leather of the bag startled the boys. They listened to the bag creak back and forth on its chain.

"Whoa," Brian muttered.

"Anytime you're cornered by a group of bullies, you pick the biggest guy and WHAM," Waldemar hit the bag again. "Punch him in the nose!"

Dale and Brian's eyes were wide as the bag swung wildly.

"Geesh," Dale gasped.

"You'll never have a problem again." Waldemar smiled broadly at his boys.

They spent the entire evening punching that bag. Dale pretended it was the bully who had scattered his jellybeans and hit that bag as hard as he could. Gerry watched as the boys smacked the bag again and again.

The trouble subsided at school the first time Dale and Brian threatened to use their boxing moves on the bully. Dale also asked his mom to start packing tuna sandwiches with no cookies, no fruit and absolutely no chocolate.

*

Gerry cried out again in his sleep. Ruth rose, bleary eyed, fumbling for her glasses on the nightstand. It was the third time tonight she had been up. She had only been asleep for a half-hour since her last trip down the hall. She went to the boys' bedroom and sat on the edge of Gerry's bed. He was crying as his legs spasmed wildly. She rubbed them firmly, trying to stop the cramping.

"It's okay, sweetheart," she soothed. "It's okay."

He continued to cry as she rubbed.

"I'm sorry, Gerry. We'll get through this one too."

Life had been one challenge after another for Gerry. The night symbolized his endless struggle in life. Nothing was easy, not even sleeping.

She thought of the day when Herman had delivered the wheelchair. Gerry was furious. She had sat him in the chair. He had clearly expressed his disgust. He had angrily spelled out a message, 'trapped.'

"You're not trapped," she said. *"You'll figure something out. We'll figure a way for you to get around on your own. We just have to think about it a bit."*

"Na," Gerry replied, scowling at her.

Gerry had been able to push himself around in his half-chair all these years and suddenly he was belted into a chair that, although it had wheels, was completely immobile for him. He was so mad that he jerked his leg, which pushed his toe against the floor. The wheelchair shot back.

Ruth smiled. "See, you solved your problem already."

Gerry had glared at her and pushed himself backwards, down the hall to his bedroom. If he could have slammed the door behind him, he would have.

Ruth prayed again that God would heal Gerry. Since his diagnosis, she had not stopped asking God to take away the Cerebral Palsy. It had been more than ten years of being up at night, massaging muscles, drying tears and soothing his frustrated ego. Every night she sat in the dark and prayed that God would intervene. If God could take Gerry's pain away — she would do anything. As a child, her father had made her study the Bible and memorize countless verses. In these quiet, dark moments in Gerry's room, the verses flooded her mind.

Tonight she thought of the woman who merely touched Jesus' cloak for healing. She remembered the verse, "Take heart, daughter," he said, "your faith has healed you."

"I have faith," she whispered. "I know you could heal Gerry if you wanted to. Where are you? Just look down on us and touch Gerry. Heal him, please God."

Another verse, Matthew 11:28, came to mind, "Come to me, all you who are weary and burdened, and I will give you rest."

Ruth sighed. She was weary. She was weary of Gerry's pain. She was weary of the battle against society. She was burdened with the judgment that fell on her and on Gerry. She was physically weary. Her back and knees ached from the constant lifting and carrying.

How could she care for Gerry as he aged? Would he always live at home? Would she be taking care of his daily needs until she was an old woman? She almost laughed as she thought of herself, old and frail, stooped over, carrying Gerry to bed. She was mentally weary. Endless questions swirled through her mind. What would their future look like if the Cerebral Palsy wasn't healed?

"Where is my rest, Lord?" she questioned into the darkness. Gerry's cries had subsided. He was back asleep.

She looked at him laying there, a grimace of pain on his face. She put her head in her hands and cried. "Why?" The storm raged within.

She headed back to her room and crawled into bed next to Waldemar. She put her cold feet on his warm legs and shuddered. One last verse floated into her mind as she tried to fall back to sleep.

"For I was hungry and you gave me something to eat, I was thirsty and you gave me something to drink, I was a stranger and you invited me in, I needed clothes and you clothed me, I was sick and you looked after me…"

She turned her face into her pillow and cried again.

Next to her, Waldemar listened as his wife battled their reality. He ached to take it away. He felt helpless against the torrent of her pain.

He prayed silently that God would bring her peace. The peace that only God could bring.

The next morning, Waldemar told Ruth he was going to be at home during the day and suggested that she should go do some shopping downtown. Ruth was delighted. It was a sunny fall day. She took the bus from their suburb into the city. All day she walked through the shops, admiring the latest fashions and purchasing the things she needed. There were functions with the RCMP that required formal wear so Ruth spent the day trying on gowns and losing herself in the search.

On the way home, she sat on the bus, looking out the window. The sun shone through the dirty windows. Ruth watched the dust float through the air. Her hands clutched her packages tightly as the bus bounced along the road.

She thought of her fury and frustration last night. All these years she had been drowning in a sea of hardship that Cerebral Palsy had cast over them.

A scene from the Bible came to her mind. She could almost taste the sea air in her imagination as she pictured the panicked disciples in the storm.

"Lord, save us! We're going to drown!"

He replied, "You of little faith, why are you so afraid?" Then he got up and rebuked the winds and the waves, and it was completely calm.

On the bus, as passengers came on and off, she felt that calmness inside her.

As she sat there, a wave of peace — indescribable peace — flooded her. The storm of anger, frustration, guilt and denial that emanated from her heart for the last ten years finally ceased.

In her mind she prayed, "God, I can now accept what has happened to Gerry and all of us. I commit all this to you. Now give me the strength to go on from here."

Chapter 15

"When justice is done, it brings joy to the righteous but terror to evildoers." Proverbs 21:15 NIV

November 5, 1960

Waldemar

Constable Morgan shook his head, "Can you believe this, Sarge?"

"There it is," Waldemar smiled, "just what we were looking for."

They had been working on this case for nearly a month. Waldemar was head of the General Investigations Branch and he and his men had been fortunate enough to come across a potential crime *before* it happened. Informants, intercepts and good old-fashioned patience had connected them with six men that were plotting a robbery, and now, he knew as he listened to the wire tap recordings, also plotting a homicide.

"This telephone intercept was genius, Pete," Morgan commented.

"It did work out in our favor, didn't it? Now we're not only on a level playing field, I think we have the home team advantage."

Moran laughed.

"We've got some work to do if we're going to get everything lined up before these guys make their move."

"What first?" Morgan asked.

Waldemar tapped his pencil against his notes. "We need to figure out the target. We need to start asking around and find out who has sold their land in the area."

"Right, and it sounds like they must be an older couple, no children, based on some of the conversations they've had."

"Let's take a drive out to the Morinville area and start asking around. I'm sure it won't take long to narrow down." He closed up the file on his desk, and grabbed his notebook and badge from his drawer. He pulled on his wool winter coat and leather gloves. "Ready?"

Morgan nodded as he pulled on his coat. "Let's go."

The two drove out to the farms around Morinville and within a few stops they were able to confirm that Mr. and Mrs. Snell had sold their family farm. Even the neighbors knew that the Snells had stashed their fortune in a safe on their property.

"Why don't we go and have a conversation with them?" Morgan suggested.

"That sounds great, let's tell them that they need to get their money secure. Then we'll start setting up the sting."

The Snells lived in a two-story farmhouse. There were a few steps leading up to a covered porch. Two small, square windows flanked the heavy wooden front door. On the left side of the house were three large windows on the main floor and three on the second floor. Morgan knocked on the front door.

Mrs. Snell hesitantly opened the front door. "Hello?" She was a petite old lady with white hair and half-framed glasses. She wore a floral skirt and a gray sweater.

"Afternoon, Mrs. Snell. I'm Sergeant Peterson with the RCMP. This is Constable Morgan."

"Afternoon, gentlemen." She smiled as she smoothed her sweater. "We don't get too many visitors calling. I'll put a pot of coffee on. Please, come in."

"Thank you, ma'am." Waldemar stepped inside the house, followed by Morgan.

"Afternoon, Officers," Mr. Snell rose from his rocking chair and stretched out his hand for a handshake. "What brings you out today?"

Waldemar explained the information they had uncovered and the possible danger that the couple was potentially in. He asked for their cooperation as they set things up and staked out the property.

The Snells were happy to comply and agreed that they would secure their safe and its contents right away.

Waldemar and Morgan spent the day searching the property. After a few hours, Waldemar found tire tracks in the fields. He followed them to some large hay bales. He poked around in the hay with a large stick until he eventually heard the ping of the metal as his stick made contact.

"I've got something," Waldemar called out to Morgan who was looking through the trees behind them.

"What is it?" he asked.

Waldemar pushed aside the loose hay until he saw what he had suspected. There was a stash of weapons.

"I don't suppose those belong to Mr. Snell?" Morgan said, smiling.

"No, sir. Why don't we give our friends a nice surprise when they come back?"

The next morning, Waldemar sat at the breakfast table with his three boys.

"Dad, why do we have to have oatmeal again?" Dale groaned.

Waldemar looked at his son as he took another spoonful of his hot cereal. "Because I love it."

"I love it too." Brian smiled at his dad as he ate. "Gerry too, right, Gerry?"

Gerry smiled.

"Eat up, Dale, we're going into my office this morning."

"Really?" Brian's eyes were wide.

"It's boring," Dale sighed.

"You guys can type on the typewriters while I do a little work."

"Great!" Brian exclaimed.

"Okay," Dale said as he began to eat.

After breakfast, Waldemar packed the kids up in the car and drove downtown to his office. He tried to give Ruth as many Saturdays as possible to rest and take some time for herself. If he was curling, he would take the boys to the rink and let them explore. He would buy them a coke and they would sit on the sidelines and cheer. Last week he had taken the three of them for a ride on the toboggan. All around their house were farmers' fields. It was the perfect place for him to run, full steam, with the three boys screaming and holding on for dear life. He still loved to run. He loved to hear the sheer joy of the boys as they bumped through the snow. Gerry sat in the front with Brian behind him, holding him tightly. Dale sat at the back, clutching onto Brian. Waldemar loved athletics and adventure. He tried to get the boys as involved as possible, but they didn't have the same passion that he had as a child. Gerry had been interested in skiing so Waldemar made skis that could strap onto the bottom of the wheelchair. They had only tried it once. He had accidentally let go and Gerry had sailed down the ski hill on his own. Ruth hadn't been terribly impressed, even though Gerry came out no worse for wear. He had promised that he and Gerry wouldn't ski anymore.

In the car, on the way to the office, Brian took a message from Gerry.

"A, B, C..."

Gerry stopped him at J.

"You miss Jet?"

"Aye," Gerry sighed.

Jet had left home about three weeks ago. He was prone to run off but had never been gone for so long before. It had been a particularly mild fall and the temperatures were warm enough for Jet to survive. Waldemar and Ruth, however, were concerned that Jet was not going to return this time.

"He'll be back," Brian said reassuringly.

Gerry vocalized.

"I know he's been gone a long time but he loves us and he'll come home soon."

Brian had spent the summer with the dog, showing an interest in him that previously wasn't there. He had always been Gerry's dog but Ruth had allowed Brian to start taking Jet for walks in the ravine. Brian had built a rapport with Jet, taking him off his leash and letting him explore. The dog would come back to Brian and allow him to clip the leash back on before they returned home. Brian felt like he was finally making his own special connection with the dog. Then he disappeared.

They parked at the office. Waldemar carried Gerry while Dale and Brian followed behind. Waldemar balanced the wheelchair in his free hand. He set it down for a moment, careful not to get the wheels dirty, and unlocked the door.

"Anyone else here today?" Dale asked.

"I don't think so, buddy." Waldemar held the door open as the boys filed in. He unfolded the wheelchair and buckled in Gerry.

They walked down a narrow hall. Brian looked at each door they passed. They went through a door marked 'General Investigations Branch' to a cluster of metal desks.

"Wow," Brian breathed. He looked at his dad's desk and read the title on his dad's business cards out loud, "Look it says, 'Staff Sergeant Peterson, Head of General Investigations Branch.' Cool."

Waldemar unlocked his desk drawers and laid out his files on the desktop. He settled Brian and Dale at a different desk and loaded paper into their typewriter. He pulled Gerry up so that he could watch.

"Go ahead, boys, type to your heart's content. I'll be at my desk. I've just got a few things to do."

"Okay, Dad," Brian and Dale chorused. Brian began to push the heavy typewriter keys down. He tapped out 'Zorro is my hero' and grinned as he saw the words appear on the paper. "Cool!" Dale walked around the office taking it all in.

Waldemar looked over the details of the Snell case. He had been working on having a blacksmith make a steel bulletproof vest for Morgan. Morgan would be waiting for the killers in Mr. Snell's rocking chair.

After a few phone calls, Waldemar confirmed that the vest was ready to be picked up. The telephone intercepts had revealed that everything would take place that night. The vest was ready just in time. He called all of the officers involved and let them know that they would be meeting at the Morinville detachment at noon. Everything was in place.

"Okay, boys," Waldemar stretched in his chair, "are you ready to go?"

Brian continued to pluck away at the keys on the typewriter, typing a letter for Gerry. Dale stood staring at the board of criminals.

"Are these all bad guys, Dad?" Dale asked.

"They aren't bad guys, Dale, they're regular guys who have made bad choices." He paused and looked at his young son. "Some more than others."

Dale studied the grim faces on the wall. "Oh." Waldemar put his big hand on Dale's shoulder.

He turned to the other boys and asked, "Brian, Gerry, are you ready?"

"Aye," Gerry said.

"Come and see, Dad!" Brian exclaimed, "I wrote the coolest letters!"

Waldemar walked over and studied Brian's typing. "You're pretty good at that!"

The four of them headed back to the car with Waldemar pushing Gerry down the hall and locking up the office as they left.

Several hours later, Waldemar sat in the Morinville RCMP detachment with the Chief Superintendent of Edmonton's K Division, listening to their men on the police radio. Morgan sat in Mr. Snell's rocking chair and another officer, Matthews, was in Mrs. Snell's chair. A third officer, Harper, was in the kitchen with his weapon ready, and a fourth, Wilkins, was sitting in a large haystack in the front yard. Waldemar heard the radio crackle.

"We've got movement," Wilkins, the officer in the haystack, alerted everyone that the perpetrators were on the property, collecting their stashed weapons.

Waldemar sat on the edge of the chair, staring at the police radio, waiting to hear what would happen next. The whole situation was very risky. *If the perpetrators decided to aim for Mr. Snell's head instead of his chest, then Morgan* – Waldemar dismissed the thought.

"They're heading for the door," Wilkins whispered into his radio.

Within seconds, Waldemar heard gunshots over the radio and a sequence of yelling, screaming and grunting.

"They're under fire in the house," Wilkins exclaimed over the radio.

"Stay where you are," Waldemar commanded.

"I've got one coming out!" Wilkins shouted into his radio.

Waldemar waited for an agonizingly long time before he heard, "One suspect in custody."

Each minute went by painfully until eventually Waldemar got a report from Morgan.

"Peterson, we've got the location of the three other conspirators in Edmonton. Matthew and Wilkins are going to pick them up. Harper and I are bringing Baker, Hammond and Franklin back to you at the detachment. We'll need transport to the hospital from there."

"Roger that, Morgan. Who are the injured parties? Over."

"Franklin has lost his ear — everything else is minor. Over."

"We'll be ready. Over."

Morgan and Harper arrived with the three criminals. Franklin was taken immediately to Edmonton for treatment on his ear. It had been shot off. The other two men were locked up in the RCMP guardroom and charged with attempted murder and attempted armed robbery.

While another officer worked on processing Baker and Hammond, Morgan sat down with Waldemar to explain what had happened.

"The first shot was fired at me, in the chair — just as they had said. It hit the vest, knocking me to the floor. Harper and Matthew started shooting back and boy the perps were surprised!"

"Did they have a lot of weaponry on them?"

"Yes, they tried to use the weapons they'd stashed but when they realized we took their ammo, they used their revolvers. I'm guessing that Franklin had always planned to use the revolver to kill Mr. Snell, for accuracy, I guess. It hit me square in the chest. We exchanged gunfire and once Franklin was hit, Baker tried to leave the property. Wilkins grabbed him in the front yard."

"I heard that part over the radio."

"Then we had a bit of a wrestle with Hammond before he surrendered. Franklin was bleeding badly so he gave up quite easily. Hammond's got a black eye and some scrapes and bruises. Baker has a dislocated shoulder."

"Well, it ended well. I got word from Edmonton that the other three were picked up. They've charged them with attempted murder and conspiracy to commit armed robbery."

"Fantastic operation, Sergeant Peterson. I'm glad I was a part of it."

"Likewise."

When Waldemar climbed into bed that night, he whispered to Ruth to see if she was still awake.

"Yes, I'm still awake. What's up?" she rolled over to face him.

"Not much, I haven't talked to you all day. What did you do today?"

Ruth smiled and said, "You must not be too tired."

"No, we had a busy night and I'm still wide awake."

She looked up at the ceiling. "Well, we had supper, the boys played downstairs while I cleaned up. Story time. Bed time — you know, the usual."

"Sounds fun."

"Oh and the strangest thing, Gerry told me that he could hear Jet's dog tags. He told me that he can hear Jet coming home."

"Poor guy."

"I know, I feel bad. That stupid dog."

"He's not stupid. He's probably lost his way and someone's taken him in."

"Well, I wish he knew how much Gerry needed him!"

Waldemar smiled. "You never know, maybe he does."

The next day, the family drove home from church in the Ford Fairlane.

"Tired?" Ruth asked Waldemar as he yawned.

"Yes. I couldn't fall asleep last night. Once I did, Gerry woke me up."

"That's hard. I hate when I'm up and I can't get back to sleep."

Waldemar glanced in the rearview mirror as he slowed to enter the traffic circle. "What's that?" he remarked. "Something is following us!"

Brian, Dale and Ruth all turned around in their seats while Gerry vocalized hysterically.

"Slow down, Pete," Ruth said.

He slowed down the car and circled around the traffic circle completely while the black speck came into view.

"It's Jet!" Dale exclaimed.

Ruth laughed as Jet caught up. "Well what do you know?"

Jet barked as he ran alongside the car. Gerry vocalized excitedly. Brian jumped up and down in his seat. "He's back!"

Waldemar stopped the car. "It's not far but I guess we can give him a ride."

Brian flung open his door. The dirty dog jumped in. His coat was filthy, matted and had sticks embedded in it.

"Oh he stinks!" Dale groaned as Jet leapt over the three kids. Gerry's arms were flailing everywhere as his excitement grew.

Brian wrapped his arms around Gerry. "Whoa, Gerry, slow down!" He laughed, "I'm excited too!"

Jet licked Gerry excitedly, knocking off his glasses.

Brian grinned as he settled Gerry's glasses back into place. "Jet's excited too!"

On Monday, Ruth drank her coffee and unrolled the morning paper. The boys were in school. Gerry was watching TV. The breakfast dishes littered the counter and table. Ruth pushed the dishes aside and looked at the picture on the front page. There was her handsome husband holding a revolver and a black garment. She read the words under his photo. *'Officer Displays Bullet Proof Vest.'*

Her eyes darted to the large headline, *'Gun Battle Halts Robbery Attempt, Six Taken In Custody, Steel Vest Saves Detective As Armed Men Walk into Trap.'*

She read the article regarding the events at the Snell farm and the subsequent arrests.

"No wonder he couldn't sleep," she mused aloud as she snipped the article from the paper. "That's one for the album."

*

The following January, Waldemar was given the Commissioner's Commendation. He read the letter to Ruth as they sat in the living room.

Dear Staff Sergeant Peterson:

> *I take great pleasure in enclosing my commendation for the part you played in organizing and supervising operations in the case of Roger Franklin and for your consistently outstanding work since assuming your charge of Edmonton Sub-Division General Investigation Section in May 1960.*
>
> *While the case of Roger Franklin is worthy of special mention, I am not unmindful of the many other investigations that have been successfully concluded during the past few months.*
>
> *This commendation was published in Part I of General Orders of January 7, 1961.*
>
> *Yours very truly,*
>
>   *G.P. Harvison,*
>   *Commissioner.*

"Good for you, Pete!" Ruth gave him a hug as she sat next to him on the couch.

"And," he smiled, "it came with a twenty-five dollar bonus!"

"Wow! That's fantastic!"

"It's been a great couple of years for me," Waldemar said, smiling. "A lot of high-profile cases I've been able to be a part of."

"I always knew you were capable of great things, Sergeant Peterson," she winked at him.

Chapter 16

"Blessed are they who maintain justice…"
Psalm 106: 3 NIV

July 1961

Brian, Dale, Waldemar and Gerry

    Waldemar and Ruth waited in the parking lot of the Cerebral Palsy Clinic. Brian and Dale were waiting in the back seat of the car, with the windows down. For the last week, Gerry, now twelve, had been away at Camp Isle, a special camp for Cerebral Palsied children. Gerry had been elated to go. He was an independent spirit, something that Waldemar and Ruth had nurtured. Seeing him go off on his own for the first time had been exciting.

It had been a quiet week with Brian and Dale. They took Jet for walks, explored the ravine, played camping in the backyard and rode their bikes around the neighborhood. After twelve years of getting up in the night with Gerry, both Ruth and Waldemar appreciated the break. It was nice to sleep in a bit, especially with Dale and Brian being off school.

Gerry came off the bus in the arms of one of the volunteers. Waldemar walked forward to take him.

"Hi, buddy!" Waldemar hugged Gerry as he took him into his arms.

Ruth was right behind. "Hi, Gerry!"

Gerry vocalized excitedly.

"Did you have a good time?" she asked.

"Aye!"

"That's great!" Waldemar replied. "Ruth, can you locate his wheelchair?"

Ruth looked at the wheelchairs being unloaded off the back of the bus. She spotted Gerry's and went to collect it. She opened it up. Waldemar set Gerry down and buckled him. He then went to collect Gerry's suitcase. They all loaded up into the car where Brian offered Gerry a big hug. "I missed you!" he said happily.

"Hey, Gerry," Dale offered.

Gerry vocalized.

Ruth smirked. "Brian was worried about you all week!"

Gerry vocalized.

"Do you have a message?" Ruth asked.

"Aye."

"About camp?"

"Aye."

"About your activities?"

"Aye."

"Did you swim?" Dale asked.

"Aye!"

"Did you hike?" Brian asked.

"Aye!"

"Did you make new friends?" Waldemar asked.

"Aye!" Gerry vocalized.

Ruth knew he had something to say that they weren't getting. "A, B, C…" Gerry stopped her at I. He slowly spelled out 'in love.'

Ruth smiled. "In love?"

"Aye," Gerry sighed.

"Oh dear," Waldemar laughed. "Like your dad, huh? You like every pretty girl you see?"

Gerry laughed. "Aye!"

*

Waldemar hadn't even started his breakfast when the phone rang.

"Hello, Peterson residence."

"Good morning, Pete," Waldemar's superior greeted him.

"Morning, sir."

"I have an interesting case for you this morning. I need you to meet me at the Alberta Legislative Building right away."

"Yes, sir, I'm on my way." Waldemar hung up the phone and headed to the bedroom to let Ruth know that he was leaving.

He arrived at the Legislative Grounds within a half-hour, on an empty stomach. He approached the Chief Superintendent, who was standing with a few other officers.

"What's happening, Chief?" Waldemar asked.

"Hello, Staff Sergeant Peterson. I've got a high-profile case for you. Have you had your coffee?" he joked. "You're going to be on this one for a while."

"Yes, sir."

"The Civil Service Savings and Credit Union offices have had a robbery. The thieves have removed a safe containing quite a bit of cash."

"What exactly are we talking about here?" Waldemar looked up at the window.

"They must have lowered the safe down from the second floor — out the window by the looks of things."

"And the safe?"

"Upwards of fifty thousand dollars."

Waldemar touched the brim of his hat and said, "I can understand the urgency."

"Yes, Peterson. The perpetrators threatened the night watchmen with knives. They were bound and gagged and left on the first floor. It's seven a.m. now," the chief looked at his watch. "And the night watchmen say they came around four-thirty a.m."

"Did the watchmen get a look at these guys?"

"No, they were masked."

"Do you have any description?"

"Young, four males, slight builds."

"I think I have a few guys who might be good for it. We've been waiting for them to pull a job. I'll gather up my men and we'll start trying to find out where they are headed with the safe. I imagine that if they took the entire safe then they must be somewhere trying to get it open. Let's hope it takes them awhile to crack it."

"I don't have to tell you that this is an embarrassment to the city. We need you to wrap this up as swiftly as possible."

"Yes, sir."

Waldemar went to the group of police cars where Morgan and Matthews were standing. "Hello, gentlemen. Are you ready for a busy day?"

"Yes, sir," they chorused.

"A, B…" Ruth asked.

"Aye," said Gerry
"B?"
"Aye."
"A, B…"
"Aye."
"A?"
"Aye."
"A, B, C…" Ruth carried on until she reached P. "Bap – Baptist?"

Gerry vocalized in such a way that she knew she was close.

"Bap – ah baptism?"

Gerry vocalized enthusiastically.

"What about it? Do you have a question?"

"Aye."

"Okay, sweetheart," Ruth started up the alphabet again. "A, B, C…"

Gerry stopped her at M and then E.

"You? You want to be baptized?"

"Aye!"

"What made you decide this?"

Gerry vocalized.

"Church?"

"Na," Gerry frowned.

Ruth thought about it. "The Bible?"

"Na."

Ruth sighed. "Spell it out for me. A, B, C…"

Gerry stopped her at C.

"A"

Gerry stopped her.

"A, B, C…" Ruth continued to M. "Camp?"

"Aye," Gerry vocalized eagerly.

"Do you know what it means?" she questioned.

Gerry vocalized.

"It's a serious decision to make. It's not something to do because the other kids are doing it."

Gerry agreed.

"If you really want to then we need to discuss it further. God already knows your heart but I want to hear what's on your mind."

Ruth and Gerry spent nearly an hour while Gerry spelled out how he was feeling. He told his mom that he believed that Jesus was his personal Lord and Savior and that he had died on the cross for his sins. Gerry knew that the only way to eternal life was through accepting Jesus into his heart. He understood that baptism was a sign of obedience.

"It's not only a sign of obedience, Gerry," Ruth explained. "It needs to be accompanied by faith and repentance. It's a way of telling God that we accept Christ's gospel and that we wish to have our sins washed away. We die to ourselves and we are reborn in Him. At the point of baptism, we make a conscious decision to dedicate our lives to Christ and live in obedience with His word."

Gerry agreed.

"Okay then. I'll talk to your dad and we can set up a meeting with the church deacons." She gave him a hug. "I'm proud of you, Gerry, this is a really big step."

Waldemar, Morgan and Matthews discussed who they thought might have committed the crime. Michael Thomas had convictions for theft, breaking and entering, and possession of stolen property.

Morgan commented, "He would have the audacity to pull off a stunt like this."

"They must have had a big vehicle. We're looking for something that's going to be able not only to fit the safe in the trunk but be able to tolerate the weight load."

Morgan added, "Not too many cars like that will have gone unnoticed."

The four officers split off to canvas the area, to see if anyone had heard or seen such a car. They spent the next two days tracing down the direction of the cars and talking to informants about the whereabouts of Thomas and his crew. Through word of mouth, they were able to determine that the vehicle had headed east out of the city, toward the town of Sherwood Park. Waldemar knocked on dozens of farm doors and had driven for hours before he finally talked to someone who had spotted the car.

"Yes, sir, I did." The old farmer nodded his head slowly. He pointed out to a dirt road, running alongside his property. "It went south along the road. I remember it because it was five a.m. and the back of the car was practically scraping along the road."

Waldemar jotted the information in his notebook. "Go on."

"And — I thought, who the hell would load a car like that with such heavy cargo?"

Waldemar nodded.

"Also, there aren't any vehicles that come this way that aren't someone we know. Four young boys — going way too fast if you ask me."

"Of course," Waldemar agreed.

"If you carry on down the road you'll find the Hewitt property. You can see if they happened to see the same fellas."

"Yes, sir," Waldemar tipped his hat. "Thank you for the information."

He carried on down the dirt farm road and radioed to Morgan, who was in the area. Morgan agreed to meet him at the Hewitt farm as soon as he could.

Waldemar went to the farmhouse and spoke to Mr. Hewitt. He had been up that morning but hadn't seen a car matching the description go down the road.

"No, Officer, I would have noticed. I am right out that way in the early morning. I would definitely have noticed if such a vehicle were going by."

"Do you mind if a few of us search your property?"

"No, sir, that wouldn't bother me any."

"Thank you. We'll be in touch."

Morgan arrived at the farm. Matthews radioed to say that he was on his way. The men spent all afternoon searching the Hewitt property and neighboring farms, looking for signs that the vehicle in question had been there. They walked up and down the farmyards until they came to a cluster of trees and a big brush pile in the corner of the Hewitt property.

Waldemar started kicking the brush aside. Morgan grabbed a large stick and started pushing aside the loose debris. At the same moment they heard the plink sound of Waldemar's foot hitting a hard metal object.

"What have we here?" Morgan smiled.

"Pay dirt," Waldemar chuckled as he uncovered a large safe with the words 'Civil Service Savings and Credit Union' on the side.

"I believe this is exactly what we're after. Is the money there?"

Waldemar looked at the firmly locked doors with spinning combination locks on the front. "Well, we won't know until we find someone who can open it. They either figured out the combinations or they ditched it, thinking they could come back to try to pry it open."

"Let's hope it's the latter."

Morgan and Waldemar waited for Matthews and Harper to try to move the safe. It was a beast of a thing and so Mr. Hewitt agreed to load it up onto his truck. The officers drove the truck back to Headquarters, excited about what they had found.

A representative from the parliament came to open the safe. He had the combinations in his hand from the Civil Service Savings and Credit Union.

"I'll get this open and we can see if it still has the cash," he declared as he spun the dials to the left and then to the right and back again.

Waldemar stood with his Chief Superintendent. They were to witnesses the opening of the safe and the counting of its contents, if there was any. If any of the funds were missing, it would be evidence in the case against the perpetrators.

The safe clicked as the parliament representative spun the final dial. He opened the door cautiously.

"It looks like a lot of cash," he remarked.

"Let's hope it's the entire sum," said the chief.

"Yes, sir," agreed Waldemar.

The parliament representative spent the next three hours counting out $58,000 that was mainly in small denominations. He let out a large sigh as he counted the last of the bills.

"That's it, men, it's all there."

"Well done, Pete!" the Chief Superintendent shook Waldemar's hand vigorously.

"It wasn't my work alone, Chief. It was our entire unit."

"Good work nevertheless. Another case wrapped up by Staff Sergeant Peterson."

"We've still got to pick up our men but I've got a few officers out at the Hewitt farm, keeping a lookout for our friends to return. We'll be sure to give them a warm welcome when they come back for their loot."

Chapter 17

"Peter replied, 'Repent and be baptized, every one of you, in the name of Jesus Christ for the forgiveness of your sins. And you will receive the gift of the Holy Spirit.'" Acts 2:38 NIV

August 1961

Gerry with Uncle Victor

The deacons had come to meet with Gerry at the Peterson home and had asked him countless questions regarding his faith and understanding of the ritual of baptism. When they were satisfied that this was something that Gerry really wanted to do, and something that he was spiritually ready for, they began to discuss the details of the day.

The Baptismal Sunday dawned with a bright blue sky. Herman and Edith had driven from Leduc to witness the event.

Pastor Roberts stood in the baptismal tank at the front of the church. He began with a verse from Matthew 28:19: "'Therefore go and make disciples of all nations, baptizing them in the name of the Father and the Son and of the Holy Spirit.'

"As we know, baptism is an act of obedience symbolizing the believer's faith in a crucified, buried and risen Savior. It symbolizes death to sin, the burial of the old life and the resurrection to walk in the newness of life in Christ.

"Let's welcome Gerry into the waters this morning as we celebrate his journey of faith and his public declaration that the Lord our God is his risen Savior."

The congregation clapped as Waldemar, dressed in a white gown, stepped into the water holding his son, also in a white baptismal gown.

Pastor Roberts spoke, "Gerry, have you received Christ as your Lord and Savior?"

"Aye," Gerry said.

Pastor Roberts put a hand on the back of Gerry's neck and another on Waldemar's arm. He looked Gerry in the eye. "I, therefore, baptize you in the name of the Father, and of the Son and of the Holy Spirit."

Waldemar and Pastor Roberts lowered Gerry under the water and brought him back up as Gerry's Cerebral Palsy limbs spasmed wildly in the cool water. Waldemar held Gerry tightly against his chest.

"Praise God!" Pastor Roberts declared.

"Praise God!" the congregation echoed as they clapped.

*

It was the end of the summer and the family was taking their annual vacation. Almost every year they had gone to the Rocky Mountains, but this year Waldemar had announced that they had a different destination in mind.

"Lac Du Bonnet!"

"Lac Du where?" Dale asked.

"Lac Du Bonnet," Brian explained, "you know where Dad grew up."

"Oh," Dale thought about this for a minute, "what do you do there?"

"Well," Waldemar smiled, "we're going to stay with your Uncle Victor. He still runs the farm and I think it would be a lot of fun to spend some time there."

Ruth added, "It's really old fashioned there, almost like camping."

Dale rolled his eyes, "But it's not camping."

Brian looked at his dad and tried to reflect his excitement. "Sounds good."

Two days later, the car and the tent trailer were ready to go. It was early in the morning. Jet wagged his tail excitedly as he watched Ruth and Waldemar go back and forth between the house and the car, loading up. Ruth was looking forward to seeing the Peterson family again but it was a twelve-hour drive and they would be cooped up in the car all day. She knew the day would not be without a lot of complaining.

Once on the road, the boys met all of Ruth's expectations. They complained for the majority of the journey. It was too hot, too boring, too uncomfortable, the dog was drooling on someone's leg — on and on. Ruth and Waldemar tried to tune them out. Finally, they declared that the last few hours of the trip would be silent. With the silence came sleep as the three kids finally decided that a nap would pass the time faster than anything else.

It was almost dark when they pulled into the Peterson farm. The property had changed. Gone were the thick woods that used to surround the farm and the neighboring properties. The house stood as though caught in a time warp. The wood was more weathered than it had been forty years ago, but aside from that, everything looked as it always had.

Victor, Waldemar's older brother, sat in a rocking chair on the screened in porch. He had a kerosene lamp on a small table next to him. The bright headlights of the Peterson's Ford flooded the front of the small house. Victor's dog, Buster, barked loudly.

"Here we are," Waldemar whispered to Ruth, "home sweet home."

Waldemar parked the car and tent trailer in a suitable spot next to the house, near the summer kitchen. He got out of the car and greeted Victor with a warm hug.

"Hello!" The crickets, the hum of mosquitoes, and the far-off sound of the cows lowing in the barn, greeted Waldemar.

Victor spoke in Swedish, "*Halla, Broder!*"

"How are you?"

"I'm vell." Victor had a thick Swedish accent. "Vonderful to see you, Ruth."

Ruth grinned. "Good to be here. Thanks for having us."

"I'm afraid I can't do too much entertaining — you know farm life goes on."

"We completely understand," Ruth smiled reassuringly. "The boys are here to help. Perhaps even Pete," She looked over at Waldemar. "I'm sure he still knows how to milk a cow."

Waldemar laughed. "I'll never forget."

They spent the next hour setting up the tent trailer and getting the boys to bed. Victor showed Ruth to the outhouse behind the house.

"I built it, brand new just for you." He gave her a kerosene lamp. "You can hang the light on the peg here and it's almost like city living."

Ruth looked at the outhouse and smiled. "Perfect."

The next morning, Ruth went into the Peterson farmhouse and started working in the kitchen. The small house was divided into thirds. The entrance to the home was on the left-hand side of the house. It led into the kitchen. The kitchen had one window facing out front of the house and one out the back. At the back of the kitchen was a large wood stove and a large holding tank for water, all the same as it had always been. Ruth made breakfast for all of the Peterson men: Victor, Waldemar, Gerry, Brian and Dale. Buster and Jet waited out on the porch. Victor and Waldemar had been out in the barn since dawn, milking the cows and cleaning stalls. They came in with an appetite.

"Thank you, Ruth," Victor said as he sat down.

"My pleasure." She smiled at Waldemar as he sat down. "Back in the barn before breakfast again? Did you miss it?"

"Yes, like I've never left. I'm still faster than Victor at cleaning out a stall."

Victor laughed and shook his head. The three boys sat silently, eating their bacon and eggs. Brian looked at Victor intently. He looked a lot like his dad, only skinnier. He wore overalls and a cap, tilted to the side. His weathered, tanned face was creased with wrinkles from years of working in the hot sun. Brian thought about the fact that his dad had once been a little boy, eating from this same table with Victor. They had been brothers who played together and worked together. He had never thought of his dad this way before. Suddenly, as he looked around the small kitchen, he wanted to know more.

Dale and Brian spent their days playing Cowboys and Indians in the field between the house and the barn. There were two broken-down wagons that were half buried in the tall grass. It was the perfect setting for Western play. They explored the property, the decrepit barn, the hayloft where Waldemar had slept as a young boy and the tiny house. Ruth spent her days cleaning the house and trying to get rid of mice and insects. She made wonderful meals despite the challenges of the wood stove and lack of plumbing. One afternoon she went through Victor's chest of drawers. She found shirts that she had mailed to him for Christmas five years ago, unopened, never worn.

The other two thirds of the house, aside from the kitchen, were the living room and the bedroom. The living room was nestled in the center of the house. It had a heater with pipes that ran up to the roof and hung suspended. The pipe ran through the wall into the kitchen, connected up with the kitchen stove and then ran across the kitchen ceiling out the chimney. The living room, the same as the kitchen, had a window facing out the back of the house and a window facing out the front of the house, onto the screened-in porch. In the last third of the house was the bedroom where the entire Peterson family had once slept. In the bedroom were three windows, one on each exterior wall. Another door led out from the bedroom onto the porch but it hadn't been opened in decades. The kitchen had a flat roof over it, sloping slightly away from the house. The roof over the living room and bedroom was gabled with a window at each end. Ruth had scrubbed every inch of the place in a way that would have made Sister Saint Christine, her nursing headmistress, proud. She organized every drawer and cupboard.

That night at supper, she asked Victor about the unopened shirts, "Why haven't you ever worn the shirts we sent you, Victor?"

"My old ones haven't worn out yet."

Ruth smiled, "You can wear a new shirt even if your old one hasn't worn out."

"No need to be vasteful."

"I suppose. Is there anything we can buy you when we're in Winnipeg? Anything at all that you need?"

"No, ma'am, I've got everything I need right here."

Victor didn't waste anything. He still plowed his fields the old way, ran the farm the old way and of course hadn't given in to any modern conveniences as the neighbors had. He didn't need fancy farming equipment to harvest his fields. He did it the way that he and Waldemar had always done it.

"Have you ever thought of painting the walls in here?" she asked.

Waldemar chuckled as he listened to Ruth.

Victor smiled and said, "No, ma'am, no need."

"I suppose, but it could brighten up the place."

Victor laughed, "I'm fine the vay I am. 'Preciate it though. It's a nice thought."

"I've got some fences to mend, would you like to come, Gerry?" Victor asked.

"Aye," Gerry answered.

"That means 'yes,'" Brian explained.

Victor winked at Brian. "Thanks, Briney."

Victor scooped up Gerry and carried him out to the pick-up truck. He belted him in. He took him out all morning. He sat Gerry on the ground while he fixed the fence; he lifted him into the tractor and rode around, letting Gerry see the farm from the farmer's perspective. Gerry grinned broadly all day.

Later that day, as Dale and Brian played, Dale wondered aloud, "Do you think Uncle Victor's ever seen a kid in a wheelchair before?"

"I dunno," Brian mused, "do you think he's ever left the farm?"

"Maybe not."

The week in Lac Du Bonnet was wonderful. Waldemar explained to the boys how the land had once been heavily wooded and how he had set his trap line. He took the boys down to the river for a swim, showing them where he had taught his younger sisters to swim so long ago. He and Victor exchanged countless stories of their childhood. In the evenings, when the kids were in bed, Victor sat at the kitchen table and shared with Ruth and Waldemar how he had cared for their ailing father.

"Pappa was lovesick after Mamma died," Victor said sadly.

Waldemar nodded.

"It was as though he were no longer here on earth, but partially heaven bound. He pined after her, night and day. I had him cut logs for the wood stove nearly every day, right up until the end."

"Margaret shared with me a letter he had sent to her. It was awfully sad."

Victor ran his hands over the worn wooden table. "He was ready to go home and be with the Lord when the time came."

"What a reunion he and your Mamma must have had," Ruth said.

Victor smiled. "*Ja*."

"I have a lot of respect for you, Vic…caring for Pappa right up until the end. I know it couldn't have been easy."

"Ah," Victor shrugged, "you would have done the same."

"I don't know," Waldemar admitted, "it must have been hard to see him that way."

"Yes. But he is happy now. In the arms of his bride, in the presence of God…"

"What more can we ask for?" Ruth asked.

Victor was happy to take the kids under his wing as he did his farm work. He took Brian out in the pick-up truck one afternoon, through the fields.

"Where'd you get your dog?" Brian asked tentatively.

"Buster?"

"Ya."

"Vell one day I was farming near the road and I see this handsome dog. The dog saw me and at the end of the day he followed me home. Been with me ever since."

"Oh."

"He's a good dog."

Brian looked at his uncle and moved closer to him. He was quiet but kind and seemed to enjoy having them there, even if he didn't say too much. Brian loved his Swedish accent and the way he called him 'Briney.' He was going to be sad to leave. Gerry, too, loved the farm. There were many new things to see and do, and Uncle Victor had been happy to take him everywhere he went, in the barn with the animals and in the field on the big red tractor, every day. Uncle Victor would even hold Gerry's hand on the steering wheel of the tractor, so Gerry could feel like he was driving.

On their last day, as Waldemar packed up the tent trailer, the two brothers lamented about the distance between them.

"It's too bad," Waldemar sighed, "I wish we lived closer to one another."

"It's been great to have you. Thanks for everything."

"Thank you for letting us invade the farm!" Waldemar laughed and gave his brother a hug before they loaded up the boys into the car. Jet was reluctant to leave his new friend Buster, but when Brian called he jumped into the back seat.

Their next stop was Winnipeg to visit Annie who was married to Gus. Annie, Gus, Ruth and Waldemar spent their time together chatting about Peterson memories on the farm.

As they drove back to Edmonton, Waldemar asked the boys, "Did you have a good time?"

"Oh yes," Brian and Dale answered at once.

"Aye!" Gerry agreed.

Chapter 18

"...Christ Jesus came into the world to save sinners – of whom I am the worst. But for that very reason I was shown mercy so that in me, the worst of sinners, Christ Jesus might display his unlimited patience as an example for those who would believe in him and receive eternal life." 1 Timothy 1:15 & 16 NIV

<u>February 1962</u>

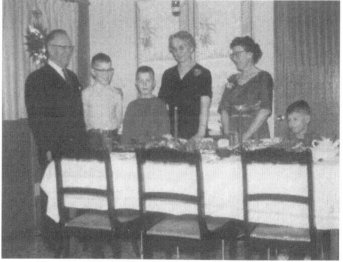

Herman, Dale, Brian, Edith, Ruth and Gerry

"It's something I'd really like to do," Ruth said as she laid out the travel brochures on her dad's kitchen table.

"I would never go back there."

"The war is over, Dad. There are a lot of valuable things we could learn from the Europeans. They have integrated disabled children into their society in varying degrees. I could research their programs and bring back ideas to help our schools develop access for children in wheelchairs."

"It sounds idealistic, Ruth, but Europe is not a place I'd ever like to go back to. I'm happy to finance the trip since it will be to Gerry's benefit. I would not be a good traveling companion. You should ask you mother."

"Mother?" Ruth stared at her father.

"She's always wanted to go. Perhaps she would accompany you." Herman called to Edith who was in the living room listening to a radio program. "Edith, can you come in here?"

Edith came into the kitchen and looked at all the brochures. "What's all this?" she asked.

Ruth replied, "I'd like to go to Europe to study how they help people with disabilities."

Edith's eyebrows shot up, "Europe?"

"Yes, they're really quite ahead of us Canadians. They have done well to integrate disabled citizens into schools and public facilities.

"Oh."

"I'm looking for a traveling companion. Would you like to go?"

Edith's eyes grew even wider. "Me?"

"Well what do you think?"

"I'd certainly like to do that. I've always wanted to see Europe." Edith smiled warily at Ruth.

"Dad will never go so maybe this is the best opportunity for both of us."

"I think you're right. We could also find out information for Gerry, like you said."

"Yes, that will be my main goal. We can go see the sights. Landmarks, museums…all of that."

"I think people will understand why we are going if it is primarily to help Gerry."

Ruth rolled her eyes. "I don't think it is anybody's business why we are going."

Edith shifted uncomfortably, "Well I don't want people to think we're being extravagant."

"Mother, we have to do what's right for Gerry."

"The ladies at church will talk is all I'm saying. I want them to know that we are on a mission of education. Trips to Europe are generally reserved for the rich and famous, and I certainly am not famous."

"Whatever makes you comfortable, Mother."

"When should we go?"

"This year sometime — the sooner the better."

"How long do you think?"

"Well let's figure out all the cities and countries we want to see and then we can lay out a timeline."

Edith nodded slowly. "Sounds wonderful." She looked Ruth in the eyes. "Just wonderful."

*

"That *is* frustrating!" Ruth exclaimed as Gerry burst into tears yet again.

"I'm sorry, sweetheart, I don't know how we can make this easier."

Waldemar came into the living room. "What's going on?"

"There has to be a better way."

"Communication?"

"Yes," she raised her hands in surrender. "It's difficult for him to get his point across. I've tried many things — hand signals for different words, head nods but nothing is working…he doesn't have enough control. He was just telling me that he was trying to tell the people at the CP clinic what he needed but they weren't understanding him."

Gerry cried in his chair.

"It's hard for him! And he needs to be able to communicate not only with us but with everyone. How do we make that work?"

Waldemar sat silently for a few minutes, contemplating the answer. "Have you prayed about it?"

"Of course I have, but I'm still not seeing the answer."

"Well then we wait, right, Gerry?" Waldemar went and put a hand on Gerry's shoulder. "We keep thinking about it and we wait."

*

There were many hard things in police work. There were dead bodies, notifying family members of a death, unsolved crimes that ate away at you…but this, this was the most difficult. In a small city like Edmonton, you were eventually bound to have a crime committed by someone you knew. Waldemar had hoped that day would never come.

It was a cold, wintry afternoon. Waldemar was driving out to the office of his lawyer friend, Ronald McGovern. The case had come across his desk. Waldemar had been told by his superiors that there were plans to arrest McGovern in a full spectacle of police force. Waldemar asked if he could handle the case, assuring his superiors that he would handle the case with professionalism. As a friend, Waldemar hoped that he could bring McGovern in while still allowing McGovern to maintain his dignity.

He parked at Ronald's office building and took a deep breath before getting out of his car. He shook his head as he looked over the evidence in the manila folder. Damning. All of it.

He went into the office building, up three flights of stairs to Ronald's office. He entered. Ronald looked up and smiled.

"Hey, Pete! What brings you by today?"

Waldemar sank into the chair on the opposite side of his friend's desk. He tossed the folder at him.

"What's this?" he asked slowly as his eyes darted over the documents.

Waldemar sat silently for a few minutes.

His friend read the papers in the folder. His face turned ashen. His knees began to shake under his desk. "I…what is this?"

"Don't…don't bother, there's too much there to dispute."

"I don't know anything about this," Ronald's voice was unsteady. Sweat began to bead on his forehead.

"Don't make this harder than it needs to be." Waldemar ran his hands through his hair. "Did you or didn't you?"

The clock ticked loudly on the wall. Waldemar listened to the traffic on the street below. He could hear the tapping of typewriters in adjacent offices.

Eventually Ronald looked up at Waldemar. "I'm sorry."

"Damn it."

"God — I am sorry!"

They both sat in stony silence, contemplating the situation.

"Am I going to prison?"

"That's for the courts to figure out."

"Shit!" Ronald smashed his fist against his desk.

"I could handcuff you and haul you in or you can come in on your own."

His friend looked down into his lap. He swiveled his chair to look out the window. With his back to Waldemar, he said, "I'll come in."

"When?"

"I'll go home and put my affairs in order and then I'll meet you at the station."

Waldemar rose up from the chair, gathered the contents of the folder and walked out of the office. He shut the door gently behind him.

The musty hallway felt like it was closing in on him. He closed his eyes for a minute and listened to the din of noise from the other offices that opened up into the hall. He went to the stairwell and began his descent back to the parking lot.

Once outside, he lit a cigarette. He stood smoking in the winter air. He watched the cars go by, down the busy street. He opened the car door and threw the file onto the front seat.

He slammed the door shut and kicked the tire of his car. "Damn it!"

A few months later, Waldemar sat in his car with Ronald. He had been sentenced to three years in prison. The two friends were quiet for most of the drive.

"Is there anything I can do for you?" Waldemar finally asked.

The lawyer's voice cracked, "You've done enough. I appreciate you driving me in. I'd hate to be with some rookie cop — you know, judging me."

"No point in judging."

"You're right, but they do. People don't even have to say anything — you can feel it."

"I'm sorry. Anything you want to get before you go in?"

"Maybe some smokes."

Waldemar stopped the car at the next gas station they came to. He and his friend went into the store. Waldemar bought him a drink and a pack of cigarettes.

"This is hard, Pete."

"I know."

"I don't know why — it was stupid."

"It's okay."

"Do you ever do anything wrong? You seem like the perfect guy."

"Sure I do. We've all fallen short. Some mistakes have bigger consequences. Unfortunately, your mistake broke the law."

"Damn. I can't believe I've got myself into this mess."

After McGovern finished his drink and his cigarette, they got back in the car and drove to the prison. Waldemar took McGovern inside and handed him over to the custody of the prison guards. He watched his friend be processed and escorted down a long hall to the medical room.

Waldemar let out a long shaky breath as he turned and walked out of the prison. He drove back to Headquarters with the events of the day weighing heavily on his mind.

He walked in the main doors and went straight to his desk. He began to unlock his drawers when the chief approached.

"Peterson."

"Yes, sir," he stood up and greeted the Chief Superintendent.

"I've got a special assignment for you. Why don't you come into my office and I'll go over the details."

"Yes, sir."

"I'm sending you to Hamilton, Ontario. I've got a very important situation on my hands. It's something that I need solved quickly and with professionalism. When they told me the problem, I knew you were the right man for the job."

"Yes, sir."

"I don't need to tell you that without a resolution…well let's just say it would be very beneficial to you if you come back with everything sorted out."

"I will do that, sir."

Ruth woke up and went to the kitchen to make breakfast. She looked out the kitchen window. The struggle for Gerry to communicate with outsiders was always on her mind. She felt like she was missing an obvious solution.

"God," she prayed, "I've had it. I can't help Gerry in this crucial area. I'm angry, disheartened and thoroughly exhausted by this whole problem. So, God, you'd better show me what I'm to do because I've run out of ideas. I'm tired. It's over and out, so you take over, Lord." Tears ran down her cheeks as she cracked the eggs into the frying pan. She listened to them sizzle as she thought about Cerebral Palsy. The quest for quality of life was exhausting and there were moments where she wanted to give up.

"Hi, Mom," Dale smiled as he walked into the kitchen. "What's for breakfast?"

Ruth walked over to Dale and hugged him. "Eggs, sweetie."

"Thanks, Mom."

She watched Dale sit at the table and tap his fingers while he waited. She served him eggs and orange juice to drink. Brian came into the kitchen shortly after Dale and joined him at the table. Ruth got him settled with his meal. She went down the hall to get Gerry. She dressed him, took him to the washroom and combed his hair. She washed his face, cleaned his glasses and placed them over his ears and firmly on his nose.

"All set, sweetheart."

Gerry vocalized 'Thank you' to his mom.

"You're welcome." She wheeled his chair down the hall and pushed him into the kitchen table. She fed him each bite of his eggs with a heavy heart.

After supper, Ruth washed the dishes. Brian and Gerry were downstairs playing while Dale read in his bedroom. When the last dish was dried, she hung up the towel and retreated to the living room. She could hear Gerry and Brian laughing downstairs.

"Lord," she prayed, "I don't know what the answer is for his communication, but I'm glad you're listening. I know you see my anxious heart. I have such sorrow for Gerry. I am tired of seeing him frustrated. Thank you, Lord, for your goodness. I know you will uphold me with your righteous right hand."

The evening paper had fallen through the mail slot in the door while they were eating. She grabbed it and sat down in the armchair.

She read the headlines, always looking for stories about the RCMP, specifically about Waldemar. It was always exciting to see him looking out at her from beneath the headlines. She wondered how he was doing in Hamilton. Her eyes scanned over the words on the newspaper.

Suddenly she jumped up, yelling, "I've got it, I've got the answer! Oh thank you, Lord!"

Dale came out of his bedroom to see what the commotion was about. Brian popped his head up from the basement. "What's going on?" they asked.

"Just a second and I'll explain," she said breathlessly.

Ruth ran downstairs and picked up Gerry. She rushed back up and sat him on the couch with the newspaper on the coffee table. Brian and Dale gathered round.

"God just showed me how Gerry can talk to us! While I was reading the paper I noticed how the individual words came into my vision."

The boys looked at their mom, perplexed.

"I realized that we could take the most common words that Gerry says and put them on a board, alphabetically, so that Gerry can point to them! Isn't that great?"

"Aye!" Gerry agreed.

"Good one, Mom," Brian said as he looked at the paper and smiled.

After the boys were in bed, Ruth sat at the kitchen table coming up with different word sheets that Gerry could use. As she jotted down common words and phrases, the phone rang.

"Hello?"

"Hi, Ruth."

"Pete!"

"How are you?"

"I'm great! I've had a revelation."

Ruth proceeded to tell Waldemar all about the idea she had for a word board. He offered that once the two of them picked the words, he could lacquer them onto a board.

He talked about his progress in Hamilton, that his time there was nearly through and that he would be back by the end of the week.

Waldemar drove home nervously, dreading his conversation with Ruth. He parked the car in the garage and went in through the backdoor.

"I'm home," he called.

"We're downstairs," he heard Ruth yell.

He went down the basement stairs to where the boys were playing. Ruth was sitting on a chair, looking rather uncomfortable.

"Hey, honey," he smiled at her. "Hello, boys."

"Hi, Dad," Brian and Dale said softly. Gerry vocalized.

"Are you okay, Ruth?"

"Gerry and I had a little accident."

Waldemar's eyes widened with concern. "What?"

Dale piped up, "They fell down the stairs."

"You did?" he gasped. "Are you okay?"

"A bit sore."

Waldemar looked over at Gerry. "Is he…?"

"I protected him with my body."

Brian added, "They fell all the way from the top, boom, boom, boom."

Waldemar shook his head and said, "I am sorry!"

"It's okay," Ruth grimaced, "we're both relatively unharmed. It could have been worse."

"Can you come upstairs? There's something I need to talk to you about."

Ruth winced. "Sure."

Waldemar gave her a hand up from her chair. He walked behind her up the stairs and once at the top he turned around to the boys and said, "You stay put."

"Yes, Dad," they chorused.

Ruth sat at the kitchen table. Waldemar poured Ruth a glass of water and then joined her.

"He's thirteen. Maybe he's getting too big for you to carry up and down the stairs."

"It's fine."

"He's getting harder to carry now that he is taller."

"I know, I know, but what can I do? He wants to play with his brothers."

"You could have smashed your heads on the concrete floor."

Ruth grimaced. "I did. But I was able to protect him with my body."

"I worry about you…"

"It was my knee, okay? It gave out. It turned back the opposite way and then – next thing you know we're at the bottom."

"You need to get it checked."

"I will."

"Will you?"

"Yes," she sighed. "Now, what did you want to talk to me about?"

"Well, I have some good news and some bad news."

"Okay," she looked up at him. "What is it?"

"The good news is that I've been promoted to Inspector."

"That's great!"

"Because I was able to resolve things in the Hamilton case I was given a promotion."

"Good for you!"

He paused. "And the bad news is that I'm being transferred."

Ruth was completely taken off guard. "Really?"

"I found out today that we're going to be posted in Saskatoon."

"Saskatoon?"

"They say that there is a school there for Gerry. I'll be promoted to Officer Commanding of the F Division."

"Wow," Ruth fingered her water glass.

"You knew this was a part of being an officer, right?"

"I do — it's hard to imagine being away from Dad."

"And the church."

"And the neighbors."

"And the CP clinic."

"The boys will have to make new friends at school." Ruth looked around the kitchen. "And we'll have to find a new home."

"It's a lot for everyone."

"But..." Ruth said, more to convince herself than Waldemar, "we'll get through it. We'll make the best of it."

Waldemar smiled at her. "Thanks. I know it will be hard for everyone but we're fortunate we haven't been moved in the last ten years. The force has been very accommodating regarding Gerry. They say the school is excellent."

Ruth took a slow drink. Slowly she said, "That's great."

"When should we tell the boys?"

"Not yet. We'll tell them a few weeks before the end of the school year. No need to ruffle feathers ahead of time."

Chapter 19

"So in everything, do to others what you would have them do to you…" Matthew 7:12 NIV

July 1962

Gerry and Taffy

    The mood in the car was grim as they pulled into the city of Saskatoon, looking for the motel. The news of the transfer didn't go over well with any of the boys. No one wanted to leave their friends or their community and the safety of predictability. All three sat in the back seat, pouting.
    "Dad, I just don't understand why Jet couldn't come!" Brian complained.
    "The new place we're going to doesn't allow dogs."
    Gerry vocalized angrily.
    "This is the worst!"
    Dale asked, "What are those things everywhere?"

"Grasshoppers," Waldemar answered, "there's a plague of grasshoppers in Saskatchewan this year."

"Just great," Brian mumbled. He hated bugs. He couldn't think of anything worse than a plague of large, ugly, jumpy insects.

Dale cringed. "Gross."

Gerry grumbled.

"Listen, kids," Ruth sighed, "I know this is hard but this is how it has to be. We're lucky we haven't been moved before now."

"It doesn't help," Dale barked.

Waldemar and Ruth exchanged a look.

"I think I see the motel," Waldemar pointed. Cheerily he added, "Welcome home, guys!"

No one answered.

"I think they have a pool," Ruth announced, "Your dad can take you swimming this afternoon once we're settled. It's like a vacation!"

Everyone sat silent in the back seat. Brian and Dale had their arms crossed over their chests. Gerry had his head turned away.

Waldemar pulled the car into the motel parking lot and went to check in. They would be there for about two weeks while the Force completed the arrangements on their new home and would move their belongings from Edmonton.

Waldemar returned with the large motel keys in his hand. "All set. Let's go find our room."

They drove around and parked in front of their door. Waldemar unloaded the suitcases and the wheelchair and then pulled Gerry from the back seat. Inside the room were two double beds covered in loud, floral bedspreads. There were two chairs and a flimsy table with a phone and a glass ashtray on top. Next to the table and chairs were a dresser and a television. The curtains were green and dingy but they blended with the orange shag carpet. At the rear of the room was a vanity and bathroom. Waldemar, Ruth and Gerry went into the room while Brian and Dale sat glumly in the car.

After a few minutes Dale said, "It's getting hot in here."

"Ya," Brian agreed.

"This is awful."

"The worst. I hate the RCMP," Brian announced.

"Me too," Dale agreed. "I'm too hot, let's go inside."

Brian shuddered as a large grasshopper crashed against his window. "Ugh!" He quickly flung open the door, slammed it behind him and ran inside the hotel room. He felt grasshoppers crunching under his feet as he ran inside. He immediately kicked off his shoes and jumped onto the hotel bed. "Ahhhh!"

Dale was right behind him. He slammed the hotel door to keep the grasshoppers out. "I think one got inside," he announced.

Brian buried his head in a hotel pillow.

"I'll get it," Waldemar trapped the jumpy grasshopper in his hands and flung it out the front door.

Ruth looked at her children. Dale sat grimly looking at the hotel floor. Gerry was slumped over in his chair, his head hung low, with tears running down his face. Brian was sobbing into the hotel pillow. She desperately wanted to make it better for them.

"Why don't you boys get your bathing suits on and I'll take you to the pool," Waldemar offered.

Dale begrudgingly agreed. Gerry answered with a half-hearted, "Aye."

Brian was not willing to leave the room again.

*

A few weeks later, the family had moved into their new house at 64 Megan Crescent. It was a short drive across the University Bridge to the police detachment.

Dale set out on his bike on a daily basis to explore the new neighborhood and nearby parks. He loved to venture far out into farmers' fields, exploring old barns and dilapidated buildings. From time to time, he invited Brian to come along but Brian could not be convinced to face the grasshoppers.

One afternoon while Dale was out for a bike ride, Ruth encouraged Brian and Gerry to venture out as well. "Why don't you boys go for a walk?"

"Too hot," Brian answered.

"You can't stay inside all summer, Brian. Why don't you and Gerry go down to the strip mall? It's only a few blocks and I'm sure there won't be too many grasshoppers."

"Fine," Brian sighed. He went to the back door, tied on his sneakers and threw on a baseball cap. Ruth helped get Gerry out the door in his wheelchair. She waved as they headed down the sidewalk.

Brian pushed Gerry as the hot sun beat down on him. "Hot, huh, Gerry?"

"Aye."

"I'm not too crazy about Saskatoon. I miss the ravine."

Gerry agreed.

"I don't know why we had to come here."

Gerry started to cry.

"I'm sorry, Gerry," Brian immediately felt bad for upsetting his brother. "It's okay. We'll get used to Saskatoon."

Gerry vocalized.

"You have a message?"

"Aye."

Brian began, "A, B, C..."

Gerry stopped him at J.

"You miss Jet? Me too. I can't believe he couldn't come."

The pair continued on glumly to the strip mall. When they arrived, they saw a coffee shop with tables and chairs on the sidewalk out front. Happy patrons ate pastries and sipped their beverages, unaware of the pain of the two young boys approaching.

Next to the coffee shop were a dime store and a pet store. Brian wheeled Gerry past the coffee patrons to the pet store. A man at one of the tables had a large snake wrapped around his forearm. He sneered at Brian as they went by, a cigarette hanging limply from his grimy mouth.

This is hell, Brian thought as he pressed on toward the pet store. Heads turned watching the little nine-year-old boy with his brother in the wheelchair. Brian could hear people commenting on them as they went by.

"Where's their mother?" was repeated in harsh whispers.

Brian opened the pet store door and held it with his backside as he backed Gerry in. The din of the coffee shop faded as chirps, yips and growls filled the air. The pet store was inviting, crammed full of cages and pet supplies. In the center of the store was a fence with three small caramel-colored dogs inside. The smell of animals was rich and pungent. Brian breathed in deeply.

"Afternoon, gentlemen," the shopkeeper greeted them warmly.

"Afternoon, sir," Brian answered. He smiled at the man behind the counter.

"Anything I can help you find?"

"No, we're new in town and we want to have a look around."

The man gestured around the shop with a smile. "Look away."

"Look, Gerry," Brian commented as he wheeled Gerry up to the fence enclosure where the puppies were, "aren't they cute?"

"Aye!" Gerry exclaimed.

"Do you think…?"

"Nay," Gerry shook his head.

"Well maybe. I know they *said* no dogs — but maybe…I mean you *need* a dog to keep you safe. Right?"

Gerry slowly agreed, considering the matter, "Aye."

The shopkeeper walked over and commented, "They're not quite old enough to go home but by next week they'll be ready."

For the next week, Brian laid out his case to his parents. All three boys took daily trips to the pet store to see the dog they had already named Taffy.

"Mom and Dad, it's been a really hard summer for all of us," Brian said.

Ruth nodded. "We know."

"And Gerry misses Jet badly. He has no one to keep him safe."

Waldemar smiled. "Is that so?"

"Aye," Gerry agreed.

Dale added, "The shopkeeper said that the dog is part Chihuahua. He said the dog will always be small."

"Well, that is an advantage," Ruth agreed.

"And Dale and I will take care of it," Brian promised.

"Yes we will!" Dale said excitedly.

This conversation had repeated itself all week as Waldemar and Ruth considered the request. Finally, the persistence of the boys weakened their parents to a point of agreement.

The following Saturday, the five of them drove to the pet shop and picked up Taffy and all of the equipment they needed. They bought a red leash, a dog bed, dog food and a dish. Taffy bounded around the backseat on the short drive home.

"Thanks, Mom and Dad," Brian laughed as Taffy nibbled at his fingers.

Gerry laughed as the dog jumped all over, licking all three of them.

*

Brian was true to his promise. He spent the summer caring for the dog, which was actually growing much larger than the shopkeeper had promised. No one seemed to mind as Taffy worked her way into their hearts. Taffy and Gerry formed a bond. She spent much of her time sleeping beneath his chair. She tolerated his wild arms and his tightly clasped hands that would sometimes yank on her fur.

On September 1, Ruth drove Gerry to his new school. There would be an interview with the doctor in charge. They were planning to tour the facilities and see how the program operated. The fall term started on the following Monday.

The school was on the outskirts of the town, near the airport. Gerry's eyes were wide as they pulled up in front of the old World War II hangar. He vocalized to his mother.

"Pretty amazing, isn't it?" She smiled over at him.

"Aye."

"Are you nervous, sweetheart?" she asked.

"Aye." Gerry looked at his mom. They caught each other's gaze.

Ruth unloaded Gerry and placed him in his wheelchair. She pushed him through the dirt parking lot and through the doublewide sliding doors.

Before they were inside, a warm voice called out, "Welcome, Petersons!"

Ruth's eyes adjusted to the dimness inside the old hanger and smiled as a kindly looking dark-haired man approached.

"Good morning! I'm Doctor Buckle, the kids call me Dr B." He took Gerry's hand in his own and shook it. "You must be Gerry. It's a pleasure to meet you." He then offered his hand to Ruth.

"Good morning," Ruth responded.

"I'm going to show you around the building and introduce Gerry to some of the activities he'll be doing." Dr. Buckle smiled at the pair of them. He had straight white teeth. He was young and full of energy.

"That sounds wonderful," Ruth agreed.

"Aye," Gerry said.

"You're thirteen years old, are you, Gerry?" Dr. Buckle asked.

"Aye."

"And how do the two of you communicate?" he questioned.

Ruth answered, "Well we use the alphabet and Gerry stops me when I get to the letter he wants. We spell out his messages. We also use 'twenty questions' where we try and guess what he wants to get across. Gerry also has a word board where he can point out the words he wants to say."

"And how is that for you, Gerry?"

Gerry vocalized.

"It works well," Ruth spoke, "but it can be frustrating. Also it can take awhile to get complex thoughts and ideas across."

"Well that is certainly something we can work on. Why don't you walk with me while we talk?" Dr. Buckle pushed Gerry's wheelchair toward some large tables where there were rows of typewriters. "Have you ever used a typewriter before, Gerry?"

"Nay." Gerry shook his head.

"Well you'll be using one before Christmas. We're going to teach you how to type."

Gerry scoffed.

Ruth said, "That would be tremendous."

"You will be surprised what we can accomplish when we put our minds to it!"

They continued through the building to an eating area, resting area and an area with tables set up, facing a chalkboard. There were maps on the wall, pictures of the solar systems and artwork from the students.

"Tell me, Mama, what muscles does Gerry have the best control over?"

"Well he can use his right foot to push himself back in the wheelchair. And he has good control over his neck muscles. His arms are the most spastic."

"Have you ever tried writing with a pen in your mouth, Gerry?"

"Nay," Gerry shook his head again.

"It wouldn't work," Ruth interjected, "we've tried many things to make communication easier but nothing has worked."

"Well we'll keep praying about it and hopefully God will lead us to the right answer."

They stopped in front of a very large elevator. "Let's go up to my office," Dr. Buckle said as he pushed the elevator button. "We can talk about Gerry's medications."

The large steel doors moaned as they opened. Dr. Buckle pushed Gerry inside. Ruth hesitantly stepped in behind. Dr. Buckle pressed the button to the second level of the building. "This elevator is a bit of a beast — but it serves its purpose!"

The elevator made all sorts of troubling noises as it began its slow ascent. At the top, they exited and went into Dr. Buckle's office. His office was filled with bookshelves that were crammed full. He had two worn chairs on the opposite side of his desk. There were degrees on the walls and photos of his family. Dr. Buckle parked Gerry next to one of the chairs and motioned to Ruth. "Please, have a seat."

"What medications do you have Gerry on?" he asked.

"Nothing."

Dr. Buckle looked surprised. "Have you ever tried a sedative? That has been used before in CP children. Perhaps it could be helpful for Gerry."

"We've never been steered in that direction but perhaps it's something we could try."

Dr. Buckle touched Gerry's tightly clenched fists. Gerry's arms were curled toward his body. "You get a lot of cramping, Gerry?"

"Aye."

"Well hopefully this will help," he reached into his pocket and pulled out a prescription pad. "We'll start with something mild and then work from there."

The three of them talked for another half-hour about what Gerry's goals would be over the upcoming semester. Dr. Buckle stressed that communication would be their biggest focus so that Gerry could be independent apart from his family.

*

It was a beautiful fall night. Ruth and Waldemar were dressed in their formal wear for a government-sponsored dinner. Ruth had hired a babysitter for the boys and was looking forward to a night out. She wore an emerald gown and her finest jewelry. Waldemar wore his best black suit. When they arrived at the party, they were caught up in the music from the band, the delicious food and the sparkle of the guests. Another officer from Saskatoon was introducing them to the various guests, one of them being the Minister of Health.

"Nice to meet you," Ruth shook hands with the minister.

"Hello, Mrs. Peterson, pleasure to meet you."

Another guest spoke up, "Mrs. Peterson is an advocate for disabled children; she has a son with a disability."

The minister raised her brow, "Oh, and where do you keep him?"

Waldemar squeezed Ruth's hand. "At home," Ruth replied.

"Oh my," the minister gasped, "How could you? Do you have other children?"

Ruth squeezed Waldemar's hand back as she tried to hold her voice steady, "Yes, two other sons."

"Oh my!" She looked around at all the other guests in the circle of people who stood with them and gave Ruth a condescending look. "Do you realize what you are doing to them?"

Ruth tried not to sound as angry as she felt, "Yes I do in fact. Hopefully they will grow up to be loving, decent, tolerant human beings."

Everyone who stood around them gasped.

The minister walked away, offended.

Ruth smiled and looked up at Waldemar. They didn't need to exchange any words. He nodded subtly.

One of the guests in the group patted Ruth on the shoulder. "You're right, Mrs. Peterson. Absolutely right."

After they left the party, Ruth let out a big sigh. "Welcome to Saskatchewan."

Chapter 20

"And you saw how the LORD your God cared for you all along the way as you traveled through the wilderness, just as a father cares for his child. Now he has brought you to this place."
Deuteronomy 1:31 NLT

September 1962

Edith, Brian, Ruth, Gerry, Dale and Waldemar

Ruth and Edith sat next to one another on the plane. Edith clutched her armrests tightly. They had landed in New York City. The plane was being unloaded.

"Okay, Mother," Ruth said quietly, "get your carry-on, let's get ready to get off."

Edith nodded as her eyes darted to all the different passengers from every culture and walk of life.

Ruth gripped Edith's elbow as she led her off the plane. The pilot smiled as they left the plane, "Good day, ladies."

"Good day. Thank you," Ruth replied as they walked by.

They funneled into the bustling airport with all of the other passengers. Edith stayed right behind Ruth as they pressed through the crowds.

"Come on, Mother, we need to get our bags." Ruth grabbed an available luggage cart and pushed through to the carrousel where everyone waited anxiously for his or her bags.

"Good grief," Edith muttered as people bumped and jostled her to reach their suitcases.

Ruth pulled each of their heavy suitcases off the belt and loaded them onto the cart. Out front of the airport, they got into a waiting taxi. Ruth gave the address of their hotel and the taxi driver lurched out into the heavy airport traffic.

Their pastor was in New York at the time and agreed to meet and escort them around the city. They had booked a nice hotel among New York's high-rise buildings. Ruth was glued to the window as they drove through the city. The sound of the traffic, the people walking everywhere and the looming buildings were a magnificent sight. She had read so many books as a child about places all over the world, and now, finally, she was seeing it for herself.

The taxi pulled into the hotel's loading zone. Ruth paid the taxi driver. They got out and unloaded their bags. A bellman greeted them warmly.

"Good afternoon, ladies," he gestured toward their bags, "can I be of some assistance?"

Ruth smiled. "Yes, please."

The bellman followed Ruth and Edith inside where Ruth checked into their room. Once they were settled, Ruth pulled out the phone number for Pastor Roberts. They made plans to meet the following morning. For the next two days, he was going to take them to all of the major tourist attractions in New York.

That night as Edith and Ruth prepared for bed Ruth said, "Goodnight, Mother." The room was still and quiet. They both sat on the edge of their double beds, wondering what the other was thinking.

Finally, Edith spoke, "Goodnight, Ruth."

"Are you okay?" Ruth looked over at Edith before turning out the light.

"It's been such a busy day." Edith frowned, "So many new experiences."

Ruth smiled and sighed. "Wonderful, isn't it?" She switched off the light and promptly fell asleep dreaming of the adventures that the next six weeks would hold.

"Welcome to the Big Apple!" Pastor Roberts exclaimed as he met Ruth and Edith out front of their hotel. "We've got a lot of things to see today, are you ready?"

Ruth nodded enthusiastically. "I sure am!"

They spent the next two days touring the city seeing the UN Building, the Empire State Building, Central Park, Rockefeller Center and the Statue of Liberty. Ruth marveled at all of the different types of architecture and the pulse of the city. She loved the rich history. Edith was unusually quiet as they went from place to place — content to listen to Pastor Roberts explain what they were seeing and where they were going.

After touring New York for two days, they flew to Paris, France. They were taking a bus tour with the Thomas Cook & Sons Ltd. Company. It was a circle tour through seven different countries. A tour guide met them at the airport and they met the other people who would be touring with them. They checked into the Hotel St. James. It was a three-story, chateau-style building in the heart of the city.

They went to The Opera House, Notre Dame, the Eiffel Tower, Les Invalides, the Solate Chappelle, Place a la Concord along the River Seine and much more.

From Paris, they took the tour bus to Brussels, Belgium, where they toured the tomb of the unknown soldiers and four liberties, the Basilica of the Sacred Heart and the Maisons des Corporations.

From Brussels, they went on to Amsterdam in the Netherlands and then south into West Germany where they toured Cologne and Heidelberg. Ruth loved to imagine her ancestors who had come from this extraordinary place. After seeing the sights in West Germany, the tour bus took them to Lucerne, Switzerland and Insbruk, Austria.

After Austria, they went on to Italy, first stopping in Venice. They toured Sighs Bridge, the Basilica of St. Marcus, The Grand Canal and Doge's Palace. Ruth loved the city on the water and adored getting in and out of the boats that took them up and down the city's canals. Edith was unsure of all of the foreign countries, new foods, languages and people, but she took it all in, listening to Ruth explain the significance of the landmarks they toured.

In Italy, they also went to Florence, Rome and La Spezia. They saw the Pantheon, the Coliseum, the Arch of Constantine and the Place Despagne in Rome. They toured many remarkable basilicas and the Leaning Tower of Pisa.

After nearly a week in Italy, they returned to France and toured through the cities of Nice, Avignon, Nevers and back to Paris. It had been nearly a four-week tour, and Edith and Ruth had thoroughly enjoyed themselves. In every city, Ruth looked for children with disabilities. She was thrilled to see that in Europe there were many children with disabilities that were out, and that the various countries had accommodated their special needs in public facilities. Many places had ramps, wheelchair-accessible washrooms and other accommodations that were unheard of in Canada. Even the fact that a child could be pushed in a wheelchair without attracting stares and negative comments was amazing to Ruth. She collected ideas wherever she went, jotting them down in a notebook she carried with her.

After four weeks, they bade farewell to everyone in their tour group. Ruth and Edith planned to spend a few days in Paris while Ruth toured a few schools that were wheelchair accessible. They were also planning to go to the Louvre for a day before they caught a plane to London. Ruth collected souvenirs for the boys in every city and sent a postcard home nearly every day.

"Dad," Brian called in a panicky voice, "Dale's throwing up again!"

"Hang on," Waldemar yelled from the bathroom where he was bathing Gerry.

"It's pretty bad!" Brian shrieked from the hallway.

"Just lean over the bucket, Dale! Brian, you stay away from him!" Waldemar called. He wiped his brow with his arm, smiled at Gerry and finished washing the shampoo from Gerry's hair. His knees were on the hard linoleum floor. He leaned awkwardly over into the tub to hold Gerry's spastic body while he bathed. "I think we're about done, Gerry. It looks like it's going to be a short bath for you today."

Gerry vocalized.

Brian came into the bathroom, breathless, "Dad, I think he missed the bucket."

Waldemar groaned, "Okay…no problem, buddy. I'll come clean it up. What time did Irene say she'd be back?"

Their Edmonton housekeeper had graciously agreed to come and stay with them while Ruth was away in Europe. She now had her own two-year-old daughter who had come along. This afternoon Irene had gone grocery shopping for the family and on a few other errands.

"I dunno!" Brian stepped out of the bathroom, "I'm going downstairs; it smells too gross for me in our room."

"You need to stay away from him anyway."

Waldemar's strong arms heaved Gerry, nearly fourteen, from the tub and onto a waiting towel that Waldemar had laid out on the floor. He wrapped Gerry, dried him and dressed him. He poked his head into Dale and Brian's room to encourage Dale who sat on the edge of his bed with his head held over the bucket.

"Good job, pal, I'll be right there! Hang in there!"

Waldemar carried Gerry to the basement where he could play with Brian. He dashed back up the stairs, two at a time, and down the hall to Dale.

"Hey there, buddy. Are your pajamas dirty?"

Dale nodded weakly. His cheeks were flush and his hair clung to his face in sweaty wisps.

"Let's get you to the bathroom and clean you up." Waldemar picked up Dale and carried him to the bathroom. He ran fresh, cool bath water and stepped out while Dale climbed in. Dale shut the sliding glass doors. Waldemar came back into the bathroom. Dale had the measles, for the second time, and was not doing well. Waldemar wished that his wonderful wife, Nurse Peterson, was there but he wasn't faring too badly on his own.

"Dad," Dale croaked from the tub, "I thought you could only get the measles once."

"Well, that's what I've heard but Irene said that in rare cases you can get it again. Thankfully, the others have all had it already. Hopefully they won't get it again too."

Dale groaned as he sat in the tub. "I feel awful."

"I know," Waldemar felt bad for his son. "I'll go get you a glass of water."

"Okay, Dad."

Ruth and Edith walked through the Louvre slowly, admiring the works of art. Ruth looked at her map of the museum.

"Denon, ground floor in the Rotonde de Mars. That's where we're headed, Mother." It was busy. People bustled all around them, speaking in different languages.

"Oh my," Edith gasped. "It sure is busy here."

"Hang onto my elbow, I know where we're going." She led Edith to the area of the museum where the Venus de Milo was. They pressed their way through the crowds and stood, admiring the mind-boggling statue.

Edith looked disapprovingly at the half-naked woman who had somehow lost her arms. "Is that the lady who owns the place?" she asked in a loud voice.

Ruth turned to her mother, her eyes wide in disbelief, and hissed, "Mother! It is the timeless masterpiece, the Venus de Milo!"

Edith shrugged and whispered back, "Is it necessary to show her top like that?"

Ruth rolled her eyes. She stood, taking in the moment. The woman's face was expressionless, her body relaxed. "She's the Roman Venus, the goddess of love and beauty. She was said to be born out of the foam of the sea. It's an honor to see it in person. It's much bigger than I imagined."

Edith shrugged again and after a few minutes asked, "Where to next?"

Ruth looked up the location of the Mona Lisa on the tour map. "Follow me."

They walked under marble columns, magnificent archways to elevator C that took them to the first floor. They followed the map to the Galerie d'Apollon where they stopped to admire the works of art on display there. At the far end of the room, they went through a door leading into the Salon Carre. From there they entered the Grande Galerie. Ruth stopped to admire the statue of Diana the Huntress, then seeing the crowds to the right she knew she had reached the Mona Lisa.

They waited for their opportunity to approach the painting. Once up close, Ruth nearly pinched herself, in total disbelief that she was there.

"Outstanding, isn't it?" Ruth breathed.

"Who is this lady?" Edith asked in a loud voice.

"Mother," Ruth whispered, "it's the Mona Lisa! The most famous painting in the world!"

Edith's eyes widened and her brows raised. "Oh, of course."

Ruth went through as much of the museum as she could, quietly explaining to Edith what the different works of art were, before she had a chance to make another silly comment. They saw the portrait of Lisa Gherardini, wife of Francesco del Giocondo, The Wedding Feast at Cana by Veronese and Jacques-Louis David's famous painting, The Coronation of Napoleon.

They admired the Winged Victory of Samothrace statue, The Oath of the Horatii painting and they paused for only a moment at the painting Odalisque.

Edith muttered, "So much nudity."

Ruth smiled and let herself enjoy it all. The museum itself was a marvel, let alone all its treasures inside.

They finished off the day by seeing more famous paintings: The Raft of the Medusa and July 28, Liberty Leading the People. They took the grand staircase back to the ground floor and found the Italian Sculpture gallery. Edith spent most of her time in the sculpture gallery with her eyes on the map.

They took the tube elevator out to the exit at the end of the day. Ruth sighed dreamily, "What amazing history."

They had finished their stay in Paris and were on their way to London. They arrived at the airport a few hours early and checked in for their flight. The airport was busy and people rushed all around them, hurrying to catch their flights.

"We've got some time to spare, Mother, let's find our gate. Perhaps after that I'll look in some of the shops. Maybe I can get some information on some schools in London that we could tour."

"Sure, Ruth," Edith clutched her handbag tightly.

"Follow me." Ruth had Edith take her arm. She pushed the luggage cart to their gate. They checked in their luggage. Ruth found a comfortable seat for Edith to rest.

"I'll be back in a bit, okay?"

Edith looked warily around at all the strange people waiting for the plane. Some spoke in foreign languages or with strange accents. "Okay."

Ruth went off to find a tourist office that might be able to give her the names of some good London schools. She poked her head into a few of the airport shops looking for treats for the kids and after a little over an hour, she headed back to the gate.

Before she got there, she could hear Edith's voice hollering, "RUTH! RUTH PETERSON, WHERE ARE YOU?"

Ruth looked all over to see where Edith's voice was coming from. She spotted her coming down an escalator toward her. Edith had tears streaming down her face. Airport personnel were approaching the frantic woman, trying to determine what the problem was.

Ruth ran to head them off and called out, "MOTHER!"

Edith spotted Ruth and ran to her, crying. "You tried to leave me!"

The airport personnel approached Ruth and Edith. One of the men asked in a thick French accent, "Everything alright, mademoiselles?"

Ruth smiled reassuringly, "We're fine. Merci."

"Good day then."

After the airport personnel walked away, Edith wiped her face with a handkerchief. "Why did you leave me?"

"I didn't – "

"You tried to trick me!" she continued to cry.

"Mother," Ruth sighed, "I did not. I told you exactly what I was doing."

Edith continued to cry. People were staring at the pair as they walked by.
"Let's go. Let's get back to our gate. Stop crying. You're being ridiculous."

Gerry vocalized.
"Do you have a message, Gerry?" Brian asked.
"Aye."
"A, B, C…"
Gerry stopped Brian at M.
"Mom?"
"Aye."
"I miss her too."

"Aye."

It was Saturday and the boys had spent the morning with their dad at the curling rink while he practiced with his team. He not only bought them a cola but a hot dog and French fries. Now it was evening and all the good television shows were over. They were played out and even listening to the radio didn't sound fun.

"What do you think she's doing over there?" Brian wondered.

Dale said, "I hope she brings us something."

Gerry vocalized again.

"A, B, C…" Brian began again.

Gerry stopped Brian at P, E, T, E, R and S before Brian guessed.

"Petersons? Ya, she said she was going to see some old Peterson people."

"What are you talking about?" Dale asked.

"You know, Dad's relatives."

"I thought they all lived in Manitoba and BC."

"Not those kinds of relatives," Brian sighed. "Old, old relatives."

"Like senior citizens?"

Gerry laughed and vocalized to Brian indicating that he had something to add.

"A, B, C…" Brian started.

Gerry stopped him at G, R, A, N, D, P until Brian guessed.

"Grandpa?"

"Aye."

"Grandpa Peterson?"

"Aye."

"Yes," Brian caught on to Gerry's train of thought. "They would be Grandpa Peterson's relatives. You know he used to live in Sweden a long time ago?"

Dale had lost interest while Brian continued to decipher Gerry's message. "What?" Dale asked.

Brian sighed, exasperated. "That's what Mom's doing! She's on her way to Sweden by now, visiting Grandpa Peterson's relatives — you know aunts, uncles, cousins…that sort of thing!"

"Oh." Dale flipped through the postcards that Ruth had sent. "She's been all over. Looks like a lot of boring churches and museums."

Brian grabbed the postcards from Dale. "I think it looks really interesting."

Once in London, Edith and Ruth joined another tour group. They went to Westminster Abbey where they watched the changing of the guards, Buckingham Palace, London Bridge, the Tower of London, Piccadilly Circus, Bloody Tower, Traitor's Gate at St. Thomas Tower and more churches and museums. After several days in London, they flew to Stockholm, Sweden.

They stayed at the Grand Hotel across from the palace. The hotel was a luxurious building. It had extraordinary chandeliers, muraled ceilings and a breathtaking view of the water. Ruth spent their first day in Sweden arranging school tours and dates when they would meet the Peterson relatives.

The schools that Ruth toured were astounding. There were ramps, an elevator and large washrooms with grab bars. The door handles were not the knob kind but a lever that could be easily opened by someone with limited control. Children in wheelchairs were integrated into regular classrooms and given special aids to help them.

A mix of hope and dread filled Ruth as she saw how far ahead Sweden was. It felt insurmountable to make the two worlds meet. Children with disabilities were not shunned here. They were accepted as they were. This was not something that Ruth could take back to Canada.

After their six days in Sweden, they flew back to London. From there they went for a weekend in Glasgow and took their final flight from Prewsick, Scotland, back to Saskatoon.

It was mid-October. Herman had driven from Edmonton to pick up Edith. He and Waldemar waited at the airport with the three boys. To Waldemar it had been a lifetime since he last saw Ruth. Irene and her daughter had headed back to Edmonton that morning. Waldemar was happy to see them go because it meant that Ruth was coming home.

Out of the arrival area of the airport came Ruth, wearing her mustard-colored wool coat. She ran toward Waldemar and the boys, smiling and laughing. She hugged them all at once. "Oh it's good to see you!"

Edith came behind Ruth a moment later. She and Herman exchanged a hug. "Good to see you." Herman squeezed her hand gently. "Shall we find your bags?"

They picked up their luggage and all headed back to the Peterson house. Ruth and Edith spent the evening telling everyone all about their trip and the wonderful things they had seen. Ruth showed the boys all of the trinkets she picked up for them along the way.

Brian held a tiny Eiffel tower in his hand. "Thanks, Mom! This is great!"

She smiled. "My bags were so heavy I had to fill my coat pockets with souvenirs!"

Gerry laughed.

"How did you all manage without your mom?" she winked at Waldemar.

All three boys began to speak at once, "Dale threw up…"

"We didn't wash behind our ears…"

"Ya, and we wrestled in the basement a lot!"

Chapter 21

"…Speak, Lord, for your servant is listening…"
1 Samuel 3:9 NIV

October 1962

Gerry

Gerry sat at the typewriter with tears in his eyes. He had been trying to type all through the fall. The teacher encouraged Gerry to use a wand in his teeth to type. It was painful, tedious and he felt hopeless. The wand would fall. The keys would jam and the tears would start, again and again.

"There has to be a better way, Gerry," Ruth lamented.

"Aye," he agreed through teary eyes."

"If only we could stick that wand to your head somehow. I wish you didn't have to hold it in your teeth."

"Aye."

Brian added his thought, "You could tape it to his head."

"That's stupid," Dale disagreed. "It would get all stuck in his hair."

"Boys…" Ruth warned.

Gerry vocalized.

"Dr B. says the best way for you to communicate is with your head, Gerry. We've got to figure that out."

Ruth was happy with Gerry's progress but she knew she could always make it better. She never wanted to stop striving for his independence and his sense of self-worth. Daily, as she went about her routine, she thought of Gerry's struggles and prayed for ways to make life easier for him.

*

Waldemar sat at his desk in the Saskatoon Detachment smoking a cigarette. He looked at the title on his desk. 'Officer Commanding Saskatoon Division.' Who knew it was going to be like this?

The days were long. There was very little criminal activity. The officers in his division were sluggish and unmotivated. Everyone sat around the office, smoking, filling the air with blue haze. The phone barely rang. When it did, it was a neighbor complaining about their property line, or a car parked illegally or some other nonsense. Waldemar felt he was being dragged into the sluggishness of the Force. The endless smoking made him feel ill. Since he was a little boy, he had taken the path of greatest challenge. Now he was forty-six, wasting away his talent in a small detachment. Throughout his twenty-two years in law enforcement, he had moved at a running pace. Suddenly, he was standing still.

"It's not about me," he sighed as he looked around the room. He put out his cigarette and tossed the entire ashtray in the trashcan. "I'm done with this!"

He looked around the detachment. "Something has to change," he said to himself.

Meanwhile, at home, Ruth immersed her hands in the soapy dishwater. She was once again praying that God would show her a solution to Gerry's communication problem. She kept thinking of how Gerry could somehow hold the wand to press the typewriter keys. Taffy lay on the kitchen floor, sleeping in a spot of sunshine. Ruth looked at the dog and sighed.

"God, I am not content. I feel like there is an answer for Gerry. I just can't see what it is. Even his teachers don't know. I've asked everyone I can think of and no one knows the answer. Even Pete, who can usually think up a gadget to help Gerry, he is stumped too!" She pulled out a plate and rinsed it off, then placed it on the counter.

She sighed and continued, "Don't you think this is important, Lord? I mean…if he could type on his own then he could say whatever he wanted — more than the word board can. Please, Lord, you're not showing me what I should do here."

She continued with her prayer, as she washed and rinsed more plates and bowls, cups and cutlery. She laid them all out to dry on the dish rack and toweled off her hands. She hung her apron over the kitchen chair and went to the living room to investigate the racket outside.

There were city workers in front of the house, digging up a small bit of Waldemar's lawn. They wore yellow hard hats and blue coveralls. Some of them were deep in conversation while others were busy digging.

Ruth stood there and watched them, wondering what they were up to.

One of the workers stopped for a break and took off his yellow hard hat. The interior of the hat was turned toward Ruth.

She continued to think of Gerry while she watched the men. He was frustrated every day by the matter. If only — suddenly the inside of the hat caught Ruth's eye. She rushed out the front door and across the lawn. The cool fall air bit at her cheeks.

She approached the workman who was holding his hat. "Please, may I see your hat?"

The man looked confused but passed his hat over to Ruth. "Sure."

Ruth turned and ran inside the house, calling over her shoulder, "I'll bring it back! I need to make a phone call!" All of the workmen stopped and watched the woman who had abducted their co-worker's hat.

Ruth ran into the kitchen and dialed the number for the school.

"Hello, may I speak to Dr. Buckle?"

"Yes, ma'am, I'll get him on the line. Who may I ask is calling?" the receptionist asked.

"Mrs. Peterson, Gerry's mom."

"One moment please."

Ruth waited, all the while looking at the hat.

"Dr. Buckle here," said a cheery voice.

"I found it! I found it!"

"Found what?" he asked, perplexed.

"I've found the answer to attaching the wand to a headpiece!"

"Okay, tell me…" he encouraged.

"I was praying about it and there were these workmen on the lawn. One of them took off his hat and I saw the inside. It's a plastic set of straps that conform to the head!"

"Right," Dr. Buckle listened intently.

"If you could take those straps, attach the wand and have a piece that goes under the chin...then we've got it!"

"Wonderful!" Dr. Buckle exclaimed.

"He could use it at the typewriter and at his word board!"

Ruth and Dr. Buckle discussed making a prototype and finding someone who could put it all together.

"Let's meet after school, Mama, and we can talk all about it."

Ruth hung up the phone, elated. Then she realized she was still holding the worker's hat.

"Oh!" she laughed and she ran outside. She proceeded to explain her discovery to the workmen. They all smiled and congratulated her.

As soon as everyone was home from work and school, Ruth shared her idea with them.

"That's great!" Waldemar agreed from his spot at the kitchen table.

Gerry vocalized excitedly.

"Good idea, Mom," Brian agreed as he sat on the floor, petting Taffy.

"How will the wand stay on?" Dale asked.

"Well we'll find someone who can figure that out. Dr. B is going to look into who might be able to make it for us."

"That will be great for his word board as well," Waldemar added.

"Yes, I was even thinking that maybe he could have a smaller word board that he could take when he's out so that he can communicate with anyone."

Waldemar sat, looking thoughtful. "Let me think about that. Perhaps we could figure out a way to attach it to his wheelchair."

"Isn't it great, Gerry?" Brian touched Gerry on the arm.

"Aye!"

*

Christmas 1962 came and went in a flurry of school plays, church plays, curling tournaments, baking and gifts. Ruth took sketches of her idea to Dr. Buckle who found someone to make the headpiece a reality. On a cold day in February, Gerry brought it home from school with him.

Ruth exclaimed as she pulled it out of Gerry's bag, "Oh wonderful! It's finally ready!"

Brian and Dale arrived home from school. They looked at the white plastic straps with the wand coming out the front.

"Hmmm," Brian looked skeptically at the headpiece. "How does it work?"

Ruth looked at Gerry, "Shall we show them? I'm going to put it on you."

"Aye," said Gerry.

Ruth put the headpiece on Gerry and wheeled him down the hall to his bedroom where his typewriter was.

"Now we get to hear Gerry's first message — typed on his own!"

Gerry looked pensive as he stared at his typewriter. He took a few minutes before he finally started to type. It was a difficult process as Gerry figured out how to press one key at a time. He kept making mistakes. The process was incredibly frustrating.

"It's okay, Gerry," Ruth encouraged, "you'll get the hang of it." Dale and Brian left the room. Ruth felt it was best if she gave Gerry some time alone to figure it out. "Just call me when you're ready — no rush."

She went to the kitchen, poured Brian some milk and got him a cookie. He sat at the table happily telling her about his day. Dale disappeared to listen to the radio. After fifteen minutes, Ruth heard Gerry call.

She returned to his bedroom, anxious to see what was on Gerry's mind.

Brian stayed at the table, enjoying his snack when he heard his mom start to cry. He got up from the table slowly and peered down the hall. He saw his mom go in her bedroom and shut the door, tears streaming down her face. He crept down the hall and listened. His oldest brother wept.

He went into Gerry's bedroom. He found Gerry next to the window. Gerry's back was turned to Brian. He walked over to take a look at Gerry's message.

Brian gasped silently as he read the words, "Why did you let me live?"

Ruth didn't answer that question that day. She cried through the night, had a long talk with Waldemar and decided how she was going to approach it.

The next day she sat down with Gerry.

"Why would you say that?"

Gerry looked at his mom with tear-filled eyes.

"God let you live. We love you. You're our son and you are precious to us. We can't understand God's plans. We wanted you to live." She sat for a moment to let the words sink in. Gerry sat in his wheelchair, angry and crying.

"You'll have to discover God's purpose for your life on your own. That's something I can't do for you."

No more was said. Ruth left the room and spent the rest of the day listening to Gerry cry. She cleaned the house with a vengeance while Brian and Dale stayed in the basement, avoiding the drama unfolding upstairs.

As Ruth tucked a tearful Gerry into bed, she added one more thought, "I don't need this, Gerry. I've done the best for you that I could. You can lay here and cry for the rest of your life or you can move on.

Cerebral Palsy doesn't define you. It is simply something you have to endure. I am not willing to see you cry for yourself any longer."

She got up, turned out the light and stood in the doorway.

Before she left she quietly added, "Blessed is he who preservers under trial because when he has stood the test, he will receive the crown of life that God has promised to those who love Him."

Gerry laid there thinking of his mother's words. The tears continued to fall as he re-played the verse over and over in his mind.

*

February gave way to a warm spring, followed by the start of another summer. The family was planning their annual trip to the Rocky Mountains. It was two weeks before the end of the school year. The kids were anxious to have a break. They were all sitting around the kitchen table, looking at the calendar and trying to decide which weeks were best.

"I don't want to go," Dale announced.

"What are you talking about?" Ruth said as she frowned at Dale.

"I don't want to go. Family vacations are stupid and I'm sick of them. I don't want to spend my whole summer with you."

Waldemar rubbed his stubbled chin. "Really?"

"Oh yes," Ruth said sarcastically, "vacations are *so* difficult."

"Well," Waldemar said as he looked at Dale, "let's hear what you have to say. What would you do if you weren't coming with us?"

"I don't know."

"This is ridiculous, Dale, you're only twelve. When you're older you can skip out on family vacation but for now — you come."

Waldemar thought of his summers on the Carlson farm picking blueberries, "How about you get a job for the summer?"

"Sure," Dale agreed.

"Really?" Ruth gasped in disbelief. "You would rather work all summer long than go on a two-week trip with us to the mountains?"

"Yes," Dale responded. "I think I would."

Brian sat glumly at the table. He looked down at his hands in his lap. He sucked in a deep breath, trying to stop the tears that threatened to fall.

"Fine then," Ruth conceded. "Your dad will find you a job."

Waldemar held true to his promise and found a job outside of Edmonton where Dale could work on a dairy farm. He would be fully immersed in farm work for eight long weeks and, Waldemar hoped, he would be anxious to join the family on the next vacation.

Despite Waldemar and Ruth's best intentions, Dale was happy to board a Greyhound bus to Edmonton on July 1. Herman would be meeting him at the bus stop and would drive him out to the Richards' farm.

Ruth called the farm a week after Dale left, wondering if he might be ready to come home.

"Hi, sweetheart."

"Hi, Mom."

"How's the job?"

"It's great!"

Ruth raised her eyebrows. "Really?"

"Yes."

"What kinds of things are you doing?"

"Well there's a truck and I can drive it around the property. Mr. Richards let me take his rifle and I get to shoot gophers from the truck window."

"Wow, that sounds exciting."

"And every morning and night we clean stalls, feed the cows and bring them water. I'm even pretty good at milking a cow."

"Well what do you know…"

"When all the chores are done, I can do whatever I want and the food here — it's great!"

"Are you having Mrs. Richards wash your clothes?"

"Yes, she takes them on the weekend and gives them back when she's done."

"Are you missing us?"

"No, not really," he replied honestly.

"Brian is sure missing you. Do you want to talk to him?"

"Okay."

"Hi Dale," Brian came on the line, his voice quivering.

"Hey, Brian. How are things?"

"Pretty good. So, you like the farm?"

"Yes, it's really fun. I can do whatever I want. It's like being grown-up."

"That sounds neat."

"It's cool."

Brian felt the tears rushing to his eyes. "Here's Mom."

Ruth took the receiver back from Brian. "I'll tell your dad you said hi. Any messages for him or Gerry?"

"No, I don't think so."

"Okay then, I hope you have a good week and I'll call you next Sunday. Just give us a call if you need anything."

"Sure, Mom."

"Love you, Dale."

"Love you too, Mom."

Chapter 22

"Do you not know that your body is a temple of the Holy Spirit, who is in you, whom you have received from God? You are not your own; you were bought at a price. Therefore honor God with your body." 1 Corinthians 6:19 NIV

April 1964

Ruth and Waldemar

The following spring on a wintry April day, Waldemar sat at his desk, looking at an old case file. The last few months had been good. He had breathed new life into the detachment, polishing up the entire squad. He had relocated people who didn't have enough work to do. He had pulled out old, unsolved cases and assigned people to reinvestigate. He had cleaned the entire detachment, ordering new desks and cabinets. He had thrown out everyone's cigarettes, declaring that all smoking was to be done outside. In the last few months, he brought national attention to

Saskatoon with their success rate on closing cases and keeping crime at a minimum. They had finally come to accept that being in Saskatoon was in Gerry's best interest and he could make it work if he had to. There were many social functions. Ruth loved every one. She hosted dinner parties at the house with distinguished guests. There was a dinner or a ball almost every other weekend.

 Gerry had been doing well too. The school was good for him. Dr. Buckle was incredibly helpful. Gerry was adapting to the headpiece. He could successfully type and point to his messages on his word board. Waldemar made a smaller version of the original word board that could be attached to the wheelchair. This allowed Gerry a whole new freedom of communication. The word board had about 200 words and phrases as well as a typewriter keyboard alphabet. Gerry could talk to people at school and church. He celebrated his fifteenth birthday with a new level of independence that he desperately needed.

 The phone rang, disrupting his reflection.

 "Saskatoon RCMP," Waldemar answered.

 Ruth filled the prescription for Valium. She and Dr. Buckle had tried other medications for Gerry, with no success. This medication had come on the market last year and Dr. Buckle felt it might be worth a try. It was a strong sedative that had been helpful for other kids with Cerebral Palsy.

 Before bed that night, she gave Gerry a tablet.

 "We'll see, Gerry, hopefully that will do the trick and give you some rest. Dr. Buckle thinks that if we can get your muscles to relax you might be able to sleep through the night."

 "Aye," Gerry agreed.

 Gerry grew drowsy almost immediately. Ruth hurried through his bedtime routine. She got him into bed just as he was no longer able to keep his eyes open.

"Wow," she commented, "that sure makes him tired."

She told Brian and Dale to get themselves to bed and went to the kitchen table to write a letter to her childhood friend Artrude.

Dearest Artrude,

How are you and your family? We are doing well. We are completely settled in Saskatoon. Gerry's school has been very good for him. His doctor there has been a gift from God. Can you believe he is already fifteen? It seems the time has passed in a blink of an eye. We were the same age when you moved away from Leduc.

Waldemar is busy with the Force and with his curling. He's still a champion, winning tournaments and having a wonderful time. He also keeps busy building and improving the house.

Dale is thirteen now, in grade eight. He is an exceptional student. We are proud of him. He spent last summer working on a dairy farm outside of Edmonton and will be doing the same this summer.

Brian is our artist. He loves to paint and sing and is very creatively inclined. He is eleven now and despite a rough transition has come to love Saskatoon.

Have you heard that the Glenrose Hospital in Edmonton is opening? It is a direct result of the growth of the original Cerebral Palsy Clinic. It is exciting to see other parents finding answers and hope where there once was none.

I am still striving to integrate disabled children into regular schools as I witnessed in Europe, but it is an uphill battle.

I hope this letter finds you well,
                                    Love, Ruth

Ruth stretched her arms and folded her letter. She placed it in an envelope and addressed it to

Artrude. She put the letter by the back door so that she could mail it tomorrow.

The house was quiet. She went to Dale and Brian's bedroom and found them both fast asleep. She went into Gerry's room where he too was sound asleep.

"I guess I should get myself to bed," she said to herself as she looked at the clock. "It's already ten o'clock; I'm sure I only have a few hours before Gerry is up."

She went to her bedroom and changed into her nightgown. She brushed her hair and put her glasses on the night table.

Waldemar crept into bed, after work, sometime in the early morning. Ruth slept on. The sun rose and light shone through the gap in their bedroom curtains. Ruth stretched and yawned, feeling well rested.

"Good morning," she whispered to Waldemar. "Thanks for getting up with Gerry."

He also stretched. He answered in a gravely voice, "I didn't."

Ruth sat up. Her heart was pounding. She jumped out of bed yelling, "He's dead! He's dead!"

Waldemar was right on her heels. They both burst into Gerry's bedroom where he lay perfectly still, in the same position, as he had been the night before.

Ruth ran to him and shook him, crying hysterically, "Oh God! I've killed him! I've killed my son!"

Just then, Gerry's eyelids fluttered open and he smiled at his mom. He vocalized.

Ruth buried her head in the bed covers and bawled. Waldemar let out a deep breath. "Gerry, you scared us!"

Gerry vocalized.

"That's the first night you've ever slept all the way through!" Waldemar collapsed onto the foot of the bed. "What happened?"

Ruth wiped the tears from her eyes. "I gave him a new medication last night, Valium."

"Well it seems like it works."

"A little too well! I better call Dr. Buckle."

Ruth made the phone call and Dr. Buckle agreed.

"You know best, Mama. If you think he needs less, then we'll give him less."

*

"Boys, come to the kitchen please," Ruth called as she came in the door one Sunday evening.

Gerry, now sixteen, wheeled into the kitchen with Dale, now fourteen, and Brian, twelve behind him. Dale and Brian came to the table and sat down.

"What's going on, Mom?" Brian asked.

"I've been teaching classes at the church all weekend and I figured it was something that I needed to talk to you about too."

Dale looked quizzically at his mom. "On what?"

"Sexual education."

Brian groaned, "Oh no! No, Mom!"

Ruth laughed, "It's perfectly natural."

"No, no, no…" Brian covered his face with his hands. "Please no."

"Okay, I won't talk to you about it but I have a leaflet I made up. Why don't you have a look and then you can ask me — or your dad — anything you like."

Dale took the leaflet and headed off to his room to take a look. Brian took the piece of paper. He grasped it with only two fingers, closing his eyes so he couldn't see the diagrams. Once in his bedroom, he dropped it in the garbage can. Then he reconsidered. He fished it out and jammed it under the bed where it could never be seen again.

Gerry sat in the kitchen with his mom while she matter-of-factly showed him the contents of the leaflet. He indicated that he had a message.

"A, B, C…"

Gerry stopped her at W, H and Y.

"Why am I doing this?"

"Aye," Gerry answered.

"Because the sixties are a time of freedom — so you kids think — and many teenagers don't know the first thing about any of this. As a nurse, I teach these young girls anatomy and sexual education from a Christian standpoint."

Gerry sat quietly listening as Ruth carried on, "The love between a husband and a wife is a beautiful thing, but sadly many kids your age are being influenced by society. If I can help by showing them God's plan then I've done the right thing."

Gerry agreed.

"Now, let's put these away," Ruth chuckled. "I've got company coming tomorrow night and although it may make for lively dinner conversation, I don't think your dad would approve."

Gerry laughed as Ruth scooped up her papers and carried them to her bedroom.

Ruth had everything ready: the roast was nearly done, the potatoes were mashed, the vegetables steamed and the table set. The dishes had been washed and the kitchen was spotless. Waldemar had invited three high-ranking RCMP officials for dinner. Everything had to be perfect. Waldemar was in the bedroom, changing into his suit. She was ready, hair curled, skirt and blouse pressed. The children had been banished to the basement.

She polished the counters and sink with the cloth one last time. She turned on the water to rinse out some offending crumbs. She noticed a bit of grime on the underside of the faucet. She took her cloth in one hand and the faucet in the other. There was a snapping noise. Suddenly, the faucet came off in her hand and water started spraying everywhere.

"PETE! PETE!" she started shrieking as she tried to push the faucet back on. As she pressed the faucet against the pipe, the water pressure built, spraying water further. It sprayed the ceiling, the walls, the cabinets, the table and worst of all, Ruth. "PETE, GET IN HERE!"

Waldemar was down the hall in a flash. He took in the scene. Ruth had her hand over the spraying pipe sending the water in every direction. She was soaked from head to toe. He calmly walked to the sink and turned off the taps. He started to laugh as he looked at her, water dripping from her nose.

"Problem solved," he laughed.

Ruth was on the verge of crying when a bubble of laughter welled up inside. She started to laugh uncontrollably. "Look at me!"

"I'll dry things up, you go get changed." He chuckled, "If you wanted to clean the kitchen there are easier ways!"

Chapter 23

"For wisdom is more precious than rubies,
and nothing you desire can compare with her."
Proverbs 8:11 NIV

January 1967

Dale

Dr. Turner looked at Ruth and Gerry across his desk. He spoke calmly, "Gerry, you're eighteen now. Ultimately it's your choice."

Gerry agreed, "Aye."

"It's not your mother's choice or your father's choice, but yours. It's between you and God."

"If it was you, Dr. Turner," Ruth asked, "would you do it?"

"It's too hard to say. I can only give you the facts. I haven't had to live with an uncooperative body for the last eighteen years."

Ruth nodded, looked at Gerry and then turned back to Dr. Turner. "Can you tell us more about the procedure?"

"Trepanation is an ancient practice." He paused to straighten his tie. "However, in the context of

Cerebral Palsy, it's a new idea. We would be using a rotating disc to enter the skull in an attempt to relieve the pressure. We'll be putting electrodes on the brain to try to stimulate the parts that are giving Gerry a lot of trouble. There are no studies on such a procedure but in some patients it has lessened their Palsy symptoms for a period of time."

Gerry vocalized.

"And in other patients?" Ruth asked.

"In some patients it has made it worse. There is the danger of becoming more athetoid on one side of your body. It's hard to say what the best thing to do is."

Gerry grumbled.

"I suggest," said Dr. Turner, "that you think about it. If you decide to go ahead, I will write your name down on a waiting list. The hospital will call you when it is your turn to go in."

"Thank you," Ruth looked over at Gerry. "Any questions, Gerry?"

"Nah."

That night the entire family sat in the living room and discussed the pros and cons of the operation. There were moments when Gerry was certain he was ready to call Dr. Turner and the next he was ready to walk away from the whole idea.

"You'll never know unless you try, right, Gerry?" Dale challenged.

"Aye."

"But it could be risky," Brian added.

"Aye."

Waldemar looked at his eldest son. "Take it to God, Gerry. That's the best thing you can do."

"I agree," said Ruth. "It's your body. It's your life. You've never relied on us to make choices for you. We've always encouraged you to be independent and that hasn't changed. We trust you to do the right thing for you."

"We're behind you in whatever you choose, Gerry," Waldemar reassured.

Gerry sat quietly for a long time, thinking the matter over. Everyone else sat and reflected on the situation. Finally, Gerry vocalized.

"Do you have message?" Brian asked.

"Aye."

"A, B, C…"

Gerry stopped Brian at I.

"You?"

"Aye."

"New word?"

"Aye."

"A, B, C…"

Gerry stopped Brian at A and then M.

"Am?"

"You want to go ahead?" Ruth interrupted.

"Aye."

It was a sunny Easter morning when the phone finally rang, summoning Gerry to the hospital. Ruth, Dale and Brian were at church. Gerry was in his room listening to the radio when his dad poked his head into the room.

"Guess who called?" Waldemar asked.

Gerry vocalized.

"The hospital."

Gerry hesitated and said, "Nah…"

"They called to say that they have a spot open this Friday."

Gerry vocalized.

"Do you have a message?"

"Aye."

Gerry and Waldemar slowly spelled out 'I'm not sure it's a good idea. What if it gets worse.'

"You're right, it could get worse. But it could be better."

All afternoon, Gerry worried about what he should do. He didn't want to be worse; he couldn't imagine anything worse. The daily pain and frustration was already as much as he could bear. But, he thought, there was the slim chance he could be better.

Dale wandered into Gerry's bedroom late in the afternoon.

"Hey, Gerry, I heard you're going into the hospital on Friday."

"Nah," Gerry responded.

"Are you scared?"

"Aye."

"Scared it could be worse?"

"Aye."

"If your God is in fact who you say He is, then He will keep you and give you peace."

Dale sat for a minute. He left the room saying, "Good luck."

Gerry considered Dale's words for quite some time. As he prayed, he felt the Lord's presence and a sense of peace.

Ruth sat in Gerry's hospital room on the day after his surgery. His shaved head was bandaged. His body was limp from the medication they had given him. Brian had come up with her today at Ruth's request.

Brian's eyes grew wide as he looked at his brother.

Ruth reassuringly patted Brian's arm. "He's okay. There is always swelling and bruising after surgery."

Brian looked down at Gerry's hand, resting on the blanket. Instead of being tightly curled, it was open, relaxed. The vile smells of the hospital rushed over Brian, threatening to make him ill. His knees felt weak as he looked at his oldest brother. He was too still, too relaxed.

Ruth sensed Brian's unease. "It's okay, Brian, he won't be like this for long."

"I'm okay," Brian lied.

They sat and talked for a while before Brian took the bus back home. Ruth stayed at Gerry's bedside, waiting for him to wake up.

About a week after the surgery, Gerry came home, and sadly it seemed, the surgery had been unsuccessful. Gerry told Ruth that he felt his left side was slightly worse. They both cried, sharing their frustration and pain.

"Gerry, I'll always be here for you, no matter what."

*

The following summer, Dale, who had finished grade eleven, made an announcement to his mother as she folded laundry in her bedroom.

"Mom, I really love Sharon."

Ruth raised her eyebrows. "You do?"

"Yes, we've been dating for a few months and I know I am in love."

"In love, huh?"

"I want to marry her."

Ruth scoffed, "No. I don't think so."

"You can't decide that for me."

"Actually, I can."

"I want to be with her all the time."

Ruth rolled her eyes. "That's lovely, Dale. While you're living with me you're going to have to cool it. You're not even finished school."

"Maybe I don't want to finish school."

Ruth stopped folding and glared at her son. "And what would that accomplish? You're going to drop out and just be in love?"

Dale crossed his arms across his chest. "Maybe I won't live here anymore then."

"Really."

"Yes. If you won't let me do what I want then I'll leave."

"Fine. Leave."

Dale stormed out of the bedroom.

Ruth looked in the mirror with a grim expression etched into her face. She was no doubt getting older. The boys were nearly grown and Dale already wanted to leave home. She examined every laugh line on her face. Where had the years gone?

If he wanted to go, so be it. She wasn't going to stand in his way. If Mr. Independence thought life was such a breeze then she would let him experience it. She loved and loathed his independence all at once.

Dale did indeed follow through with his threat. He worked at the local nursing home, washing dishes, and this afforded him meager accommodations. Within a week he found a small studio apartment, partially furnished with a dingy shag carpet, tattered drapes, burn marks on the couch and a dresser with the drawer fronts missing.

"I'm leaving tomorrow," he announced at the supper table one night.

Waldemar answered, "Really? All this for a girl?"

"Yes, Dad, all this for Sharon."

"It sounds like you have your mind made up," Ruth said and exchanged a look with Waldemar.

"I do. I've found a great place. I've already put down one month's rent."

"And school…" Ruth spoke at the same time Waldemar said, "How much is that?"

"Nineteen dollars a month."

"Good for you."

Brian ate his supper quietly, surprised and annoyed that Dale was leaving home. Gerry laughed as he ate his supper.

"What is it, Gerry?" Brian asked.

Gerry vocalized.

"A, B, C..." Brian began.

Gerry spelled out, 'No more home-cooked meals.'

Ruth and Waldemar smiled as Dale said, "I can cook."

The following day, Dale spent his day at the nursing home washing dishes. At the end of the day, he was worn out. When he came in through the back door, he nearly tripped over a lineup of boxes. He took a minute to examine them. There were towels, sheets, dishes and other household items. On the side of the box, Ruth had written DALE.

He looked at his mom sitting at the kitchen table, reading the paper.

"Hi, Mom."

"Hi, Dale. How was work?"

"It was fine."

"Are you hungry?" She kept her eyes on the newspaper.

"Yes actually, I am." He pulled out a kitchen chair and sat down next to her.

She looked up at him. "I'll make you something."

"Sure."

She got up from the table, went to the refrigerator and pulled out some eggs, green onions and ham. She heated up the frying pan and proceeded to make an omelet. Neither one said a word as she cooked. Dale let his eyes skim over the paper. Ruth kept her focus on the omelet.

She served it up for him and brought it to the table. "So, are you staying here tonight or are you going to your new place?"

Dale hesitated. He thought of his dirty, pathetic studio apartment with the old mattress. "God knows what's in that mattress," he mumbled. He looked at his mom and shrugged his shoulders. "You know, it's cold...I'll stay."

Ruth said nothing, folded the paper and headed down the hall to her bedroom.

The next morning, Ruth carried the boxes to the basement. She smiled as she pushed the boxes into storage under the stairs. "Another day."

*

Waldemar sat in the armchair in the living room, listening to the radio. The family had returned from a vacation in British Columbia. Brian was up in his room reading. Gerry had gone out to a friend's house. Ruth was at the grocery store.

Dale had not come on vacation with them, as usual. He stayed home, working and spending time with his girlfriend. He never did move out. He didn't even bring the subject up to his mother again. He only mentioned it to his dad because when he went to get the rent money back from the landlord, the landlord had refused.

"Can't you get the money back for me, Dad?" he had asked. *"You're a cop. Just make him give me the money back."*

Waldemar laughed and said that no, he could do no such thing.

Brian had spent the weeks before their vacation house sitting for a neighbor. He often invited friends over to keep him company. Before they had left for the mountains, Brian handed off his house-sitting duties to one of his close friends.

There was a sharp knock at the door. Waldemar got up to answer it. When he opened the door, he was met by two young constables.

"Good afternoon, gentlemen. How can I help you?"

One of the young constables spoke up, "Sorry to disturb you, Inspector Peterson, but we were hoping we might be able to ask you a few questions."

Waldemar was perplexed. Perhaps it was regarding a case he had been working on. "Certainly, why don't you come in?"

The pair nervously came in and sat down on the couch.

"It's regarding your son," one of the constables began.

Waldemar's brow furrowed. "Which one?"

"Brian."

Waldemar nodded. "Okay, do I need to call him in here?"

"Well, sir, the Baxters returned from their vacation and found that their car has been stolen. We were able to recover the car but it is totaled. It appears the robbers crashed the car and abandoned it on a farm road a few kilometers east of the city."

"Hmm. We've been away. Brian has been house sitting for them all summer, prior to us leaving. Why don't I call him in here?"

Waldemar left the room and went to Brian. "Brian," he said in his most stern police officer voice.

"Yes, Dad," Brian looked up from his book nervously.

"There are some constables here who would like to ask you a few questions regarding the Baxters' car."

Brian went white. "Okay, Dad, I'll be right there."

Waldemar returned to the living room. The constables told them the information they had regarding the car and the possible young men who could be involved. Waldemar waited for Brian to join them. He could hear he had made a stop in the bathroom.

A few minutes later, Brian joined them in the living room looking pale. "Good afternoon."

"Afternoon, Brian. We have a few questions for you."

Brian nodded and smiled, trying to sound upbeat, "Sure."

"Were you staying at the Baxters'?"

"Yes, sir."

"Did you ever see the keys to their Volkswagen?"

Waldemar studied his son intently.

"Yes, sir. They were on a hook by the backdoor."

The other constable broke in, "And how old are you, Brian?"

"Fourteen," he squeaked.

"And have you ever driven a car?"

Brian shook his head. "No, sir."

"The Baxters' car was taken for a ride. Do you know anything about that?"

"No, sir. We've just returned from vacation."

"We're going to need the name of your friend. The one who took over the house-sitting job when you were on vacation."

"Ah – okay. It's Thomas Sullivan."

The constables looked at Waldemar who turned to his son.

"Anything else you'd like to say, Brian?"

"No, Dad."

Waldemar looked at the constables. "I guess that's all then." He looked Brian in the eyes. "If he says he doesn't know anything about it then he doesn't. Right, Brian?"

"Yes, Dad."

The constables got up, looking uncomfortable. "Yes, Inspector. Thank you very much for your time."

Brian went to his bedroom before Waldemar had even finished closing the front door. He turned around to say something to his son but upon his disappearance decided to wait for Brian's next move. He opened the newspaper and held it up, listening for movement.

Within five minutes, Brian did not disappoint. Waldemar heard him creep across the hall into the master bedroom. He heard the rattle of the rotary spinning on the telephone. He listened to frantic whispers and pleas.

That night, Waldemar and Ruth went for a walk. They strolled hand in hand, waving away the summertime mosquitoes.

"I love you, Pete," Ruth said warmly.

He smiled down at her, "I love you too."

"Tomorrow you're back to work?"

"Actually, work came to me today."

Ruth looked puzzled. "What are you talking about?"

As they walked, Waldemar explained the afternoon visit and the fate of the Baxters' Volkswagen.

"We weren't here though…"

"True," Waldemar agreed, "but he's involved somehow."

"He's only fourteen — he can't even drive."

Waldemar stopped walking and turned to face Ruth. "I've been doing this for a long time." He looked her in the eyes. "I know when someone is lying. He may not have crashed that car but I'll put money on it that he knows exactly who did."

The couple began walking again. Ruth mulled their conversation over. "Why didn't you say something then? Why didn't you confront him? Make him tell you what happened."

"He should come forward on his own."

"But what if he doesn't!"

"I don't want to get involved. This is between Brian and the law."

"But you are the law!"

Waldemar laughed. "It may seem that way." He was silent for a while as they started to head back toward the house. "What will he learn if I make him do the right thing? He needs to find the right way on his own."

Chapter 24

"The Lord will keep you from all harm – he will watch over your life; the Lord will watch over your coming and going both now and forevermore."
Psalm 121:7 & 8 NIV

September 1968

Brian

"I'm sorry, Dale, but this isn't going to work for me." Ruth was out in the backyard, hanging laundry on the line.

"I hate it, Mom." Dale sat on a patio chair, watching his mom. He had come home from school. He was in his first year at the University of Saskatchewan.

"Is this something you're going to regret down the road?" She pulled a clothespin from her apron and hung up Gerry's pants.

"I always thought I was destined for university — but maybe I'm not."

Ruth shook her head and stopped hanging clothes. She put a hand on her hip and studied him. "You're smart, you're motivated…what's the problem?"

Dale looked at his hands, folded in his lap, as he thought things over. "It started this summer."

"How so?"

Dale had spent the summer in Halifax working as a civilian in the RCMP division. It was a job that was exclusive to sons of RCMP officers. He had been a deckhand on a boat doing a lot of cleaning, painting and washing dishes. He had plenty of downtime on the job to connect with the other young men who were working there. They played cards, swam in the ocean and talked about their girlfriends. Dale loved the freedom, despite the hard work. One particular night had made him feel like he could never go back to do anything ordinary again.

"It was the night of the storm," Dale began. "We got the call that a boat was in distress. Atlantic Air Search and Rescue wasn't able to get to it fast enough so we were called. We got on our rain slickers and the boat left the harbor in minutes. As long as we didn't get in the way, we civvies were invited to come along. The wind was howling and the rain was pelting us. The waves were at least twenty feet high. We had to hang on for dear life."

Ruth watched her son, lost in his story.

"The RCMP vessel pulled up alongside the sinking ship just as a wave pushed the other guy's boat up. As it went down into the sea, two big RCMP officers reached over the side of our boat and grabbed the fisherman. It was unbelievable!"

"It sounds amazing," Ruth agreed.

"The thing is…" Dale looked at his mom earnestly, "I love being an adult. I love the freedom. I don't want to be a student. I don't want deadlines and papers and all of the stress that university brings. I want to be out there — taking risks and experiencing life."

Ruth sighed and asked, "You're going to quit school?" She went back to hanging laundry on the line.

"Yes."

"And do what?"

"I don't know — the possibilities are endless."

"What about all the money you've paid for tuition?"

"If you drop out before October 1, you don't have to pay."

"Well if you're going to live with us then you have to be working. I will not aid your life of adventure with free accommodations."

"That's fine. I can work until I figure out what I want to do."

She picked up her empty laundry basket, shaking her head as she went inside.

That night after Waldemar got home from work, he and Ruth sat in the living room listening to the news on the radio. When their program was over, Waldemar switched it off.

"Our kids are growing up," Ruth said.

"What makes you say that?"

"Dale made an announcement to me today."

Waldemar looked at her quizzically. "Good or bad?"

She sighed. "I don't know. Bad, I think, but I'm sure Dale would say good."

"Tell me."

"He's quitting university."

"What!" Waldemar exclaimed.

"Yes, if he drops out now he can get his tuition money back."

"What about his future?"

She shook her head. "I don't know."

Waldemar sat quietly, thinking things over before he spoke, as was his way. "My parents wanted me to be a teacher. Pappa even bought me the books."

"I guess we each make our own choices."

"How about Gerry?" he asked.

"He told me today that he wants to move out."

Waldemar raised an eyebrow. "Really?"

"Yes. It's true. He's ready to leave the nest."

"How is that going to work?"

"I know it sounds crazy but it is something we have to face at some point. What are we going to do for Gerry in the long term?"

"I don't know," he sighed.

"The options in Canada are nursing homes, for the elderly, but frankly I didn't fight for his rights for the last nineteen years to put him in an institution now."

"Exactly," he agreed.

"We need to figure something out."

"What do you have in mind?"

"In Sweden, Mother and I toured some 'Group Homes' for adults with disabilities. Depending on the disability, they adapt the homes to be accessible for independent living. That sort of thing would be perfect for Gerry."

"Yes, he would do well on his own if he had the personal care."

"True."

"Do they have these types of homes anywhere in Canada? Perhaps I could request a move."

"No," she paused. "Sadly, no."

They both sat silently, thinking of their three boys.

"And Brian?"

Ruth laughed. "No news on Brian. Thank goodness."

Waldemar sat quietly for a while. Finally he said, "It's hard to believe but I guess we're at the point in their lives where we have to sit back and watch them make their own choices. The big choices."

"It's scary. We've always let them be independent — now they're starting to make their big life decisions."

"Yes, but I guess that's when we have to realize that they are really and truly in God's hands. All we can do now is pray for them."

She looked at Waldemar and smiled. "Is that enough?"

"Yes." He reached over and hugged his wife. "It's time to let go…just a little for now."

*

Dale went back to the nursing home where he previously worked part time, through high school. He asked for a full-time position. They were happy to offer him head dishwasher for $1.25 an hour. It wasn't exactly the adventure he had longed for.

He spent a lot of time with Brian and his friends. Tonight they were going to a school dance. It was Thanksgiving and Dale invited his girlfriend, Sharon. Brian's age group, although hardly younger than Dale's, had a much greater propensity for trouble. Someone added liquor to the punch, making the party wilder by the hour. Dale and Sharon weren't too interested in it but Brian was.

Brian staggered home with his friends, laughing at everything and nothing in particular. They all had their coat pockets filled with bottles of hard liquor and beer.

"What a great night," Brian slurred.

"Good times!" his friend agreed.

Brian gave a whoop and opened his coat, exposing his pockets full of liquor. "Anybody need some more?" He laughed hysterically.

Suddenly, a car approached. Blue and red lights flashed. All but one of Brian's friends ran off.

"Man, that is bright!" Brian's remaining friend commented as the headlights of the car shone in their eyes.

Brian stood with his coat open and grinned broadly. He swayed on his feet and then fell to the ground, laughing, "Whoa!"

The officer got out of his car and approached the two young men. "Evenin', boys," he said with a thick Scottish accent.

Brian lay on the ground, smiling. "Evening."

Brian's friend laughed and said, "Evening."

The officer shook his head. "Ye're not lookin' so good, son. Have a seat with ye're friend there." The friend sat next to Brian who was now sitting on the curb. "What's ye're names?"

"Thomas Sullivan," Brian's friend answered.

"And you?" The officer looked sternly down at Brian.

"Brian Peterson."

The officer's brows raised. "What's ye're father's name, Peterson?"

Brian laughed again, giddy with drunkenness and answered, "Waldemar!"

"Ja-heezus Christ, sonny, what were ye're thinking?"

Brian promptly passed out on the curb.

The officer shook his head. "List'n, Sullivan, ye're going to help me get this kid in the back of my car. Got it?"

Thomas agreed. The two of them picked up Brian and laid him on the back seat. "Get in the front," the officer instructed Thomas. "I'm driving ya home."

"Yes, sir."

"And give me ye're liquor." The officer took all of the alcohol from the boys and locked it in his trunk. "Ja-heezus."

He dropped Thomas at his parents' house with a stern warning. Then he drove to the Peterson's home. He rang the doorbell and waited.

Waldemar opened the door. He saw the officer, and his heart started to race. "Hello. What can I do for you?"

"Evenin', Inspector Peterson." He waved his hand toward the back of the police car. "I've brought ye're son home. Brian."

"Thank you," he replied.

Without another word, Waldemar walked to the police car, opened the door and pulled Brian out roughly. He heaved him over his shoulder in a fireman's hold and carried him straight in the house, to his bed. The officer waited in the living room with Ruth, both saying nothing.

Waldemar returned to the living room and shook the officer's hand. "My sincerest thanks."

"Yes, sir."

The minute the door shut behind the officer, the pair headed to Brian's bedroom. Ruth charged at him. "WAKE UP! WAKE UP!"

Brian rolled over, groaned and smiled at his mom. "Hi, Mom."

"How could you do this? How could you disgrace your dad? What were you thinking! I am so angry right now…"

Waldemar put up his hand. "Stop. Just stop, Ruth. There's no point."

"He has made a fool of himself! Under-age drinking!"

"Stop," Waldemar said again calmly. "Let's go." He led Ruth from the room and shut the door behind him. "I'll deal with this."

*

Ruth stood in front of the other parents, "It is not an option. These children of ours need their independence."

"Yes," a young mother spoke out, "we can't be their caregivers indefinitely. They need options."

"Who's going to make it happen?" another parent argued.

Ruth looked around the room at the exasperated parents. Tonight's meeting was to discuss a pilot project for a group home in Saskatoon. Everyone was interested but had different views on what a group home should look like.

"I think," said one father, "that it should be two to a room. It would save costs — and these kids could have a roommate."

"No," said Ruth adamantly, "the whole idea of a group home is to foster independence. These aren't children, they are adults, needing an adult home."

The parents commented to one another.

"Yes," Ruth continued, "they are our children but they are soon to be our adult children. They should have large rooms, like an apartment, and the only common spaces should be eating spaces."

"Who would pay the staff?" someone piped up.

"Yes and how would they be regulated?" another asked.

"There are many questions," Ruth nodded reassuringly, "I know. I had these questions myself. I've toured in Europe to see what these facilities were like. We need to take these ideas and adapt them to life in Canada, and to what our government and private sector are willing to accept."

One man scoffed, "No one will accept a home for the disabled."

"I know," Ruth reassured. "We've all faced these judgments, but if we stand united, as a group of parents, all with the same objectives, we can make something happen."

"Are we united?" the youngest mother asked. "Do we all want the same thing?"

Everyone spoke at once, clouding the room with opinions.

"Now, now." Ruth addressed the parents. "One thing at a time. We need to come up with our expectations, on paper, and meet with members of the government. We need to speak as one to anyone who will listen. The details will come, in time, but for now we need to get through the red tape and be acknowledged."

"How did it go?" Waldemar asked as Ruth came in the back door.

She let out a big sigh and plopped her briefcase down on the kitchen floor. "Ugh. People. Honestly — sometimes I think I should make a home for Gerry with a live-in caregiver. It would be easier than trying to negotiate with everyone."

Waldemar took a long drink of coffee, his hands dropping the newspaper he had been reading. "That good, hey?"

"Everyone thinks that we'll never be heard, that funding will never come. Some think that the members of the group home should share rooms, common areas — well everyone has an opinion…"

"And," he asked in his quiet way, "what are you going to do about all this, Mrs. Peterson?"

"I am going to take the information I've gathered tonight, write a brief and submit it to anyone who will listen."

He nodded knowingly.

"And then I'll pray. I'll pray like crazy that someone will listen. Somewhere, somehow God will connect me with people who will be willing to make it happen." She laughed, "Hopefully they'll want to do it my way."

Waldemar chuckled, "That's usually the way you like it done."

She leaned in and kissed him. "I sure do, Pete."

He pulled her into his lap. "It's good to have you home."

She fingered his hair. "And you, Mr. Peterson, how was your day?"

"Not quite as eventful but good all the same."

She grinned at him. "Glad to hear it."

Chapter 25

"Not only so, but we also rejoice in our sufferings, because we know that suffering produces perseverance; perseverance, character; and character, hope. And hope does not disappoint us, because God has poured out his love into our hearts by the Holy Spirit, whom he has given us." Romans 5:3 NIV

October 1970

Waldemar drove the car down the familiar stretch of highway. Ruth felt nervous and excited, all at once. There were many questions, still weighing on her mind, as they had for a lifetime. Her mother, her birth mother, had been wrapped in a shroud of secrecy for nearly fifty years. As a young girl, she had always imagined that one day her father would sit down and talk about her mother, about his marriage to her and the Lessing family. But each year passed and the subject became more unapproachable.

When she was seven, she had found photos of her mother in boxes in the garage, along with other items that must have belonged to her mother and father as a young couple. She assumed that her dad would give them to her — perhaps, as she became a nurse and started working at the Misericordia — the very place her mother had died. Perhaps on her wedding day, she had thought, he would speak of her mother. Perhaps when she herself had children, maybe that would spark a conversation…but there were none. The only thing she did have was her mother's name, Ruth Lessing.

She couldn't imagine her mother as a real person because she didn't know what her mother was like. She didn't have any of her father's memories. She didn't have anything that belonged to her mother. She didn't even have a photo of her. Nothing. There was a cavern of emptiness regarding her life and her death.

This summer had been full of change. Waldemar had been given another promotion. They returned to Edmonton where he was posted to the Officer in Charge of Edmonton Sub-Division. Saskatoon was amazing. They had a school for Gerry, a place where they had connected with wonderful friends and where their boys had grown into young men.

Now Ruth's energy shifted from Gerry's education to his long-term living situation. In Saskatoon, they had formed a coalition of parents who were lobbying politicians to open a group home. They faced a lot of opposition but had gone ahead with the initial stages of planning. Her son, now twenty-one, needed to feel like any other man his age — independent.

Upon returning to Edmonton, Waldemar and Ruth found that only a few of the couples that had once formed the original Cerebral Palsy Clinic were still in tact. The majority of marriages had failed with the husband leaving the wife and disabled child. Ruth felt both proud and sad.

They were able to buy their house back and made plans to re-landscape and remodel extensively. Dale decided to remain in Saskatoon. He would study Geography at the University of Saskatchewan. He had met a lovely girl, Marlene. He realized after nearly a year of washing dishes at the nursing home that going back to university was probably the best choice for his future. Last June, he applied for a cook position in a hotel in the Rogers Pass, British Columbia. After a summer of work, he was able to finance his following year of school. Marlene left her family in Vancouver and moved to Saskatoon to attend university with Dale.

In one of their late-night conversations, Ruth expressed her frustration and sadness over losing her mother and never being able to grieve her loss. Waldemar, Mr. Matter-of-fact, had simply said that they should go to her graveside and pay their respects. Ruth had never been before but she knew her mother was buried in the Fredericksheim Cemetery outside of Leduc. As they came into Leduc, Ruth's stomach flipped.

They drove down the noisy gravel road to the gates of the cemetery. Waldemar got out to open the gate and they drove in. The cemetery was long and narrow. Waldemar parked the car, unloaded Gerry and the three of them walked through the markers, searching for the Lessing or Schindel name. There were large headstones, clustered together in the center of the cemetery and the further back they went, the older the graves were. The earliest Leduc settlers were buried there near the back of the cemetery. As she walked, Ruth saw many German family names on the headstones. There were large headstones, family plots, and tiny grave markers for children who had died. They went up a small rise and there Ruth's eyes caught an inscription. The words were worn with age.

Ruth Lessing
Beloved Wife of
H. F. Bohlman
Born August 18, 1901
Died Dec 13, 1921.
We will meet again.
Bohlman

"Here," she called out to Waldemar and Gerry. "Here she is." She ran her hands over the marker. "Here she is…" she whispered. The wind rustled through the trees. A dog barked at the neighboring farm. Emotions swept over her. A lifetime of longing for a mother she had never known. A lifetime of wondering… "Here I am," she breathed.

Waldemar pushed Gerry up the incline. He stood back, letting Ruth be alone. She said the words in her mind, my mother…then out loud, "My mother." She stood still. *What would life have been like if this young woman had lived?* Her eyes went to the dates. Her mother was twenty when she died. Twenty. She barely had a chance to live.

She looked at her mother's date of birth, August 18. She had never realized that her mother's birthday was only one day after Waldemar's. She looked at her mother's date of death, December 13. One week. She had lived one week with her mother. What happened that week? She remembered the wonder she had felt when she had first laid eyes on Gerry. What had her mother felt when she laid eyes on her baby girl? Had her mother nursed her, held her and cradled her?

She looked at the dates again. She was young. Really, just a child. Sadness washed over her. Tears ran down her face. She was nearly fifty and she still had so much to see and do.

    A tornado of sadness and longing rose up inside her again. Why had her father and Edith made this such a taboo subject? She already had to face the pain of losing her mother, why did the memories also have to be suppressed? She could have had the stories, her mother's things and the memories…if nothing else.

    She tried to imagine the day of the funeral, here in this very small piece of prairie. She tried to stand in her father's shoes. He had a newborn baby at home. He stood on this very spot, on what must have been a bitterly cold winter day. What had happened? What words were spoken? What hymns were sung?

    She looked to the left and read the next stone. It read 'Lessing' across the top. Underneath it said, 'In Memory of Frederick, Born July 15, 1873, Died June 12 1921.' At the bottom it simply said, 'Father'. Her grandfather. He laid here. He had not died much earlier than his daughter. What a year that must have been for her Grandmother Lessing. She began to wander the area and found another family marker. It was white with black etching. It read, 'Heir Ruht Martha Lessing, Born Dec 12 1898, Died June 22 1908.' Martha must have been her aunt. She too had been a young girl, laid to rest in this small patch of Alberta earth. It was fantastic to be here, among her family.

    Waldemar called out when he found the markers for Amelia and Gottlieb Schindel, her great grandparents. Ruth walked that way, down an incline to a double plot. She read each side of the stone.

Gottlieb Schindel   *Amelia Schindel*
Born 1845   *His Wife*
Died Jan 10 1942   *Born Sep 5 1842*
    Died July 5 1922

Blessed are the dead which die in the Lord and their children do follow them.

"These would be your mother's, mother's parents?" Waldemar asked.

"That's right." Ruth ran her hand over the cold stone. "I met Grandmother Lessing a few times. Her name was Pauline. These are her parents." She looked up at Waldemar and smiled. "Remarkable, isn't it?"

"So from Gerry to the Schindels is five generations," Waldemar figured.

"Great Grandfather Schindel didn't die until 1942. His house was only a few minutes from mine," she said quietly.

He said softly, "You could have known him."

"Could have, except for…"

Waldemar shot her a warning look. His eyes went to Gerry. "Ruth."

A tear rolled down her cheek. "What a shame."

They walked through the cemetery reading the other names and dates. So many babies and young children. The oldest grave seemed to be from 1896. Along the backside of the cemetery were many unmarked graves. She wondered who might have the records. Was anyone else from her family buried there?

The dog on the neighboring property barked. Ruth looked around. Waldemar and Gerry were sticking to the main path reading the stones along the way, chatting about the names and dates.

Finally, Ruth decided it was time to go. "I'm ready," she called to Waldemar.

They headed back to the car. Waldemar carefully loaded Gerry into the back seat, folded the wheelchair and placed it in the trunk. They quietly drove out of the cemetery. Waldemar got out and closed the gates behind them. Ruth sighed and stared out the window. So many questions, so few answers.

The following Wednesday, Edith and Herman came up from Leduc for supper. It had been a longstanding tradition. Now that Waldemar and Ruth were back in Edmonton, they resumed their weekly visits. Ruth could sense something was up with Edith from the moment she walked through the door.

"Hello, Mother." Edith joined Ruth in the kitchen while Herman went outside with Waldemar to discuss the landscaping.

"Hello, Ruth."

"So, how was your week?"

"Fine."

The conversation paused awkwardly. Ruth continued, "How are things at the church?"

"Fine."

"Any events going on?"

"No."

"Anything happening with your social club?"

"No."

Ruth sighed and folded her arms. "What is it?"

"What is what?"

"What is the problem? Something is wrong. Now what is it?"

"I don't know what you mean," Edith looked at Ruth with steely eyes.

"Give it up, Mother, what is going on? Is it Dad? Is something wrong with Dad?"

"No."

"Well, are you upset with me?"

"Not upset…"

Ruth raised her eyebrows. "What?"

"Just disappointed."

Ruth rolled her eyes. She turned her back to Edith who was now seated in a kitchen chair. "Do you want some coffee?"

"Yes, please."

Ruth poured the pair of them some coffee, then came and joined Edith at the table. "Are you going to share with me why I have disappointed you this time?"

Edith was quiet. She dropped a spoonful of sugar into her coffee. She poured some cream in as well and stirred. The spoon made a tinkling noise as it hit the edges of her cup. She took a drink and placed the cup back onto the saucer.

"You were seen."

Ruth was baffled. "Seen?"

"Yes, the neighbors saw you."

"What neighbors?"

"They recognized the chair."

"What chair?"

"You can't expect to go places with Gerry and not be recognized."

Ruth was completely exasperated. "What are you talking about?"

Edith met Ruth's gaze. "I don't know why you insist on pressing this issue."

Ruth took a drink of coffee, trying to understand what Edith was getting at. *The issue*, she thought, *what issue?*

"What are you trying to find out?" Edith drilled.

"About?"

"About the Lessings?" Edith spat out the name Lessing like it was poison.

Understanding dawned on Ruth. "Oh…"

"What are you going there for?"

Ruth sat quietly, took a drink of coffee and carefully considered her answer. Finally, she replied, "To grieve."

"Grieve what?"

Ruth shook her head. She clenched her jaw as she responded, "My mother."

Edith looked into her coffee. "*I* am your mother."

"Yes, you are. But she was my mother too and I have never been there."

"There's no need."

"You and Dad have never told me anything about her. You cut me off from the Lessing family. You hid her photos and personal items and," Ruth's words caught in her throat, "and now you are saying that I can't even go to the cemetery and pay my respects?"

The pair sat silently at the table. The clock ticked loudly on the wall. The women could hear the low voices of the men outside.

"I don't understand…" Edith began.

"That I want to know about my mother?"

"What does it matter now?"

Ruth sat silently, trying to push back the rage that was boiling up. She didn't look at Edith. Her eyes were fixed on a spot on the wall. She said softly, "I had a family with aunts, uncles, cousins, grandparents and great grandparents. You took them away from me."

"Death took them away."

"*They* didn't die — only my mother. There was no reason I couldn't have…"

"I did what was best for you."

Ruth glared at Edith. "Best?"

"Yes, the best I could — given the circumstances."

"I remember my grandmother coming to try to see me! She wanted to know me! You stepped in between us and sent her away!"

"A child doesn't need the confusion of all of these things…"

"I am not a child anymore. I am forty-eight! Why don't we talk about it now?"

Edith shook her head and took another sip of coffee. Her hand trembled slightly. "You're going to upset your dad if you continue."

"I can never get back that connection that you broke."

"You don't understand," Edith retorted.

"No. I don't."

"What will the community say when they see you lurking around the cemetery? Your father is a respected member of the church – "

Ruth seethed, "Lurking?"

"People talk, you know."

"Apparently," Ruth snapped back. "It's not a secret that my mother died. Everyone in Leduc knows the Lessings. Everyone knows my mother died. I bear her name!"

"*I* am your mother."

"Yes, you are my mother but you didn't give birth to me! I have a right to mourn Ruth Lessing!"

"You didn't even know her!" Edith said menacingly.

"It doesn't matter!" Ruth spat.

"I don't understand your need to pursue this…"

"No," Ruth interrupted, "And you never will."

Chapter 26

"Each of you should look not only to your own interests, but also to the interests of others."
Philippians 2:4 NIV

June 1973

Ruth, Waldemar and Gerry

Ruth faced the members of the community. "Welcome. Thank you for joining me this evening. I've come to you today to talk about a pilot program that the Alberta Rehabilitation Council for the Disabled is planning. I want to discuss with you the possibility of the first group home in Alberta being opened right here in this community."

It had been five years since Waldemar and Ruth first started talking about the eventual need for Gerry to move out and live on his own. The battle for the group home began after they moved back to Edmonton from Saskatoon. As she found with all her experiences with Gerry, there was opposition in every possible way. Nothing could be straightforward. Receive a donation and build a group home. No, that could not be, it was much too easy. She had been in endless meetings and presentations, and finally now, things were underway.

The Alberta Rehabilitation Council for the Disabled, the ARCD, had been the beneficiary of the Milton Elmer Elves Estate. She approached the executor and submitted a proposal for the group home pilot. They had agreed. It was one tiny step on a long journey. The City of Edmonton was involved. The Minister of Social Services, Architects, Planning Committees — all of these groups had to come together for this sole purpose. Opposition erupted. Questions came forward and Ruth faced each one with prayer and dependence on the Lord.

Tonight she was in the community where the group home was proposing to build.

"My name is Ruth Peterson. I've been working on the council for some time and I am the coordinator for this Group Home project. Allow me to tell you more about the disabled community.

"Currently, disabled adults in Alberta are institutionalized in nursing homes with the elderly. As a mother of a disabled young man, I can tell you that this is not an option we wish to pursue. My son has Cerebral Palsy. He is highly intellectual and fiercely independent. He has a right to have his own home, just as we all do. He is twenty-three and, as many of us were at this age, he is ready to leave the nest. He is not physically able to care for himself, but certainly with the right support he could live independently.

"The home that we are looking to build here would be a multi-bedroom facility with common living areas and a large yard. The home will be privately funded. The department of social health and development will pay for operating costs. I've come to you today to answer any questions you may have regarding the facility and to gain your trust and acceptance as we move forward.

"Please feel free to ask anything you like and I will answer as best as I can."

"Mrs. Peterson," a resident of the community asked, "are there other homes like this in Alberta?"

"No. This is the first home like this in Alberta."

Another person stood. "What is Cerebral Palsy exactly?"

"Cerebral Palsy is a disability of the neuro-muscular system, which results in the in-coordination of the muscles. It is the result of an injury to the brain, before, during or after birth."

"Is this your idea?"

"Yes, I hope to be responsible for opening up the first group home in Alberta. I've based my ideas on models from Europe."

Someone else stood. "And what would these people do at this home?"

"It would be a residence, primarily. It would also be a place of transition for those who need extended physical care after an accident or injury, which has left them incapacitated. It would be a place where independence is encouraged and residents can be given the support to learn life skills, essential for living apart from their parents."

"Are people with disabilities a danger to the community?"

"Absolutely not." She smiled reassuringly. "Most people with disabilities have lived a normal life under the care of their parents. Because of age and infirmity, parents cannot carry the burden of personal care any longer. This setting will be the natural transition from home to independent living. I can also assure you that the board will screen all residents.

There is an application process to verify that all residents accepted will be able to handle the challenges of independent living."

Ruth answered questions from the residents of the community for nearly an hour. They were polite and receptive. Most had never seen or heard of anyone with a disability before. Many were surprised and amazed that there was a need for this type of facility. Some simply said nothing but smiled politely at Ruth as they left, shaking her hand and thanking her for the information.

After the last person left, Ruth walked around the church, tidying it up. Her knees ached as she bent down to pick up a discarded piece of paper. They had been giving her a lot of trouble lately and her doctor had indicated that knee surgery would not be too far off.

Over and over, she reminded herself that *'Without me you can do nothing.'* She took every burden and question to God in prayer. How could this work? Who would pay? How would it be funded? Was this whole idea feasible? Waldemar stood silently behind her, immersed in his career but ever faithful to her cause.

The last few years since returning to Edmonton had been eventful. Ruth had been wrapped up in Gerry's housing situation. Now that Gerry had graduated high school, he was often plagued with boredom. Ruth tried to find creative ways to enrich his days. She offered him books on tape and encouraged his interest in gardening. He took an interest in geology and began a rock collection with Waldemar's help. He tried various programs that were offered through the community. Because of his physical limitations, most had been inappropriate.

She spent time with her aging parents. It was good to be back in Edmonton and close to Leduc. She spent a lot of time walking with her father, telling him her struggles. He listened intently and counseled her on the best way to help the boys, now that they were growing into men.

 She was occupied with Brian who was having a difficult time. He was involved with other young men who were into drugs and alcohol. Despite the negative influences in his life, he was a promising young man with many things going for him. Brian had been involved with drama in school and met a sweet young lady named Margaret. Ruth tried to encourage him in his drama clubs, encouraging him to live a lifestyle pleasing to God. She would help him practice his songs for his shows, tapping out the beat on the table saying, "Come on — your timing is terrible! A – one – two – get with it!" They would laugh. Brian would sing his heart out in the living room. All of this led up to performances where, like herself, he thrived under the spotlight.

 Dale and Marlene had become more seriously involved throughout the fall of 1970 and Dale proposed before Christmas. Marlene had been terribly discouraged to find that her year at Simon Fraser University in British Columbia was not transferable to the University of Saskatchewan. She was told in the fall of 1970 that she would not only lose the year of credits that she had already completed but she would need to retake grade twelve. She decided to drop out and take a job at the Hudson's Bay Company. The pair of them made plans to marry in the summer of 1971. They had driven out to Vancouver for the ceremony on August 28.

 It had been a glorious time. Ruth and Waldemar had enjoyed meeting Marlene's soft-spoken parents, Dick and Dorothy Minchin. They loved being out on the coast, staying with and visiting Ruth's brother Lorne and his wife Shirley. Waldemar and Ruth were both happy that Dale had settled down with Marlene. She was a nice Christian girl who seemed to bring out the best in Dale. She took an immediate interest in Gerry. She confided to Ruth that she had never known anyone with Cerebral Palsy before and was fascinated by his intellect, his humor and his outlook on life. She played cribbage with him at the table whenever she visited and was eager to take a message on his word board. She even mastered the A, B, C method for talking on the phone to him.

Amidst the joy of the wedding, she ached for Gerry. For Gerry, life had been one long competition between him and Dale. For him it was the ultimate sign of things he might never achieve. During the days leading up to the wedding, he was angry and inconsolable. Lorne and Shirley tried to offer Gerry their sympathies but he was unwavering in his self-pity. She had watched him struggle with self-pity over the years. He had always found a way out. But she could see that this time was exceptional.

Dale and Marlene moved to Edmonton in May after Dale graduated from university. They had found a duplex to rent on 106 Street and had settled in quite comfortably. Also in May, Marlene had announced that she was expecting their first child. Ruth thought of her father who had always loved being a grandfather. Now she knew first hand his elation as they prepared for the newest member of the family.

Before she left the community meeting, she rolled up the architect's blueprints. She dropped them into a cardboard tube and snapped the lid on. She looked around the empty church building and sighed. One more step complete.

*

"That," Ruth sighed, "was amazing!"
Waldemar glanced over at her while he was driving. "You liked that, did you?"
"What a once-in-a-lifetime opportunity!"

"I know."

"The venue — just tremendous, have you ever seen such enormous arrangements of flowers?"

Waldemar laughed, "No, can't say I have."

"And the gowns? The hair-do's…" her voice trailed off dreamily. She grabbed his free hand. "Did you see the detailing on the silverware?"

He squeezed her hand affectionately. "Yes! You showed me."

"I loved her hair, and her outfit. She is such a sharp lady. She really has it all together."

"I guess she does."

"I am proud of you. Chief Superintendent of K Division."

"And you like the perks that come with it?"

"Yes, the parties, the balls, the entertaining…"

"Even better than our glory days of entertaining in Saskatoon?"

"I loved that."

"This one takes the cake though."

"Dinner with the Queen of England. Who would have thought? Me, a little German Baptist from Leduc sitting right across from the Queen, eating supper."

Waldemar laughed, "I'm glad it meant so much to you."

"It almost makes all the hardships of being an officer's wife worth it."

"Almost?"

"It wasn't easy."

"I know."

"Hearing about the dangerous things you had been involved in on the news, wondering if you were going to come home in one piece…."

Waldemar nodded. He kept his eyes on the road as he drove back to the Calgary hotel they were staying in.

"It took its toll in the early years. Always wondering when the phone was going to ring, calling you out to a homicide. Wondering if you were okay on your undercover work…not knowing."

"You didn't want to know."

"No, I didn't. It was better that way."

Waldemar nodded.

"We made the best of it."

"What did you think of the program tonight?" She looked over at him and smiled.

"It was good."

"And the dancing?"

"I had the prettiest girl on the dance floor." He smiled coyly.

"You bet you did," Ruth chuckled. "And, you're not so bad yourself."

Waldemar laughed, he raised his eyebrows and said, "Not bad, eh? I've got some moves, if I do say so myself."

Now it was Ruth's turn to laugh. "As long as you don't mind slow dancing with a girl with a bum knee, then I've got it made."

"You'll do."

"All kidding aside, I want to say thank you. I had a great time. All in all, I am thankful you are a member of the Royal Canadian Mounted Police. You've been able to provide for us more than adequately and you've given me the opportunity to meet many, many wonderful people whom I might never had met otherwise."

Waldemar smiled as he pulled into the hotel parking lot.

"Thank you, Pete. Thank you for all of your hard work over the years."

He put the car in park and leaned over for a kiss. "I love you, Ruth."

Chapter 27

"Enter his gates with thanksgiving and his courts with praise; give thanks to him and praise his name. For the Lord is good and his love endures forever; his faithfulness continues through all generations." Psalm 100: 4 & 5 NIV

<u>December 3, 1973</u>

Ruth, Wally and Keith

The wind howled and whipped at Waldemar as he walked from the car to the main doors of the hospital.

Waldemar pulled open the door and felt the fans blowing hot air down on him. He went to the information desk and made an inquiry.

"Hello," he said as he adjusted the bouquet of flowers in his arms.

A friendly receptionist looked up from her papers. "Hello, sir."

"I'm looking for Marlene Peterson. She's just had a baby."

"She'll be on the fourth floor then, postpartum. Just ask at the desk when you get up there."

"Thanks." Waldemar headed to the elevator.

The hospital was busy. People rushed by him. It was Monday afternoon and Waldemar had made this special trip on his own, without Ruth. She was very jealous that she couldn't join him. She had knee surgery a few days earlier and was stuck in bed, hardly able to move around the house, let alone out in a blizzard and to the hospital. Waldemar promised he would bring back as much information as possible and that he would definitely take pictures of the newest Peterson.

Once on the fourth floor, he enquired again and was directed down the hall to Marlene's room. He passed a gentleman in the hallway who was smoking.

"Afternoon," the gentleman greeted him.

"Afternoon," Waldemar replied.

"What room are you looking for?"

"419," Waldemar answered.

"One more — on your left."

"Thanks," Waldemar shifted the flowers in his arms. He turned and went through the next door.

"Hi, Dad," Dale greeted Waldemar warmly. Dale motioned his dad over to their curtained-off area. Three other women shared the room. The space was abuzz with excited voices and babies crying.

"Hi!" Waldemar walked up to Marlene, who was lying in the bed, and gave her a hug. He presented the flowers to her. "From Mom and me."

"Thank you!" Marlene said excitedly. She admired the flowers and then passed them to Dale who placed them on a small table next to the bed.

Waldemar looked around the room. "Where is the little guy?"

"He's down in the nursery," Dale answered. "We can go down and get him. Marlene needs to feed him right away anyway."

"That sounds great." Waldemar looked at Marlene who was pale and looking incredibly tired. "Are you okay?"

Marlene nodded and smiled bravely. "I am."

Once out in the hallway, Dale explained, "She lost a lot of blood. They say her hemoglobin is very low. They are giving her iron to try to help her recover."

Waldemar nodded in understanding. "Poor thing."

They went to the nursery and Dale let the nurse know he needed to take their baby back to the room. She went to the bassinet labeled 'Peterson' and wheeled it to Dale.

Waldemar looked at the tiny baby, all bundled up. He had dark hair and a pink complexion. "Wow. Isn't he something?"

They wheeled the bassinet down the hall back to the room and behind Marlene's curtain. She had her eyes closed but opened them and smiled when they came in.

"How is he?" she asked.

"Good," Dale answered. "He's sleeping. Did you want to try to feed him?"

"No," she looked at Waldemar. "Let Dad have a chance to hold him."

"Sure," Dale said as he passed the baby over to his dad.

"How's Mom?" Marlene asked.

"She's in a lot of pain. She's not up on her feet yet. The knee is very swollen so she's been in bed mostly."

"Sounds awful," said Marlene.

Waldemar looked down at the tiny baby. He was peaceful. It didn't seem that long ago that Gerry,

Dale and Brian were this small. "What did you decide to name him?" he asked.

"Keith," Dale answered, "but we haven't decided on a middle name."

"Hello, Keith," Waldemar said softly. "No middle name?"

"How about Waldemar?" Marlene offered with a smile.

Waldemar looked up from Keith's sleeping face and smiled. "It's a good solid name."

"Keith Waldemar Peterson it is then," Dale agreed.

Keith stretched and his arm burst from the blankets. Waldemar offered his big finger. Keith wrapped his tiny fist around it. He wiggled, squirmed and opened his eyes. He looked up into Waldemar's eyes.

"Hello," Waldemar said softly, "I'm your Grandpa…" He reflected on the word 'Grandpa' for a minute. He took a deep breath and said, "You and I are going to have a lot of fun together."

A week after Marlene and Keith were out of the hospital, they went to visit Ruth and Waldemar at their home. Waldemar opened the front door when he saw them approaching.

"Come in, come in…" he called, "it's cold today!"

Dale and Marlene hurried inside. Marlene was holding Keith, wrapped tightly in a warm blanket. They stomped the snow off their shoes. They greeted Waldemar with hugs.

"Hi, Dad," Marlene offered Keith to him. "Will you hold him while I take my coat off?"

"Of course!" He took Keith into his arms.

"Hi, Mom," Dale waved to Ruth who was sitting in the armchair with her leg propped up on an ottoman.

"Hi, kids! I can't wait to see that little boy! Bring him to me, Pete!"

Waldemar walked over to Ruth and unwrapped Keith. She pulled the baby from the heavy blanket and brought him into her embrace. "Oh, he's beautiful!"

Marlene and Dale came into the living room and sat on the couch. Waldemar took their coats and hung them in the front closet. Marlene looked at Ruth who had her eyes locked on Keith.

Ruth said, "I've been waiting for this moment for so long! I was sad I couldn't come to the hospital."

"We understand," Marlene soothed. "How are you feeling? How's the knee?"

Ruth grimaced, "It's terrible. It is really painful."

"Oh," Marlene winced, "I'm sorry."

Keith began to fuss. Ruth rocked him gently in her arms. "How is everything with you?"

Marlene sighed. "To be honest, I'm a little lost. He cries a lot and I'm not sure why."

"Tummy pains?" Ruth asked.

"I don't know. His arms are all over and he gets mad."

"Are you swaddling him tightly?"

"Swaddle?"

Ruth smiled. "Here bring me one of his receiving blankets and I'll show you."

Dale spoke up, "Is Brian home?"

"Yes," Ruth answered, "He's sleeping downstairs. Why don't you go and get him? I'm sure he'd love to meet Keith."

"Sure." Dale got up from the couch and went to the basement in search of Brian.

Marlene got up from the couch and came to Ruth with one of Keith's blankets in her hands.

"Lay it on the floor," Ruth suggested. "My dad always told me that the best thing to do is to wrap them up nice and tight. Keep those little arms from waving."

"Okay," Marlene laid out the blanket.

"Now fold over one of the corners. That's where you'll place his head."

"Sure." Marlene folded over the corner as instructed.

Ruth passed Keith to Marlene. "Put him on the blanket. Take the right corner and tuck it under the left side."

Marlene did just that.

"Good. Now bring the bottom up and the other side over. Just tuck the end in so it doesn't come loose."

"That's great." Marlene looked at Keith, wrapped securely in his blanket. "Nice and cozy."

The pair spent the next hour talking about all things baby. Ruth encouraged Marlene with his feeding, his tummy troubles and the best ways to rub his abdomen to help relieve his gas. She showed Marlene to touch Keith's opposite elbow and knee together gently, which would help keep things moving. Ruth assured Marlene that it would get easier, especially once she was feeling better herself.

"Are you nursing him?" Ruth asked.

"Yes, it's going well."

"In my day, nursing was not the thing to do. They really discouraged it. It's one time I wish I hadn't listened to the advice I was given."

"Did you have a tough recovery with Gerry?"

"Oh yes," Ruth answered, "I had to have fourteen transfusions after he was born."

"Oh my goodness!" Marlene exclaimed.

"Yes, it was quite traumatic."

"I should say. My hemoglobin is low. I'm tired and the iron I'm on — oh, it's terrible."

"I had the same trouble. I can sympathize."

"I'm glad we came today," Marlene smiled at Ruth. "I've really been missing my mom. I'm happy that you are here to help me through all this."

"After we had the three boys, I wanted to try for another, for a girl. My doctor and Pete said no, but I've never stopped wanting a daughter." Ruth looked Marlene in the eyes. "Now I have one."

"Thanks, Mom." Tears came to Marlene's eyes. "It's funny how when you become a mother you find you really need your own! It seems like Vancouver is too far away."

"How are your mom and dad?"

"They're good. They can't wait to meet Keith. Mom said that they're planning to make a trip out in the summer."

"That will be nice."

Marlene stifled a yawn. "Sometimes I feel like I may never feel rested again. I have no motivation to do anything. I'm trying to figure out the basics!"

"Give yourself time to heal," Ruth comforted, "This is the hardest job in the world. You can't expect to know everything right away. You'll learn as you go."

"I never realized how much there is to learn. Oh, and we really appreciate the buggy you bought. It's been working wonderfully."

Ruth and Waldemar bought a carriage for Keith. It could be used as a stroller or a place to sleep. "That's great."

"At night I rock him back and forth in the buggy until he stops crying."

"Poor little guy." Ruth looked at Keith. "He looks peaceful now."

Marlene looked down at her son. "He is amazing. It makes you realize how meaningless all of your other accomplishments are."

"Yes, children certainly are God's greatest gift to us. And especially grandchildren," she winked.

A week later, Ruth was in Leduc, checking on her mother and dad. Her dad had not been feeling well lately. She knocked on the front door and entered. Herman sat on the sofa, reading his Bible. Edith was upstairs, resting.

"Hi, Dad," she said as she joined him, taking a seat in a chair opposite him.

"Hello, *Schatzi*," he said wearily, closing his Bible and setting it aside. "How are you?"

"I'm doing fine."

"Tell me about everything with you." He crossed his hands in his lap. "What's the latest news?"

"Well, the plans for the group home are coming along nicely. It looks like we'll be able to have the sod turning ceremony this summer."

"Fantastic!"

"It's hard to believe that we've overcome another hurdle with Gerry."

"God has guided you," he said.

"Absolutely. I think God gives us government bureaucracy to test our faith."

"You do, do you?" Herman chuckled.

"Honestly, the amount of hoops I've had to jump through…I've been close to giving up. Between the pain in my knees and the red tape — it has seemed impossible. Once again, God gave me the strength to persevere."

"Is Gerry excited?"

"Yes. You know it's really lifted his spirits lately. Since Taffy died he's been so down. It's given him something to plan for and look forward to."

"He and that dog were inseparable. I feel for him."

"We all miss her but it's true, she and Gerry had a special connection.

"And how is Brian?"

Ruth sighed heavily. "He worries me."

"How so?"

"He seems lost right now. He's getting into all kinds of trouble — with drugs and alcohol. He is crossing the line over and over. Pete keeps bailing him out again and again and it infuriates me."

Herman nodded knowingly. "We don't all have the same approach to a problem. That isn't a bad thing. Pete has his own way. He has many things to consider."

"I know, Dad, but there are days when I'd rather have Brian locked up than be wondering if he's going to hurt himself — or worse, someone else."

"It is hard."

"I keep feeling like this is just a phase. That he'll learn his lesson and give up the lifestyle, but once again he goes off track."

"And yet we love them anyhow. Just as God loves us."

"It gives me a greater appreciation of God's love. Even though we sin over and over. He loves us, despite our failures."

"Brian knows that. He knows that there will never be a failure too big."

"I wish it was easier. I wish he'd make the right choices."

"Child, he'll be alright."

"I hope so."

"And Dale and Marlene? How are they doing with Keith?"

"He's a fussy baby, but they're learning. It's always hard at first. It's a big adjustment becoming a parent! I have to say, I love being 'Grandma'."

"Yes and I am Great Grandpa Bohlman," Herman laughed. "Sounds good, doesn't it?"

"You've certainly earned it!"

"I can't wait to meet him."

"Christmas is not too far away. It will be fun to have everyone all together at our place."

"And Pete? How is he doing?"

"Great. He's busy, busy. I am proud of all of his accomplishments. He's got a curling tournament this weekend."

"Can't keep that man away from the rink," Herman smiled.

Ruth smiled at her dad. "Enough about me, how are you doing?"

"Well," he nodded, his tone suddenly more serious, "I had some news this week from the doctor."

A look of concern passed over her face. "What is it?"

"You know I haven't been feeling well."

"Yes."

"They told me that it's cancer."

Ruth took in a sharp breath. "Cancer? What kind?"

"Colon cancer."

"Oh, Dad," Ruth looked at her dad, with deep concern. "I'm sorry. What did they say?"

"They think that surgery will prolong my life."

"Is it localized?"

"Yes. I'll have radiation as well."

They sat silently for a while. Each of them thinking over life's surprises.

"Are you worried?" she asked.

He shrugged and pushed up his glasses. "Should I be?"

Ruth reached out and took his hand. "No."

"I am an old man. I am in God's hands."

She looked him in the eyes. "Not too old."

Ruth cried as she drove from Leduc to Edmonton. She was not ready to say goodbye to her dad. Cancer was such a menacing word. Would he survive? Would he die? Would he be able to handle the treatments?

"What am I going to do?" Ruth asked Waldemar that night as they got ready for bed.

"There's not much you can do."

"I'm not ready to lose him." Tears began to roll down her cheeks again.

Waldemar looked at her compassionately. "I don't know that you ever will be. You and your dad have a special connection."

"And there is the other matter to consider…"

"What do you want to know?"

"Everything!" she exclaimed as she brushed out her hair.

Waldemar smiled and slid his feet into his slippers. "More specifically…"

Ruth sighed and put the brush on the dresser. "Really, is he ever going to tell me?"

Waldemar shrugged. "Perhaps not. Maybe he has a reason. Maybe there is something that is better off that you don't know about."

"Oh for heaven's sake, Pete! You sound like one of them."

He chuckled, "Okay, okay. Why don't you ask him?"

"Just march in there and tell him to tell me the story? Tell me the truth about her? Give me her things? Her photograph?"

"You've done a lot of things that took a lot of gumption. Asking your dad for your history can't be the most difficult. You've marched into a lot of situations and given your opinion."

She smirked. "True. I have."

"So go, visit him and ask him. The time is now. With his surgery coming up…well, you don't want to wait too long."

*

Ruth took a deep breath before entering his hospital room. She saw her dad, looking small and fragile in the hospital bed.

"Hi, Dad," she approached him and gave him a hug.

"Hello, child."

"How are they treating you?" She sat in a chair next to his bed.

"Just fine," he adjusted his glasses, looking over his daughter, "I'm scheduled for this afternoon."

There was silence for a moment. Ruth asked, "Where is Mother?"

"She'll come after it's all over. There was no point in her waiting around here."

"Oh." Ruth paused before saying, "I need to talk to you about something."

"Sure, go ahead."

"Why have I never been told about her?"

He looked puzzled for a minute, then understanding dawned on him. "Your mother?"

"Yes. I need closure. I need to know something about her. Anything."

Herman lay there, stony faced, thinking over what he could say. "It's complicated…"

"Why?"

"It was a difficult time for me…"

"I know."

"It's a hard thing to explain to a child."

"Dad," Ruth sighed, "I'm fifty-two. How much longer do I have to wait?"

"What can I say?"

"You can tell me about her. What was she like? What happened? How did you meet? Where were you married? Why did you love her?"

Herman was silent. Ruth waited for her father to speak. She could hear the staff in the hallway, the sound of a phone ringing, patients being discussed and beds being pushed down the halls. Still, he said nothing.

"Do you have her wedding ring?"

He nodded.

"Where is it?"

"Mother has it."

"Mother?" Ruth was taken aback.

"She was meant to give it to you years and years ago."

Ruth took a deep breath and let it out slowly.

He spoke in a shaky voice, "She died, Ruth. She died." He fingered the edges of the hospital blanket that covered him. He took a deep breath. It rattled through his throat as he let it escape. He felt an enormous weight on his chest. He felt the room closing in. His voice cracked with emotion, "My Ruth died." The last three words came out in a whisper, "A lifetime ago."

"Tell me about her…" Ruth begged in a frantic whisper.

"It's too hard." A tear slipped from his eye and ran down his wrinkled cheek. Ruth watched it fall from his jaw onto his chest, above his heart.

Chapter 28

"Do not store up for yourselves treasures on earth, where moth and rust destroy, and where thieves break in and steal. But store up for yourselves treasures in heaven, where moth and rust do not destroy, and where thieves do not break in and steal. For where your treasure is, there your heart will be also."
Matthew 6: 19 – 21 NIV

May 1974

Ruth

    Ruth finished up the lunch dishes and dried her hands. Everything was coming together on the group home project. It had been a long road but they were now planning the sod-turning ceremony for October 18. There had been times along the way where she had wanted to give up but now it was near completion.

This Sunday afternoon she, Waldemar and Gerry were going to Leduc to visit with Herman and Edith. Herman had battled his cancer with surgery and radiation and was now in remission. He had many difficult days in the hospital following his surgery, but he had come around with what was, so far, a positive outcome.

Ruth grabbed her cane that was hanging on the back of the kitchen chair. She hobbled down the hall to Gerry's bedroom.

"Hey, Gerry," she smiled as she found him sitting, looking out the window, watching the birds.

"Huh," Gerry said.

"Ready to go to Grandpa and Grandma's?"

"Aye."

She walked up to his wheelchair, hung her cane over the handle and wheeled him down the hall. Waldemar was already outside, polishing the car in the garage. Ruth went out the front door, down the ramp and around the side of the house to the garage.

"We're ready, Pete," she said as they approached the garage.

Waldemar smiled as they approached. "All set?"

"Aye."

Waldemar lifted Gerry into the back of the car, folded the wheelchair and loaded it into the trunk. Ruth climbed into the passenger seat. They drove out of the city and down the highway to Leduc.

Herman greeted them at the front door and watched as Waldemar skillfully maneuvered the wheelchair backward up the steps. Once inside, Herman hugged everyone warmly.

"And how is everyone today?"

Ruth answered, "We're good. And you?"

"Very good," he nodded, "very good indeed. We had a lovely service today at church. Your mother has been busy this afternoon making supper."

The men went into the living room and took a seat while Ruth excused herself to see if Edith needed a hand.

"Hello, Mother," Ruth said as she entered the kitchen.

Edith turned around, her hands in the sink, mid-peel of a carrot. "How are you?" she asked.

"I'm well, and you?"

"Just fine."

"Do you need some help?"

"Sure. Can you check the roast? It should be nearly done."

Ruth grabbed the oven mitts and pulled the roast from the stove. She put the thermometer in and checked it. "Yes. Nearly done. Maybe ten more minutes."

Edith nodded, her eyes on the carrots. "Why don't you get the platter for me and cut up these carrots."

"Sure, I can do that." Ruth moved around the kitchen with her cane, finding what she needed, and sat down with the carrots and cutting board at the kitchen table. She sliced them into fine sticks.

"How have you been feeling, Mother?" Ruth noticed that Edith looked thinner than ever. "Have you had an appetite?"

Edith responded curtly, "I'm fine."

"Are you doing okay? Something on you mind?"

Edith looked at Ruth. "I'm fine, child. I'm fine."

Ruth backed off. "Alright, I was just asking. You seem a little preoccupied."

"I am busy making dinner for my guests. Now if you're finished with the carrots you can carry them to the table. Then you can take out the roast and make the gravy. If you'd like to be helpful you can do so in a practical way."

Ruth's eyebrows raised. "Yes, Mother."

Supper was quiet; Ruth kept an eye on her mother. Father seemed tense too. He and Waldemar chatted about politics and spelled out messages for Gerry.

"How's the group home going, Ruth?" Herman asked.

"It's great. We're nearly there. Not everything has gone my way but I guess that's par for the course. The plans are nearly complete. It will be a few more months of red tape, signing contracts and perhaps in a year we might be moving Gerry into his new home."

Gerry agreed, "Aye."

"Won't that be wonderful?" Herman smiled at Gerry. "Good for you."

After supper, Edith and Ruth went to the kitchen to wash dishes and clean up. Gerry joined them, finishing his coffee at the kitchen table.

Herman and Waldemar sat down in the living room. Herman asked Waldemar about his plans for the yard this summer.

"There's some bushes I'd like to rip out. They're getting a little overgrown."

"I see." Herman looked around the room, making sure they were alone.

"Something on your mind, Dad?"

"I have something to tell you."

Waldemar's brow furrowed. "Sure, Dad. Go ahead."

"It's something I've been needing to say for a long time but it's never the right time — or situation. And Mother — she isn't too keen on talking about it at all. She'd rather deny that Ruth ever existed than talk about this. So between you and I, man to man…"

"Sure, Dad, I understand."

He cleared his throat. "I loved her more than anything," he said softly. "She and I met at church. She was vibrant and energetic…"

Waldemar listened intently, wondering what Herman was about to reveal.

"It wasn't until I was sick that we really connected. Her family cared for me. I was a young bachelor then. When she turned eighteen, I proposed."

It was then that Waldemar realized that Herman was talking about his first wife, Ruth.

"We had a lot of fun together. Life was good. Oh…oh I loved her. And then it all changed."

Herman looked down at his hands. He took a deep breath. It came out in a shudder.

"The doctor," his tone turned angry, "he was a drunk. I should have done something. I should have stopped him…he killed her."

Herman squeezed his hands together, his body tense. "We had a midwife. She tried all night but the baby was too big — twelve pounds. She had me go and get him. I should have known…there was no one else to help."

Waldemar shook his head, watching Herman as he told his agonizing story.

"He didn't wash his hands. He went straight in the room and he killed her. If he had been a different man…not a drunk…he would have washed his hands. She died a week later from Septicemia."

He cleared his throat. "She was very ill. She was sorry that she didn't have a chance to know her daughter."

Tears rolled down Herman's cheeks. His emotion was as raw as the day Ruth died. He took his handkerchief from his pocket and dried his face.

"It's been fifty-three years and not a day goes by that I don't think that…" Herman stopped. The words caught in his throat, "…maybe, things could have been different. If only…"

Herman sat, the tears coming steadily down his face. Waldemar said nothing. He looked at his hands folded in his lap.

"I wonder what could I have done? I should have noticed…I should have said something" He paused. "She was only twenty years old. We had so much living ahead of us."

"I'm sorry, Dad," Waldemar said gently.

"And then…and then it only got worse. Mother Lessing left with baby Ruth and everyone told me that a man could not raise a baby. Not without a wife…I just wanted my baby back."

Waldemar got up from his chair and sat next to Herman on the couch. He put a hand on his back. "I'm sorry, Dad. That must have been very difficult for you."

Herman nodded. He cried into his handkerchief. He took a deep breath. He dried his face.

"Let's talk about something else then. Before the others join us," said Herman.

"Okay, Dad," Waldemar agreed. He thought for a minute. He said. "Tell me about your garden this year. What will you plant?"

"Ah…this year I think I'll add forget-me-nots and daisies…"

After Edith and Ruth finished in the kitchen, they joined the men in the living room and chatted for a bit before Waldemar decided they should get on the road. As everyone prepared to leave, Edith looked at Ruth. "Can I see you for a second, before you go?"

"Sure."

Waldemar looked at Ruth. "Dad and I will take Gerry outside. We'll get him loaded in the car." He looked at his son. "Right, Gerry?"

"Aye."

The three men walked out the door, Waldemar expertly navigating the wheelchair back down the front steps. Edith reached into her pocket and pulled out her hand, close-fisted.

"Give me your hand," she ordered Ruth.

Ruth put out her hand. "What is it?"

"I should have given this to you a long time ago."

Ruth felt a cool metal touch her palm. She looked down and saw a gold ring, with three small diamonds. Ruth looked at Edith.

"It should be yours."

Ruth closed her fist over the ring. Stunned, she turned and walked out the front door. Edith shut the door behind her. Ruth's heart was pounding. She walked past her dad who was smiling, holding the front door of the car open. She got into her seat without speaking.

"Goodbye, Ruth," Herman smiled at her, as he was about to shut her door.

She looked up. "Goodbye, Dad."

He shut the heavy car door and waved at the family as Waldemar pulled away from the curb.

Ruth held the ring tightly in her fist. The ride home was completely silent.

That night, Ruth and Waldemar were lying in bed. Both had been quiet for a long time. Then Waldemar whispered, "Are you still awake?"

Ruth rolled over and faced him. In a sleepy voice she said, "Yes."

"Your dad talked to me today."

"About?"

"He told me about your mother."

"He told you she was supposed to give it to me a long time ago?"

"What?"

"She gave it to me!"

"What are you talking about?"

"As we were leaving! She just put it in my hand and said, 'I should have given this to you a long time ago.' I mean, how long have I been waiting for this?" She reached over into her night table drawer and pulled out the ring. "This was on my mother's finger. It's my first physical connection to her. A symbol of their love! Can you believe it?"

"No…I mean that's great." Waldemar looked at her with a puzzled look on his face. "He didn't say anything about that. That wasn't what I was talking about."

She propped herself up on her elbow, completely awake now. "What are you talking about?"

"He told me about your mother."

"Edith?"

"No, your birth mother, Ruth."

"Really!?" her eyes were wide.

"Yes."

"What did he say?"

Waldemar recounted as much as he could from the conversation, trying to be certain he hadn't missed anything that Herman had said.

He stared up at the ceiling and said, "You should have seen him. He was heartbroken. I could tell it was hard for him to tell me."

Ruth lay there for a while. She replayed the conversation over in her mind. She wondered why he had told Waldemar and not her. Finally, she said, "I'm glad he was able to trust you with all of that."

*

"Today," Mr. Nelson spoke to the crowd, "October 18, 1974, has been a long anticipated day for many of us with the Alberta Rehab Council for the Disabled. We are proud to be gathered for the sod-turning ceremony for the McQueen Residence. I'd like to introduce the woman behind the vision, Ruth Peterson, Chairman of the Adult Section of the A.R.C.D."

The people gathered around the grassy lot applauded. Ruth stepped forward, cane in hand, and stood next to Mr. Nelson.

She spoke in a clear, strong voice, "Thank you everyone for coming to celebrate with us today.

This day has been a long time coming. I have fought for independence for the disabled for the last twenty-five years. It has been an uphill battle, to say the least. But today, as we turn the sod for the new McQueen Residence, I feel as though all of our struggles have come together for the good of all of those who will be living here.

Our vision at A.R.C.D. is to make a difference in the lives of people with disabilities and special needs. With community support and collaboration, we want to provide resources and services that enhance the quality of life for individuals and their families with disabilities and special needs. All of us at the A.R.C.D. feel that this is a big step in the right direction.

I'd like to introduce Mr. Les Young, MLA from the Jasper Place riding. He is our provincial government representative."

The crowd applauded again as Mr. Young stepped next to Ruth.

"Thank you, Mrs. Peterson. Indeed this is a remarkable day. With the passion of people like you, visionaries in our community, these types of projects go from being a dream to a reality. I am thrilled to be able to join you for this special occasion.

"This will be Canada's first accessible group home for adults with a physical disability. It will be a community-based group living experience for nine adults with physical disabilities. We are proud to have this innovative, groundbreaking project here, in this neighborhood."

Ruth spoke up again, "Thank you, Mr. Young. Also joining us today is Commissioner Savage, a representative from the City of Edmonton."

Mr. Savage acknowledged the crowd. "Thank you, Mrs. Peterson. It is a great honor to be here today and to be a part of history. We all have dreams and aspirations, and the city is proud to have a resident like Mrs. Peterson. She is someone who is willing to volunteer her time and energy to pull all of the required bodies of government into action to support these valuable members of our community."

Ruth smiled and said, "Thank you, Commissioner Savage. And now it is my great pleasure to invite my dear friend Reverend Douglas Moffatt who will pray for this site."

Doug Moffatt stepped toward Ruth. "Thank you. I'd like to begin with a verse from Proverbs 31: 8 & 9.

"Speak up for those who cannot speak for themselves, for the rights of all who are destitute. Speak up and, judge fairly; defend the rights of the poor and needy."

"Let us pray,

Heavenly Father, we are gathered here today to bring honor to you. We know that you have created each of us in your image. Whole and loved. We thank you for organizations like the A.R.C.D. that are willing to support these children of yours.

"Thank you for the work of everyone involved to make this residence a place where You can be honored.

Amen."

"Amen" the crowd chorused.

"And now," Ruth chuckled, "The part we've all been waiting for." She gestured toward the small Bobcat, front-end loader behind her. "Now I actually get to turn the sod!"

Doug Moffatt gave her a hand up into the seat of the Bobcat. One of the men gave her a quick explanation on the controls. Ruth turned the key and brought the Bobcat to life. It took a few minutes and some maneuvering. Eventually, she got the scoop to dig into the earth. Everyone cheered as the earth showed its dark black underbelly.

Ruth stopped the Bobcat and climbed out with Waldemar's assistance.

He hugged her tightly. "Good job, sweetheart!"

She hugged him back. "This is great, isn't it! A day I'll never forget."

They mingled with the guests as the cool October air coaxed everyone into the reception room in the McQueen Community Building. The late afternoon turned into evening. Eventually, everyone gave their congratulations and headed home. Waldemar and Ruth stood in the aftermath of her success.

"I'm terribly proud," he smiled at her.

"Thank you. It is wonderful to know that this is the first group home in Canada. Gerry will have a place to live. It's everything I could have hoped for."

Chapter 29

"For I am convinced that neither death nor life, neither angels nor demons, neither the present nor the future, nor any powers, neither height nor depth, nor anything else in all creation, will be able to separate us from the love of God that is in Christ Jesus our Lord."
Romans 8: 38 & 39 NIV

August 1974

Wally and Keith

Waldemar bent down and picked up Keith. "Boy you're a chubby little guy, aren't you!"

Keith squealed and clapped his hands. "Ma, ma, ma..."

Ruth said, "Mommy's gone to the store for a few things. She'll be back soon. Do you want to play cars?" She rummaged around in the diaper bag to look for a toy. She came up with a small container of Cheerios. "Do you want a snack instead?"

Keith reached out his chubby arms toward the container. Ruth laughed. "Yes?"

"I think that's pretty clear," Waldemar laughed.

"Let's go to the kitchen then." Keith smiled and put his little fingers in his mouth and chewed them.

"Yummy fingers?" She smiled. "Are you getting another tooth?"

Waldemar sat down in a kitchen chair and popped open the lid on the container. He balanced Keith on one knee and fed him Cheerios with his free hand.

Gerry came down the hall, backwards, pushing himself with his foot.

"Huh," he said.

"Hi, Gerry." Ruth looked at Keith. "It's your Uncle Gerry. Can you say hi?"

Keith continued to stuff the Cheerios in his mouth. He looked wide-eyed at Gerry.

"Isn't he cute?" Waldemar asked.

"Aye," Gerry laughed.

Waldemar kissed Keith's cheek. He smiled up at his Grandpa in return.

"I think that after his snack we should go out in the yard," Waldemar suggested. "What do you think?"

"Aye," Gerry agreed.

"You can show him your favorite birds," Ruth said to Gerry.

Waldemar said, "We can also check the bushes and see if there are any raspberries. Maybe we can send a container home with Marlene."

The three sat at the table, admiring Keith. He was content to eat his snack. Afterwards Waldemar gave him his bottle. They watched his eyelids grow heavy as he drank. Eventually, he fell asleep in his grandpa's arms.

"Isn't he peaceful?" Ruth said softly.

"Aye."

"You know we've had a little practice at this," she said.

Gerry laughed.

"Three boys and now a grandson."

"Aye," Gerry vocalized.

"Yes, I always wanted a girl. It seems God wants to bless me with lots of little boys."

Gerry laughed.

An hour passed and Keith woke up and stretched in Waldemar's arms. His arms were tired of holding Keith but he wouldn't have moved for anything. He loved feeling his warm body against him. He loved watching Keith's closed eyes and his open hand — each finger completely relaxed.

Ruth checked Keith's diaper and they all went out into the backyard. Ruth laid out a big blanket on the grass. Waldemar put Keith on it so that he could roll and move around.

"Ah, I love summer."

"Aye." Gerry vocalized, indicating that he had a message.

"A, B, C…" Ruth asked.

Gerry stopped her at G.

"A, B, C…"

Gerry stopped her at R

"A, B, C…"

Gerry stopped her at O

"Group home?"

"Aye."

"I was there a few days ago. Everything is coming along nicely. The foundation is poured."

Gerry vocalized.

"Rooms?"

"Aye."

"I say six. The government says twelve. Twelve is too many. It will be less of a home and more of an institution if you have twelve people. Also, twelve is too many for personal care. You'd need a much larger staff and so on…I'm telling you, six is appropriate."

"Aye."

"However, it looks like we may need to meet in the middle. The architect has agreed on nine bedrooms and the government has conceded that they would be willing to accept nine."

"Aye."

"Sometimes you have to know when to agree. We'll see though — at some point they may be telling me I was right."

Waldemar and Gerry laughed.

Ruth chuckled, "I do know a thing or two, you know."

Gerry laughed.

"Look at Keith," Ruth pointed to Keith who had rolled himself to the edge of the blanket. "He's on the move." She went over and picked him up, sitting him on his solid bottom. He pulled off his shoe and began to chew on it.

Marlene came before supper and joined them in the backyard. She nursed Keith in one of the patio chairs while they all visited.

"How was he?" she asked.

"Oh he was wonderful." Ruth replied, "He had his snack, slept for a bit and now he's been happy to be out in the yard, soaking up the sun."

"That's great," Marlene ran her hand over Keith's brown hair. "Thank you very much for watching him."

"It's my pleasure. I'm happy we live so close. How's Dale?"

"Ah," Marlene paused, "he's busy. School is a huge time commitment for him. I do my best with work and balancing taking care of Keith. Dale has a hard time when Keith is fussy. He's never too sure what to do. We're both still learning I guess."

Ruth nodded knowingly. "It's hard when life pulls us in all directions. It will get easier; you'll never stop being a mom though." She looked at Gerry.

"Right, Gerry? I think I'll always be worrying about my three boys."

"Aye."

"How has Grandpa Bohlman been feeling?"

"He's not doing too badly. I'm starting to feel like the house might be too much for them. It's hard. They don't want to leave but it would be easier if they were here in Edmonton so I could check on them every day."

"Yes, that's true," Marlene agreed. "Have you talked to them about that?"

"No," Ruth sighed. "Not yet. But I need to. Perhaps the next time I see them."

Waldemar interrupted, "I was going to ask you. Did you want some raspberries?"

"I'd love some!"

Waldemar went in the garage and pulled out a bucket for picking. He headed down the side of the garage to the bushes and picked all the ripe ones he could find. He returned victorious and went inside to find a container to send home with Marlene. Waldemar carried Keith out to the car with Marlene once she was ready to go.

"Thanks again, Dad."

"No problem, when do you need us next?"

"Wednesday?"

"See you then." Waldemar waved goodbye as she pulled away in the car.

*

There was a stony silence in the car. The call had come in just before midnight. When the phone rang, it was typically for Waldemar, calling him to the scene of a crime. Tonight he was still in his uniform, having returned from a ceremony that he had been required to attend. When the phone had rung at such a late hour, he had been surprised.

"Your son, he's in rough shape. We just put him in the back of an ambulance, you should meet him at the hospital."

The caller had been an officer who knew Brian and knew that he was Waldemar's son. He had been the first to arrive at the scene of the accident. Waldemar had woken Ruth. They jumped in the car and sped to the hospital. Each one thinking over everything that had been happening with Brian over the last five years, the alcohol, the drug abuse and all of the illegal activity. Each of them wondering if Brian's downward descent had finally hit rock bottom. Each wondering if Brian would get a second chance to turn things around.

Waldemar thought about his youngest son. He was lost right now. Truthfully, things had been bad for a long time. The night before they moved from Saskatoon to Edmonton, Brian spent the night out partying with his friends. They had gone from bar to bar getting more and more intoxicated until everyone was laughing, hugging and crying all at once. They had been walking downtown and when passing a funeral home Brian decided he would get up and dance on the roof of the hearse. Everyone had been laughing and having a great time until the police spotlight lit up the show. Brian was booked, interrogated and placed in a cell. After hours and hours of questioning, Brian told the officers his name, and — his father's name. He also told them that it was their last night in Saskatoon and that because of his father's promotion they were headed for Edmonton. The officers drove Brian back to the hotel where they were staying at around five o'clock. He stumbled in, exhausted and drunk. A few hours later, Waldemar and Ruth went to wake him for breakfast only to be greeted by the foul smell of body odor, vomit and stale alcohol.

Ruth was outraged. She yelled at him to get up. Waldemar decided that it was better to eat with Gerry and come back to collect their drunken son when they were ready to leave the city.

They had no idea of Brian's antics the night before, other than it was obvious that he was tired and hung over. He didn't say anything the entire day as they drove back to Edmonton. At the end of the day, Waldemar pulled Brian aside and simply said, "This cannot go on. You have a chance to start over. Take it."

Brian swore that he would. He would stop the drinking, the drugs and everything else. He would find good friends, get involved with the church and point his life in a positive direction.

Waldemar learned about Brian's last night in Saskatoon much later. At the end of the summer, several months after taking his new post, a letter came across his desk — a letter he would have rather not read. It was from the Saskatoon City Police, stating that Brian had been involved in this serious act of vandalism. Waldemar confronted Brian and the story of the night had come out, how he had been booked, interrogated and held in a jail cell. All of the young men involved had been given the same choice: pay for a new hearse or be arrested. Waldemar had the embarrassing task of contacting the other parents and trying to arrange the money to cover the cost of the vehicle.

Now Brian was in an accident. Nothing had changed. Waldemar parked the car in front of the emergency room doors and helped Ruth out.

"I'll be inside in a minute," he said.

She walked slowly inside, being careful not to fall on her unsteady knee.

The hospital emergency room was busy. Ruth waited to approach the admitting desk.

Finally, it was her turn and she said, "I'm looking for Brian Peterson."

The lady looked up. "Brian Peterson?"

"Yes, he was hit by a car."

Waldemar joined her.

"Oh, yes. Right, Peterson. He's in trauma 2. The green room, second door on the right."

"Thank you." Ruth took Waldemar's elbow. They headed toward the room.

"Oh, Brian," Ruth gasped. She approached his bed. A nurse was adjusting his equipment.

"Hello," she greeted them. "Are you his parents?"

"Yes," Waldemar answered.

"He's stable for now."

A few hours later, Brian was in a ward bed, awaiting surgery. Waldemar sat on the edge of the bed, his uniform a stark contrast to the situation.

"How did it get this bad?" Ruth whispered to Waldemar.

"He chose this on his own," he whispered back.

"You kept bailing him out of trouble. He could have — should have — been arrested and locked up years ago! At least he wouldn't be here!"

Waldemar looked at his wife. He respected her deeply and had always admired her outspokenness but tonight he was angry too. "Do you think it would have been easier to have a son that was incarcerated?"

"I don't know..."

"What do you think the prison population would do to the son of the Chief Superintendent? My colleagues did me a favor by letting me handle things. You can't pin this on me. Brian's choices brought him here...not mine."

Ruth sighed. She was silent for a minute and then said, "I don't know what to say."

"Then let's leave it alone."

"I'm sorry. This isn't your fault. I'm just..."

The monitor beeped with each of Brian's heartbeats. The couple sat watching the IV bag drip.

Ruth switched gears and asked, "Why haven't they taken him into surgery yet? What is the holdup? Why aren't they giving us any information?"

"Relax."

Ruth paced back and forth. She walked down the length of the small room. "I can't. I need to go find his doctor." She turned and left the room, her knee throbbing as she walked out the door.

Brian's eyes flickered open. Waldemar touched Brian's hand. "Hey, Brian."

He tried to say, "Dad," but his voice was raw and broken.

"It's okay, don't say anything. I'll get you some ice." Ruth had left a cup by Brian's bed. Waldemar carefully pulled an ice chip from the cup and put it in Brian's mouth.

"Dad..." he croaked, "I'm..."

"Brian," Waldemar sighed, "you've really messed things up this time."

Brian closed his eyes and grimaced. He couldn't bear to look at his father, sitting there in his uniform.

"What happened?" Waldemar asked.

"I don't know."

"The officer says you were drunk."

"Yes, we were drinking."

"Were you high this time?"

"No...maybe...I don't know."

"Did you tell the hospital what you're on?"

"No."

"You need to."

"It was a long time ago...we were getting high this morning."

"I don't care. You need to tell them."

"Okay," Brian sighed, "I will."

Waldemar shook his head. Ruth re-entered the room. Once she saw that he was awake, she swung from being worried to being furious. She charged at him. "Brian, you could have killed yourself!"

"I know…" Brian turned his head to the side, looking out the hospital window into the darkness of the night.

"What happened?"

"I was riding my bike…they tell me…and I rode out in front of a car…"

"What are you on?"

"I don't know."

"You could have killed the people in the car! Innocent people!"

"I know!"

Waldemar touched Ruth's arm. "Enough."

"He never thinks! He never thinks about the consequences of his actions! I'm sick of it!"

"I know, Mom," Brian moaned.

"He knows…" Waldemar looked Ruth in the eyes. "He gets it."

"You always say that! You've been saying that since he was a little boy getting lost in the woods…he's learned his lesson. He won't do it again." She turned to face Brian. "Have you? Have you finally learned your lesson or are you going to end up dead before that happens? Are you going to ruin your father's career? Are you going to tear apart this family?! What is it? What has to happen to us for you to get it?"

"Mom…" Brian groaned.

"You've crashed your father's car, stolen your brother's Valium, crashed our house parties — coming in drunk and swearing, embarrassing yourself…You've disappeared for days on end, brought drug dealers into our home; you've lied to us and caused us endless worry! When is this going to end?"

"Mom!"

"When, Brian! Where's your turning point? When will you realize?"

He grimaced in pain.

"Where?" She stopped her tirade. "Where does it hurt?"

"Everywhere."

"You need to get into surgery. We're going to get you into surgery." Hot, angry tears rolled down her face.

Waldemar touched Brian. "Look at me."

Brian turned his head and looked at his father in the eyes.

"When are you going to love yourself? We all love you. When are you going to love yourself?"

Tears began to roll down Brian's face. "I don't know."

"What are you after?" Waldemar questioned, "What are you looking for?"

"I don't know."

"You've got a lot of talent. You have a lot of promise. You could do anything you want. What do you want to be?"

"I want to be you," Brian sobbed.

"Me?"

"I want to be you."

"Why?"

"You've done everything right."

Waldemar shook his head. "No, Brian, you're wrong. I don't want you to be like me." He sat quietly as the monitor beeped to the rhythm of Brian's heart. Finally, he said, "I want *you* to be *you*."

Chapter 30

"...For if God is for us, who can be against us?"
Romans 8:31 NIV

June 1, 1975

Ruth and Karen

It was a day that they had been waiting a lifetime for. The warm sun radiated through the windows and the building was alive with anticipation. The group home was complete, and Waldemar and Brian had been busy moving Gerry's things over and setting up his room. Ruth was busy talking with the staff and meeting the other residents and their families.

"Mrs. Peterson?" an older lady wearing a floral print dress approached Ruth.

"Yes."

The lady stuck out her hand. "Gladys McFinn. Such a pleasure to meet you. I am very thrilled that our son has an opportunity to be a resident here."

"Pleasure to meet you as well."

"Honestly, when Roger was born I didn't know what we'd do. If it wasn't for people like you and the Easter Seals — honestly, nothing would be done."

"I'm glad that the residence can be a benefit for your son as well."

"Won't it be great for Roger and Gerald to be friends?" Gladys gushed.

"Friends?"

"Yes, like roommates!"

Ruth nodded. "Of course, yes."

Gladys continued to talk and then Ruth saw Waldemar at the door, his arms full of boxes. "Excuse me, Mrs. McFinn, I must be going."

Ruth walked over to Waldemar and looked at him intensely.

"What?" he asked light-heartedly.

"How old is Gerry?" she asked quietly as they walked down the hall to Gerry's room.

"Ah," Waldemar looked puzzled, "is this a trick question?"

"Twenty-five. He's twenty-five."

"I know."

"Well I've told the government that the rooms should be big and the common areas small because Gerry is an adult. Isn't he?"

"Yes."

The pair entered Gerry's room. It had a sliding door to enter in, another part of the planning that Ruth had argued against. On the wall to the right of the door was a large window with a door that led out to a patio and onto the vast gardens. Gerry had a double bed, a desk for his typewriter and wardrobes for his clothing. Ruth had argued for closets but the government had not stated it was necessary.

"It really irritates me that the other parents see this as summer camp or something."

"What happened?"

"Oh this mother came up and asked me if her son and Gerry were going to be friends… so patronizing. She sounded like we were talking about our preschoolers."

"I'm sure she didn't mean anything – "

"When are people going to start treating the handicapped with respect? When?"

"Ruth, I'm – "

"If we were moving grown adults into an apartment complex, no one would…"

Brian entered the room, pushing Gerry.

"Hi, Mom, hi, Dad."

"Hello," they both answered in a cheerful tone.

"We've taken a tour and Gerry's ready to oversee the unpacking," Brian announced happily.

The conversation fell and Waldemar filled the wardrobe, hanging all of Gerry's slacks and shirts. Brian plugged in a television and pointed it toward Gerry's bed. After he finished that task, he lovingly arranged all of Gerry's glass birds in a cabinet for him to admire.

"How does that look, Gerry?" Brian asked.

Gerry used his word board to explain to Brian that some of the birds should be arranged differently, according to their types. Brian listened attentively and then worked on rearranging them to Gerry's satisfaction.

"Well, Dad," said Brian, "now that you're retired you should have plenty of time to help Gerry in the garden."

He nodded. "Yes, I plan to. I'm looking forward to this summer."

"Can you believe your policing days are over?"

Waldemar paused, thoughtfully for a moment. "Yes I can. I've got a wedding to look forward to, a new grandchild, a trip next year to plan for and plenty of projects I've been putting off for the last thirty-five years."

Gerry laughed.

"And you, Mom?" Brian asked.

"I'm pleased too. I've been waiting for this day for a long time. Now I have him all to myself."

Gerry indicated that he had a message.

"A, B, C..." Brian began.

Gerry spelled out, "How are your wedding plans?"

"Well it's mostly up to Margaret."

"I am really happy for you, Brian," Ruth said.

"Thanks, Mom."

Gerry then explained how he wanted his clothes organized and which books he wanted where. With all of them working together, the room was in order in no time. Ruth clapped her hands as she looked around the room with a satisfied smile. "Well, boys, we've done it!"

Gerry smiled broadly at his mom. "Aye!"

She went to him and slid his glasses up his nose. She kissed him firmly on the cheek. "You're finally home."

Tears sprang to Gerry's eyes. "Aye."

"What a day. We've all been fighting for your independence for the last twenty-five years and now you have it."

Waldemar cut in, "We're real proud of you, Gerry."

*

Marlene studied the newest member of the Peterson family. She was perfect. Tightly bundled in a pink blanket she lay in her bassinet, breathing in and out slowly, in perfect rhythm. Dale had brought Keith up to meet his new sister a few hours before with her mom and dad, Richard and Dorothy. Now everyone was gone and although exhausted, Marlene peered over the edge of the bassinet, not wanting to take her eyes off this magnificent little girl.

She had gone in for a routine doctor's appointment, driven by her dad who was in town along with her mother to help out. As soon as the doctor examined her, he exclaimed that she had better get over to the hospital right away. She and her dad had driven over and her dad, terribly out of his comfort zone, had whisked her up to labor and delivery. A short time later, Karen Louise had arrived on the scene greeted by her dad and her maternal grandparents.

Tomorrow morning she would be leaving the hospital to go home and face life with two kids. She sighed as she leaned back against her pillows. Could she do it?

The phone rang, interrupting her thoughts.

"Hello."

"Hi, Marlene!"

"Hi, Mom," Marlene smiled. "How are you? How's Kelowna?"

Ruth squealed, "I am so happy! I am happy to finally have a girl! Dale called us with the good news but I just had to talk to you myself!"

Marlene laughed, wrapped up in Ruth's excitement, "It's great, isn't it?"

"I always wanted a girl. In fact, if I had it my way I would have had three more, just to have one!"

"Well a granddaughter is the next best thing."

"Yes, I had to call it quits as it was getting risky for me to have anymore but now — now I feel complete. A little girl to buy dolls for, to have tea parties with and to love and adore."

Marlene looked over at Karen; it was hard to imagine all that yet. "It will be wonderful, won't it?"

"Dale said you're coming home tomorrow, we'll let you get settled but can we come by next weekend when we're back and meet our precious darling?"

"Of course. Any time is fine."

"When are your parents going back to Vancouver?"

"Next Wednesday."

"Oh that's good; you'll have a bit of help while you recover."

"Yes, I'll need it I'm sure."

As promised, the following weekend Ruth and Waldemar came to Dale and Marlene's duplex, armed with gifts and full of excitement and joy to meet Karen. Dale opened the front door, greeting his parents, "Hi, Mom and Dad!"

"Hello," Waldemar stuck out his hand, "congratulations."

Dale shook his dad's hand vigorously. "Thanks, Dad."

Waldemar ushered Ruth through the door. He helped her to a chair in the living room. They greeted Marlene's parents and exchanged small talk.

Once settled, Marlene brought Karen to Ruth.

"Hello, little lady." Ruth stroked Karen's soft cheeks. She was tiny and delicate, with large blue eyes that drew Ruth in. "Oh, Marlene, she's beautiful."

Marlene smiled, crouching next to Ruth. "Thanks."

Ruth touched Karen's tightly curled fists and wiggled her arthritic finger into Karen's grasp. "Hello, sweetheart, I'm your grandma."

Dorothy spoke, "Can I get anyone some tea or coffee?"

"Yes, please," Waldemar answered.

The others gave their orders of tea or coffee. Marlene and Dorothy went to the kitchen.

"Where's Keith?" Waldemar asked Dale.

"He's sleeping. He should be up soon."

"What does he think of his little sister?"

"He's actually quite enamored."

"Not like Gerry," Ruth laughed, "He wouldn't even look at you when we brought you home."

Dale shook his head and smiled. "No, Keith doesn't seem to mind at all. He'll be happy you're here when he wakes up."

"We've brought a big brother gift for him," said Waldemar.

"He'll love that."

Waldemar and Richard visited for some time, discussed politics and the weather, the summer's harvest and chatted about the upcoming hockey season. Dorothy and Marlene brought out coffee, tea and refreshments and set them all on the coffee table.

About an hour later, Keith emerged from his room, rubbing his eyes.

Waldemar got up and scooped him into his arms. "Hello, buddy."

Keith's eyes lit up. "Grandpa!"

"How are you?"

Keith smiled.

"Are you a big brother?"

Keith pointed at Karen. "Baby."

"Yes she is, she is your baby sister."

"Baby." Keith looked around the room at all his grandparents.

"Do you love her?"

Keith nodded. Then he buried his face in his grandpa's shoulder as Waldemar gave him a big hug.

Waldemar put Keith down. He toddled about the room, playing with each grandparent. He went over to his Grandma Minchin and crawled up in her lap. She rubbed his back affectionately.

"You're a pretty lucky guy," Richard said, "Lots of grandmas and grandpas here to love you."

Keith smiled, scrunching up his nose, and said, "Love."

Dorothy kissed him on the nose.

Ruth looked at Waldemar. "Why don't you get Keith his gift?"

"Oh yes, Keith, we have something for you."

Keith came over to his grandpa who was holding a small, flat box. He began to tear into the paper. He pulled out the dark blue jersey with the orange trim.

"Hockey!" he exclaimed.

Everyone in the room burst into laughter. "Hockey indeed! Yes, Keith," Waldemar answered, "your very own hockey jersey!"

*

A year-and-a-half later, Ruth and Waldemar were vacationing in Israel. They were on the fifth day of a ten-day tour. Ruth stood on the edge of the Sea of Galilee and felt the breeze whisper against her face. She tried to imagine Jesus here nearly two thousand years ago.

"Amazing, isn't it?" Waldemar commented softly.

"Really." Ruth leaned on her cane and adjusted her footing. The water was a rich shade of blue. Several fishing boats were out in the water. She imagined Jesus in a boat on these very waters.

The tour began in Jerusalem with a vast panoramic view of the Old City from the Mount of Olives. Then the tour bus took them to Dominus Flevit, the Church of All Nations and the Garden of Gethsemane. Ruth pictured the old olive trees as young saplings when Jesus had been there, the night of the Last Supper. She could imagine his inner struggle as he sat in the olive grove.

After that, they had been to the Temple Mount, scene of Abraham's offering of Isaac. Then they saw the Western Wall, the Western Wall Tunnels and the City of David. The first day ended with a trip to Mount

Zion, the Church of St. Peter in Gallicantu, King David's Tomb and the Room of the Last Supper. Again, the couple had been incredibly moved to be in the room where the Last Supper had been eaten. It brought a deeper connection to the practice of communion.

The second day, they went to Lion's Gate, the Pool of Bethesada, the site of Jesus' healing of the paralyzed man. Following this, they walked the Via Dolorosa, Jesus' journey through Jerusalem where he walked on the day of his crucifixion. It surprised Ruth that it was busy, bustling with vendors and tourists. There were old stone buildings on either side of the street and endless stone steps ascended through the city. It wasn't as she had pictured it. The journey through the city led not to a hill but to a church where Jesus' crucifixion was said to have taken place.

The third day, the tour group went to the Israel Museum, the picturesque village of Ein Karem, birthplace of John the Baptist, with the Church of John the Baptist and the Church of the Visitation.

The fourth day was in Tel Aviv. They had toured Jaffa, the ancient seaport mentioned in the story of Jonah and the whale. After that, they toured Caesarea National Park on the Mediterranean where Paul was imprisoned. At the end of the day, they crossed the Galilee Mountains stopping at Arbel National Park for an overview of the Sea of Galilee.

All the bible stories seemed alive and renewed in her mind as she stood along the shoreline today.

"Is it how you pictured it?" Ruth asked.

"Yes, I think it is. Bigger perhaps, more concrete."

The tour guide called out, "Is everyone ready to get back on the bus?"

The group slowly moved toward the tour bus. Once seated, Ruth read the items on the itinerary. "We're going to The Mount of Beatitudes where Jesus preached his Sermon on the Mount. Following that we'll see Capernaum, Tabha, Benedictine church, Bethsaida and finally The Yigal Alon Museum."

"Sounds good." Waldemar stretched in his bus seat. "Another busy day."

At lunch, Waldemar sat across from Ruth, eating a thick sandwich.

"We've had a pretty terrific year for travelling," said Ruth.

"Yes." The couple had also been to the Netherlands in the spring where Waldemar discovered more of his family history.

"I think it was amazing to see the palace where your mother worked…"

"And the house where Pappa was born…still standing."

"I loved meeting so many relatives of yours."

"Do you like their accents?"

Ruth laughed, "Nothing like it!"

"Retirement is so far pretty exciting."

"Yes, I think we have a trip planned every spring and fall for the next few years."

"It's nice to have the freedom to do this now."

"I wish my knee didn't give me such a hard time."

"It is what it is…not much you can do about it."

"No, but it does cramp my style…you know the cane and all."

Waldemar laughed. "I see."

"You know, Dad and I had a funny conversation before we left. I don't think I told you about it."

"No, what did he say?"

"I was talking about our trip to the Netherlands, saying how remarkable it was to be in the birthplace of your dad and he got really upset."

Waldemar wiped his face with his napkin and pushed away his plate. He took a long drink of his ice water. "About what?"

"Well," Ruth picked at her pasta lunch and took a bite. "He said, 'Promise me one thing.'" She paused to chew and swallow.

"What?"

"He said, 'Never got to Tuzcyn.'"

"His birthplace?"

"Right, I said that I couldn't promise him that."

"What did he say?"

"He was upset. He said that the Polish people are fearful that you will reclaim your land."

"No worries over that. I'm quite certain we don't want any Polish land."

"No — it's funny though, he still has such hard feelings against the old country."

"Well he's had a different life experience than you."

"True. Still — it seems strange to me." Ruth changed the subject. "The fiftieth anniversary party was better than I expected."

"Yes it was a successful event."

"They were so thrilled to have Keith and Karen be a part of it."

"Yes, I can't imagine having great grandchildren one day."

Ruth laughed, "That will be something!"

Waldemar picked up his cup and raised it in the air. "A toast."

Ruth picked up her glass. "A toast," she repeated.

"To travels and adventure with the woman I love. To health and happiness for another thirty years of marriage."

Ruth clinked her glass against his. "To health and happiness."

Chapter 31

"The Spirit of the Lord GOD is upon me; because the LORD hath anointed me to preach good tidings unto the meek; he hath sent me to bind up the brokenhearted, to proclaim liberty to the captives, and the opening of the prison to them that are bound; to proclaim the acceptable year of the LORD, and the day of vengeance of our God; to comfort all that mourn; to appoint unto them that mourn in Zion, to give unto them beauty for ashes, the oil of joy for mourning, the garment of praise for the spirit of heaviness; that they might be called trees of righteousness, the planting of the LORD, that he might be glorified."

Isaiah 61: 1 – 3 KJV

Fall 1979

Ruth stood at the front of the church, ready to share with everyone who had gathered.

"Thank you for having me today. I was asked by one of the elders to share with you about my life experiences and how God has taught me about His faithfulness."

A murmur went through the crowd. Ruth shuffled her papers into place.

She took of sip of water and placed it gently back down onto the podium. "Isaiah stated centuries ago, 'He gives us beauty for ashes, joy instead of mourning, praise instead of heaviness.' I read that passage often, but was unaware that God meant for me to experience Him in a special way so that I can say most empathetically — He gives joy instead of mourning.

"Our eldest son, now thirty years of age, was born a victim of Cerebral Palsy — a lack of control to the muscles due to brain damage. Often there are also difficulties with speech, hearing and vision. It is a long-term disability. It can be caused by a variety of factors. Gerald's was due to a lack of oxygen at the time of birth. In Canada, the prevalence of Cerebral Palsy is estimate at two per one thousand.

"Gerald has never walked, is unable to communicate verbally but is mentally alert. He is unable to feed himself or look after his personal needs, bathing, dressing and that sort of thing. He has received a basic education, has a great many interests and hobbies, and enjoys life to the fullest. He is a witness in a special way, displaying his love of Christ. Gerry and I simply refused to accept the traditional way that people related to the severely handicapped. For example, they were not to be educated, just dumped into institutions and forgotten! Our family is proud of Gerry's acceptance of his life but that's another story." Ruth looked up at the crowd and smiled.

"Our first born arrived in this world handicapped, but loved. Months went by before our pediatrician found the courage to make a diagnosis, at which time his advice was to 'place this baby in an institution and forget you ever had him!' And then came the mourning — my grief gave way to tears, to denial, to bargaining with God, isolation and withdrawal. Finally, after a bitter struggle, to acceptance. Acceptance not of the child — he was mine and loved — but acceptance of something I could not change, that — yes God had indeed permitted this child to be born into our family. During those dark days, my husband was my sustainer and stabilizer. He had his struggles, but because of our two very different natures, his acceptance came earlier than mine.

"I have been God's child from early childhood but now came the time for entering into a totally different relationship with God. I had always believed — more or less — that God keeps His promises, that his word is indeed truth. But the adventure with God had begun anew. His word literally became "a lamp unto my feet."

"God does not promise any of us a carefree existence on earth. I firmly believe God does not inflict punishment on us in the form of serious illness, or permanent physical or mental disabilities, but that suffering, unique as it is, is the ultimate triumph in living."

"Isaiah 41:10 reads, 'So do not fear, for I am with you; do not be dismayed, for I am your God. I will strengthen you and help you; I will uphold you with my righteous right hand.' To read it is mind boggling. To believe it is to experience healing. To live it turns mourning to joy.

"That verse became my anchor over the years.

"God enabled me to mourn for my child, to deal with my negative guilt feelings, to cope with rejection. He granted me a unique serenity in accepting my role in the unfolding drama of a unique position — the mother of a severely physically handicapped son.

"How does one accept the fact that your child will never walk, or worse still, be unable to communicate verbally? Certainly not in one's own strength. I knew all things work together for good for those who love God, but I asked God in all honesty — how could anything good come from this? Little did I know or understand 'His upholding by His hand' but I learned it with great difficulty."

Ruth paused, took a sip of her water and carefully set it back down.

She continued, "I strongly believe it is my Christian responsibility to be aware, search intelligently, and use all known channels available in obtaining help. God never does for us what we can do for ourselves. God uses people to help people. Thirty years ago, there was no available help. There was neither the knowledge, nor the skills. There were no special schools, no specially trained teachers and neither was there acceptance, public or private of the handicapped. These were the grim facts.

"Where did the quest for help lead me? Back to God. He did say 'Fear not' and oh how I feared that Gerry would not receive an education. But he did — because God opened doors for me. How I feared he would someday have to live in an institution — and that fear was groundless. Gerry lives in a group home with eight other severely handicapped young adults, all because God put me in the right place at the right time. There he is assured of a quality of life that's unique. He's independent, in the real sense of the word.

"God said 'be not dismayed.' I was dismayed: by the attitudes, by ignorance so often callously displayed.

"I was dismayed at the deepest level of being viewed as "the crazy lady" who was out to change attitudes and gain acceptance for the disabled; dismayed by the long struggle to have education available to the disabled. Dismayed that it took me so long to develop the word board, which enabled Gerry to communicate with us, by pointing to words and thereby constructing sentences. Gerry is able to type with a head wand and uses this method of communication. Now through modern technology, God has provided through others the 'Handi-Voice,' which actually speaks for Gerry. It has opened a whole new world — the spoken word!

"I have been dismayed and ashamed at that dismay, but God has helped me, upheld me and strengthened me, just as He stated He would. He has often confronted me with seemingly impossible tasks and often impossible people to work with in order to break barriers of ignorance, to change societal attitudes, to fight for acceptance and win!

"There were many struggles, many remain. Housing for the disabled is inadequate. Why must most of our disabled live in institutions? There are alternative solutions, less expensive; that's been proven. Where are the people to speak for those who are voiceless?

"I recognize that God placed me in a unique position and called me to serve in this area. For this I praise Him. I've stumbled, I've fallen on my face — and on my knees time and again, but He was always there upholding, helping to calm my fears. If anyone would boast let him boast of what the Lord has done.

"Rejoice with me — He has indeed given me joy instead of mourning."

Waldemar got out of his car and shut the door. The sound of it closing echoed across the vacant property. The services were over, the family was gone. Now only the hollow task of wrapping up the estate loomed before him.

Waldemar looked around the farmhouse one last time. His fingers danced over the worn tabletop in the kitchen. Victor had died. He had come to wrap up all of the details surrounding the sale of the farm and the estate. It had been strange to be alone in the old house with only the echo of their voices in his memory. He still saw his Mamma in the kitchen, rolling out dough, feeding the furnace and wringing out the laundry. He could still imagine his Pappa in the yard, sawing logs, even until the very end.

It had been a good life here.

He went to the bedroom, the one they had all shared as a young family, and opened Victor's dresser drawers. There were shirts that Ruth had sent, fancier than an old farmer would have cared for, with the tags still on. There were woolen socks, nearly worn through but still with the tiny VP embroidered on the side, made lovingly by Mamma so many years ago. On the dresser top were items for shaving and a comb. He packed it all into boxes and loaded it into the trunk of his car.

He was selling the furniture with the house. The realtor had promised he would take care of everything else. Waldemar had one more trip to the bank in Winnipeg and then would be heading back to Edmonton.

He walked out the front door and stood on the sagging porch. He remembered the summer he had worked so hard, screening in the porch, trying to get a cool, bug-free place to sleep on the nights he had stayed out late.

Victor was not yet an old man, only in his sixties. Waldemar had only just recently learned that he had a heart defect, one that had plagued him his whole life. Mamma must have known. Waldemar wondered if that was why Mamma had always been so easy on Victor as a young boy. Before he died, Victor had explained that he and Alice had both suffered from the same condition. Waldemar swatted a mosquito that hummed loudly by his ear. The porch groaned as he went down the steps and to his car.

Waldemar finished up his meeting at the bank in Winnipeg, closed all Victor's accounts and split his assets with the other members of the family. He stopped at a local restaurant, ate a late lunch and began his long drive back to Alberta.

As he drove, he reflected on the last few years. Retirement had certainly been an adjustment. Good and bad. The trips were amazing. At home — that was a little harder. He tried to help Ruth with the household chores and things but she had her own way of doing things. She was independent and wasn't used to him being around all the time. It had taken awhile to find his own new routine.

Brian was turning his life in a positive direction. He had completed a degree at the University of Alberta in 1977. He and Margaret moved to Wolfville, Nova Scotia, where he was studying theology at Acadia University.

Dale was in the ministry and had become a youth pastor at Trinity Baptist in Vancouver. It had been very difficult when they had moved away. He and Ruth had such a great connection with Keith and Karen. It was hard to believe they were going to grow up so far away. Marlene had been faithful with weekly phone calls from the kids. Keith wrote the cutest letters and sent pictures keeping them up to date with his life. There was one letter in particular Waldemar especially loved. It was typed out on the typewriter. "Dear Family, I'm having a hard time at this age. Especially with Karen. She bugs me but I am trying YES I AM. So can you please HELP ME? Love Keith." They promptly called and talked to Keith about how much his little sister was getting on his nerves. It was fun to be a part of their lives. They also welcomed a new granddaughter into the family that year, Shauna Marie.

Ruth continued to be active with ARCD and had won the President's Award that year. It had been an honor to see her recognized for all of her good work.

Waldemar had been working with the Baptist Union of Western Canada for some time now and was up for presidency for the next two years. It was something he enjoyed immensely.

During the summer, the two of them had taken a long awaited trip across Canada, starting from Tofino on Vancouver Island and ending in Cornerbrook, Newfoundland. They stopped to see baby Shauna in Vancouver at the beginning of the trip and ended with seeing Brian and Margaret on the East Coast. Ruth had thoroughly enjoyed Prince Edward Island and touring the Anne of Green Gable's property. It was a favorite story from her youth. The entire trip took seven weeks. It was a real luxury to travel without children, take their time and enjoy exploring Canada together.

When he returned to Edmonton, Waldemar had plans to re-do the back yard. Next summer, Keith and Karen were going to fly out on their own. He wanted to add a gazebo and a small pond with a bridge over it. He had already made a little boat from his scrap lumber. It was great to have time to do all these wonderful things for the grandkids. Amidst his sorrow, there was much joy.

*

"This is an impressive event," Ruth smiled up at Waldemar. She was wearing a fitted evening gown with long gloves.

It was three years later, in the fall of 1982. The couple were spending the evening with Waldemar's peers, from his RCMP days.

"RCMP functions always are."

"Do you miss the Saskatoon days? Parties all the time…"

"These reunion dinners are enough for me."

The crowd hummed with excitement as officers reunited and exchanged stories. Ruth and Waldemar found a table and sat down with their drinks. Before long, Waldemar spotted a friend and excused himself. Ruth sat quietly and listened to the conversation at the next table.

"…Speaking of brushes with death I had one of my own," an older gentleman said.

A neatly dressed woman in a pink gown responded, "Tell us about it, Clive, what was your moment of glory?"

"Well, I wasn't in the line of duty, no, nothing so heroic."

The guests at the table laughed politely.

"I was a young man, working at the sawmill in Northern Alberta."

"Did you almost die of frostbite?" another younger man cut in, laughing.

"No," Clive laughed, "Just listen. I was cleaning some equipment when my pant leg got pulled in, nearly severed my leg."

Everyone at the table groaned.

"It was awful, I mean really awful. The foreman got me out of there and called the local law enforcement. They planned to try to get me on a train to Edmonton."

Ruth eavesdropped intently.

"Well I made it part of the way. The train stopped in Kinuso. The Mountie knew of a nurse who worked there who might be able to help me."

"Did they figure she could come along on the train?" the lady in pink asked.

"I don't know," Clive responded. "From the sounds of things they didn't think I would live to make it to Edmonton. They were desperate."

"What's a nurse going to do?" the lady in pink asked.

"It was different then, they had skills, real-world skills, and I was lucky enough..." Clive answered, "Now," he laughed, "let me tell the story! The best part is yet to come!"

The guests at the table all smiled.

"So the Mountie and the foreman take me to the nurse's cottage. It's the dead of winter — freezing cold and they've only got a few hours to get back to the train to try to get me to Edmonton...perhaps with my leg, perhaps not. So this young thing opens the door, rubbing the sleep from her eyes and the foreman, well he thinks this Mountie's made a real mistake! I mean this little thing, she's not going to know up from down, let alone what to do with a nearly severed leg! Maybe a few months out of school, if that."

"Oh my," another party guest at the table gasped.

"Turns out she was a sensational student, indeed, only just barely out of nursing school. She turned her cottage into an operating room, laid me out on the kitchen table, had the Mountie deliver the anesthetic and the foreman hold up the lamp while she operated!"

"Are you telling me there wasn't any power?"

"I am indeed! Simply a coal oil lamp, my dear. Not only did she stitch the leg back together in a little over an hour, she did a pretty damn good job!" He laughed as he slapped his leg. "Like it never happened! The surgeon in Edmonton said he'd never seen anything like it! He said she had the hands of a surgeon twice her age."

"That is sensational!" the lady in the pink dress gushed. "Thank God she was there! She must have been your guardian angel!"

"Indeed," Clive took a long drink. "I never did thank her. I don't even know her name. Makes me think it was an angel."

Ruth slowly put down her drink that had been hovering in mid-air the entire time Clive had been retelling the night of his injury.

"Excuse me," she cut in as she approached the table, "I couldn't help but overhear your conversation…"

"Evening, ma'am," Clive smiled at Ruth. "Captivating story, isn't it?"

"Well, yes. For more than one reason though."

Everyone looked at Ruth expectantly.

"Are you Clive McIntyre?"

"Why yes I am."

"I only knew your last name," Ruth looked at him, "and your face."

Clive was puzzled.

"I worked in Kinuso in 1944. As a district nurse…I was twenty-three at the time."

Clive jumped to his feet. "Holy Mackerel! You've got to be kidding me!"

Ruth laughed, "I assure you, I am not!"

Waldemar returned and joined in the conversation, "Good evening."

"Good evening, officer," Clive shook Waldemar's hand. "I was telling a story of mine…about a night in Kinuso and it turns out your wife here — oh excuse me…"

"Ruth, Ruth Peterson."

"Your Mrs. Peterson saved my life, and my leg back in 1944!"

"Wow! It's a small world," Waldemar responded.

"Indeed!" Clive exclaimed.

"I could not believe it as I listened to you tell your story!"

"I know, what are the chances? Well, Mrs. Peterson, I must officially say thank you for saving my life, and my leg. God bless you and all of your good work."

"Truly a miracle from God."

"Skilled hands, sharp mind, faith in God. I am a lucky fellow." Clive looked around the table, picked up his glass and said, "Shall we drink to miracles from God?"

"Cheers," everyone chorused as their glasses met in the center of the table.

The evening went on with the others around the table sharing their exciting career stories. Ruth kept looking over at Clive and reliving that night in her cottage. After dinner and dancing, Ruth and Waldemar bid their goodbyes and headed back to the car.

"What a night for you," Waldemar said, smiling.

"Yes."

"You are quite the woman. And don't worry," he teased, "I don't forget it."

"It wasn't me that night."

"What do you mean?"

"It was God, Pete, God saved him. I was just the instrument."

Chapter 32

"I will repay you for the years the locusts have eaten…" Joel 2:25 NIV

July 1983

Ruth and Wally

Ruth clipped out the article in the paper about herself. She laughed as she read the headline from the *Edmonton Journal*: "Doors flew open for feisty Ruth Peterson, written by Marg Pullishy."

If one were to select a single adjective to describe ARCD's past President Ruth Peterson, that word would surely be 'feisty..'

Mrs. Peterson, who looks forward to retirement once she completes her two-year term on ARCD's board of directors, hasn't retreated yet. Her final post will be as chairman of the committee responsible for ADL and EHB.

But is it possible for a woman who has spent more than half her life working for and with disabled persons to pull back, to be content to take a less than active role in the constant battle for equality?

According to Mrs. Peterson, whose arthritis has necessitated the use of a cane for several years, the answer is 'yes'! "I'll always be interested in what progress is being made," she explains, "But I know that we all have our time, and when our time is up, we have to turn the reins over to capable people in the agency now."

Mrs. Peterson became involved with a disabled person more than 30 years ago, after her first child was born with Cerebral Palsy. She was shocked and appalled to find that the province offered no services or special programs for disabled children. When she approached her physician and voiced her concerns, her doctor was quick to tell her that there are no children with Cerebral Palsy in Alberta, that's why there are no special services or programs for them. Mrs. Peterson's quick response to the doctor: "Well there are now, because I have one, so what are you going to do about it?"

Apparently, the medical man was not prepared to do a great deal; as a result, Mrs. Peterson decided to do it on her own. Using the press to reach other parents with disabled children, a parents group was quickly formed.

Mrs. Peterson became one of the original founders of the organization that has since evolved into ARCD, as it is known today.

"Besides having no services available in the early 1950s," Mrs. Peterson recalls, "We [the parents and the disabled individuals] had to deal with the social stigmas attached to disabilities. Right from the beginning, I knew my son was socially acceptable, and under no circumstances would he be locked away."

"We kicked open a lot of doors in those early years," she continues, "And every time a door flew open, we found more problems...education, housing, transportation, everything."

But through it all, she never tired. At best, she would feel frustrated, at worst angry. She laughingly tells the story of the day she went to a government deputy minister's office, seeking his final approval on an innovative program to be implemented. When the minister showed considerable reluctance at the last moment, withholding his necessary signed approval, Mrs. Peterson brought her cane through the air with considerable zeal, whacking it emphatically on the minister's desk. In short order and without further discussion, the minister signed the precious document.

Undoubtedly, Mrs. Peterson has ruffled a few feathers in her many years of active service, but all for a good cause. "Looking back, I realize we have come a long way, from virtually nothing to a considerable number of services and perhaps most importantly, a social awareness of disabled people and the very real contributions they make," she says.

"Sometimes, I think we have almost arrived. I look around the agency's [ARCD] offices and think about the progress we've made, but the fight will never be finished, though I think it will take on a different focus."

"There will always be a need for public awareness; every new generation that comes along brings with it built-in attitudes, so the need to educate the public will always be there. And I think our primary focus right now must be to work with the medical profession, to make them realize that whether they are dealing with a congenital disability or a traumatic injury, there is still no smooth transition into the community. We have to make them understand that there is a great need for the proper support systems that will make the transition from dependence to independence smoother for everyone concerned. We've made tremendous strides in this area, but there's still room for improvement."

Mrs. Peterson feels more than comfortable leaving ARCD in good hands. "We have a very committed group of people here and that's probably the most important element, not only in the agency's continued growth, but in their future development. The main focus of the agency has always been to help disabled citizens become as independent as is possible, in whatever form that takes; we're prepared to give them the skills no one has ever bothered to teach them in the past. And finally, the agency will always, I hope, act as the facilitator in housing or whatever it takes to make disabled persons as independent as possible."

She tucked the article into a red photo album that was full of other newspaper clippings from her journey with Gerry. She looked up at the clock. Brian was due any moment. She picked up the box of photos.

Ruth spread out the pictures on the kitchen table. She heard a knock at the door and let Brian in.

"Wow, Mom, impressive," Brian said as he looked at the photos.

"It was really amazing."

Brian nodded enthusiastically.

She looked into the distance. "Such a warm group of people, they welcomed me with open arms…"

"Tell me about it," Brian encouraged.

"Well," she looked him in the eyes. "I arrived at Walter's place and he introduced me to all of the family. Then, after a little visit, we took a drive over to the old Lessing house. I mean — can you imagine! My mother was born there. It was rich with history. My history! I walked through the rooms where mother grew up, and oh, Brian, to hear Walter tell it, I felt like I had lived it."

Brian smiled, "I am so happy for you."

"He showed me hundreds of photos, explaining who was who on the family tree. He gave me all these pictures of my mother. I am sixty-two years old and this is my first picture of my mom." She waved one of the pictures in the air. Tears sprang to her eyes. She brushed them away and smiled. "I never thought this day would come."

"Anyway, after he explained the whole family history he told me all about the immigration to Canada, how our families settled where they did and why we were Germans living in Russia. He told me the personalities of all the family members and it was almost — almost like knowing them. We talked for hours and hours. I took notes and soaked up everything I could."

"What was your mom like?"

"He said she was energetic, talkative, a devoted Sunday school teacher. She was passionate about everything she did. In a lot of ways like me." She paused and looked longingly at her mom in the photo. "And, Walter says, she and Dad were desperately in love. He told me about her death — and what it did to Dad. He said it changed him profoundly in ways they couldn't understand."

Ruth pulled out a faded picture of her father and mother. They were laughing as he tugged on her arm. "Look at this, I mean, this is a side of my dad I can't imagine. So carefree."

Brian examined the photo closely. "Wow. Just fantastic, Mom."

"He gave me her obituary from the paper and the words that were read at her funeral service. Listen to this, "Her death was a triumph. Her relatives and dear husband stood at her death bed and were witness to her glorious home going. She saw heaven standing open and she saw the relatives that preceded her to heaven. With her marvelous singing voice, despite her weak condition, she sang the hymn 'Jesus, Lover of My Soul.' All present, her relatives and the nursing staff at the Misericordia hospital were admonished to lead Godly lives. She prayed for them all. It was an astonishing scene for all those who were present at her death. We can be assured they experienced a never-to-be-forgotten scene. Truly that is not death, to go to God in such a way."

Brian rubbed his arms and wiped the tears from his eyes. "Gives me goose bumps."

Ruth had tears rolling down her cheeks. Softly she said, "It was hard. She was awful to me."

Brian's eyebrows knit together as Ruth continued. "Nothing was ever good enough. Nothing. I wanted to be loved."

"What do you mean…"

"Mother — Mother Edith. It was awful. From the first day I met her I had visions of a wonderful mother, someone like Artrude's mom — boy, was I mistaken. I tried to please her, tried to know her, to be loved. She was so hard on me. The things she said — you'd never believe it. I still have dreams about it."

"Really?" Brian struggled to imagine his sweet Grandma Bohlman in this way.

"She cut me off from the Lessings. We lived in the same communities and yet I wasn't able to see them, to socialize — anything! What would my life have been like if I had been able to know my aunts, uncles…Grandma…" Ruth cried quietly into a tissue. "She never loved me. Never — always Dad, Lorne, but never me. She loathed me — what I stood for. Even when I was grown, she still kept things from me. Dad has never been able to speak freely about my mother. She chastised me for visiting my mother's grave. I was a grown woman! Even now — she wields this unseen cloak of shame and secrecy over my mother. It makes me so angry and so sad all at the same time."

"I had no idea."

"Why wouldn't she let me mourn my mother…why have I never been able to grieve my loss? Why can't we speak about who she was?"

Brian looked stunned. "Mom…"

"I never knew my mother's face, or how she died — anything…it was all kept from me. I only just received my mother's wedding ring in 1974! All she said was, I should have given this to you years ago…" Ruth shuddered as she cried.

"My grandmother, she tried — she tried to visit me and Mother stood in between us and sent her away. My grandmother raised me for the first year of my life. Can you imagine how close she must have been to me? She visited me after that, every time she was in from Oregon. Once Dad remarried, Mother cut her off. Grandma couldn't see me after they were married, when I was four. That must have been so hard for her. Walter said it was her greatest heartache."

Brian's eyes danced over the photos of his grandmother. Her soft eyes, her radiant smile…he suddenly felt the enormity of what his mother had lost sixty-two years ago. He felt his grandpa's pain anew as he looked at the photos of the happy couple. So much heartache. So much pain.

Finally, Brian spoke, "Tell me more about the immigration."

Ruth blew her nose and set her tissue down on the kitchen table. She went into the story of long ago, back in the eighteenth century when Germans left Germany and settled in Russia. She explained to Brian where the family had lived and told him how the Lessings, Schindels and Herman made their way to Canada, so bravely, leaving everything they knew behind, following their pastor to a new country, where they could worship freely. She recounted everything she could about all of her aunts, uncles and cousins.

"Don't get me wrong, Brian, I have happy memories with Mother. But this, this subject was always my greatest source of heartache. I guess we can't understand why people do the things they do. Maybe one day I'll have it figured out."

"Thanks for sharing all of that with me, Mom." He looked at this woman wiping away her tears, this woman he had always known as the toughest, most courageous person — and wondered, could little Grandma Bohlman really make her feel this way?

*

The kids came out of the gate, Keith looking excited and dragging Karen along behind him. She clutched his hand. "Hi!" Waldemar and Ruth rushed forward and embraced the two kids.

"Hi, Grandma and Grandpa!" Keith beamed.

"How was your flight?" Ruth asked.

"It was fine," Keith answered. "We had a snack, peanuts, apple juice — you know."

"That's great," Waldemar put out his hand to take Karen's. "How are you, Miss Peterson?"

Shyly she said, "I'm okay." He took her small hand in his and pulled her into a warm hug.

"I'm glad you're here."

The flight attendant that had been accompanying them took Ruth and Waldemar's information and surrendered the kids over to their care. She carefully unbuttoned the large 'UM' buttons from each of their coats. She said goodbye to the kids and turned to Ruth and Waldemar. "They did really well. True pros at this flying all by themselves business. Have a great time together."

"We will," Keith responded.

They all walked out of the airport together. Keith, now eight years old, chatted with Waldemar about how excited he was to go to a baseball game with him this week. Ruth sensed Karen's apprehension.

"Are you okay, sweetheart?" Ruth ran her arm around Karen's shoulders.

"I'm okay."

"It's the first time you've been away from your mom. That can be hard."

Karen nodded.

"I promise I'll take very good care of you. How's Shauna?"

Karen smiled. "She's good. I like to take care of her and teach her things. We play together all the time."

"I bet you are the most wonderful big sister a girl could have."

Karen nodded and turned to smile up at her grandma. "Thanks, Grandma. I think I might be."

They all got in the car and drove back to the house together. Once they had turned into the alley, Waldemar stopped the car and put it into park. He turned around and looked at Keith. "Want to drive?"

Keith's eyes widened. "Sure!"

Keith unbuckled and pushed open the heavy back door. He shut it and jumped onto Waldemar's lap in the front seat.

"Alright now," Waldemar put the car into drive. "...off you go."

Keith put his small hands on the big steering wheel. He carefully drove the car down the alleyway and watched his grandpa's big hands envelop his own as together they steered the car into the garage.

"Good work, Keith!"

Ruth turned to Karen in the backseat. "Tomorrow it can be your turn." She smiled, wide-eyed.

They all got out and went into the backyard. Waldemar showed the kids his raspberry patch along the side of the garage. He showed them the gazebo in the yard where they could play and best of all, a small pond with a bridge he had built so they could walk over it.

"This is great, Grandpa!" Keith exclaimed as he raced back and forth over the bridge. "Do you have that boat you were telling me about?"

Waldemar laughed, "How about we eat some lunch and then we can go look for the boat."

The kids went inside, washed their hands and sat at the table. Ruth made sandwiches for each and let them choose candy for dessert. After lunch, they went over their plans for the week. Waldemar was going to take Keith to a baseball game. All of them were going to go to the zoo, Fort Edmonton Park and various other Edmonton attractions. There would also be plenty of time for play. Ruth was ready with an assortment of toys for Keith and Karen.

The rest of the afternoon they spent in the backyard playing with the boat. They sailed pinecones back and forth under the bridge, delighting in the cool pond water. Karen and Ruth played in the gazebo, cutting pictures of food from Ruth's old magazines so that they could play restaurant together.

"And what would you like to order?" Karen asked Ruth after the cutting-out job was complete.

Ruth's eyes scanned over the cut-out food. "A bit of shepherd's pie, chocolate cake and chocolate milk to drink."

Karen carefully wrote the order down on a notepad that Ruth had given her. "Okay," she cocked her head and looked up at her grandma, "what's shepherd's pie?"

Ruth pointed to the magazine cut out. "That one. That meat pie."

"Okay. So you want meat pie, chocolate cake for desert and chocolate milk. Got it."

She went to work arranging her dishes and pretending to cook.

Ruth watched her granddaughter intently as she whisked herself away into an imaginary kitchen. She looked outside to Keith, carefully stacking pinecones on the boat. Oh how she had missed these kids since they moved away to Vancouver. She adored being a grandma and she was going to make sure that they had the best week together.

Karen brought over a tray of food carefully arranged on toy dishes.

"Oh thank you, waitress," Ruth said sweetly, "This looks like the best meal I've ever had!"

"Eat your meat pie before you eat your cake," Karen looked at her grandma with big serious eyes, "the cake is for dessert."

Ruth laughed, "Yes, ma'am, I will."

Waldemar sat down on the ground next to the pond and watched Keith.

"How's school?"

"Okay."

"Are you excited about grade three?"

"Yes. I like school."

"How many pinecones can the boat hold before it sinks?"

Keith looked at his grandpa and laughed, "I don't know!"

"Shall we figure that out?"

"Okay — I'll look for more pinecones." Keith got up and began looking around the yard for more pinecones.

Ruth was ready for bed, in her housecoat, reading at the kitchen table. The kids were asleep in the basement, in the spare room. Waldemar had already gone to bed, leaving the house still and quiet.

"Mom!" Karen cried out from the basement.

Ruth jumped up, nearly knocking her chair over. She went down the stairs as quickly as her old knees would allow her. She burst into the bedroom and found Karen sitting up in bed, white as a ghost.

She was crying, "My tummy hurts so bad!"

Ruth grabbed the garbage can and put it under Karen's chin. Just then, Karen heaved out the contents of her stomach. When she finished retching she cried, "I need my mom!"

"It's okay, sweetheart, Grandma's here." She ushered Karen from the bed and took her upstairs. Keith slept soundly. Karen looked down at her pajamas and fingered her hair.

She burst into tears again. "Oh no — I got it on my jammies and in my hair!"

Ruth shushed her, "It's okay, we can fix all that." She lovingly took Karen into the kitchen and had her climb up on a kitchen chair next to the sink. She helped her lift her nightgown over her head. She gave her a big towel to wrap around her shoulders.

"Here we are. Now you stay right here. I'm going to get my special shampoo." Ruth went down to the bathroom and brought back her shampoo. She had Karen lean over the sink and began to wet Karen's long brown hair. She then massaged in the shampoo, making plenty of suds. Karen relaxed and stopped crying.

"Thanks," she sniffled.

"Think nothing of it, my dear."

After it was washed, Ruth wrapped Karen's hair up in the towel. She went downstairs to see if Marlene had packed a spare set of pajamas. Sure enough there were. She brought them up to Karen. She helped her into the bottoms and then buttoned each button on the top. After that, they went into the living room where Ruth combed out Karen's long hair.

"Were you feeling sick after supper?" Ruth asked gently.

"No."

"Were you feeling sick before bed?"

"Yes."

"Are you worried about something?"

"It's kind of scary downstairs."

Ruth nodded, understandingly. "I see. Do you want to sleep upstairs?"

Karen shrugged.

"How about I set up some blankets on the couch for you. I can make it nice and cozy."

Karen nodded.

Ruth made a bed on the couch and tucked Karen in. She stroked Karen's hair until she fell asleep.

Ruth looked down at Karen. She bent down and kissed her on the cheek.

She sang softly, "May the Lord bless you and keep you. May the Lord make his face shine upon you. And give you peace, and give you peace forever."

Chapter 33

"Therefore, as God's chosen people, holy and dearly loved, clothe yourselves with compassion, kindness, humility, gentleness and patience. Bear with each other and forgive whatever grievances you may have against one another. Forgive as the Lord forgave you."
Colossians 3: 12 & 13 NIV

May 1985

Herman and Edith

"Well, Mother, I think we're almost through here," Ruth called from the kitchen.

It was a warm spring day. The buds were bursting on the trees, the grass was changing from its dull brown to a brilliant green. The birds were calling to one another and the members of the community were out, emerging from their winter hibernation. Neighbors were greeting each other. Yards were tidied. New annuals were planted. Ruth had been inside all day in the small one-bedroom apartment that Herman and Edith had called home for the last few years. They had come to Edmonton to be closer to Waldemar and Ruth, but now they needed to be somewhere where their medical and personal needs could be met, around the clock. Ruth had suggested a few places in Edmonton but Herman had been anxious to return to Leduc, to his community and his home for the last sixty years.

    A few weeks ago, the majority of the furniture and personal items had been moved or sold. As the month came to an end, Ruth was preparing the apartment for the next tenants.

    They were packing the few belongings that remained and giving the home a thorough cleaning. Edith had come from Leduc to wrap things up. She was perched on the last remaining chair, near the front door, watching her stepdaughter lean on the mop handle.

    "The floors look as clean as they can get, and if not, this old knee of mine has just about had it." She grimaced as she reached for her cane. She smiled at Edith. "Good enough, shall we say?"

    Edith looked at Ruth. At last she said, "Thank you."

    "It's no trouble. I can have one look around and make sure we haven't missed anything."

    "That's fine."

    Ruth limped down the hall to the bedrooms, leaning heavily on her cane, her arthritis screaming out from every joint. She opened every cupboard, searching for any last items. Edith stood up, went to the window and looked out on the patio that had become familiar over the last few years.

    Ruth came up behind her and studied the pots with flowers already brimming over. Herman had started his seeds indoors a few months earlier. Waldemar had helped him plant them outdoors at the beginning of the month. "Dad's sure going to miss his gardening, isn't he?"

Edith sighed, "Yes, Ruth. Yes he is."

Ruth turned and looked at Edith. Her gaze was fixed outside.

"Are you okay?" she asked.

A heavy silence filled the room.

"We've had to sell most everything."

Ruth nodded.

"All of your things, they — they don't mean as much any more."

"It must be hard." The room was heavy with silence.

"You know, when you have to let it go, you realize — it never meant anything anyway."

Edith walked away from the window and went down the hall, retracing Ruth's steps, walking into and out of every room. She came back to Ruth, still standing at the window. The keys were clutched in her white-knuckled hands. She looked into Ruth's eyes.

"It could have been so different."

Ruth was quiet for a moment. She knew exactly what she meant. "Well, it was out of my hands, Mother."

"I wished you had been mine," Edith whispered. Edith handed Ruth the keys and sighed, "You've got to forgive me."

Ruth looked at the old woman in front of her. Just a shadow of the lady she had once been. Neither woman said a word. Ruth rolled the statement over in her mind again and again. "I do," she whispered. Silence rolled in between them.

Finally Edith spoke. "Do what you want with it, it doesn't matter now." She turned and walked out the door.

As Ruth looked around, she noticed one final box, left for her. On the top was marked "Ruth" in Edith's precise handwriting. She took the box and carried it out to the car where Edith was waiting.

"What's this, Mother?"

"It's yours, Ruth," reluctantly she added, "always should have been."

Ruth tried to imagine Edith lugging this box from house to house, wondering what had kept her from simply giving it to her.

She placed the box on the top of the trunk and carefully pulled back the tape to open it. Edith leaned against the passenger side door, looking away.

Upon opening the box and unwrapping the contents, Ruth found beautiful black dishes with gold edging.

"What are these?"

"They belonged to your father, as a wedding gift," Edith spat out the words.

Understanding dawned on Ruth. "Oh. I see."

Ruth looked at Edith, leaning there with her arms crossed. Her hair in tight gray curls, her sweater pulled across her chest. She was rigid. Ruth tried to think of something to say. Some way to address the conversation they just had — some way to make peace. She wanted to say thank you for this gift.

She packed the dishes back up and placed them carefully in the back seat on the floor.

"Ready to go?" she asked as she opened the front door.

Edith nodded, opened the car door and got in. The women drove in silence back to Leduc.

*

"…She was a quiet woman," Ruth looked up at all the guests in the church, "a woman who was faithful and true to Dad. A caring mother for Lorne and I, and a wonderful grandmother to Mark and Byron, Gerry, Dale and Brian. Above all, she was a woman who was deeply devoted to her church and community.

    I want to thank you all for coming today to pay your respects to my mother. A friend to us all and a woman we won't soon forget."

    It was September 1985. Edith had gone home to be with the Lord. The organ started up. The organist pounded out the hymn, *Great is Thy Faithfulness*. Ruth sang whole-heartedly.

    After the service, everyone proceeded to the graveyard where a short ceremony was held. Ruth kept her eyes on the casket as the minister spoke. Waldemar stood behind her with his hand on the small of her back. She steadied herself on the back of a chair where her dad sat.

    At the end of the ceremony, Ruth watched the casket as it was lowered into the ground.

    "Earth to earth, ashes to ashes, dust to dust. In sure and certain hope of the resurrection into eternal life." The pastor scattered a handful of earth onto the casket.

    Ruth dabbed at her cheeks. She rubbed her father's shoulder. He blew his nose loudly into a handkerchief.

    This week had been a flurry of helping to clean out Herman and Edith's double room and relocating Herman to his own single room. Ruth had been busy ordering flowers, preparing the order of service and coordinating all the details of the reception. Some of the church ladies made sandwiches. Others made desserts until everything had come together. Lorne and Shirley had flown out with their kids. Dale and Marlene had come in from Vancouver. Edith had passed suddenly, in her sleep. Since then Ruth had been in full planning mode, avoiding the emotions that were suddenly sweeping over her.

The service was at Temple Baptist, down the street from Herman and Edith's old house. Many friends had come from Salem Manor as well as family from Saskatchewan, and all of the people who had known and respected Herman and Edith as members of their community and church.

The pastor finished his final prayer and dismissed everyone from the graveside. Ruth lingered with her father. Gerry was crying as Brian pushed him back to the car. She watched them go.

Ruth rubbed her dad's shoulder. "Whenever you're ready."

"I just need a minute," he said softly.

Herman stared into the hole where Edith's body was to lay. They had bought a plot here together a long time ago — in preparation for this day. He would miss her constant presence, her attention to detail. Her concern for him. Her love for him. It had been a good life together. They were like a well-worn pair of shoes…comfortable and purposeless without the other.

"What now?" he said quietly. "What now?"

He had been here before, at the graveside of his first wife. Sixty-four years ago, he had not been ready to say goodbye. Now his reunion with her, his time, didn't seem so far away. He knew the hope of seeing all of those who had gone before him. His wives, his family, relatives he had lost in the old country. His mother and father, his little sister Martha. Soon they would all be reunited in God's Kingdom. Thank God.

Herman blew a kiss toward the casket. "See you soon."

*

It was Christmas, four years later and Ruth was busy preparing a turkey for dinner that night. She picked up the baster and carefully squeezed the juices out over the top of the turkey. The sweet aromas of turkey, potatoes, casseroles and pumpkin pie filled the condominium.

 Shortly after Edith died, Waldemar and Ruth sold their Ottwell home and moved into a downtown high-rise. It was a stately building on 100th Avenue. It had an old-fashioned brick exterior and an opulent lobby. Their suite was enormous, boasting a large entrance, two bedrooms, two bathrooms, a living and dining room as well as a wonderful screened-in balcony. They were on the tenth floor and had a peek-a-boo view of the river valley. There was a family room that connected to the living room where they had a large TV and piano. Off the kitchen was a cozy eating area with a large pantry space.

 It was the right time to downsize. Owning a home at their age no longer seemed practical, and although Waldemar would miss his garage and garden, the upkeep was time consuming. Ruth realized that she desperately needed her life to be on one level as her knee and arthritis were worse than ever. Their new condominium had the luxury that they loved.

 The grandkids had been out from Gibsons, British Colombia to visit. First, Keith on his own and then the girls together. They came many times during the first two years that they moved in. The girls especially loved sleeping in the king-sized bed and playing games out on the balcony.

 In the summer of 1987, Dale and Marlene relocated back to Edmonton. Dale was called to pastor a church. Waldemar and Ruth left Braemar Baptist, where they were very involved, and began to attend Dale's church.

 Brian and Margaret divorced. Brian remarried a young lady named Darlene. They lived in a small house in Edmonton with a couple of dogs. Brian was a key part of Gerry's life, helping him in any way he could. Darlene had taken to Gerry, enjoying his company and assisting him with his day-to-day needs.

Gerry began to write and published his first book, *Accepting Reality*. Ruth had collaborated with him in his personal record of his struggles with Cerebral Palsy. He sold copies at church and in local bookstores.

Today Waldemar was off to Leduc to pick up Herman. He was looking forward to an afternoon with his great grandkids. He had a particularly soft spot for Keith who he had grown to know so well. Brian and Darlene would be joining them later that afternoon. Ruth made up some games for the children and had wrapped a few small gifts and placed them under the tree. Trays of chocolates and desserts lay out along the buffet. The condominium sparkled with tiny Christmas lights and ornaments.

Ruth opened a can of cranberries and plunked its jiggly contents into a serving dish. She carefully covered it with plastic wrap and carried it to the table. She made up sandwiches for Waldemar and her dad for when they returned. She looked at the clock on the kitchen wall. *They should be here any time now.*

Before long, she heard the click of the key in the front door and in came Herman with Waldemar behind him, gripping Herman's elbow. Herman leaned heavily on his cane. He was ninety-four and doing remarkably well. Waldemar gently helped Herman down into an overstuffed chair near the door and helped him with his rubber-soled shoes, then eased his coat off his shoulders.

"Hi, Dad!" Ruth gave him a hug and a kiss. "How are you?"

Herman smiled at Ruth, his hand smoothing down his gray hair, "I'm well. And you?"

"Just fine. Come on in. Can I get you some lunch?"

Waldemar hoisted Herman to his feet. The pair followed Ruth to the kitchen table where their sandwiches were laid out.

Herman went and sat in the blue wing-backed chair in the family room after lunch. Waldemar turned on the radio to some Christmas carols. Before long, Herman was fast asleep.

Soon all of the other family arrived: Gerry, Brian, Darlene, Dale, Marlene and the three children. The turkey had been basted for the last time and was resting on the counter. The food was coming to its point of perfection. The coffee was hot. Everyone found their place around the large dining room table. Waldemar gave thanks.

"Heavenly Father, we come to you today with a spirit of thanksgiving. We thank you that we can all be together on this day, the birth of your son. We acknowledge your incredible gift to us. Thank you that we can spend time with one another, sharing in the joy that this season brings. Thank you for this meal. Bless all those who partake in it. In your Holy name we pray, Amen."

Everyone around the table echoed, "Amen."

Everyone feasted. Afterwards the children helped themselves to the heaps of chocolates and desserts. The table was covered with trays of Nanamio bars, peanut butter squares, bowls of nuts, oranges and every imaginable chocolate. Nothing was off limits today. The adults chatted and drank coffee and tea. Karen and Shauna visited quietly and gobbled up as many treats as possible.

Ruth suggested that the children play a game after supper. They could try to count all the angels in the house. Ruth had a particular fondness for angels so this was no easy task. With notepads and pencils in hand, the three of them moved about the house, carefully counting. The winner, Karen, was awarded a prize for finding nearly all of the 176 angels. After the game, they opened gifts and played board games.

Keith found himself seated on the sofa next to his great grandpa as the night wore on.

Herman patted Keith's hand. "You're becoming a young man now, Keith."

"Yes, Grandpa," Keith nodded.

"There is a lot of responsibility for a man your age. Tell me, what are you going to do with yourself?"

"Do you mean for school?"

Herman nodded.

"Well, I'm going to go to university, to study business perhaps."

"Ah, a wise choice. You know I had my own store for many, many years."

"Yes," Keith smiled, "yes I do."

"It was a labor of love I tell you. Many hours at the counter, many hours behind my desk, placing orders…" his voice trailed off. "Make sure, Keith, that family comes first for you." He looked Keith in the eyes. "I mean when you have a family one day."

"I will."

"And God, make God the center of everything you do. Then you will be successful."

"I will, Grandpa."

"I am proud of you. You have a quiet, humble strength that I admire. I know you will do great things."

Keith wiped a tear from his cheek. He loved this old man so fiercely. He was quiet and kind, God-fearing and humble. He had accomplished many great things and yet boasted about none.

"I love all my great grandchildren. I am a rich man to know you and your darling sisters. God has given me the gift of knowing not only my children, my grandchildren but also my great grandchildren. I am a blessed man."

"I love you, Grandpa. Merry Christmas."

Herman squeezed Keith's hand. "Merry Christmas, Keith."

Chapter 34

"In my Father's house are many rooms; if it were not so, I would have told you. I am going there to prepare a place for you. And if I go and prepare a place for you, I will come back and take you to be with me that you may also be where I am." John 14: 2 & 3 NIV

<u>February 1989</u>

Byron Bohlman (Grandson) with Herman

Brian came down the familiar hall in Salem Manor, pausing for a moment at his grandpa's door. He visited almost every week. Some weeks were better than others. If Herman was sitting up in his chair, he could be very lucid and they could carry on a reasonable conversation. When he was in his bed, however, his thoughts were in another place and time. Sometimes he was sleeping, and if not he would doze in and out of the conversation. Brian paused for a moment inside the door. The chair was empty.

"Hello?" he called softly, not wanting to startle his grandpa, as he bent down to tie his shoe.

"Ruth? Is that you?" he called weakly from the bed.

Brian was about to say no when Herman began to speak.

"I love you."

Brian came into the room quietly and said nothing. Herman's eyes were half-open and his gaze was away from the door, toward his window. He was about to say that he loved him too when Herman went on.

"You're beautiful." He paused. "I love you."

Brian looked around the room, and said nothing.

"You're the only woman I've ever loved." Herman's gnarled hands moved over his blankets, smoothing the unseen wrinkles. "We were young. So in love. The future was ahead of us. I would have given anything to be with you."

Brian's eyes widened as he realized that Herman thought that he was Ruth. He started to say something and then Herman's eyes shut.

"You're the only woman I've ever loved. I love you. We will meet again."

Brian's heart quickened. He slowly backed out of the room. He walked down the hall replaying the scene in his mind.

*

Ruth walked down the hospital hallway. She took a deep breath in and squeezed Waldemar's hand before they entered the room. He smiled down at her reassuringly.

"Hi, Dad," Ruth called out as she entered.

Herman stirred.

She approached his bedside and patted his hand. "How are you?"

His eyes met hers. "I've been better."

"How is the pain?"

"Manageable."

Waldemar helped Ruth into a chair that was next to the bed. "Hi, Dad."

"Hi, Pete."

"Are they taking good care of you?" Ruth asked.

Herman shook his head. "I want to go home."

"I know, but this is where you need to be."

"I want to go home," he said softly.

"I'll talk to the doctors again and see what we can find out. Okay?"

Herman nodded and closed his eyes.

"I hate it here."

"I know."

"No you don't."

"Okay, fair enough, I don't know."

"I want to go home," he agonized, his face twisting into a knot of panic.

"Dad," Ruth said softly, trying to soothe him.

"Please, Ruth, pray for God to deliver me." He began to cry.

Waldemar and Ruth exchanged a glance. Ruth began to sing softly. It was an old German hymn from her childhood. Herman gently squeezed her hand. Tears rolled down his cheeks as she sang each verse.

When Herman was sleeping soundly, the couple left the room.

Ruth hugged Waldemar. "I hate this."

"He's had a good life. A full life."

Ruth sniffed, "I know, he seems so fragile now."

"He's ready to be with God. The cancer is everywhere now. He's ninety-four — his body just can't do this anymore."

Ruth cried, "I know."

*

"Hello, Mr. Bohlman," one of the nurses at Salem Manor sang out as she popped her head into his room. "How are you feeling?"

Herman adjusted the oxygen in his nose. "I'm okay. And how are you?"

She laughed, "I'm fine, thank you. Are you going to sing me a song today?"

Herman smiled. "I think I can hum a little tune." He started tapping his fingers on his blanket that was wrapped tightly over his thin legs. His tenor voice, still clear, hummed out a tune. He had been in hospital for twenty-seven days and he was glad to be back in his own room, with people who knew him.

The nurse checked his oxygen tank and assessed his other medical needs. "How is the pain?"

"It's bad. It's hard to breathe."

She listened to his breathing for a minute with her stethoscope. "It sounds like you're having a tough time. Should I call the doctor?"

He looked at her, long and hard, and with as much authority as he could muster said, "No, ma'am."

She raised her eyebrows. "Okay, I won't for now but I'm going to come and check on you in a little bit."

He closed his eyes, laid his head back and began to hum his song again. The nurse watched his fingers tap out the rhythm of the song.

The nurse walked back to her desk and dialed Ruth's number.

"Hi, Mrs. Peterson?"

"Yes," Ruth answered as she picked up the phone.

"This is Phyllis."

"Hi, Phyllis. What's going on?"

"Well his breathing is really laboured. I have some concerns."

"Did you want Pete and me to come?"

"Not yet, he insists he's fine. But I'm going to keep a close eye on him."

"Okay."

"I wanted to give you a heads up. I will be monitoring him closely."

"Thank you, Phyllis, I really appreciate it. Keep me posted."

"Will do." Phyllis said goodbye and hung up the phone.

In the night the alarm sounded. Phyllis rushed down the hall to Mr. Bohlman's room. "Mr. Bohlman?" Herman lay very still in his bed, his heart rate monitor beeping loudly.

"Mr. Bohlman!" Phyllis gave him a shake. "Can you hear me?"

His eyes fluttered weakly.

Phyllis hit the page button on the wall. "I need an ambulance."

A few days later, Ruth visited her dad in the hospital yet again. He was breathing better now and his pulse rate was back up thanks to some medications they had given him. He was quite alert and more himself than ever before.

"Ruth, I do not want to be here. I can't be here anymore. Night and day I pray for deliverance."

"Dad," Ruth sighed, "please."

"I am ready. I am an old man, Ruth. The pain — and I am weary. So weary. I want to be back in my own room and wait for God to take me."

"You need to be here, Dad."

"I'm not going to make it to ninety-five."

"Yes you are. We've got a big party planned. Lorne and Shirley are coming."

"That will be nice. I won't be there."

"Dad," Ruth pleaded. The room flooded with silence.

"The food is awful," he said brusquely.

"You said the same thing at Salem Manor."

"It's worse here."

Ruth nodded. "Okay."

"I don't have an appetite. I don't want to eat and the things they bring me. Ruth — it's terrible."

"Okay, Dad."

Herman shifted in his bed. "How's Keith? How is his trip going? Has Marlene talked to him?"

Keith was away in California on a Spring Break bus trip with his school.

"He's having a great time. He has loved the independence. They've been to Disneyland, the beach, and Universal Studios."

Herman smiled. "Sounds fun. Wish I was there."

Ruth chuckled.

"And Gerry? How's Gerry?"

"Gerry's good. He's coming to see you tomorrow."

"Oh, he doesn't have to come all this way in the cold for me."

"He wants to, Dad. You know I couldn't stop him if I wanted to."

Now it was Herman's turn to laugh. "No you couldn't."

"Brian and Darlene?"

"Good," Ruth smiled at her dad, "both working hard."

"And the girls? Karen and Shauna? Tell me what they are doing."

"Karen is keeping busy with her church youth group and Shauna has some really close friends at school that she spends all her time with. A neighbour girl and one other who Marlene says must be joined at the hip to her."

"Good. Good for them. Where's Pete?"

"He was just here, right?"

"Oh yes. I'm getting forgetful in my old age." He laughed again. "Has he gone to buy me a coffee?"

"No coffee for you I'm afraid — but yes, he's gone to get one for himself."

Over the next few days, endless visitors came to see Herman. Walter and Rose Lessing, Dale, Brian and Gerry, Keith, and many others from the church and community.

After a little over a week, Herman was allowed to go back to Salem Manor.

The plans were made, the cakes baked and in the freezer. The guest bed was made up for visitors. The gifts were bought and ready for the big day. It was three days until Lorne and Shirley arrived and Ruth and Waldemar were planning a trip to the store to pick up some last-minute food items.

Herman called at nine a.m., as he did every morning. He always talked to Waldemar because he had trouble hearing Ruth. She listened in on the extension. This morning he had said he was not feeling well and Ruth wondered if it was any worse than usual.

They had last been there five days ago and had a pleasant time. At the end of the visit, as was their custom, they wheeled him into the dining room where Ruth kissed him goodbye. They were planning to go back tomorrow to see him again. She was hoping to get a better sense of what exactly was bothering him.

Today the nurses and staff were having a birthday lunch for him in the sunroom. Ruth was grateful that he would have some distraction from the pain.

"Happy birthday to you, happy birthday to you, happy birthday dear Mr. Bohlman, happy birthday to you."

Everyone applauded as Herman weakly blew out his candle.

"Thank you." He looked around the room. "Thank you for your outstanding care and concern. I value you all."

All of the residents began to recount stories of their youth. Herman told everyone about the night that he had first arrived in Leduc.

"There was only one street light…I was bound and determined to take the next train back east!"

Everyone laughed.

"I wasn't going to land myself in a small bit prairie town and get stuck — and now look at me!"

Everyone exchanged their own stories of immigration and settlement, childhoods long ago in distant countries and the bountiful opportunities and freedoms they experienced in Canada. Herman grew tired. He bade goodbye to his friends. One of the staff members wheeled him back to his room.

"Here are your pills, Mr. Bohlman," the young lady passed him a cup of water and his six pills in a small Dixie cup.

"Thank you." Herman waited until her back was turned. He slid the pills out of the cup and into his sleeve. He took a drink of water and tapped the cup on the bedrail. "Here you are."

"Have a good rest then. Call if you need anything."

"I will." Herman smiled as he prayed once more for God to take him home. He thought of the words on his first wife's tombstone. *We will meet again...'* "Soon, my love, soon."

Chapter 35

"He will wipe every tear from their eyes. There will be no more death or mourning or crying or pain, for the old order of things has passed away."
Revelation 21:4 NIV

<u>April 13, 1989</u>

Herman

At 1:10 a.m. the phone rang. Ruth sat up straight. Before she reached for the phone, she knew what the news would be.

"Mrs. Peterson?"

"Yes."

"This is Dr. Baker. Your father is no longer with us."

"No," she inhaled, "no."

"I am sorry for your loss."

"What happened?"

"He went peacefully, in his sleep."

Tears sprang to her eyes. Waldemar was now rubbing his eyes and moved to wrap his arm around her.

"Thank you for calling." Ruth hung up the phone and fell into Waldemar's arms. "Oh, Pete…"

She shook as she wept, replaying the last visit in her mind.

"We should call Lorne."

"You're right," Ruth dabbed her face with a tissue.

They woke up Lorne.

"Lorne, it's Ruth."

"Ruth, what's wrong? Is it Dad?"

"Yes, he's gone home to his Saviour."

Lorne was silent but for a gasp.

"Lorne?"

"When?"

"Tonight. Just a few hours ago."

"What happened? How?"

"He died in his sleep, peacefully, as he wanted."

"We were going to see him tomorrow."

"I know. I'm sorry."

"We should have come sooner."

"You didn't know. No one knew…"

"His birthday…" Lorne began to cry.

"Dad always said," Ruth recalled as she wiped the tears from her cheeks, "children, when you receive the call that I am no longer here — rejoice with me."

Later that day, Brian met Waldemar and Ruth at Salem Manor. Brian carefully folded all of Herman's clothes and placed them in boxes. As Ruth wrapped each photo and placed it in a box she felt as though she were looking at the world through a kaleidoscope — all crazy and out of control; surreal, unimaginable. Pain swept over her in tidal waves.

It was a sunny, windy spring day on the day of the service. His casket was covered with spring flowers and pussy willows.

The congregation finished singing 'To God be the Glory.' Byron, Lorne's son, moved to the front of the church to read his grandfather's eulogy.

"Good afternoon. I would like to share some things with you about my grandfather."

"He was born April 15, 1894, in Tuzcyn, Russia, to Frederick and Julianna Bohlman. He accepted Christ as his Saviour and was baptized in 1911 at seventeen years of age in Russia.

"Herman immigrated to America in May 1913. After staying four years in Minnesota, at the urging of friends from his home in Russia, he moved to Leduc. He said he planned to take the next train to anywhere the next morning, but he remained here for seventy-two years. He left his mother, sisters and brothers in Russia and never saw any of them again.

"He worked in a hardware store and a general store and became a member of First Baptist Leduc (Fredericksheim). There he met and married Ruth Lessing in 1920. Ruth died in 1921 and for four years he was a single parent. In 1926, he met and married Edith Fleck of Yorkton, Saskatchewan.

"Herman went into the hardware business on his own in 1931 and operated Bohlman's Hardware until his retirement at age seventy.

"In 1927, Herman and Edith founded Die Zweite Deutsche Baptisten Gemeinde, which later took the name of Temple Baptist in Leduc. Herman served his Lord faithfully through good times and bad, and throughout his lifetime his leadership qualities were enjoyed by young and old. He served as Sunday school superintendent for thirty-five consecutive years — twelve months a year. He served as deacon for many terms of office and at his passing was an honorary deacon. He also held many different offices in the North American Baptist Conference and was instrumental in the founding of CIT, which is also now known as NAB College. He served many years on the board of directors. He sang in the tenor section of the choir for many years.

"Herman also found time to serve on the local school board as well as the Chamber of Commerce. He sang in a glee club and acted as an unofficial counsellor to all that needed a listening ear.

"During the war years, his was the only car that was operational twenty-four hours a day, and many a Leduc baby was born in an Edmonton hospital due to Herman's availability to all who needed him.

"His Bible was well worn from reading. He endeavoured to live out his life in a God-honouring servant fashion.

"His formal education was minimal but he assured his children and grandchildren that God's word was the truth — a light unto his path — and that Jesus Christ was Lord of his life. He worshiped the risen Lord and always invited others to choose Christ as their Saviour. He left his family with a tremendous legacy, for which each member will be eternally grateful."

Reverend Hoffman addressed the church and read from the book of Psalms. After that, Brian stood to read a tribute that he and Gerry had prepared. Brian began with Gerry's words.

"I remember when I was a little boy. I remember going to visit with our grandparents. I would often be sitting on my grandpa's knee. We didn't talk too much, but he held me and I felt safe on his knee.

"Once we were visiting in Leduc and I went shopping with my brothers. I bought some grapes but by the time we went back to my grandparent's home, I had reconsidered. I didn't want the grapes anymore. I wanted to return them.

"My brothers wouldn't return them for me. Even my parents didn't want to do it. But my grandpa did do it, taking my grapes back to the store and returning with my money. He would do those kinds of things for his grandsons because he loved us.

"I think the first thing I really noticed about my grandpa's life was his walk with God. I recall being a child and my grandparents would come into Edmonton to shop for their store. This happened each Wednesday afternoon. They would stay for dinner at our home but then they would go back to Leduc for a prayer meeting.

"Perhaps we couldn't understand why they didn't stay and visit with us. But now I look back and that was the greatest example in my life, the importance of having fellowship with other Christians. To this day, I cannot miss my midweek Bible study. Grandfather knew his Bible and that is why I study mine. I want to know the scriptures as my Grandpa did. I want to have faith like him, and for that I am grateful I am one of his grandsons."

"And now," Brian addressed the crowd, "Thoughts of my own. Well, Grandpa, you have left us but your memory will remain. You will be missed. May we learn from your example that no matter what, even now in this time of sorrow and loss, we too can open our hearts. We too can wait patiently and we too will be led to greener pastures. We too will be taken to still waters. We too will experience restoration for the soul. Grandfather, this is the legacy you have left us. This is the gift you have given us. We shall cherish and nurture it. This gift is the greatest inheritance of all."

Next Dale came to the front of the church, and began to sing *Lamb of God*.

"*Your only son, no sin to hide but you have sent him from your side…*"

Ruth dabbed at her eyes.

Following Dale, the reverend gave a short message and then the service ended with the hymn, *Blessed Assurance.*

Ruth sang while tears streamed down her cheeks. Her eyes were fixed on her father's casket. She sang to him for the last time.

*

Over a year later, in September of 1990, Ruth stood in front of the town well in Tuszyn, Germany, and smiled for the photograph.

"Can you believe it?" Waldemar asked.

"Here I am. It's hard to imagine Dad here."

"This is where he grew up. Where he came from."

"Amazing." Ruth looked around at the strip farms. They were a long and narrow shape. They snapped many photos of the interesting farmhouses and buildings. The native Polish people seemed leery of the 'Americans' here to see their land.

They had travelled from Edmonton to Toronto and on to Stockholm where they had visited with sixty-three members of Waldemar's extended family. Next they rented a car in Stockholm and crossed the Baltic to Gdansk, Poland. Following that they had stayed in Torin, toured Lodz where Ruth's grandparents, Frederick and Julianna Bohlman had been born and married in 1888. Tonight they were staying in Kalicz where Ruth's grandmother Pauline Lessing had been born and where the Lessings had left from to come to the 'New Country' in 1896. Tomorrow it was on to tour Auschwitz.

At the end of the day, Ruth sat down and wrote an entry in her travel journal.

September 9 1990. You have been gone now 1 year and 5 months, Dad. I am finally here where you were born. This part of Poland belonged to Russia when you were born. It has been a wonderful experience to be here. People have been living in this area since the year 1000 and your mother and father were born not far from here. How sad that both Grandpa Lessing and Grandma Bohlman had such short lives 39 years and 48 years; and here I am at age 68, seeing this land. You too were foreigners here, your grandparents arriving here as colonists. A lot has changed in that time, war, oppression and yet somehow one gets a sense of history — the land provides food each year, people are born, live and die and pass on their values to their children. The quiet fields belie the fact that war ceased only 45 years ago — communist rule for 45 years and once again freedom. People with dreams, dreams of a better life — and you made it, Dad. I shall be eternally grateful that you and my grandparents Lessing left this land for a new future far from this land. They risked all — and I am the inheritor of their dreams. #1003 Edmonton is a million miles away — in every sense, and our sons and grandchildren have such a good life. Dad, I am grateful that you were brave enough to venture forth and how happy I am to be able to be in Tuczyn — the village of your birth — the chickens, geese, cows, sheep and people live in close proximity to one another. The stables connected to the houses here become garages but I see the land is farmed in long strips behind the houses on the edge of the town. I thank God that I have had this experience and that He granted me health and strength so I could come to Tuczyn, Lodz, Kalisz and Lublin. I really have found my European roots!!!

The tour guide spoke. "Welcome to Auschwitz Museum Site. Today I will show you around the camp and give you some of the notable facts. This is a place where we can learn from history. Many parts of this tour are sad and horrifying, but if you can take your mind to a place of remembrance and reflection, I do believe you will walk away today," she paused, "changed. Let's begin."

Ruth walked across the cobblestone pavers. She read the German words, *Arbiet Macht Frei*, Work Makes Free. She felt a chill go up her spine. The buildings were unassuming, speaking nothing to the horrors they had seen. She leaned on her cane and held Waldemar's arm tightly.

The tour guide pointed to a large, old tree inside the gates. "This tree is where prisoners would be tied and tortured. The building behind the tree is the prisoner administration building and to its right, the camp kitchen."

Ruth looked up at all the two-story brick buildings. The great trees shaded the gravel roads.

"You'll note the guard tower," the tour guide continued. "If you can take a look you'll see the area beyond the guard tower in the distance. It is the location of Krematorium I. The rows and rows of barracks were built with slave labour. Each barrack slept hundreds of people who were worked to death or waiting to die." The group walked along until they were told to stop at the electrified fence. "These fences were made by prisoners, ironically. If you'll notice the quality in which they were made, the precision in each concrete post, each twist of the wire, you can appreciate the Nazi's philosophy of order."

The group carried on into an open square, talking as they walked.

"This is the infamous Roll Call Square. Every morning and evening, each prisoner was accounted for, dead or alive. If someone was missing, then everyone stood here, even if it took all night. Here also the selection process was made. It was decided which prisoners were fit for work and which ones would be sent to be gassed."

Ruth whispered to Waldemar, "It's awful."

He nodded solemnly.

"This," the tour guide gestured toward another brick building, "is one of the many 'hospital' buildings. Prisoners were taken here to die of natural causes — many came off the trains very ill from the journey. They could also be coming to the hospital to be given a shot of phenol in the heart or they would be held here until they could be gassed. They were certainly not cared for."

The group walked on for some time until they were in a small, unappealing concrete courtyard between two barracks.

"This is the courtyard of the camp jail, so named Block 11. The cells were in the basement and you'll notice the concrete walls built around the cell windows to further isolate prisoners. On the opposite side you will see the boarded windows of Block 10 where Dr. Carl Clauberg conducted sterilization and other abominable experiments on women prisoners. Let's come down to the end of the courtyard now."

Ruth felt ill.

"This is Death Wall. Mostly Polish political prisoners were shot here. Also, leaders would have been executed here, members of the underground organization and anyone who would have been involved in planning escapes or anything of that nature."

The group came out of the courtyard. "This low wooden building is the camp laundry and where the confiscated items of the prisoners were kept. Anything that could be saved and credited to the cause of the Reich would be. Gold teeth, glasses, jewelry…" The group walked through the building where there were displays of glasses, shoes and other personal items that had been surrendered either before or after death. "Behind this building are warehouses where poison gas was stored. Now we'll tour the cells in Block 11."

After a facility tour and countless stories of brave women and men who died, the group re-emerged into the sunlight.

"Next I'll take you to the Krematorium." A murmur ran through the group. Once inside the small concrete room, the tour guide pointed to the ceiling. "You'll notice that there were small holes where the poisonous agent 'Zyklon B' was poured in. Many, many prisoners met their fate in this very room. Special prisoners were given the gruesome task of moving bodies from here into the furnaces for cremation. They used these rail cars on these tracks to transport them from one area to the next."

The group stood quietly, staring at the rail cars, the tracks and the furnaces where so many had lost their lives.

"January 27, 1945, the Red Army of the Soviet Union freed all prisoners still remaining in Auschwitz. That brings me to the end of the tour and from here you are free to wander the camp grounds. You'll find information signs throughout the camp and if you have any questions please come and see me in Roll Call Square."

Waldemar and Ruth broke off from the group and found a place to sit.

"What do you think?" he asked.

"Monstrous. You know, you've heard about this for so long, you've imagined it, you've seen photos of it but to be here…it hits a nerve."

"It does," he said.

"What bothered you the most?"

"The Krematorium. And you?"

"The glasses. The pile of glasses. Each pair had a face, a story, a loved one."

Waldemar shivered. "Let's get out of here."

"Yes, I think I am done for the day myself."

The couple walked to the gate of the museum site and took one look back. "Can you imagine the day they were set free, I mean those who endured this hell?" she asked.

He paused and said, "I'm sure you can never be free from this."

"That was a memorable day," Waldemar said as he sipped his wine.

"Indeed. We witnessed a historic event. The final fall of the Berlin Wall."

"And we have a piece to take home."

"I love being here, hearing the language." She cut into her steak.

"You still remember it all?"

"Yes, it really is second nature. Some of the slang is a bit different…and the accent but I understand it all."

"I'm lucky to have my German from Leduc to guide me through Berlin."

Ruth laughed, "The waitress asked me what part of Germany I was from while you were in the washroom; she couldn't pinpoint my accent."

Waldemar laughed, "I bet she was surprised!"

Ruth nodded and took a bite of her supper.

"And tomorrow…"

"Yes, on to Hamburg, Lubeck and by ferry to Trelleborg, Sweden. Then a week in Voxjo with your cousin Ingvar Peterson and finally Stockholm."

"And back to reality — Edmonton."

"It will be good to see the family."

"True." He took her hand. "Although the only family I need is right here." He leaned in for a kiss. "I love you, Ruth."

"I love you too."

They sat in silence, eating their supper and taking in the view along the River Spree.

"All this makes me think of my dad, as a young man. It makes me think of all of those, so many generations back, the Lessings, the Schindels, even your family. All of them left their homes, sometimes their families, everything they knew…and for what?"

"A promise. No guarantees."

"A promise of a better life, a better church, a place to freely worship and prosper." She sighed as she looked out at the boats on the river. "Could I have done it? Made the journey, I mean?"

"I know, it is such an extraordinary gift they gave us. Sometimes I think we, and especially our children, take it for granted."

"Being here makes me appreciate their journey so much more. I can't even imagine my dad walking from Tuszyn to Amsterdam. It's nearly an eleven-hour drive."

Waldemar twirled his pasta onto his fork. "He always was haunted by the day he left, wasn't he?"

"Yes, his younger sister, Martha. When I went to Auschwitz it made me consider their journey, dying in a cattle car on the way to a Siberian work camp. Maybe they were better off freezing to death than being worked to death or gassed. I can't imagine the burden my father must have carried, knowing he wasn't able to save them."

"What a life…what a tragic life of loss he had."

"His father, his mother, sisters, brother, in-laws, wife…"

"And you — I mean he had to give you up for a year…"

"And he was very brave to take me back. It speaks of his devotion to me. How many single fathers would have made the effort that he did?"

"Not many."

"What a lot of questions I will have when we reunite."

"Are you happy about his street?"

"Bohlman Way," she laughed, "how appropriate." She thought of the street in Leduc, newly named after her father.

"Quite an honor."

"He gave so much to his community, he deserved it."

Waldemar nodded and pushed back his plate. "Delicious."

Ruth put down her utensils as well. "I'm stuffed." She stretched out her aching legs.

"Do you feel like you found what you were looking for?"

"My roots?"

"Yes, your roots."

"Somewhat — so many questions still."

"And now, your parents are gone."

Ruth was pensive for a bit. "Wednesday afternoons will never be the same again. God gave him ninety-five years of a long, full life. He had his fair share of heartache and joy. Children, grandsons, great grandchildren — each one treasured."

"Yes he did."

"They say the death of the saints is pleasing to God…the way I miss him, suddenly I am a little girl again." She fingered her napkin. "He left me many memories — some painful, many happy. I guess one can never measure a relationship — on this side of the Jordan. It is one of the mysteries of life. He was a product of his day and generation — as indeed, each of us is, I of mine, my children and grandchildren of theirs…I miss him." She looked Waldemar in the eyes. "I always will. I was his darling daughter."

Waldemar touched her cheek and wiped away the tear that was falling. "It's okay."

"He has gone on to a better place…been reunited with his loved ones waiting there."

Waldemar squeezed her hands. "Yes he has."

Ruth looked up at the heavens, the night sky full of millions of twinkling stars. She wondered what he was doing right now. She thought of all the loved ones that had gone before her. The ones who would be there to greet her when it was her time.

She blew a kiss heavenward. "I miss you, Dad."

Chapter 36

"Who of you by worrying can add a single hour to his life?" Matthew 6:27 NIV

July 1992

Ruth and Waldemar

"I'm sorry, Mrs. Peterson. The tumor is cancerous."

Ruth and Waldemar looked at one another. The doctor sat quietly with Ruth's chart in his hands.

"What does this mean?" Ruth asked, her heart pounding.

"You're going to need a mastectomy, right away."

Ruth's hand went to her breast involuntarily.

"I've already scheduled you a surgery date at the University Hospital."

Ruth nodded.

"It's going to be next Tuesday, six days from now."

"Okay," she said, her voice quivering.

"I know this is a lot to take in. Take your time, think about it and if you have any questions, please don't hesitate to call." The doctor looked over at Waldemar who was staring at his hands. "You too, Mr. Peterson. If there is anything I can do, let me know."

Waldemar looked up and extended his hand. "Thank you, Doctor."

In a blur, the couple left the doctor's office and drove home. They said nothing as they entered their home. Waldemar hung Ruth's coat in the closet and helped her with her boots. They both went into the den and sat down.

"Who should we call first?" Ruth asked.

Waldemar shrugged.

"Dale?"

"Sure. Call Dale."

Ruth picked up the phone and carefully picked out the familiar seven digits to reach him.

"Hello," Marlene picked up the phone cheerfully.

"Hi Mar. It's Mom."

"Hi Mom. Everything okay?"

Ruth cleared her throat. "Your Dad and I need you and Dale to come by tonight. It's important. Can you do that?"

"I'll check with Dale but I don't see it being a problem."

"It's important," Ruth stressed. "We need you to come without the kids."

"Okay, Mom," Marlene said. "We'll be there."

Ruth hung up the phone and began to cry. Waldemar moved next to her.

"I couldn't say it."

"I know." He rubbed her back gently. He too began to cry.

Dale and Marlene came that evening. They too cried at the news. They prayed together, asking God for his wisdom and peace as Ruth sought treatment and faced radiation. After that, they called Brian and Gerry. Dale calmly broke the news to each of his brothers and answered any questions they had.

That night while Waldemar was in the shower and getting ready for bed, Ruth held her bible in her hand, struggling. Her fingers went over her favorite verse. "So do not fear, for I am with you, do not be dismayed for I am your God, I will strengthen you and help you. I will uphold you with my righteous right hand."

"God, I know the verse," Ruth said aloud, "I know and have experienced your righteous right hand. You say do not fear, Lord, this goes beyond fear." She trembled. "I'm terrified. You tell me not to be dismayed — God, you know I'm devastated by what is happening to my body."

Her hand went to her breast, which she was about to lose. Tears fell freely. She set her bible aside and laid her head in her hands. She wept.

Into her mind came a verse she had memorized as a small child. "Who of you by worrying can add a single hour to his life?"

On Saturday night, Ruth and Waldemar drove to Dale and Marlene's house.

"Are you sure you want to go ahead, given the circumstances?" Waldemar asked, his hands clutching the wheel.

"Of course. Who knows how I'll be feeling after surgery and radiation? Maybe my voice will change."

"Okay."

"How do you think the girls will be?" She twirled her cane that lay on the seat next to her.

"I don't know," he said, his eyes fixed on the road, "upset, I presume. They may have questions."

"I hate to burden them with this."

"It's not like we have a choice."

"I know. I'm just saying." She looked out the window, her agitation clearly showing. "Are you alright?"

"I'm fine," he lied.

They pulled into the driveway and Waldemar put the car into park. He sighed and flung open his door. He walked to the passenger side and opened her door. He helped her out. They were there to rehearse for this upcoming Sunday. Ruth and the girls planned to sing Amazing Grace during the church service.

"Thanks." She looked at him and smiled. He didn't meet her gaze.

They went to the front door and knocked. Karen opened it.

"Hi, Grandma and Grandpa. Come in."

Everyone else was seated in the living room and exchanged hugs and kisses. Waldemar sat on the couch. Ruth sat down on a dining room chair Marlene had moved next to the grand piano.

"Can I get you anything?" Marlene asked. "Some coffee for you, Dad?"

"Sure. That would be nice."

"Mom? Tea?"

"Please."

Marlene left for the kitchen. Dale sat quietly on the piano bench. The grandkids looked at their Grandma.

"So…you've heard the news."

Shauna nodded.

"Yes," Karen answered.

"I'm in God's hands, right?"

"Yes," Keith replied.

Shauna nodded again, her eyes filling with tears.

"Are you scared?" Karen asked quietly.

"Yes. A little bit." Ruth looked around the room at her family. "But, I know that God has promised me something."

"What?" Shauna asked.

"That He knows how many days I have. He knows my fear and he is going to take care of me. I know that whether I get more days here, with my family…" she wiped a tear that ran down her cheek, "or…if it's my time to go home, then I will be okay."

Shauna cried. Marlene came in the room with coffee and tea. She served Waldemar and Ruth. She sat next to her youngest daughter and rubbed her back.

"When is your surgery?" Karen asked.

"This Wednesday."

"Why don't we pray together?" Dale asked.

Everyone nodded.

"Dear Heavenly Father. We pray for Mom. We trust that you are with her for this journey. We pray that you will give her peace and comfort as she faces surgery and radiation. Please help us all to remember that you are in control. In your Holy Name, Amen."

Ruth looked at the teary faces of her granddaughters. Keith sat quietly. She tried to sound upbeat, "Now, let's begin our practice. It's not every day I get to sing at church with my two beautiful girls."

Keith and Waldemar went downstairs to Keith's bedroom so that they could talk while the others practiced.

Ruth held the hymnal. Karen and Shauna stood on either side. They worked out who would sing which verse. Dale sat at the piano and began to play.

At the end, as Ruth moved to her seat, she wiped the tears from her eyes. "Well done, girls. Very well done." She hugged them both.

Six days later, Ruth was ready for surgery. She looked at the young anesthesiologist with great trepidation. She prayed over and over in her mind, as she met his eyes.

"I am highly allergic to many, *many*," she emphasized, "chemicals. The reaction can be very severe. Do you understand? Are you taking notes? I have it written out here but I need you to know them — memorize them and assure me that you will not jeopardize my life with carelessness." She spoke with the sharp tongue of her headmistress from nursing school, Sister Saint Christine.

"I hear you, Mrs. Peterson. I have read all the items on your allergy list. I assure you that I understand your misgivings."

Ruth looked him over skeptically. She wanted to ask how old he was, how long he had been practicing medicine and if he was even qualified, but she held her tongue.

She simply nodded her head.

She was wheeled into the operating room. All of the hospital staff buzzed around her. Nurses and doctors were talking, preparing equipment and going about their daily routine. Ruth's heart pounded. This was it — could these be the final moments of her life? Did anyone care? She had said a tearful goodbye to Waldemar who had assured her over and over that she would be okay. Still, she had a bad feeling.

The young anesthesiologist was getting his things organized when suddenly he said, "Oh my, I have to go! It's three o'clock! I'm due at a meeting now!" He whipped off his rubber gloves and left the room. Ruth began to panic. *No, no, no…don't go…*

How can this be happening? Would she have time to explain to the next doctor about how severe her reactions could be? Was this it? She prayed over and over in her mind, not sure of what to say. *Help me. Help me.*

"Mrs. Peterson," one of the nurses came to talk to her, "we've had a delay with the anesthesiologist. You're all ready to go. We've paged another doctor to come in. We don't want to hold this process up any longer so as soon as he gets here we'll begin."

"Will he know about my allergies?"

The nurse looked at Ruth's chart and asked, "Ah, which allergies?"

"To the anesthetics? It's very severe."

"I don't know…I guess I can check."

Ruth grabbed the nurse's arm before she walked away. She gripped it tightly. "It's very important."

"Of course, dear."

Ruth took in a deep breath.

She heard people in the room talking about who was available to fill in.

A few minutes later, the surgeon came in with the second anesthetist. He was much older. The surgeon smiled at Ruth. "Sorry about that, Mrs. Peterson. This is Dr. Clements. Don't worry, he's the best and I've filled him in on all your allergies."

Ruth looked up at him. In her mind she thought, *God, for whatever reason for the switch — I'm yours.*

Several hours later, Ruth opened her eyes. She looked around. She was in the recovery room.

"Hi," said a familiar voice.

Ruth turned her head and saw Waldemar, sitting in a chair, watching her.

"Hi," she croaked.

"How are you feeling?"

Ruth tried to move. "My chest hurts."

"Do you remember anything?" he asked.

Ruth looked at him quizzically. "Should I?"

"I was just wondering."

"What? Oh, the doctors."

"What about the doctors?"

"They switched the doctors at the last minute. I was worried..." she closed her eyes and laid her head back. Sleep took her away before she could finish speaking.

The following morning she was feeling more alert. The nurses had been attending to her needs all night. She was sitting up in bed with a tray of breakfast foods when Waldemar came in.

"Good morning, love." He came to her bed and kissed her.

"Morning, Pete."

"How are you feeling this morning?"

"Everything hurts. They've given me pain medication but it's not helping. I feel like the dog's breakfast."

Waldemar laughed, "That good, hey? Has the doctor been in yet this morning?"

"No." She picked at her cereal. "This doesn't taste very good."

Waldemar sat down in the pink, vinyl hospital chair. He looked at his wife.

"Are you okay?" she asked.

"Yes. Yes, I am. I am very grateful today."

"What are you talking about?"

The doctor entered the room. "Good Morning, Mrs. Peterson. How are you feeling this morning?"

"Sore."

"I can imagine. Did your husband tell you what happened?"

She looked at him, her eyebrows crossed. "No." He looked her in the eyes, yet said nothing.

"Well, you gave us a bit of a scare." The doctor looked at Waldemar and smiled.

"What do you mean?" Ruth asked hesitantly.

"Your heart stopped during the procedure. It took our entire team to bring you back around. We had to use CPR and the defribulators to get your heart beating again. You could say that you tried to leave — but we weren't going to let that happen."

"No…" Ruth looked at Waldemar. He squeezed her hand.

The doctor smiled at her again. "You're a lucky lady. If we hadn't had Dr. Clements with all of his experience…well, it might have been a different ending to this story."

"The second anesthesiologist?"

"Yes. He was able to think quickly about what we could use given all your complicated allergic reactions. His experience was invaluable to us."

"Thank God," Ruth said softly.

"Indeed, Mrs. Peterson. Although you are sore, you have much to be thankful for."

*

She had been checked and rechecked. The technicians had prepared her. She lay still on the hard metal table. Large steel machines were all around her. The lights went out and the technicians left the room. The machine whirred to life, humming loudly.

Ruth felt God's presence all around her as the nuclear rays attacked her cancer. She felt tremendous peace. So far he had taken care of her better than she could imagine. As she lay there now, in this dark room, she felt Him and the angels, calming her, reassuring her.

Even as her breast was gone and her body was being exposed to radiation, she knew she was blessed.

"Thank you, Father," she whispered.

Chapter 37

"When you pass through the waters, I will be with you; and when you pass through the rivers, they will not sweep over you. When you walk through the fire, you will not be burned..." Isaiah 43:2 NIV

June 2004

Wally and Jacob

The boxes were everywhere. Ruth and Waldemar were moving again. The time had come for them finally to accept that they needed assisted living. Thankfully, there was more dignity in assisted living now. They found a facility with a large two-bedroom apartment. It had a small kitchenette. All the meals were prepared and served for the residents.

The work involved in moving was enormous. Many things had been given away, many others packed, but still there was so much to do. Ruth found that she tired easily. Her hands, no matter how she willed them, did not cooperate with her mind. Brian had come to help but she and Waldemar were both of the same stubborn mold and insisted that they could handle it on their own. Waldemar had been working tirelessly from morning until bedtime, only resting periodically for meals and taking a few minutes to watch a football game now and then.

"Are you doing all right, sweetheart?" Ruth called out from her chair in the den.

"I'm fine. Are you ready for some lunch?"

"That would be nice."

Ruth limped to the table, relying on her cane as well as the furniture and the boxes scattered along the way.

Waldemar brought her a plate with a sandwich and a cut-up peach. He also had two cups in his hands, carefully balanced, one full of milk and the other full of juice.

"There you are, my love. Lunch."

Ruth leaned up to kiss him. "Thank you. Can you get my meds?"

Waldemar went back to the kitchen and brought Ruth her pills. "Anything else you need?"

"No, that should do." She watched him grimace as he sat down in his chair opposite her. "Are you alright?"

"I'm fine."

"Karen is coming today."

Waldemar nodded as he took a large bite of his sandwich.

"I think I'll have her help me pack the china cabinet."

"That's a good idea." He took a long drink of milk.

Ruth looked at him again. "Are you sure you're alright? Maybe you should take a break this afternoon."

"I'm fine."

Waldemar went to work washing the dishes.

The last few years had been full of change. The grandkids were growing up. In 1998, Shauna married a young man she met in California. In 2002 they had a son, their first great grandbaby. Shauna came nearly every week to visit so that they could know and enjoy him. Waldemar was glad that he was healthy that he could be the kind of great grandpa that some grandpas didn't even have the privilege to be. He could be down on the floor and play. He could pick him up in his arms and pace with him. He could carry him out to the car for Shauna at the end of the visits.

He prided himself on his physical strength. He exercised every day. The athlete inside may have aged but he surely hadn't died.

Ruth loved to hold Jacob and to rub his belly when he was crying or not feeling well. His stomach often pained him. Ruth used the same methods she had used on Gerry so many years ago to rub out the aches.

Keith and Karen both married in the last year. Karen to a fellow named Dave and Keith to a young lady named Heidi. They had been blessed to be a part of the celebrations for each.

Ruth had been working on the Premiers Counsel for a long time now. She was a consultant for integrating the disabled and designating funding for various programs. She retired two years before. Even though she had been in an advisory role, it was getting to be too difficult for her to get to the meetings. She was a valuable resource when it came to rights for the disabled.

Karen knocked tentatively at the door. Shauna stood behind her, holding Jacob in her arms.

Waldemar came to the door. A wide grin spread across his face. His blue eyes twinkled. "Hello!" He motioned his arm. "Please come in! Don't mind the mess." He hugged each girl in turn and took a minute to look Jacob in the eyes. "Hello, little man."

Jacob stretched his arms out to his great grandpa. Waldemar happily took Jacob while the girls took their coats off and laid them on some boxes by the door.

"You guys have been busy," Shauna commented.

"You've really made some progress here, Grandpa." Karen looked around the apartment. "Grandma's not working you too hard, is she?"

Waldemar laughed, "No, she keeps me on task but she gives me the occasional break." He hugged Jacob tightly. "Good to have you here."

"Will you keep Jacob busy while we help Grandma?" Shauna asked.

"Of course. It will be a happy distraction from my duties."

"Hello!" Ruth called from her spot at the dining room table. The girls moved into the apartment and over to where she was sitting.

"Hi, Grandma!" Karen and Shauna called out as they approached her. They exchanged hugs and kisses.

"How are you, Shauna?" Ruth asked.

"I'm good," Shauna sighed, "Jacob keeps me busy!"

"I'm sure! I remember when I had three little boys. They can wear a mom out!"

Shauna nodded and laughed, "Yes, I can't imagine three!"

"And you?" Ruth looked at her oldest granddaughter. "How's teaching?"

"I'm good. Work is going well. It's nice that we are getting near the end of the school year. I'm looking forward to summer holidays."

Ruth said hi to Jacob. Waldemar took him down the hall to find some things to play with.

"I'd like to pack the china cabinet today. All my silver, everything in the cabinet." She waved at the large cabinet against the wall. The doors hung open, showing their bounty.

"No problem," Karen commented. "Let's get started."

The three women chatted as they packed. Ruth instructed, and Karen and Shauna did the lifting, moving and wrapping. Waldemar came in and out of the room. Jacob played in a cardboard box. After awhile, Waldemar turned on a cartoon in the den. Jacob settled happily into his great grandpa's arms.

Waldemar looked down at Jacob, fully absorbed in his cartoon. He fit neatly in the crook of his arm. What a perfect place to be.

A pain shot through his arm. He gasped, sucking in a lung full of air. Jacob looked up at him with his big blue eyes. He babbled.

"Too much moving, little guy. Just too much."

Waldemar was up in the night. He couldn't sleep. The move was scheduled to go ahead in three days. He looked around at all of the symbols of his life with Ruth. Photos, pictures, paintings, albums and treasures. Seashells, ornaments, books and awards. Dishes and collectable spoons from all the places they had been. Everything was scattered around in disarray.

They had an amazing life. They had loved, lived and adventured to the fullest. They each had their own struggles and heartaches, but together — together they had made it. Now they were entering a new phase of their lives. It wasn't going to be easy. Nothing ever was. But, they would do it together.

He went into the bedroom and watched her as she slept. He sat on the edge of the bed. He gently stroked her cheek. He got up and moved back to his side of the bed. He laid down and tried to fall back to sleep. He watched her body rise and fall with each breath. He wrapped his arm around her. God, he loved her.

The next morning at breakfast, Ruth groaned, "I'm telling you, I know when you're not feeling well."

"I'm fine," he insisted.

"Pete — really."

"I'm getting worn out I guess."

"Take a break."

"Oh be quiet. You know I don't want to, so why are you telling me?"

"Wally, listen to me — come on, sit down."

"You're no better off than I am. You're aching all over. Admit it."

Ruth looked at him sheepishly. "I'm fine."

"Sure you are."

A few hours later, Waldemar took slow steady breaths and rubbed his chest. His chest felt tight. He was lightheaded.

"Ruth," he called out weakly, "Ruth!"

She was dozing in front of the television.

"Ruth!"

Ruth's eyes flew open. She grabbed her cane and tried to bring herself to her feet as swiftly as possible. "WALLY!"

She came out of the den to find him in the living room, on his knees, clutching his chest. "WALLY! WHAT IS IT?"

"Call 911!"

If Ruth could have run to the phone, she would have. She tried to stay calm and make her way without falling. If she fell now she couldn't help him. "Big deep breaths, sweetie, big deep breaths." She picked up the phone and dialed frantically.

"Edmonton 911, what is your emergency?" the operator rolled out her greeting.

The words exploded from Ruth's mouth, "My husband, he's having a heart attack!"

"Okay, ma'am, try to stay calm. What is your address?"

Ruth recited the address.

"I need you to get him lying down, with his head propped up; make sure he is breathing and comfortable. Can you do that for me?"

Ruth nodded. "I can."

Her heart was racing as prayers flew heavenward at a frantic pace. She put down the phone and took a pillow to Waldemar, propping his head up as he lay there, white as a ghost, moaning in pain. "You're going to be okay, sweetie."

She went back to the phone and picked it up. The operator talked her through the next few minutes.

"Help is on the way, ma'am, but I need you to unlock your front door. Does your building have a buzzer?"

"Yes, it does."

"I'm going to get you to hang up the phone. I can see they are nearly there. I want you to be off the line so you can buzz in the EMS team."

"Okay."

Ruth hung up the phone and waited as each second dragged by. *Oh God, oh God, oh God...not Pete...not now...no, no, no.* "You're going to be okay, honey," she reassured him as he lay there, his eyes now shut. She looked at him lying there, helpless. *Not now, not now...not now.* "You're going to be okay, Wally — deep breaths, try to take nice deep breaths."

Finally, the phone rang. "EMS."

Ruth pressed the key to let them into the building and went to the front door, praying them to get to her suite as soon as possible. The next five minutes were a blur as they came in, assessed him, loaded him on a gurney to take him to the nearest hospital. She grabbed her purse and locked the door behind her as she hurried out with the emergency medical team. One of the paramedics held Ruth's arm as she hobbled down the hall.

"He's going to be okay, ma'am."

She looked at this man that she loved so fiercely, laying on the gurney, his eyes shut and wincing in pain. She thought of the day she first spotted him on the post office steps, the courtship, the romance, the friendship, the trials and pain, the joy and laughter...this wasn't the end, was it? Was this the end of their story? She prayed fervently. *Not today. Not today, Waldemar*, she thought. *You're not going without me.* She felt ill as they loaded into the elevator.

The doctor came in the room, "Well, sir," he shook Waldemar's hand, "I would say that you are one lucky man." He winked at Ruth. "This husband of yours has a heart of a twenty-year-old. He's in tip top shape."

Waldemar smiled at Ruth.

"In fact," the doctor noted, "now that he's had this triple bypass he should be good for a long, long time." He looked at Waldemar, "You need to eat right and exercise, young man, and your heart will thank you."

Ruth exhaled loudly, "Thank you very much, Doctor. We are grateful for your excellent care over the last week."

Waldemar ran his finger over the incision on his chest. "Thank you."

"We've been married for a long time," Ruth said, "And I wasn't ready to let him go just yet."

"You two take good care of each other."

"We will," Ruth promised.

The last week had been one trying moment after the next. Waldemar had been rushed into emergency and a triple bypass was preformed on his heart. He, as the doctor had said, really did have an athletic heart, one that had most likely saved his life. She thanked God for Waldemar's passion for athletics, his love of curling and his lifetime of being active.

*

"Well, Wally, here we are. Another Easter together."

Waldemar sat in his blue recliner and smiled at his wife. "Yes. Are you disappointed that we aren't able to get to a church service today?"

"No, I've accepted that we're not as mobile as we once were."

Ruth ran her gnarled fingers over the worn pages of her bible. She and Waldemar had long given up getting to church on a regular basis. Not long after Waldemar's triple bypass, she had suffered her own heart attack, on the unpacking side of the move. She had a failed valve that doctors were able to replace with an artificial one. It had been a very stressful year as they adjusted to a new home, a new way of community living and a major sense of loss of independence. Waldemar was no longer able to drive because of his heart attack. This aggravated him on a daily basis. It had been a humbling experience. No more parties, no more entertaining, no more cooking. All of those days were gone. They both felt fairly helpless.

Brian and Gerry came faithfully to see them. Shauna brought Jacob once a week. He was such a source of joy for them. He played cars on the floor with Waldemar and he walked Waldemar around, holding his one finger and showing him all the things he wasn't supposed to touch. Ruth gave Jacob some wooden hand-painted eggs from Poland. Jacob loved to hide them. Then his 'Papa' would look, trying to collect all nine of them back into the bowl.

They were getting to know Shauna better too now, in a different way. They saw her in the role of mother and granddaughter. She took great interest in their stories and photos and seemed to soak up the sense of history Ruth also enjoyed. She loved to tell Shauna as much as she could remember of her years as a young mother, as a nurse and of her courtship with Waldemar.

This Easter they were happy to be together. Ruth looked over at Waldemar and asked, "Do you want me to read to you?"

"Yes," he leaned his head back and closed his eyes. "Please do."

Ruth read the passage about Jesus' death and resurrection, the familiar words surrounding them.

Ruth felt a wave of emotions rush over her as she finished reading. She thought of Jesus — asking his Father to forgive those who persecuted him. After everything he had been through, he still was able to ask for forgiveness.

"Are you okay?" Waldemar asked.

"I'm just thinking, about Edith."

"Tell me."

"Have I ever really forgiven her? I mean, I've said it, but have I ever felt it?"

"I don't know," he looked at her quizzically. "Have you?"

"I'm just thinking about that day we packed up the apartment…when she asked me for forgiveness. How can I truly find peace with the way Edith related to me? Have I ever really forgiven Edith for the way she had held back her love and affection?"

"Think about what Jesus said, *'Father, forgive them for they know not what they are doing.'* Do you think Edith ever intentionally wanted to hurt you?"

Ruth thought about this for a long time. Finally, she said, "No."

Psalm 90:4 came to her mind. *'For a thousand years in your sight are like a day that has just gone by, or like a watch in the night.'* Her God was sovereign; he was in control. She would be with her mother again. She and her mother would spend an eternity together in heaven. Edith had said unkind things over the years, but in the end, did it matter? What had Edith taught her? To be strong? To be independent? To stand up in the face of adversity? She was who she was today because of Edith's influence. She was able to handle the public rejection and heartache regarding Gerry because she was a strong woman. God had shaped her into the individual that she needed to be so that she could help the disabled, bring glory to God and live her life as a testament to him.

God *had* provided for her over the years. He had given her Artrude and her mother, loving women in Christ who had cared for her and nurtured her. He had brought many dear women into her life through her work and through her church. He had not left her without the support she needed.

"Wally, will you pray with me?"

"Of course."

Ruth began, "Father, fill me with your peace. Let me feel the strength of your forgiveness. I forgive Edith — in her humanity she made the choices she did — as did I." Ruth paused, thinking of all of the anger and bitterness she had carried around for years, "I surrender it to you. In your holy name, Amen."

Chapter 38

"Because of the Lord's great love we are not consumed, for his compassions never fail. They are new every morning; great is your faithfulness."
Lamentations 3: 22 & 23

June 27, 2008

Ruth and Wally

"We're here!" Shauna's voice rang out as she entered the building.

"Hi!"

"Papa!" Jacob rushed into Waldemar's arms.

"How are you?" Waldemar bent down on one knee to hug both Jacob and Shauna's younger son Jasper, now nearing age three.

"Auntie Karen had a baby, Papa!"

"I know! That's exciting!"

"A girl!" Jacob looked over at Shauna. "What's her name again?"

"Amelie."

"Amelie," Jacob repeated.

"What a pretty name."

"Now Lucas is a big brother too!" Jasper exclaimed.

Karen had two children now, Lucas, nearly three, and a newborn daughter, Amelie.

"Are you waiting for Gerry?" Jacob asked.

"Yes, I am."

"Can I wait with you?"

"You better ask your mom." Waldemar stood up and took each boy by the hand. "What do you say, Mom?"

Shauna smiled. "Of course you can wait here with Papa, but you must be a very good listener."

"I will be," Jacob promised sweetly.

Shauna looked down at Jasper. "Do you want to come up to see Grandma with me?"

Jasper nodded.

"Okay, we'll see you in a bit."

Waldemar and Jacob settled into a chair together by the front door, where they had a clear view of the driveway where Gerry's bus would be pulling in.

Shauna went to the elevators with Jasper in one hand and a big bag of toys in the other. She rubbed her back as she waited.

Jasper looked up at her and smiled sweetly. "I love you, Mom."

"I love you too, sweetie."

"Are we going to play trains?"

"Yes, that's what I brought."

"That's good." The elevator doors made a ding sound and opened. Shauna and Jasper stepped inside. "Can I press the button?"

"Number four," Shauna pointed, "this one."

Jasper sped down the hall once he and Shauna reached the fourth floor. All the doors looked the same but he knew which one to stop at. He looked back. "Can I, Mom? Can I knock?"

"Go ahead."

Jasper knocked on the door. Ruth pulled it open, leaning on her walker. "Hello, Jasper!"

"Hi, Great Grandma," he beamed.

"Is your mom with you?"

"She's coming."

Shauna came through the door and gave Ruth a hug. "Hi, Grandma." She kissed her cheek. "How are you?"

"Not too bad," Ruth shut the door. "My arthritis is giving me trouble this week but what else is new?"

"I'm sorry to hear that."

"Come in, come in, did you see your grandpa down there?"

"Yes, Jacob is waiting with him for Gerry."

She tapped Shauna's protruding belly. "And how are you feeling?"

Shauna sighed, "Pretty awful. I feel sick all the time. I am glad this is almost over. I am really tired of feeling rotten."

"I was lucky," Ruth said as she found her seat, "I never felt too sick with any of my pregnancies."

"Yes, everyone tells you that the next one won't be too bad but so far each one has been worse!"

Ruth laughed, "Rumour, pure rumour. Maybe this one's a girl."

"Can you believe Karen had a girl?"

"I know!" Ruth gushed, "I'm thrilled for her. And what a name."

"Yes, Amelie Ruth, after your mother's sister, and you of course."

"It's so nice, such an honor."

Jasper settled on the floor and began to put together the pieces of the wooden train track.

"What have you got there?" Ruth asked.

"A train track."

"Ah, I see. Do you like trains?"

"Oh yes," Jasper nodded enthusiastically, "this isn't all the tracks we have. We have more but Mommy said it would be too heavy to bring them all."

Ruth looked at the large bag of tracks and train cars. "I think you'll have enough."

Jasper nodded and got busy with lining up the cars on the tracks.

"Has Karen been by?" Karen had delivered her second child two days earlier.

"No, not yet."

"And Keith and Heidi? I think they're coming up soon too." Keith and his wife Heidi lived in Calgary with their two sons, Caleb, aged four, and Joel, who had celebrated his first birthday in June.

"Yes, we're looking forward to seeing them."

"You have quite the handful of great grandchildren, Grandma. Did you ever imagine?"

"No," Ruth shook her head, "I'm a lucky lady, especially to have you all so close by."

"How's Gerry doing?"

"Not too well. He starts radiation soon. He's in so much pain."

Shauna groaned, "I'm sorry. That must be hard too, for you as his Mom."

Ruth nodded. "It is. You never stop worrying and loving. I don't want him to be in pain."

"Please," Shauna whispered so that Jasper didn't hear, "if you can, don't say anything in front of Jacob about Gerry. He'd be devastated."

"I understand." Ruth made a zipping motion across her lips.

Just then the front door swung open. Waldemar stepped inside and Jacob came in next pushing Gerry.

"Hi guys!" Ruth called.

"Hi!" Jacob said enthusiastically, "Gerry's here!"

"Come in, come in." Ruth waved them over. "Right here Jacob, you can park Gerry next to me."

Jacob expertly manoeuvred Gerry next to Ruth. "How's that, Gerry?" he asked.

"Aye," Gerry answered. Gerry vocalized some more.

Jacob looked at Ruth and asked, "Did he say thanks?"

Gerry and Ruth laughed. She answered, "Yes!"

Jacob gave Gerry a hug and a kiss on the cheek. Gerry's arms moved wildly and Jacob laughed, "Whoa, Gerry, be careful!" He looked at Jasper. "Nice track, can I help?"

"Sure," Jasper agreed.

The boys went to work building a bigger, better track while the adults caught up on the last week's events.

*

Gerry moaned as he drooped over in his chair.

"Have you been able to sleep, Gerry?" Ruth asked in a tense tone.

"Nah."

"Are you tired? Can you sit up?"

"Nah."

"Is it the pain? Is it bad?"

"Aye."

"Do we need to call someone?"

Ruth leaned over and pushed Gerry's glasses up his nose. "You're going to fall right out of that chair if you don't sit up! Is he belted? Pete, is he belted?" She was frantic.

"Of course he's belted!" Waldemar snapped.

"I am saying that he is going to fall right out. Sit him up. Sit him up, Pete!"

Waldemar ignored her as he stroked Gerry's back. The three of them were in the den, watching television. It was Gerry's night to visit. Today he was in terrible pain from the cancer. He hardly ever took any medication but today he had asked for a painkiller. Waldemar gladly placed it in his mouth and gave him water to wash it down.

Gerry's arms spasmed and flailed wildly. He verbalized loudly.

Ruth saw Waldemar move to the edge of his seat and eye up Gerry.

"No, Waldemar, don't…you are ninety years old," Ruth protested vehemently.

Waldemar battled inwardly. "I have to." He rolled Gerry's chair over to the couch and lifted his sixty-year-old son carefully from his chair. He sat down on the couch with Gerry in his arms.

Gerry flailed and moaned as Waldemar held him firmly. "It's okay, Gerry."

Waldemar gently rocked his grown son in his arms. His touch as predictable as the rolling tide. He spoke soothingly over and over. Ruth fretted from her chair. He said softly, "You're going to be okay. Just a matter of time now, the medicine's going to help."

Safe in his father's arms, Gerry's body finally stopped battling. He dropped off to sleep, listening to his dad's reassuring words.

Waldemar and Ruth watched the television, saying nothing. They listened to Gerry's deep breathing. Finally, it was time for his bus to come. Waldemar woke him gently and carefully lifted him back into his chair. Gerry looked into his father's eyes, tears forming.

"It's okay, Gerry." Waldemar fastened the lap belt and carefully adjusted Gerry's glasses. He smoothed his hair and helped him put on his cape.

Gerry vocalized.

"We love you too," Ruth answered.

Waldemar wheeled Gerry down the hall and to the front doors where they waited for his bus. He patted Gerry's shoulder.

"You know, Gerry, you've handled yourself in a real positive way. I've never heard you complain."

"Nah."

"And that," Waldemar looked at his oldest son, "that is really something."

"Aye," Gerry vocalized again.

"Message?"

Waldemar put Gerry's headpiece on and watched him as he spelled out a message on his word board.

"I – m-a-k-e- p-e-a-r-l-s-o-u-t-o-f-m-y-p-r-o-b-l-e-m-s." The bus pulled up.

"Yes you do." Waldemar wheeled Gerry out into the dusky night. It was late. The summer sun was setting. "Take good care of yourself, Gerry." He kissed his son on the cheek and pushed him onto the bus ramp. "Goodnight."

Gerry called out, "Buh."

*

Seven months passed. They had just celebrated the new year.

"Hello!" Shauna called as they came in through the front door.

Ruth wheeled over in her power wheelchair. "Hello, sweetheart!" She looked at each little great grandchild. "Hello, Mr. Jacob."

He smiled as he kicked off his boots. "Hi, Grandma."

"Hello, Jasper."

Jasper flung his winter coat to the floor. "Hi, Grandma!"

"And hello, little lady."

Shauna moved next to Ruth so that she could see Jenna.

Waldemar shut the front door and began picking up the carnage of winter coats, boots, mitts and hats on the floor. "Come on in," he motioned to the living room, "make yourselves comfortable."

Shauna laughed as the boys raced past Ruth and went straight for the cupboard where the toys were kept. "No problem with that. Here, let me get this." Shauna bent down, and picked up the coats and passed them to Waldemar.

"How are you?" he asked.

"Good," Shauna sighed, "Tired and busy but doing okay."

"Are you taking care of yourself?"

Shauna smiled. "Trying to!"

He put his arm around her back and kissed Jenna who was in her arms. "I'm glad you're here."

"Me too."

The kids began to set up the play dishes and take orders. Waldemar ordered his favorite, blueberry pie and coffee to drink.

"Grandma," Jacob asked, "What do you want?"

"Okay," Ruth looked up in the sky, "let's see…how about chicken, mashed potatoes and carrots?"

Jasper whipped away and went to Jacob who was cooking in the cardboard box kitchen.

"Grandma wants chicken and potatoes."

Jacob made a flurry of movements, concocting his imaginary supper. He gave Jasper the meal to deliver on the box lid tray.

"Thank you, sir," Ruth said, with utmost sincerity.

"Where's my pie?" Waldemar enquired, "I'm getting hungry."

Jasper laughed, looked at Jacob and made a silly face, "Pie! Pie! We need pie!"

After ten rounds of restaurant, Jacob and Jasper took Waldemar away to go and hunt for monsters down the hall. It was a long-standing tradition, complete with flashlights and a plastic bag for detaining monsters.

Ruth and Shauna visited in the living room while the boys played.

"I love Jenna's hair. It's much lighter than the boy's," Ruth commented.

Shauna ran her fingers through Jenna's fine strawberry-blonde curls. "So cute, isn't it?"

"Mine was the same when I was a little girl. Right up until nursing school."

"Really?" Shauna looked at Ruth's gray hair that still had bits of dark brown. "I didn't know that."

"Yes, I was skilled in the OR so they put me on a lot of rotations. Sister Saint Christine was hoping I'd become an OR nurse."

"I guess you really were able to use that knowledge in Kinuso."

Ruth smiled. "Yes, God had it all planned out. Only trouble was working with Ether all the time made my hair go brown."

"No kidding."

"Yes, it was a pretty strawberry-blonde all my life and after that — boring brown."

Shauna shifted gears, "Hey, how's Gerry doing?"

"He's okay. His pain is very bad, but he won't take anything. He never listens to his mom." Ruth smiled.

"Ah, I see, not even when they're sixty — hey? I guess I don't have any hope."

Ruth laughed, "No, he's never listened to me. He's got a mind of his own and it better be his way! That's one thing we always impressed on him. He had to be his own individual. Didn't know it was going to work against me too!"

"Those first-born kids, Jacob is the same way. His way or the highway."

She changed the subject, "Do you think the boys are ready for treats?"

"I'll go and get them." Shauna laid Jenna on the ground headed down the hall for the boys. She poked her head in the den where Waldemar was on his hands and knees, peering under the couch. "Treat time."

"Treat time!" the boys exclaimed. Jacob grabbed Waldemar by the hand. "Come on, Papa! Treat time!"

Waldemar sprang to his feet and went down the hall after the boys. They sat on the floor in the kitchenette area. Ruth dolled out mini-chocolate bars, Dixie cups full of M&Ms and Hershey Kisses. The boys were quiet as they ate.

Waldemar sat on a nearby chair and studied the boys. He was glad that he could know them as a playmate and friend. He was a very blessed man.

After treats, Jasper and Jacob sang a Christmas song for Ruth and Waldemar. They clapped their hands excitedly at the end.

"My dad would have loved that!" Ruth proclaimed.

"Your dad?" Jacob asked.

"Yes. Your great great grandpa. He loved to sing. He loved to hear singing. Most of all he loved his family. He would love to see you three precious darlings."

"See you again next week?" Shauna asked as they put on their coats.

"We'll be here," Ruth answered.

Waldemar beamed, "We'll look forward to it." He slipped on his shoes and walked Shauna and the kids down to the front doors.

"Love you," he said as he gave her a big hug.

"Love you too, Grandpa."

"I love you, Papa," Jacob said as Waldemar came down on his knee for hugs.

"I love you, Jacob." He pulled Jasper close. "And you too, Jasper. You take good care of your mom, okay?"

They both smiled. "We will."

"And that baby sister of yours…she's something special."

The boys looked at their mom, holding Jenna, all bundled for the cold weather. "We will, Papa. We take good care of our sister."

He hugged each of the kids in turn. He watched as Shauna loaded up the kids into the van and drove away.

Chapter 39

"...Forgetting what is behind and straining toward what is ahead, I press on toward the goal to win the prize for which God has called me heavenward in Christ Jesus." Philippians 3:13 & 14 NIV

September 2009

Ruth hated this. She always had to go to the washroom at the most inopportune times. She was in the middle of a dentist appointment and had to excuse herself.

Waldemar got up from his seat in the waiting room when he saw her coming down the hall in her wheelchair, being pushed by a dental assistant.

"What are you doing?" he asked.

"I need to go to the washroom."

"I'll take her." Waldemar maneuvered the chair through the washroom door. He looked at her sternly. "I'll stay and help."

"No."

Waldemar shook his head disapprovingly. "You call me if you need help. You hear me?"

She glared at him. "Just go."

Waldemar stood anxiously outside the washroom door. Finally, he heard what he had been half-expecting and entirely dreading. There was a loud clunk and then a weak, "Pete."

He opened the door and slipped inside. She had washed her hands and was trying to sit back in her chair when she had lost her balance. Now she lay on the floor, her leg twisted at a terrible angle.

"Ruth!" he exclaimed. "What happened?"

"Never mind. Just help me."

He braced himself against the wall and hoisted her under the arms and up into her chair. His back cried out as he set her down, as gently as he could.

She grimaced in terrible pain. "Good Lord!"

"We need to take you to the hospital."

"I need to finish my appointment."

"Oh no you don't."

"Waldemar, I am going to finish."

He begrudgingly wheeled her back to the dentist's chair where she concluded the last half of the appointment. Her leg and hip screamed out in agony the entire time but she suppressed the urge to say something. At long last the dentist finished, unaware of her fall, and she left the clinic.

Waldemar helped her into the car where she protested loudly. "Oh, it's bad," she groaned. He, now with his license re-instated, drove to the hospital and took her into the emergency room.

After several hours of waiting and multiple x-rays, the doctor came into the room where Ruth lay.

"Mrs. Peterson, you are one tough lady."

Ruth smiled. Waldemar shook his head in disbelief as the x-rays went up on the light.

"You have broken your hip and leg in nine places."

Ruth gasped, "Oh my goodness!"

Waldemar continued to shake his head.

"We're going to schedule you for surgery as soon as possible. I have to warn you that you are going to have a long road of recovery. It may be a reality that you won't be able to walk anymore, or live independently."

Ruth said nothing.

"Thank you, Doctor," Waldemar said.

"Why didn't you ask me for help?" he asked, once the doctor had left.

Ruth began to cry. "I don't know."

"Are you so stubborn that you will risk your life, your health, our independence because you don't want me in the bathroom with you?"

She hung her head. "I know. I'm sorry."

He reached out for her hand. "I'm sorry, Ruth, I really am. I hate this. I feel like you never listen to me."

"I don't want to bother you."

He rolled his eyes. "Bother me? It's only been a few months since you fell in the bathroom at home and I had to pick you up. Then that day at Sears last year — same thing, you wouldn't let me help you in the washroom. When are you going to get it? You need me!"

"I know."

"And I need you. We have to recognize our weaknesses. I'm ninety, you're eighty-seven…we're not able to make the same choices we always have."

"I'm sorry."

"I don't want you to be sorry."

She looked him in the eyes. "What do you want?"

"I want you to promise me that you won't do this anymore."

"I won't."

"You can't risk yourself for pride's sake. I don't want to be separated."

"We won't."

"What if they say you can't come home? Can't live independently?"

"I will."

"You may not have that choice."

"I swear to you, I will come home."

He put his head down on the edge of the bed. She stroked the top of his head.

"I'm sorry."

Waldemar picked up the phone. "Hello."

"Hi, Grandpa, it's Karen."

"Hi, Karen. How are you?"

"I'm fine. I just got a call from Cindy at the group home. Gerry's being taken by ambulance to the hospital. He was having a hard time. They haven't come for him yet but she'll call me when they do."

"Oh dear."

"I'm going to go, or call Dad and see if someone can meet him at the hospital to interpret."

"Okay. I appreciate that. I'm going up to see your grandma."

"How is she doing?"

"She's doing pretty well. The nurses are stunned. Dale says that in order for her to come home she needs to prove that she can handle herself in the washroom and that she can walk across the room with her walker. They won't allow me to be her primary caregiver. They say there is a certain level of independence she needs to have in order to stay where we're at."

"If anyone can do it, Grandma can."

"She's hell bent and determined to come home so I keep encouraging her onward. One small step at a time. We'll get there."

"Okay. Well, tell her I said hi. I'm going to make some calls and see what we can do about Gerry. I'll keep you posted on what happens."

"Thank you, Karen."

Waldemar sighed and hung up the phone. He was weary. So weary. Ruth had fallen in the spring and broken her wrist. He had cared for her, dressing her, even doing her make-up and making sure she was as comfortable as possible. Now she had recovered from that and here they were again. Going through all of this. Now Gerry.

"God," he prayed, "I've had enough. Give me the strength and wisdom to go forward."

Dale had been at the hospital all day and night. Gerry was in terrible pain. He was in spasm, doubling over, moaning and crying out. The nurses were unsure of what to do. They treated him as though he were mentally disabled. One nurse even asked Dale in a whisper while approaching Gerry, "Is he violent?"

Dale laughed, "He's a convicted killer."

The nurse's eyes widened. Then she smiled. "Oh."

Gerry laughed at his younger brother.

"Gerry needs something for the pain," Dale waved the list of medications that Gerry was on. "Now that we have this, we need to get him something, now."

"I understand, Mr. Peterson, but we have to get the doctor to look at this and then order something."

"Look at him," Gerry was curled into a tight ball, convulsing. "He needs something — now."

"I'll go and speak to the doctor."

Just then, Shauna's husband Matt came into the room with sandwiches and coffee. "Hi, guys."

Gerry looked up.

"Hey, Matt," Dale motioned to the empty chair, "have a seat."

"Thanks, Dad. I got off work and I was talking to Shauna. I thought you might like something to eat. Sounds like you've been here all day?"

"Yes. It's been a long day. Thanks for coming."

Matt looked at Gerry. "How are you doing?"

Gerry moaned.

"It's pretty bad. We couldn't find his list of medications. I tried the group home. It took them a long time to get a list of what he was on. In the meantime, he's been without anything. Not even his usual meds."

"Oh no," Matt said sympathetically.

Matt stayed and visited for nearly half an hour. He was able to make Gerry and Dale laugh despite the condition Gerry was in. Finally, it was time for him to get home.

"Well, Gerry, I better get home to the boys."

"Jacob," Gerry said.

"You want me to bring Jacob?"

"Wow, Gerry," Dale said, surprised, "no need for translation on that one."

"Yes, I knew right away what you wanted." Matt exchanged a look with Dale.

"You know, Gerry," Dale explained, "this might be a bit much for Jacob right now."

"He's sensitive." Matt added, "He would be really upset to see you in the hospital. He's already completely broken up about Grandma being in the hospital. He knows you're here. I think seeing you like this, in so much pain. He couldn't bear it."

Gerry agreed, "Aye."

"As soon as you're feeling better though," Matt promised, "I'll bring him to you."

Every step was agony. Ruth felt every nerve in her body reacting as she tried to pilot her walker across the hospital room to the bathroom. She had to do it. She had to get there.

She willed herself to lift her broken leg. She breathed in rapidly. She exhaled slowly. "I can do this."

Waldemar knocked softly on the door.

"Come in," she called.

He opened the door. "Oh, you're up."

"Yes," she grimaced. "I'm trying to work on my walking. Dale says if I can show my independence and get to and from the bathroom on my own — they'll let me go home."

"Yes, he told me that too. Just don't overdo it."

She looked at him sternly. "You haven't been here for three weeks."

"I have. I've been coming here every day for three weeks. You don't have to tell me how hard this is."

"I'm sorry. It's the pain. And thinking that some government body is going to tell me where I can or cannot live."

"It's going to be fine."

"I can't go to a nursing home."

"No you can't."

"Not yet. I can't live apart from you."

"Then get walking." Waldemar sat down in the chair. He hated to see her in so much pain. "I won't get in your way."

Inch by inch, Ruth worked her way to the bathroom. She tapped the frame of the door. "I did it!"

Waldemar nodded. "Indeed. You did."

She started to laugh. "Want to give me a ride back?"

He laughed, "Of course I will." She sat down on her walker seat. Waldemar came over and took the handles. She slid her slippers along the ground. He said, "I think this is cheating."

She looked up at him and winked. "I know you won't tell a soul."

A week later, Ruth sat in her familiar recliner and dialed Gerry's number.

"Huh," he said when he picked up the phone.

"Hi, sweetheart. It's Mom."

Gerry vocalized.

"How are you feeling?"

"Gah."

"Good? Are you in a lot of pain?"

Gerry indicated that he had a message.

"A, B, C…" Gerry stopped her at H. He carried on to ask her how she was feeling.

"I'm okay. I'm in a lot of pain. Your dad says I am not to move without his permission. I have exercises to do and also I have times during the day where he sends me to bed to rest. He's taking good care of me."

Gerry laughed.

"I can't believe you're home again, Gerry. I'm worried about you. Are they taking good care of you? Are you taking your medicines? What do they say about your kidneys?"

"I la-uv ooo, Mum."

Ruth was speechless for a minute. "Gerry! Did you hear yourself?"

He laughed.

Her mouth hung open. "I can't believe it! That's the first sentence you've ever said to me!"

Gerry laughed again, "Aye."

"I can't believe it! I've waited sixty years to hear you put a sentence together!"

"Mah."

"Message?"

Gerry spelled out: 'I'm full of surprises.'

Ruth laughed. "Yes, Gerry, you are. This isn't the first time you've scared us, thinking that you were heaven bound. I don't know if I'll ever be ready for that day."

Gerry then spelled out, 'I am.'

Ruth started to cry. "I'm your mom. I want to greet you on the other side when it's your time."

Gerry cried softly.

"The Lord knows our days, Ger. Let's count every day together as a blessing, shall we?"

"Aye."

Waldemar combed Ruth's hair before bed. He helped her slip her nightgown on and carefully eased her into bed next to him. He sat down on the edge of bed, arranging her pillows. He looked her in the eyes.

"Well, my love. You did it."

"Yes I did."

"You came home to me."

"I said I would."

"I should have never doubted you," he laughed. "You would think I'd know better by now!"

Ruth laughed. "There's nothing that would keep me from you."

Comfortable silence filled the air between them, each one lost in their thoughts.

Finally, Waldemar said, "We've been through a lot, you and me."

"We're quite a pair."

He rubbed her arm. "I don't know what I'd do without you. I was so lonely here while you were in the hospital."

"We've had a good life," Ruth said softly.

"There hasn't been a day that's gone by where I haven't been thankful to have you as my wife."

Ruth's eyes misted up with tears. "I love you, Waldemar, more than anything."

Waldemar took her hand in his. "I love you too, Ruth."

"We've learned a lot over the years."

"Humility."

"Patience."

"How to compromise."

"How to listen."
"How to love."
"How to depend on the Lord."

Ruth looked at Waldemar. "I have learned how to forgive."

"And so have I," he replied

"It hasn't always been easy."

"Certainly not. We've each had our share of heartache."

"Oh it was awful those first five years of having kids…me on my own, you at work…never seeing one another."

"But we did it."

"Losing loved ones, seeing our children struggle, seeing our grandchildren struggle," Ruth continued.

"Caring for Gerry — fighting tirelessly for Gerry."

"Making tough choices. Sacrificing our own needs."

"Following God's Word amidst the temptations of the world."

"And now," Ruth said softly, "Here we are, still together and strong. There is nothing I can't face with you by my side."

"We are fortunate. We have our minds. We have our health. We have our faith and…" He bent down and kissed her, "we have each other."

"We have each other," she echoed.

"Until death parts us."

"Until death parts us."

Death Parts Us

Karen, Grandpa, Shauna, Grandma and Keith

    This is the end of their story and it is the beginning of mine.

    After Grandpa turned 90 I asked both he and Grandma if I could tell their life story. They were excited and over-joyed that someone would take on the job. Grandma had always wanted her story to be told. She wanted to share all of her struggles and victories, to permanently etch the past in the minds of future generations. I wanted to record their history because I knew that one day, they would no longer be there to tell me. I wanted all the stories, all the memories, told in the proper way, the proper order and with all of the lessons laid out for my children.

    Since I finished writing their story there are some key events that I want to share.

    July 3, 2010 Gerry passed away. It was a terrible time leading up to his death. His kidneys were failing, he had prostate cancer and he was in tremendous pain. He never complained. He continued to find his joy in the Lord. He met with us for visits at Grandma and Grandpa's. He emailed us regularly. He prayed for us. Mostly he kept the phone calls coming to his parents. Every night he would talk to them while Grandma and Grandpa patiently worked out his messages, using the alphabet method.

In the end Dale and Brian were there for Gerry, in the hospital – seeing him fade. During all of this Grandma had broken her leg again and was in long-term care, rehabilitating. She did get better, and was able to take a few steps, which granted her the ability to come home to Grandpa.

Grandpa told me that on one of his last visits to the group home Gerry could no longer hold himself up in his wheelchair. He kept drooping forward. Grandpa sat beside him and placed his 93 year-old hand on Gerry's chest, the entire time they were there. As they left Grandpa wheeled Gerry out to the door all the while holding him upright. Grandpa told me that he prayed. He told God that he could never let go of his son. God whispered to him to let go. Amazingly as he removed his hand Gerry remained upright. Grandpa was overwhelmed with God's presence and comfort. As he walked out the door he felt angels all around Gerry. He felt God saying to him, I will hold him now.

It was heartbreaking to hear Grandpa tell me this. I knew that he felt so helpless. He didn't ever want to see Gerry die. He didn't want to see the end of Gerry's story. However, he was comforted as he saw Gerry taken into God's loving care.

It wasn't long after that Gerry's end came. Grandpa was devastated. He said often that he wished he could have done more. All of us wondered, what more? He was an amazing father and friend. Grandma's reaction was different. She was numb. She told me that she felt so empty. She couldn't cry, but she wished she could. She could not believe that he was gone. She could not believe that he would not be phoning, or coming for a visit. As Christmas passed and then his birthday she mourned quietly.

At Gerry's viewing, the night before his funeral service, we gathered at the funeral home. Gerry looked so strange to me. He had always been tense and now he was lying flat, with his arms at rest. Grandpa and Grandma said he looked so peaceful. To me, he looked unfamiliar. The pain I felt as Grandpa prayed over Gerry and thanked God for his life was most likely only a fraction of what they were feeling. I was overwhelmed with grief for them as I watched them kiss their eldest son goodbye. The service and internment were surreal. It is impossible to describe the emotion on Grandpa and Grandma's faces as Gerry was lowered into the earth. It was the end of their purpose. It was the end of their mission. They had completed their cause, to educate, to love and to provide for their son.

In August 2012 Grandpa celebrated his 95th birthday. He didn't want a party but Grandma insisted. She was fearful of his birthday. Her own father died close to his 95th birthday and she feared that this might be Grandpa's experience as well. Grandpa spent a lot of time in 2012 talking about his end. He asked how we could care for Grandma, he asked about his financial affairs, he asked about where Grandma would live. He asked Karen and I to make sure that all of Grandma's wishes were followed and that we would care for her in the same way that he did. We promised him we would. His conversations brought a knotting grip to my stomach. I wondered if he knew that he was ill, and was not sharing.

I spent a year reading this story to them. They enjoyed it and would often tell me what was going to happen next at the end of my reading for the day. I'd laugh and say, I know, that's next week! It was an incredible experience to have a chat with the characters of my favorite story. They would add in memories as they surfaced. I loved to hear their thoughts and reflections after I read. They often said, "We've had an incredible life" or "That's it exactly, it's like you were there."

On one of these visits I asked Grandpa why he was asking so many questions about his final preparations. I asked if he was ill. He said that no, he wasn't ill but he had been very tired this last year, especially the last few months. Grandma confirmed that he slept a lot more than usual. He could finally begin to feel his age as he approached 95. Despite all of this, he cared for Grandma completely. He dressed her, did her makeup, helped her eat, helped her in the washroom and did all of the housework. No wonder he was tired! Her vision had been fading for years due to macular degeneration. In 2012 almost all had faded away for her. Her mobility was limited to pivot transfers. Grandpa lovingly helped her every step of the way. He was incredibly faithful. As I asked that question, I began to cry. I told them that I could never imagine the two of them apart. Grandma began to cry. She rarely cried and yet as she imagined saying goodbye to her beloved Wally the tears ran freely. She squeezed my hand as we sat there crying. We both looked at this man we loved dearly.

For his birthday we celebrated at Caleb Manor, where they had lived since 2006. All of the family came. We took many photos, offered gifts, had lunch and cake. Keith's son Joel was eager to blow out the candles for his Great-Grandpa. Grandpa had many smiles that day, watching his seven great-grandchildren surround him. At the end of the party he was tired. We took a large family photo together. After that, Grandpa spoke to all of us. I recorded those words and I am glad I did.

"I want to start out by saying that this has been a wonderful, wonderful occasion for me. I wasn't anticipating anything or expecting anything. I want to thank all of you. But even before I thank you I want to thank my God for looking after me for 95 years. He took me from the small farm in Manitoba and brought me to where I am here today. It's been a wonderful trail. The travelling along the journey has been beautiful every step of the way. I don't know how I can thank all of you, but I really want to thank you all. Some come from far, some from near but you all come to bring me greetings. So on behalf of myself and on behalf of Ruth, I say thank you to all of you. Please remember that I love you all, that you have been a wonderful part of my life. Thank you."

He and Grandma retired to their suite while we cleaned up the party and said goodbye to one another. I felt that this could be the last 'Happy Birthday'. I could feel it in his words.

Grandma

The fall came and went with many happy visits. There was more reading and sharing stories followed by long talks, counsel and encouragement. Leading up to Christmas we could see how tired Grandpa was getting. On the 28th of December Grandpa called us out to see them. He wanted a family meeting. This made me feel ill… something was happening. When he called and asked if I could come he was using his 'policeman' tone. I drove out to their place quickly, the ever growing knot in my gut intensifying. When we arrived Grandma did not look well. She was waxy and extremely pale. I had seen them only a week before and she had changed considerably. Karen had seen them on Christmas Eve and had mentioned that Grandma's color was poor.

Grandma looked like a young girl. Little Ruth, full of worry and heartbreak. She was angry and pouting in her wheelchair. She was angry that things were not going her way. Once Dad, Brian, Karen and I arrived they told us that Grandpa could no longer care for Grandma at home. He said that she had become so weak that she could not bear any weight on her legs. He too had grown weak and could not lift her, without her providing some assistance. They were both feeling helpless and frustrated. Grandpa was so heavy burdened with guilt. He wept as we sat around him, comforting him. Grandma said that she knew she had to go to a nursing home. We promised that we would do our best to sort out a good solution for both of them. Little did we know how warped the system for the elderly was. They didn't ever want to be apart. Grandpa wept and Grandma was stony and silent. Although Grandpa urged that he needed help quickly none of us realized how urgent things were. We left, promising to make phone calls the following morning.

That night Karen and I spoke on the phone for a long time, as was our custom, but this time solely about our favorite 'G&G' as we called them. We commented on Grandma's color and talked about taking her into a hospital that night. It was ten o'clock and we decided that they probably would be in bed. We made a plan to go out the following morning to take Grandma in for medical treatment.

I don't remember when we got the call but Grandma woke up in the wee hours and was taken by ambulance into the hospital. Karen arrived first and then myself shortly after. We spent the day in the hospital with Grandma, trying to figure out what was wrong. After some investigation, we found out that her hemoglobin had dropped to 40, so that explained her color and tone. It also explained her weakness and growing confusion. She was in good spirits over all, resting, chatting with us and asking after Grandpa. The hospital gave her many bags of blood. She had transfusion after transfusion to raise her hemoglobin. She went in and out of confusion as she slept and woke. At one point, she was speaking to us in German. Karen and I smiled at one another, wondering what she was saying. We did everything we could to keep her happy and comfortable. Grandpa was being driven to the hospital to keep her company. The days were long for him and he refused to eat or drink, he was sick with worry.

Grandma did not like the food and was having trouble swallowing or feeding herself. Karen and I took turns caring for her. Feeding her, washing her hands and face, and combing her hair. She found it very difficult to be away from Grandpa and that she could not see. We brought Grandpa up to visit her daily.

Grandma was moved to a private room where it became evident that the transfusions had caused a lot of fluid to pool in her lungs. She struggled to breathe and the confusion became worse.

Only a few days after Grandma went in to hospital Grandpa had his own troubles. He had suffered from the stomach flu back in the beginning of December and his stomach had been out of sorts ever since. He was alone in their suite one night and began to vomit. He vomited incredible amounts of blood. He struggled to the bathroom and then realized this was bad. Really bad. He pressed his call button for help. The staff at Caleb Manor rushed up, knowing that Waldemar Peterson would not ring unless it was very serious. It was. The suite looked like a murder scene. There was blood everywhere. He was covered in blood. 911 was called and an ambulance rushed to him. The staff saved his life. God intervened. He should have died.

I had just come home from a long day at the hospital with Grandma and was exhausted. We got the phone call at eleven o'clock informing us of what had happened. My husband Matt offered to go to the hospital to meet Grandpa. Matt stayed at the hospital through the early morning hours. Grandpa was in surgery. His stomach had ruptured. He had lost a lot of blood. It was a miracle that he lived to see another day.

Karen and I were at Grandma's side constantly minute by minute. Sometimes she was calm and connected to us and other times the confusion overwhelmed her. She was angry with us. She wanted to go home. She wanted Grandpa. She didn't understand that she couldn't stand, could barely breathe. One night Karen went home while I stayed. Grandma began to insist that I get her dressed, get her slippers on and take her 'down' to the kitchen so that she could make supper. I gently explained that she was sick, she had no strength and besides, she wasn't at home. She became angrier and angrier, screaming at me that I was keeping her from Grandpa. I kept trying to be reasonable but she was in another time and space. Then I tried to come into her time and space but she wasn't buying it. She continued to scream at me, that I was the villain. I had never seen her like this. I began to cry quietly as the screaming went on for over a half hour. Then she heard the sadness in my voice and was even angrier. She wanted me to get her out of bed, and boy if I could have, I would have! Finally, I had to call Karen to come back. I was crying and couldn't stop as she kept tearing me apart. All she wanted was to go home to Grandpa. I tried to explain that Grandpa was in a different hospital but that was only more upsetting to her. She started to scream 'HELP!' to try and get the staff to come in and rescue her from me.

Karen came in and was able to handle the situation. She listened as Grandma screamed at her how wicked we were. Karen agreed at how frustrating the whole situation was. After nearly two hours she finally grew weary of yelling.

Karen and I sat by her bedside quietly while she fidgeted with her oxygen tube. We texted back and forth that she was probably trying to figure out a way to lynch us both with that tube. I left weary and sad. Karen talked her through what was happening. Grandma ended the night by telling Karen how to hand wash sweaters. This soothed Grandma.

We went to their place after Grandpa had the stomach rupture and saw that he had vomited blood everywhere. Keith came up to help and cleaned Grandpa's walker while Karen cleaned the bed and sheets. I could not handle any of it. I just stood numbly watching my siblings work.

Grandpa stayed in hospital after his stomach rupture. We visited him. Grandpa and Grandma were able to talk on the phone. Grandpa was determined to get well and go see Grandma. Every day he exercised and quickly recovered.

Grandpa was discharged from the Misercordia and was able to go home. We got him settled in and took him to see Grandma every day. After one visit we both sat on a bench, near the door of the hospital and broke into tears. He said to me, "What would I do without her?". He held me in his big, strong arms while I cried. To think of the two of them apart tore me up inside. To think of my life without my Grandma – I could not imagine it.

We talked a lot those days. He cried. I cried. He told me how he was feeling. He was very vulnerable – which was a rare thing to see. He would often clasp his hand to his forehead and sob quietly.

When he visited Grandma I would give them time alone. I would go for a walk or get something to eat. On one particular day I was returning for Grandpa when I heard them talking. Before I came around the curtain I stopped to listen.

"Ruth, I love you. If it is time for you to go, you need to go."

"I can't Wally. I can't go without you."

"Have you seen angels?"

"Yes," she said quietly.

"I promise you, I'll come. I'll be right behind you. This is something you have to do alone."

Stubbornly she replied, "I'm not going without you."

"Ruth," he insisted, "the end is near. I can see that. When the angels come for you. I need you to go."

"No Wally," she began to cry, "I can't."

I stood at the door, tears pouring down my face.

"Tonight we will pray together, just as we always do at nine, so that our spirits can be together. You remember that Ruth, okay?"

"I will."

"Listen to me. This is the one thing we cannot face together. You have to go alone. Then I will come. I promise you. I will come as quickly as I can."

Grandma nodded, finally accepting what he was saying.

"If the angels come tonight, go. I'll be okay. You can go with them."

She whispered, "I will."

He prayed silently over her, tears running down his weathered cheeks. He kissed her, tenderly and squeezed her hand. "I love you. I love you so much."

"I love you too Wally."

Grandpa came out of the room, took one look at me and we embraced. We cried in the hallway, aware of all that had just transpired. She had finally accepted that this was the end. She seemed to realize that this was one thing they could not do together.

Again we went back to their home at Caleb Manor. He sat in her chair while I sat in his. We cried for a long time wondering if indeed, the angels would come for her that night.

She didn't go that night. Karen and I prayed continuously that God would take them both in their sleep so that they could run through the gates of heaven together, hand in hand.

This was not to be.

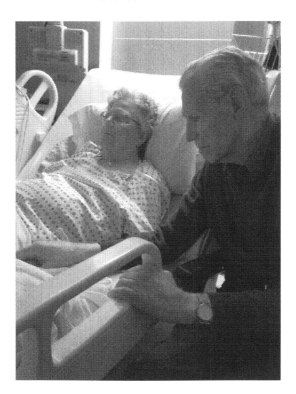

Together

After one trip to the hospital Grandpa came back to Caleb Manor for dinner. He went up to their suite and got ready for the meal. He then went down to the dining room and as he was crossing the foyer he collapsed. The people who witnessed it said he just fell straight back and smashed his head on the hard floor. Again, an ambulance was called. Again, he was rushed to the hospital.

I was visiting Grandma when it happened. She and I were chatting. A family member arrived unexpectedly and asked to speak to me outside. Grandma knew. She knew something was wrong with Grandpa. I didn't say anything to her about it. I told her I would go and get something to eat and come back. I went down to emergency to find Grandpa in rough shape. My dad was there. Grandpa was speaking but his speech was extremely slurred. He was hard to understand. Eventually I went back up to Grandma to tell her what had happened. She was worried, however, we were grateful they were both in the same building.

Karen and I were there every day. We went back and forth between their units tending to their needs. They constantly asked how the other one was doing. A day after his fall I helped Grandpa into a wheelchair and I took him to Grandma. They were so happy to see each other. Grandma was upset and worried that he was out of bed. He wanted to stand up to kiss her and Grandma and I both told him to 'sit down!' He did get on his feet and kissed her. He had the last say in that matter. They held hands and talked. I left the room to give them privacy.

They held hands and looked at one another for hours. Eventually Grandpa grew weary and Grandma insisted he go back to his bed to rest. I wheeled him back and settled him in his room.

Karen and I advocated repeatedly that they should be in the same room. We begged, we pleaded and we told anyone who would listen how much they loved each other. After a long time they were in the same room. I was so relieved.

Unfortunately, they only had two nights together before we were told that Grandma had to be transferred to long-term care.

We talked often. I asked her everything I wanted to know, so that when it is my time, I can draw upon her experience. I asked her if she was afraid, and she said no. We talked about her meeting her mother and seeing Gerry again. She wanted to see her father, Herman. She told me that I would be okay. I asked her if she could feel it, heaven that is, calling her. She told me that she dreamed of loved ones who were in heaven. For hours, while she slept, she would reach out her arms, to the heavens. Sometimes she told us that she wanted to go home. When we asked she did not refer to being with Grandpa as home… but somewhere else. Karen and I marveled at this. We could feel angels around us in those quiet moments while she slept. We could feel heaven calling her home.

Long-Term Care

The morning that she left the hospital was another heart-breaking scene. They were both upset and nervous. Grandma was transferred to a stretcher and the paramedics were kind enough to wheel her right next to Grandpa's bed. He sat up and kissed her. He sent his love and prayers with her. We rode in the ambulance together, Grandma and I, leaving Grandpa behind. It was a bumpy ride. I sat behind Grandma's head and numerous times she asked for me. I would touch her shoulder and reassure her that I was there. I wasn't going anywhere. Because she couldn't see the whole experience was overwhelming.

We arrived at Lynwood long-term care facility and Grandma was taken to her room. It was awful. It was as awful as Grandma had feared. The residents were all on death's door, with vacant stares as everyone waited to die. I sat with her and answered all of her medical questions. We met a nice doctor who listened to her and treated her respectfully. We sat together all day. She slept, I fed her and we held hands. The room was shared with another woman so it was quiet and awkward.

I texted Karen that the facility was terrible. I took a photo and showed her how bad it was. We were both grateful that Grandma couldn't see. I didn't want to leave her that day. She was disoriented and confused. She was frustrated and unhappy. She did tell me every time that we were together how much she loved me. No matter what time or space she was in, that never changed. She always was appreciative of Karen and I being there and she would always end our visit with a kiss and squeeze our hands, saying, "I love you."

The next time I came up she was in a "Geri-chair" lined up with all the rest of the residents, all of them with their vacant eyes and haunting muttering. I barely recognized her there. This was not my Grandma. I quickly wheeled her to her room where I was able to feed her, comb her hair, and hold her hand. We chatted about when Grandpa was going to join her. I promised her that we were doing everything we could.

Meanwhile Karen was at the hospital with Grandpa trying to convince the staff that he too qualified for long-term care. He may have been okay to be in a facility with slightly less care but our idea was to get them both to Lynwood. When he was being assessed for his mobility he strutted around the hospital room with a walker showing how strong he was. Despite this Karen was able to persuade the decision maker that all he wanted was to be with his wife. He was unsteady and was not able to eat solid foods so begrudgingly the hospital agreed that he could go to Lynwood. This took quite some time but eventually he was transferred there.

Again, Karen and I were at our wits end because they ended up on different floors of the facility and they were not able to see each other unless we were there to transport them to each other and back. So every day we took turns going up, taking them to each other, feeding them and making life as bearable as possible. Grandma was quite confused and flickered in and out of the present situation. We rode along with it, trying to be reassuring. We brought our children who talked to her, held her hand and brought some light into that dismal place. Karen's daughter Amelie was chatty and outgoing so she was happy to talk to all of the residents there.

We begged and pleaded for weeks to have them moved to the same floor but it all seemed impossible. Finally Grandma was moved to the fourth floor. Another discouragement was that they could not be in the same room. They were each put in a room with someone who had been at the facility for a long time. No one wanted to move so that they could be together. They were not allowed to visit in their rooms so they had to have someone move Grandma into the hall to be with Grandpa. When Grandma was too weak to get up Grandpa would sit on a chair outside her door. It was so sad to see him there, hour after hour.

Karen and I continued to come and after our visits we would agonize over the facility and the fact that they could not be together. Grandpa was going crazy, being treated like a child. He was talked down to and bossed around by the staff. To them this man was not the Chief Superintendent of the RCMP, he was not a loving father who had cared for his disabled son all his life, he was not a devoted husband who has done all of his wife's personal care for years. He is an old confused man who deserved to be told what to do. It made me so angry to see the both of them treated as children. These people have had more life experience, have done more and deserve so much more than this.

Grandpa at this point was eating pureed food so that he could continue to be nourished and be strong for Grandma. He hated it. All of his drinks were thickened and this made him the most frustrated. He put up with it to be with Grandma and to support her through her struggle.

On February 18th we went up as a family to see Grandma. Grandpa was concerned because she had been in bed all day and was too weak to get up. We went in and all the kids talked to her and kissed her. She recognized them and was thankful that they were there. Her color was poor and she was very tired. I was worried that she was near the end. The next day, Tuesday, I went up and she was sitting in her wheelchair looking much better. They were holding hands in the hallway and we talked about us trying to get them in the same room. I explained that Karen and I had been working on it endlessly but to no avail. I promised them both that we would continue to do everything we could to get them to share a room.

I said goodbye. Grandma squeezed my hands and looked me in the eyes.

"Thank you for everything. I love you."

I cried and kissed her, "I love you too."

Grandpa hugged me tightly. "I love you."

Wednesday Karen went up and said that Grandma's breathing was again labored. Thursday I had dental appointments for the majority of the day and didn't feel I could squeeze in a visit before work. I should have.

Goodbye

Friday morning I was down in my daughter's bed. She had been up in the night and I had laid down to comfort her. When the phone rang I saw the Lynwood caller information. I picked it up, my heart racing.

It was one of the staff.

"Shauna, this is Jan. Are you sitting down?"

I felt sickness wash over me. "Yes, I am."

"Your Grandma died. We haven't told your Grandpa. Can you come down so that you can be here when we tell him?"

I didn't respond. I didn't know what to say. I couldn't believe it. I told her that I was coming right away. She reminded me to drive safely. I hung up and I called Dad. He contacted Brian and made his way to Lynwood with Brian. I called Keith and tried to reach Karen. She was at work and I couldn't get through. I called Matt and my mom. We took the kids to my friend's house and Matt and I went to Lynwood. I still couldn't reach Karen.

When we walked in the room Grandpa was leaning over her body, weeping. He wept and clasped her hand, rocking back and forth. Brian and Dad stood back, watching helplessly. I came in and touched Grandpa's back. He looked up at me. His teal eyes shone with tears.

"What am I going to do?"

He stood up and we hugged. I cried into his shoulder, wishing this was all a nightmare. I sat on her bed and held her hand, her curved pinky resting in my hand. Those familiar fingers, those loving hands that had held mine so many times, lay motionless. The grief was overpowering. I felt like I couldn't breathe, I couldn't think. My head was going to explode. I kept looking at Grandpa, who was rubbing her arm, trying to keep her warm. Different family members sat next to her. Touching her, kissing her and saying goodbye. I took a place on the far side of the bed, holding her other hand. Karen was reached and she came to Lynwood right away. She and Grandpa also embraced when she arrived. He sobbed again, asking over and over, "How will I go on?"

Karen told him that he didn't have to go on. He could release us and go with her. Karen's calm presence made me feel better. We sat with Grandma for hours. Finally, the funeral home came to take her away. To think of her body being zipped up in that maroon bag, I could not take it. I cannot say that it was difficult; I don't know how to describe what I was feeling. It was agony. For the rest of the day Karen and I sat on either side of Grandpa and cried. We didn't want to leave him. We clung to him and him to us.

Keith came up from Calgary that evening and we ate with Grandpa, sharing memories. Grandpa wanted to eat 'real food' so we got it for him. Whatever he wanted. He no longer cared about choking, or pureed food. He wanted to feel normal again. We left that night, not wanting to say goodbye. He reassured us that he would be okay and that all he wanted to do was sleep.

The following day, Saturday we made funeral arrangements all day while Mom stayed with Grandpa at Lynwood. I was so angry. I couldn't speak, I couldn't look at anyone. I didn't want to make arrangements. I didn't want to pick a casket. I did not want to pick clothing for her to wear. I did not want to think of a program. I did not want to think of music, photos, or anything. I did not want Grandma to be dead. Everyone else talked on like we were thinking about what to pack on a picnic lunch. I just wanted to scream. No. No, no, no. This is not happening.

We made the arrangements. I sat there numbly wishing this was not a reality. We had a heated family discussion at the end of the arrangements. I wasn't the only angry one. We were all dealing with it in our own way.

Karen and I went to Caleb Manor to pick out an outfit for Grandma. I hated that. Grandma had told us what she wanted but Grandpa had a slightly different plan. We went with Grandpa's wish, a pink sweater and a pink skirt. We picked out some jewelry that would suit her outfit. Karen and I cried. Then we were off to Lynwood to see Grandpa. When we got there it was evident that he was not doing well. Our mom had sat with him all day and she agreed that the facility was awful. Karen and I brainstormed over what could be done. We both felt a strong urge to 'kidnap' the cop. We could not leave him there another night. Karen was able to clear it with the staff and we asked Grandpa, do you want to go home? He was happy about that. He wanted to get out of there and never look back. The whole experience had been terribly painful. He wanted to be as far away from Lynwood as possible.

The trouble was that both Grandma and Grandpa had asked us weeks ago to clear out their home, as they would no longer require it. We were nearly done the task, aside from the big pieces of furniture. All the paintings and pictures were off the walls, all the personality had been stripped… it was a mess. In Grandpa's mind, even though he knew, he still pictured home as he had left it. We struggled over how hard it would be for him to lose his wife and then go home to see it all stripped down to a shred of what he remembered. I went ahead of Mom and Karen to try and put things back in a semblance of order. They packed up his things and loaded him in mom's car. There was a traffic accident on the way back so it took a dreadfully long time to make the typically ten minute drive. When I arrived I raced up and did as much as I could to help things look 'normal'.

Grandpa came in shortly afterwards with Mom and Karen. He said he didn't mind the mess but we knew it was a shock. He walked down the hall and sank himself into Grandma's blue chair. He rubbed the armrests fondly and cried. We brought him a blanket, hand made by Grandma. He sat there while the three of us buzzed around him, setting things straight. Karen volunteered to stay the night with him. Mom drove back to Karen's house to get a change of clothes for her. Grandpa told Karen and I several times that we could stop trying to set things in order but we insisted that it was no big deal and continued to try and fix things.

As midnight approached I left Karen and Grandpa. Grandpa pulled down the king-sized bed spread and turned down the sheets for her on Grandma's side. He got his pajamas on and then Karen heard a thud. He had fallen. She went in and he was on the floor. He looked sheepishly at her. Karen asked if he was OK and he said he was that he was trying to get something off the floor. He got up and Karen tucked him into bed. I was grateful that she was there with him.

That week we got their place back to normal and prepared for the funeral. We ate with Grandpa in the dining room and realized how many people loved and cared for him. He was surrounded by staff and residents who loved him. He enjoyed having meals with us and we loved not having to cook.

March 4th. 2013 was the viewing for Grandma. Karen had previewed her to see how she looked, to make sure that Grandpa would be pleased.

When we entered the funeral home I was overwhelmed with the situation. Grandpa looked frail and weak, which he wasn't. His brokenness affected him inside and out.

Grandma was in the chapel and once all of the family arrived we went in. She looked beautiful. She looked exactly like she should. She was Grandma, not sick but strong. She looked as she had on so many other family occasions. I was happy for Grandpa so that he could see his Ruth, in this beautiful way and carry that with him. We all had our turns at the casket. We touched her hands, kissed her cheeks and whispered our final words. Grandpa sat next to her, holding her hand and kept telling her how much he loved her. There were oceans of tears as we watched his heartbreak and felt our own.

Near the end of the time Grandpa gathered the family around. He prayed for Grandma. This is what he said.

"Ruth, we all come to you with love and respect for what you have meant to us and others.

Thank you Lord God for the multitude of your blessings. Thank you for watching over us and providing. I know that you called Ruth home and she is heaven with you but Father God I am finding it awfully difficult to say my final farewell. I ask for your forgiveness if I falter or fail in any way.

I do want to thank you for my beautiful family as is evident by the way in which they've surrounded me. I thank you for each and every one Father God and I thank you for being with us, your presence not only in the later days but throughout my entire life and Ruth's.

Thank you Lord God for everything. Help me though. Help me to be able to face the reality of my life now. It is in your precious and holy name that I offer up this humble prayer and ask you please to accept it as a final farewell to this lovely person that came into my life and was with me all of my days. And now I say farewell not only on my behalf but on behalf of all my loved ones, family and friends.

Thank you Father God. Please continue to walk with them and abide with them. Please continue to love them and support them as you have me. I am saying thank you and I am offering up a final farewell to this beloved person that has been my wife for all these many 66 years but has been more than that. She has been a special person in the life of many others and has worked endlessly to be a help to others. So I am saying thank you for her and I am saying thank you for all of my family, but especially bless her. Keep her in your loving care and help me to face the reality. Amen."

He then leaned in and whispered, "Ruth, I'm coming as quickly as I can. I love you sweetheart."

He didn't want to leave. He kissed her one last time and said, "I'm never going to be ready to leave her, so take me now." He was escorted out by my dad and driven home.

After Grandpa left Karen was testing the DVD that would be played during her service the following day. I sat in the front row of the church, looking at Grandma laying there, in her casket. I didn't want to leave. I could not handle that I would never look upon this woman again. The photos played on a screen behind her, showing all of the glorious moments of her life. When the photos were done I said goodbye for the last time and walked away.

The following day we had a lovely service, honoring all that Grandma had accomplished in her life. I sat behind Grandpa, who couldn't hear much of the service anyway. He just looked straight ahead. I couldn't concentrate either. The hymns sounded hollow and the words of the pastor meaningless. The casket was closed and all I could do was picture her in there. The eulogy was read by Keith and then Brian. The photos were wonderful. A song was sung in German. At the end of the service we walked out behind Grandpa.

I was supposed to ride in our vehicle with my family but as I passed the limo where Grandpa was I opened the door. He sat there – looking stony and empty. I hugged him and we both cried. He held me and I held him. He looked at me with his tear filled eyes and said, "Please, come with me."

I got in the back of the limo and snuggled up next to him. We held hands and cried. The other family members in the limo chatted casually. I just wanted to scream at all of them to shut up. As we took the long drive to Fredericksheim cemetery I wanted to be present, with Grandpa. He kept saying over and over that he didn't know if he could do this. I squeezed his hand and responded, "I don't know Grandpa, I don't know."

He said quietly to me that he always drove this road with her, and now he was alone. He looked longingly out the front window at the hearse, where his wife lay.

When we arrived at the cemetery he exited the limo. I stood beside him, holding his hand. The casket was taken from the Hearse and carried over to the triple plot where Gerry was already buried. Once the casket was in place Grandpa made his way over and sat – staring at this box that was about to be lowered into the ground. The pastor spoke, prayed and then we placed white roses on the casket. Grandpa stood up at the end and placed his hand on the casket.

"I love you," he breathed.

He sat back down and cried. I crouched next to him and looked up into his face. He asked while he wept, "How can I ever leave her here? I can't. I can't leave her here"

I responded, my heart breaking, "I don't know Grandpa. I don't know." We cried, everyone else around us cried, taking his grief and letting it mingle with their own. Everyone knew what a special couple Ruth and Wally had been. No one could imagine

Grandpa walking away from her side. I'm sure if he could have he would have laid down next to her, in the plot already marked for him, to be with her.

Eventually he nodded at my dad and Dad took him back to the limo.

We hugged one another, each one of us experiencing our grief in our own way.

Eventually it was time to go. My second cousin, Mark, who had recently lost his father Lorne, came to me and mentioned that he had read the book, Weep Tonight. He read it in a matter of days and loved it. He told me that he particularly enjoyed reading about his Grandpa, Herman, and that most of all that Ruth and Wally's story was a love story that deserved to be told. He hugged me. I felt Herman there with us, in Mark's arms. I felt the love of all the generations surrounding us.

I went home and slept. I ached for Grandpa.

Alone

The next few days Karen and I camped out with Grandpa. We sat on his couch, assisted him to his chair and watched curling with him. He slept a lot and cried. We shared memories. I read books and tended to any of his needs that I could. Mostly we sat in silence.

We went down for meals where he struggled to swallow. He was upset at this but didn't want to go back to pureed food. He couldn't remember what had started the swallowing problem so we had to keep reminding him that he had not only ruptured his stomach but had fallen and hit his head.

On March 8th we were celebrating Matt's birthday. We received the news that Grandpa was in the ER after choking on his dinner. Karen's family was on their way to Banff for a much needed get-a-way. I'm not sure of all of the details but a CT scan was done to see if there was a bleed in his brain. There was a small one and it was discussed that Grandpa might want to have brain surgery to help the situation. The doctors explained that the brain surgery only had a small chance of helping his swallowing issues and it was not going to help his speech issues. When we were there he was not able to speak much at all. He was incredibly frustrated by this. He had so much to say to us and yet the words wouldn't form. He often pounded his fists down on the blankets and shook his head. He was able to tell us that he wanted Karen. Over and over he asked for her. I called her, explaining what had happened and after much discussion they turned around and came back to the city.

It was a long night in the ER, wondering what to do, what Grandpa wanted, and if he was in the right space to decide. After hours of labored communication with Grandpa and the doctors, he decided that the long term implications of the surgery and the lack of improvement to his speech were not worth the risks.

Grandpa was offered a feeding tube. He decided against that as well. He did not want to be in the hospital. He did not want to go back to long term care. Karen asked him if he wanted to go home. He said yes. Karen and her husband got him dressed and took him home. They helped him to bed. He wanted to be alone that night.

The next few days were hard as we tried to get him up and feed him. He was unable to communicate effectively and could not swallow. Every day it became harder to move him from his bed to Grandma's chair in the next room. One day my dad came to help me move Grandpa back to the bed for the end of the day. We struggled immensely to lift this strong man and to maneuver him back to his bed. That was the last time we moved him. It was too risky for him. He could not help us, something that frustrated him. His body would not co-operate. We realized this was the beginning of the end and worked to find a way to keep him comfortable in bed.

The home health service was increased to four times a day in order to care for him in bed. A hypodermoclysis line was started providing saline into his tissue as we could not keep him hydrated. Grandpa was no longer mobile and was bed ridden. He could not turn, sit up or even lift his head. Karen and I cared for his needs making sure to move him regularly to avoid bedsores.

Grandpa was overcome with grief, the loss of Grandma, his speech, his ability to swallow, or even move. Karen lovingly shaved Grandpa's face and washed him. To reposition him we had to stand over him on the bed to move him up. He was heavy. He laughed often as Karen and I stood in awkward positions to move him safely. He was patient with us as we learned the best way to help him. My son, Jacob, was there with me often and assisted in rolling, or moving his Great-Grandpa.

Sam, his home care nurse was loving and she treated him with respect and dignity. We were very thankful for her. Grandpa could nod yes and no, smile and squeeze our hands. He laughed often, sharing small moments of joy with us against the many struggles. Every day we sang, read and talked about his home coming. We were sure he only had a few days to live as he been without food for some time.

Without food Grandpa lost a lot of weight. He was never in too much pain and he managed it with pain medication. He was so strong. He was most frustrated that he could not speak to us. We talked to him as the kids played on the bed and around him. Life was surrounding him.

Karen and I alternated times of day when we could be there with him. It was hard to be there, to see his discomfort, but it was harder to be away. Even when one of us wasn't there we were texting back and forth about what was going on. One day as I knelt by his bedside, asking him multiple questions about how I could help him, he pulled me in with his arm. He laid my head on his chest and began to stroke my hair, just as he did when I was a child. I cried as I laid there, listening to his gentle heartbeat. Although he could not speak, he could love. You could see it in his eyes every time he looked at you, you could feel it in the squeeze of his hand.

Grandpa enjoyed as I read him stories of his childhood from Weep Tonight. I would often stop and ask him, should I keep going? He would nod, yes.

I couldn't read the chapters about Grandma. It was too hard to think of her, not with us. I read about him running as a young boy, to take him away from the present and into the past where he was free. I napped with him, held his hand and prayed for hours every day. Finally things changed.

One day when Karen was visiting he started to speak. It had been weeks. In a small raspy voice he asked for coffee and toast. She was so shocked that she ran down to get him some. He ate small bits and could suck coffee from a straw. He said, "That is good!" Karen called me right away. We were completely dumbfounded! Here was a man who had gone weeks without nutrition and he had found his voice and his appetite again!

In the days to come he told us he loved us, thanked us and expressed how grateful he was that we were caring for him. I asked him many questions. Could he feel heaven? Did he see it? He often raised his arms up when he was sleeping, or half-awake. He would get a smile on his face and a twinkle in his eye. We asked him if he saw angels. "No," he replied. We asked him if he saw Grandma, "Yes."

One conversation I was crying and telling him how much I missed Grandma. He did not say that he did too, he said, "I'm sure you do."

"Do you see her?" I asked.

He smiled.

"Is she here?"

He smiled again.

Tears streamed down my face, as they often did. He tenderly wiped them away. He smiled at Karen and me all the time and laughed frequently. He was good natured despite death overtaking him.

Five weeks had gone by since March 8th, the day that he choked and this phase had begun. Although he wanted to eat, very little food actually got down to his stomach. Mostly he liked the taste in his mouth and then spit it out when he could not swallow. We continued to check in as things got worse to see if he wanted a feeding tube, or more medical attention. He consistently said that he wanted to go home. We reminded him gently that he was home. He always shook his head, no. Some days he would understand that he was home, at Caleb Manor and then other days he would say that home was with Grandma, and therefore he was not home. Confusion and clarity would come and go. Mostly he was clear but some things were mixed up in a metaphor. Home was a confusing topic. He kept speaking about going on a trip. He would ask if his suitcase was packed, if his things were in order, what time the plane was leaving and other questions like that, the mode of transportation changing.

He often asked questions about when he would be leaving. We told him that we didn't know. He was annoyed by this. He asked why it was taking so long. We told him that the hypodermoclysis line was keeping him alive, and slowing down the process of going home. He thought about this and asked us many more questions. His body physically continued to deteriorate and his pain increased as his bones were the only thing holding him together. All his strength was gone. He was still incredibly heavy even to roll. I can't remember how the discussion came about but he questioned the hypodermoclysis line. He indicated that he didn't want it to prolong things further. We talked to many health professionals and caregivers who then talked to him to gauge his understanding and if he was able to clearly make choices. He was.

It was a Wednesday morning, April 10th when I went to see him. He was confused, which was not typical. He asked me to get him up and out of bed. I explained that he could not get up. He asked me why. I explained that he hadn't eaten in many weeks and that his body was not able to support him anymore. He didn't remember anything about himself. He did not ask for Grandma but he wasn't sure why he couldn't get out of bed and walk out of the room. For hours we talked, I cried as I told him he was dying. This was new information for him. He nodded, his face serious. He said, "Okay, it's okay." He questioned again when he would go home. I explained that there was no way to know but that he couldn't go on too much longer.

I explained that we had talked about removing the hypodermoclysis line, that day. He had more questions about that. When the health care worker came she spoke at length with him. She had known him for a long time and was kind and gentle, making sure he understood what would happen. He agreed that removing the hypodermoclysis line was the right thing to do.

"Okay Wally, we will take it out then. I can see that you are ready," she said.

Grandpa nodded. She gently pulled the line out of his abdomen. Tears rolled down her face as she tucked him back in. I could not help it, I broke down, sobbing. I was on the bed next to him, holding his hand. I laid my head down on his chest and let all of the emotions that overwhelmed me pour out. He stroked my head.

"I'm sorry Grandpa," I whispered, "I should be comforting you."

"No, this is how it should be," he whispered. He smiled lovingly and looked deeply into my eyes.

I cried on and on. The worker told me that he would likely die within 24 to 72 hours. The afternoon dragged on as we held hands and slept. I could not believe that this man would not be here in a day or two. Eventually I left the room while he slept. I thought about his words. 'This is how it should be'. As it sank in I understood that he meant that all this time I had been caring for him. He was thankful to stop having me care for him and for him to be the Grandpa again.

That night many more family members came. When Grandpa woke up he was asking when he was going home. We explained that nobody knew. I told him that God was the only one who knew the time. I suggested that he pray about it to ease his mind.

The family came around to pray with him. He begged God to take him, to send the angels to bring him to his Ruth. He prayed humbly that God would hear his prayer and release him from his body. We all said our prayers of gratitude for his life. Eventually everyone went home but Brian and I stayed, keeping Grandpa company as he drifted in and out of sleep. Around ten o'clock Grandpa asked when the bus was coming. We explained again that we didn't know. We said that he was free to go whenever he was ready. He nodded and thought about what we were saying. Brian and I prayed and listened to music as he slept. Finally at 11:30 pm we said goodnight. I left crying, wondering if I would ever see his sparkling eyes again.

I came the next morning, kids in tow. Once again he was asking me to help him out of bed. I could not believe that I would have to have the conversation with him again.

"Remember Grandpa? Remember? Your body isn't co-operating any more. You can't walk. You can't swallow food. Your body is done. You are so strong that you keep on going!"

He smiled at me, peppered me with questions for the next hour and then seemed content that he understood, yes he was finally going home. I sat, reading by his bed as he slept, ready in case he opened his eyes and needed something. He was constantly lifting up his arms while he slept, he stretched them to the ceiling, which was unbelievable since he had no muscle to accomplish this. I enjoyed watching him sleep and seeing his arms reach up to heaven. It was particularly quiet in the room and suddenly he shouted "I'm coming!" in a firm, yet annoyed tone. I nearly fell off my chair! Although he had regained speech he was usually close to a whisper and barely audible. To hear his old, strong voice was such a shock. By the way he yelled it I could tell Grandma was giving him a lecture from heaven. It comforted me.

Karen came after she was finished work. Karen asked Grandpa how his day was.

"Shauna just sat on my bed all day and drank my beer," he complained.

"That's terrible!" Karen replied.

Karen and I had a giggle, since I hate beer. We figured he must be craving a nice cold glass!

As the night went on Karen and I chatted quietly while he slept on and off. Upon waking at one point he announced that he was ready to go.

"Where do you want to go Grandpa?" Karen asked.

"Have you packed our suitcases?"

"Yes," Karen gently answered, "You are all ready."

"How about you?" he asked. "Are you packed?"

"Yes, we are ready too."

"What time does the flight leave," he questioned.

I answered, "We don't know Grandpa."

"Soon," he said, "Have you packed the pillows?"

"Yes Grandpa," Karen said, "We have everything."

"Where are my keys?"

"Keys?" I questioned.

"To my sports car, you know the red one."

Karen smiled at me. "I'll get your keys."

She went down the hall to get his house keys. She put them in his hand and he fingered them.

"My car key isn't here."

We sat quietly for a few minutes.

"Well get me out of bed then," he said sternly. "I'm driving us."

"Grandpa," I said, "you can't go anywhere. You aren't strong enough."

"We are going on a trip. On the wagon. Get your things girls."

Karen and I played along, "But Grandpa you're not even dressed!"

He thought about this. "Well get me dressed! I don't want people to think I've been robbed!"

Karen and I exchanged wide eyed glances as we laughed at his comment. We could barely slide him up the bed, let alone move him from his bed. We decided to play along, as he was insistent.

We got his pajama pants on and changed his shirt. Karen opened the window which allowed a cool breeze to come into the room. The setting sun shone brightly on his bed.

"Help me sit up then," he commanded us. "The wagon is ready. You girls need to find a seat."

"We can't go with you Grandpa," I said, trying to suppress the emotion.

"Well of course you can. I'm not leaving without the two of you."

Those words meant so much. We were holding him here while Grandma was calling him 'home'.

A few more minutes passed. "The boat is ready," he announced. "Get your things girls. It's time to go. Stop being silly, we are all going on this trip. I am not leaving without you two."

"We want to go with you Grandpa, but it's not our time," said Karen. I held my breath, waiting to see his reaction.

He scowled at the two of us.

"Let's go," he replied firmly.

We always listened to our Grandpa. I mouthed the words to Karen, "Let's try."

"Okay," Karen said, "let's go Grandpa."

The two of us used all our might to bring him up into a sitting position. Angels must have been helping us! I knelt behind him on the bed while he leaned against me. Karen swung his legs off the side of the bed. The sunlight shone on his sunken face. He felt the fresh air. We all sat silently for a while, wishing there was more we could do.

Home care workers arrived to find us with Grandpa sitting off the edge of the bed. They were surprised. So were we! We were happy to help him feel like he was going somewhere, even if for a short time. We laid him back down while the staff got him comfortable.

Karen and I went in the other room and cried. If only we could take him somewhere, or do something. We would gladly take a ride in his sports car, or wagon or even a boat. Sadly we weren't able to take this step with him. He would have to go alone.

The End

It was thirteen days before we got the phone call. His strong, athletic body of 95 years ticked on and on. His heart was strong and his body worked very hard to preserve itself.

Every night after we tucked him in we would cry thinking that this was our last kiss, our last bed time. Every morning Karen and I went and were stunned to find him alive. He continually said thank you. He said thank you more than anyone ever has. He was grateful, that is what he wanted to leave us with.

Speech left him. He was unable to close his eyes to sleep. He drifted in and out. The last few days he began to distance himself from us. He no longer looked us in the eyes or connected with us. It was as though his spirit was gone but his body remained.

Karen shaved his whiskers, we combed his hair and made him comfortable. We massaged his hands and feet, sang and prayed as we waited.

April 23, 2013 Karen was having a vivid dream. Young, handsome, strong Waldemar was in a row boat. He was paddling away from her as she stood on the shore. The lake was calm and smooth and his strong muscles rippled the lake water as he moved further and further away. He smiled at her as he moved into the blazing light. He waved and disappeared into the mist.

She woke up and looked at the clock, seven o'clock. Home care would have been in to see Grandpa by now. She rolled over and went back to sleep.

Around eight o'clock the phone rang at Karen's house. Grandpa was gone. Home care had been running behind and had come up to his suite to find his spirit gone. Karen called me. We drove together. It was perfect, just the two of us there with this man we loved so dearly, with this man who had given so much love, attention and care to us. We sat on either side of him, holding his hands. We cried, spoke to him and congratulated him on finally making it home. We told him that we would be okay and that we would come when it was our time.

On my phone I had a video that I had recorded at his 95th birthday. I played it. His strong voice came into the room.

"I want to start out by saying that this has been a wonderful, wonderful occasion for me. I wasn't anticipating anything or expecting anything. I want to thank all of you. But even before I thank you I want to thank my God for looking after me for 95 years. He took me from the small farm in Manitoba and brought me to where I am here today. It's been a wonderful trail. The travelling along the journey has been beautiful every step of the way. I don't know how I can thank all of you, but I really want to thank you all. Some come from far, some from near but you all come to bring me greetings. So on behalf of myself and on behalf of Ruth, I say thank you to all of you. Please remember that I love you all, that you have been wonderful and a part of my life. Thank you."

Tears ran down our cheeks as we heard his voice, saw his face and felt his presence. We listened to the hymn, 'It is Well With my Soul'. We were filled with immense pain and relief. We reminded ourselves that Grandma was probably questioning him, wondering what took him so long. He was finally able to run, and perhaps was going for a morning jog with Gerry. Karen shared her dream with me. I believe it was Grandpa saying goodbye. I will always have an image of him rowing into heaven.

Karen and I spent an hour with his body. Talking, sharing memories and expressing our heartache. The rest of the family came. We sat around until nearly lunch visiting, sharing memories and taking in his physical presence just a little longer.

The funeral home came to take him away. Again, the stretcher, the bag, all of it felt so wrong. They went down the hall to his room while we waited in the living room. One small young girl loaded him onto the stretcher. How she did it I can't imagine. He was so tall that she could barely make it down the hall with the stretcher. Karen and I walked out with him, like the royal guard as we walked alongside his body. There were two elevators. All of the family got in one while Karen, the funeral attendant and I squeezed into the other elevator. Grandpa was so tall that he barely fit in the elevator.

We left the building, on either side of him, as the other residents looked on. We felt their sympathy, love and support. Grandpa was loaded up and driven away.

Karen and I walked back up to the suite. It was desperately empty. I don't remember much after that. The next week we made the funeral arrangements, trying our best to make them fitting for this remarkable man. Everything was a blur as we felt the full impact of losing both Grandma and Grandpa.

We were able to have the funeral at Caleb Manor, where he had lived, and fulfilled his last wish, to die at home. It was truly the most amazing funeral service. Keith shared an extraordinary writing about how Grandpa was a hero in many ways. Brian and Dad shared, a song was sung and then photos were shown. We had many wonderful photos of his life. At the end of the photos the video from his birthday played, bringing everyone to tears.

We drove to the cemetery and laid his body next to Grandma's. It was very difficult to leave. Karen and I lingered the longest, wondering what we would do now. We cried, looking down into the deep hole where his casket had been lowered. We knelt there, feeling lost.

And Now

Time passes and I still cry when I reflect on all of those weeks where we were able to connect with our grandparents in such a special way. It was a privilege and an honor to see these two incredible people through to the end. I would not give up my involvement in their end of life journey, even though it was hard. It was beautiful, spiritual and healing to be there for each step of the process.

Now they are gone. Their legacy lives on through all of the lives that they impacted while they were here. Grandma's endless advocacy for the disabled, helping people who were treated unjustly in the First Nation's community, caring for her children and grandchildren and being a constant friend and companion to Grandpa, all this changed the world around her.

Grandpa taught everyone he met what compassion looked like. He counselled and encouraged his sons. Often, when they had made a mistake, he said nothing. He just came into the situation and began to set it right. He was a strong man of faith who prayed daily for his friends and family. He served in the Baptist Union for many years and was a faithful part of his church community. He took all of his challenges to the Lord in prayer. Grandpa was gentle and kind. He was an excellent example of God's love for us. He gave love freely, forgave easily and cared for his family unendingly. Mostly he had a spirit of gratitude. He was thankful for all of the people in his life.

I am very grateful that they shared their stories with me. I will never forget the hours and hours we spent together, me asking questions, and the two of them telling me all of their adventures. As I sifted through my recordings of our interviews I heard

Grandpa say this, "Looking back now I can see that it was all for a reason. We've had an unbelievable life."

"Viking"

"I have fought the good fight, I have finished the race, I have kept the faith. Now there is in store for me the crown of righteousness, which the Lord, the righteous Judge, will award to me on that day—and not only to me, but also to all who have longed for his appearing."

2 Timothy 7 & 8 NIV

Earthquakes and Whispers, written by Ruth Peterson
May 25, 2001

"I have been asked to speak to you today about mine and Wally's experience in the very unique role of parenting a son with a physical disability.

"Step back with me, as we travel back to January 16, 1949, the day of Gerry's birth, and from where I stand I see a series of Earthquakes and Whispers that changed our lives in dramatic ways.

"Over the past few years, we have become very aware of earthquakes around the world and especially the one this year at the west coast of North America, with aftershocks felt in British Columbia reminding us that earthquakes are a reality, a bit too close for comfort.

"When Minnie asked me to speak to you today about our experience, she asked for a title for this address. I reflected for some time and felt that "Earthquakes and Whispers" best described what life has been like for our family. We all know that those at the epicenter of a quake are most affected, but quakes have a ripple effect and aftershocks — but I digress.

"Wally and I were happy to welcome Gerald into our hearts and lives, bear with me please for those of you who have read Gerry's book 'Accepting Reality.' You will recognize the chapter I wrote in that book.

"We were not allowed to see Gerry for three days after his birth, and my professional training as a nurse should have alerted me to the signals that were being sent out, but my mothering instinct somehow refused to pick up on those signals. The doctor explained that Gerry was unable to breathe on his own for fifteen minutes or more. I learned later that the nun in charge of the delivery room had alerted all the nurses to stop by the chapel and pray for Baby Peterson. Many did just that. Mother Superior came to visit me and even though we had differing views on matters of theology, they did not shirk their responsibilities. Gerry was not expected to live so he was baptized and they committed him to the Lord. Gerry arrived and survived on the wings of prayer. His baptism, based on his confession of faith, came thirteen years later. Life took on a new rhythm but as days grew into weeks and months, we knew that the disturbed nights and his frequent illnesses were really not the norm. He slept only in short spurts, had difficulty swallowing and was prone to chest infections. Doctor visits were frequent. Gerry was having severe muscle spasms in his arms and legs. We wanted answers. The doctor was very evasive when I asked questions. Whenever I suggested that something was amiss, with my beautiful blue-eyed son, the doctor would suggest that nurses as mothers were in a category all our own — worry, worry, worry.

"When Gerry was seven months old, I took him to our pediatrician for a checkup. He carefully examined Gerry and then I bundled Gerry in his blanket for our trip home. He sat behind his desk looking at us, twirling a pair of scissors round and around, making no eye contact. So I picked up courage and said, 'Okay now tell me what is wrong with my baby.' He replied, 'You know Gerry didn't breathe unassisted for twenty minutes after his birth, he has Little's Disease, Cerebral Palsy, so named after a doctor who did research on newborns with difficulties like Gerry's. He will be hopelessly crippled due to a blood clot in his brain, which has blocked out that part of his brain that controls muscle coordination, the damage is permanent.' The earthquake hit — but he wasn't finished, 'My advice to you is to put him in an institution and forget you ever had him.' Another earthquake. I picked Gerry up, looked this man in the eyes and screamed, 'Oh no I won't, over my dead body, neither you nor anyone else will put this child in an institution!' This was our son, with the beautiful eyes who responded to our every touch, this baby boy who conveyed love and understanding to us. No, not possible. Denial, of course. I honestly don't remember the trip home. When Wally arrived home, he took one look at me and said, 'Tell me.' And then the earthquake struck, our whole world shook violently. We three were at the epicenter. We fell into each other's arms and cried. The ripple effect had begun. We had to tell our parents, Wally's and mine, siblings, extended family, friends and our pastor — and the aftershocks continued for a long, long time. I recall looking in my medical textbooks and yes, there were two lines on Little's Disease, no answers only more and more questions. I wrote letters to the Federal and Provincial Departments of Health. The answers were always, 'Sorry we can't help you.' My cry to God was always why? Why me, why us? Why our son? I yelled a lot. We were desperate. God didn't seem to hear me. I had at one time worked for the Department of Health, Alberta, so I phoned the Minister of Health. I told him I wanted to know how many children had Cerebral Palsy in Alberta. In a very condescending voice, he assured me that we had no Cerebral Palsy children in Alberta, to which I replied, 'Well my son, ten months old, has Cerebral Palsy and what are we going to do about it?' I slammed down the phone. Another earthquake. Only denial everywhere I went. What were Wally and I to do? Believe me we had a lot of Job's comforters come into our lives. The cruelest remark to come our way, as to the 'why' of this dilemma, was *Sindenschuldt*, a German word for Sin Guilt. What a guilt trip to be handed, over and over. I often responded that perhaps it was the sins of the fathers, visited upon the children.

"I am eternally grateful, that from the time I was very young my father insisted that I read and study the Bible; little did I know how important this would be for all of my life. Oh and did I have a lot to learn. Always when the earth would stop shaking and I would stop the constant flow of questions heavenward, I would turn to and read the word. The verse that became my life's rock, and is always the one I turn to, is found in Isaiah 41:10, *So do not fear, for I am with you, do not be dismayed for I am your God. I will strengthen you and help you, I will uphold you with my righteous right hand.* How did God speak to me? Always in a whisper.

"I learned early that it isn't the circumstances that we are caught up in that were most important, but God in those circumstances. In 1949, I visited the Premier of Alberta in his office, hoping to get support for help for disabled children — but none was forthcoming. Now what? Who to turn to? I was angry, so I said my piece and left. Another earthquake — caused by a person who had power to change things that would have an impact on many lives. I left his office so distraught and while the earth shook I remembered Psalm 46:10, '*Be still and know that I am God.*' Being still for me was difficult. He whispered, '*Apart from me you can do nothing.*' John 5:15. I know this to be true. I have always claimed that I trusted Him, but now trust had to be taken to new levels. Always the whispers. I was often dismayed. God knew this, and my dismay always came because of people's attitudes. How I would pray — God show me what to do, what to say. Looking back, I realize He always showed me the path to take. My first really big task was to now find someone with authority and clout, first of all, to listen, so that children of disabilities would be acknowledged, then recognized as having worth and entitlement to the best life we could make available to them. I decided to go to the leader of the opposition. There I poured out our story and frustration.

"In the early 1950s, private citizens were permitted to address the Legislative Assembly, and in March of 1950 I was standing on the floor of the legislature just below the speaker's chair and giving it my all. Yes, there were disabled children and adults in

Alberta. We as a society had to acknowledge this and provide care to them and their families. God provided and honored that request and the media was supportive. While all this was unfolding, a mother with a Cerebral Palsy son wrote a letter to the *Edmonton Journal* requesting help. I phoned her and the result, some months later, was the establishment of the first Cerebral Palsy clinic in Alberta, built and funded by the South Side Kiwanis Club. The government provided funding for staff. God's direction was very clear. This was not a problem unique to Wally and I. Proverbs 31: 8 and 9 very clearly states our response to God's teaching. '*Speak up for those who cannot speak for themselves: for the rights of all those who are destitute: Speak up and judge fairly, defend the rights of the poor and the needy.*'

"Our family grew, two brothers for Gerry. Gerry joined them and their friends at play, at church, at Cubs, on vacations camping in the mountains, doing all the things that growing boys do. We never apologized for Gerry's presence anywhere. Wherever we as a family went, Gerry was there. Oh I was called 'the crazy lady' and many other distressing names.

"Disabled children were denied an education because 'they didn't fit in.' Now it was time to take on the Department of Education. Yes, another earthquake that sent aftershocks for years to come. I prayed often and fervently for solutions to what, at times, seemed unanswerable questions. God was always there. Wally supported me in all my efforts and struggles. He is ever the diplomat — bless him. At that time, confrontation was my best tool. Gerry was home schooled. I went back to nursing for three years so that we could have a retired schoolteacher come three times a week. We knew Gerry could comprehend the spoken word — but how could he communicate with us? Again the answer came after much prayer and submission. One day when I was talking to God and suggesting that IF He heard me, please let me know — if He had the answers to this problem of communication I needed to know, because the earthquake was ever present. Three days went by and my tears were overflowing. The boys were playing outdoors and I gave a sigh of earthquake proportion. I sat down to read the paper. I began reading and suddenly I wasn't really reading, just looking at the words and then it hit me. I had my answer. Now I was crying. God was answering my prayer, right there, go do it, take the words Gerry uses most often and put the letters as they appear on a key board upon a board, so that Gerry can indicate the words and letters he wishes to use. We had the answer. Gerry's first communication tool came into being. This too is included in Gerry's book 'Accepting Reality.' In 1962, we were transferred to Saskatoon and there Gerry attended a school for the physically disabled. He was thirteen at the time. He completed his grade twelve. He learned to type using a headpiece, but therein lies another story.

"That year I visited Sweden to the schools and clinics there. When we had newly arrived in Saskatoon, Wally and I were guests of a government-sponsored dinner, and I was being introduced to the Minister of Health. On being told by one of the guests that our eldest son had a disability, she asked me, 'And where do you keep him?' 'At home,' I replied. 'Oh my, how could you — do you have other children?' 'Yes,' I said, 'two sons.' Another 'Oh my, do you realize what you are doing to them?' She gave me this drop-dead look. I answered, 'Yes I do, hopefully they will grow up to be loving, decent human beings.' All those within earshot gasped, she walked away and I just smiled. I was applauded by those who heard our conversation.

"Attitudes — are they better or worse? Both. What causes me the greatest pain? Attitudes.

"We were in Saskatoon for eight years and returned to Edmonton in 1970. I could keep you here all day. There is the story about the Group Home — it celebrated its twenty-sixth anniversary this year. The story of how God provided for this, through the estate of a farmer who wanted to build a children's hospital, but in the early 1970s citizens didn't build children's hospitals and I was instrumental in convincing the executors of the estate to build a group home here in Edmonton, in spite of government's resistance. It is a residence for nine people. The government wanted twelve. I wanted six so we compromised and built for nine. Now group homes are built for four or six at most. I have served the past three years on the Premiers Council on the status of persons with disabilities — but that's another story.

"A word about Gerry. We taught him to be independent. Gerry is unable to feed or dress himself or attend to his personal care, but he is the most independent person I know. He received Christ into his life at thirteen years of age and his father carried him into the baptismal waters. He is a leader of Junior Highs at church and much loved by the kids there. He has a tremendous sense of humor. He attended many classes at North American Bible College. He knows his Bible and has been known to quiz his mother. Both Wally and I would like to express our gratitude to the many people who have enriched Gerry's life and gone out of their way to help him in so many ways. He is an avid gardener. In 1995, he was near death and on life support for ten days in ICU. We wondered how Gerry felt about his struggle. I asked his younger brother Brian to ask him at some appropriate time, in the event that he should ever be this ill again would he want to be on life support? Gerry spelled out, 'When I am ninety-eight it will be okay to pull the plug.' In 1949, life expectancy for Cerebral Palsy children was fourteen years. Gerry is fifty-two. He finds such joy in life. He is computer literate. He phones us every day and we communicate by repeating the alphabet and Gerry stops us at the correct letter. To God be the glory…we have a new phenomena — the disabled are aging. Never before in history has this happened. There will be other earthquakes, as these problems need solutions.

"Oh, how I have learned to trust; often to wait — often to speak. The youngest of Job's comforters, Elihu, said it best, *'For God does speak, now one way, now another – though man may not perceive it.'* Job 33:14.

"One day when my final earthquake comes, I will shout, I know that my redeemer lives, and I shall see Him. It has been a long journey for Wally and me. A journey of faith. God always saying 'Trust me.'

And I think on that last day God will whisper to me, '*Ruth, welcome home.*'"

Acknowledgements:

Thank you to my heavenly Father who stirred in me the desire to embark down this road, to capture this story and to share it with others so that they may know His love. Thank you for all of the signposts along the way that led me in the right direction and that prodded me forward when I felt like giving up. All of the honor, all of the glory and all of the praise go to You for giving me the words to say.

Thank you to my supportive family who encouraged me along the second leg of this journey. To my husband, Matthew, and children, Jacob, Jasper and Jenna, who gave me the time and freedom to work, and especially to Matthew who encouraged me never to give up on this project, even when completion seemed impossible. Thank you for holding me through the tears and the dark days when writing this second story seemed like it was over.

Thank you to my mom, Marlene, and my sister, Karen, who encouraged me to the end of the finished work. Thank you for your prayers and for helping me to hear God's voice in all of the chaos of our lives.

Thank you to Brian, Dale and Gerald who shared with me their stories, from their points of view. Thank you for making the story richer with its honesty. Thank you for being willing to reflect on the past and to take my hand as we traveled into the decades of your childhood.

And finally, again, thank you to Joyce Bellous who took the time to read the manuscript. Thank you for your encouragement and guidance as I took this project to a professional level. Your dedication to superior writing inspired me to write it again and again, until it was a masterpiece. I will always be grateful for your contribution to this project.

Made in the USA
Charleston, SC
12 June 2015